PRAISE FOR *THE WEDDING SHROUD*

"All the drama and sensuality expected of an historical romance, plus a sensitivity to the realities of life in a very different time and world . . ."

—Ursula Le Guin

PRAISE FOR *THE GOLDEN DICE*

"Skillfully plotted and with vividly drawn characters, *The Golden Dice* is a suspenseful, romantic exciting drama . . ."

—Sherry Jones, author of *Four Sisters, All Queens*

PRAISE FOR *CALL TO JUNO*

"*Call to Juno* is a stirring saga of war, sacrifice, and transcendent love."

—M. Louisa Locke, author of *Maids of Misfortune*

"In *Call to Juno* Elisabeth Storrs tells a vivid story of love and war, honor and revenge set in Ancient Rome. Using a skillful blend of history and drama, and full of characters both heroic and human, Storrs transports readers to that long-ago world. Highly recommended."

—M.K. Tod, author of *Lies Told in Silence*

CALL

TO

JUNO

ALSO BY ELISABETH STORRS

The Wedding Shroud
The Golden Dice

CALL
TO
JUNO

— A Tale of Ancient Rome —

ELISABETH STORRS

LAKE UNION
PUBLISHING

Text copyright © 2016 by Elisabeth Storrs
All rights reserved.

Published by Lake Union Publishing, Seattle

www.apub.com

Amazon, the Amazon logo, and Lake Union Publishing are trademarks of Amazon.com, Inc., or its affiliates.

ISBN-13: 9781503951952
ISBN-10: 1503951952

Cover design by Danielle Fiorella
Cover image © Elisabeth Storrs
Map image © Elisabeth Storrs

Printed in the United States of America

To Natalie and Joyce

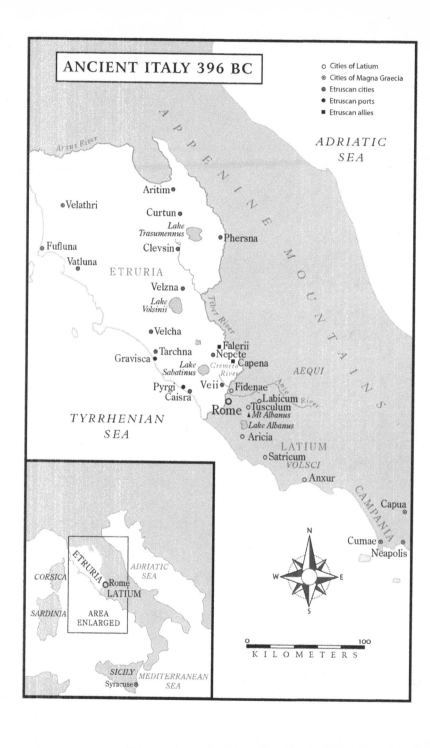

ANCIENT ITALY 396 BC

○ Cities of Latium
◉ Cities of Magna Graecia
● Etruscan cities
● Etruscan ports
■ Etruscan allies

Arnus River

A P P E N I N E

ADRIATIC
SEA

● Aritim

● Velathri

● Curtun

Lake Trasumennus

● Clevsin

● Phersna

● Fufluna

● Vatluna

ETRURIA

● Velzna

Lake Volsinii

● Velcha

M O U N T A I N S

Tiber River

● Tarchna

Gravisca ●

■ Falerii

● Nepete

Lake Sabatinus

Cremera River

■ Capena

AEQUI

Pyrgi ●

Caisra ●

Veii ●

● Fidenae

Arno River

TYRRHENIAN
SEA

○ Rome

○ Labicum

○ Tusculum

▲ Mt Albanus

Lake Albanus

○ Aricia

LATIUM

○ Satricum

VOLSCI

○ Anxur

CAMPANIA

Capua ◉

Cumae ◉

◉ Neapolis

N
W   E
S

CORSICA

ETRURIA

○ Rome

ADRIATIC
SEA

LATIUM

SARDINIA

AREA
ENLARGED

SICILY

Syracuse ◉

MEDITERRANEAN
SEA

0   100
K I L O M E T E R S

CAST

Veii

Caecilia (Aemilia Caeciliana): Born in Rome, Mastarna's wife (nickname Bellatrix)

Vel Mastarna Senior: Etruscan king, Caecilia's husband

Tarchon Mastarna: Adopted son of Mastarna

Tas (Vel Mastarna Junior): Caecilia and Mastarna's firstborn son

Larce Mastarna: Caecilia and Mastarna's second son

Arnth Mastarna: Caecilia and Mastarna's third son

Thia (Larthia) Mastarna: Caecilia and Mastarna's daughter

Tanchvil: High priestess of Uni

Karcuna Tulumnes: Sethre's cousin/guardian, a general

Sethre Kurvenas: Tarchon's beloved

Thefarie Ulthes: General, Mastarna's friend

Lusinies: General

Semni Vulca: Wet nurse in Mastarna's house

Arruns: Mastarna's bodyguard, Semni's lover

Cytheris: Caecilia's maidservant, Aricia's mother

Aricia: Novice priestess, Cytheris's daughter

Perca: Junior nursemaid

Seianta: Mastarna's first wife (deceased)

Hathli: Wet nurse

Aule Porsenna: Zilath of Tarchna, Mastarna's former
    father-in-law
Kurvenas: King of Veii (deceased)
Laris Tulumnes Junior: Former king of Veii, Karcuna's brother
Laris Tulumnes Senior: Former king of Veii, killed at the battle of
    Fidenae, Karcuna's father

Rome

Pinna (Lollia): Camillus's concubine, former prostitute
Marcus Aemilius Mamercus Junior: Military tribune, Aemilius's
    son, Caecilia's cousin
Marcus Furius *Camillus:* Patrician consular general
Appius Claudius *Drusus:* Friend of Marcus, Caecilia's admirer
Artile Mastarna: Soothsayer, Mastarna's brother
Marcus *Aemilius* Mamercus Senior: Caecilia's uncle and adopted
    father, Marcus's father
Caius *Genucius*: Plebeian consular general
Lucius Furius *Medullinus*: Patrician consular general, Camillus's
    older brother
Spurius Furius Medullinus: Patrician general, Camillus's younger
    brother
Scipio: Senator
Icilius *Calvus*: Plebeian people's tribune
Tatius: Knight
Postumius: Patrician consular general
Titinius: Patrician consular general
Sempronius: Patrician military tribune
Gnaeus Lollius: Pinna's father (deceased)
Mamercus Aemilius: Former dictator, Marcus's great uncle
    (deceased)

The Gods

Nortia/Fortuna: Goddess of Fate

Uni/Juno: Guardian goddess of Veii (Uni), warrior goddess, goddess of marriage/mothers/children, queen of the gods, wife of Tinia/Jupiter

Tinia/Jupiter: King of the gods, husband of Uni/Juno

Aplu/Apollo: God of prophecy, music, healing, and light

Fufluns/Dionysus: God of wine and regeneration (his worshippers follow the Pacha Cult)

Mater Matuta: Goddess of the dawn, mother goddess

Aita: Etruscan god of the Afterworld (his worshippers follow the Calu Cult)

Areatha/Ariadne: Fufluns's wife, made immortal

Laran/Mars: God of war

Nethuns/Neptunus: God of water

Menrva/Minerva: Goddess of wisdom, war, arts, and commerce

Latona: Divine mother of Apollo and Diana

Herculeus: Son of Jupiter, famous for his "Twelve Labors"

Mercurius: God of commerce, communication, eloquence, and boundaries

Diana: Goddess of the hunt

Atlenta: Mythological huntress

Ba'al: Principal Phoenician god

Astarte: Phoenician goddess of love, war, and fertility

Cities

Veii

Rome

Tarquinia/Tarchna

Graviscae/Gravisca

Nepete

Volsinii/Velzna
Falerii
Capena
Labicum
Anxur
Tusculum
Satricum

PROPHECY

ONE

Caecilia, Veii, Autumn, 397 BC

Red paint and small fingers are a dangerous combination. Caecilia's eyes widened on spying Arnth. Her two-year-old was smearing vermilion across his face and then holding up his hands to threaten his older brothers.

"Blood, blood!"

Four-year-old Larce squealed at the threat of his new clothes being dirtied and took refuge behind his mother's skirts. Tas, too old at seven to be terrorized, looked disdainful.

Avoiding being branded herself, Caecilia deftly seized Arnth's wrists and held him at bay. The imp wriggled, indignant. "Let go!"

"Stop this," she urged. "The paint is for the coronation ceremony, Arnth. Not for you to play with. Do you understand?"

Her admonishment only set the child into full revolt. He squirmed against her and bellowed to be released. She imagined his cheeks would be red even if not covered with crimson dye.

The noise set the baby crying. Caecilia frowned. "See what you've done. You've woken your sister."

Tas walked to the cradle and peered down to its occupant. "Thia is always whining," he said, lisping through the gap from his missing two front teeth. "It's because she's a girl."

"Nonsense," said Semni, the wet nurse, who scooped up Thia. "You boys are just as tearful when you're irritable. She needs feeding, that's all." The girl sat down on a wicker chair and offered her nipple to the babe.

As always, Caecilia felt a mixture of gratitude and regret at Semni's care for her daughter. She was thankful Thia could gain nourishment, but seeing another woman suckle her baby pained her. She was the first of her four children who she'd not put to her breast.

"What is going on here?"

Vel Mastarna's deep bass had immediate effect. Arnth ceased his noise and stood still as his father entered the chamber.

Caecilia caught her breath at the sight of her husband, dressed as he was in the robes of a king. The thick fabric of his tunic was deep, rich purple, held at his shoulder by a large amethyst brooch. He was swathed in a purple tebenna cloak embroidered with gold. Three amulets hung from heavy chains around his neck. A lump rose in her throat. She knew he would prefer to be in armor, that Vel never wanted to be costumed as a regal lucumo.

His right arm—his sword arm, was in a sling of purple cloth. Caecilia's memory of seeing his elbow broken and bicep sliced as she watched from the city wall was still vivid. Only six weeks had passed since the Battle of Blood and Hail. Six weeks since the former king had betrayed his people and Mastarna. Every day she prayed to Uni, the great mother goddess, to thank her for sparing her husband's life.

Caecilia let Arnth go. "Apa, Apa," the boy called to his father as he scooted across the room. The nobleman hoisted him under his arm, keeping sticky fingers at a distance. He winced in pain when the child accidentally bumped his injury. Sitting down on one of the large bronze armchairs in the private quarters, he settled Arnth on his lap. Every inch of the boy's face was thick with pigment. His fringe was stuck high in a cowlick. "You look like a demon." Mastarna chuckled.

"He was being naughty, Apa," said Larce, venturing forward from his mother's protection now his brother's temper and threats were contained. "You should punish him."

Mastarna signaled the four-year-old to come and sit on his other knee. Larce was careful not to bump his father's arm.

"No need. It's just Arnth's high spirits. And this is a special day, after all."

Secure that he'd avoided a spanking, Arnth grinned. Caecilia frowned at her husband's favoritism of his youngest son. He was as lenient as she was impatient with the boy's recklessness. Mastarna recognized his own temperament in him. Fearlessness.

"Be careful, Vel. He'll dirty your coronation robes."

"A few red marks won't show on purple," said Mastarna. "Besides, as his hands are already colored vermilion, he may as well help paint my face as well for this masquerade. Don't you agree, little soldier?" Arnth nodded and slid off his knee to head across to the bowl of dye that had caused the commotion in the first place.

"Me, too, Apa!" Larce slipped from Mastarna and trotted after his brother, confident now his father was prepared to condone being messy.

Caecilia was not so obliging. She gestured to her Greek handmaid to help her. "Time for a bath, don't you think, Cytheris?"

The stout servant grinned, showing her missing dogtooth. "I'll take these rascals to the nursery, mistress. Extra scrubbing will be needed."

This time Arnth did not attempt to struggle when Cytheris grabbed him, hoisting him onto her hip. He knew he had met his match. Larce was despondent, imploring his mother, "Please, Ati! I want to see Apa crowned."

Caecilia bent and kissed him. "The ceremony is not for children, my love. Apa will say good-bye to you before he goes so you can see him in his regalia."

"So I can touch his eagle scepter?"

She nodded.

"Me, too!" Arnth was adamant.

Caecilia kissed the top of his head, avoiding patches of paint. "Yes, both of you. Now go and clean yourselves."

Tas tugged at her sleeve. "I'm already clean, Ati. And I'm old enough to go to the ceremony."

Caecilia crouched before him. His oval, tawny eyes were solemn. "Not quite, Tas. There'll be a vast crowd, and the rites are long and tiring."

Some of Arnth's doggedness emerged. "I want to see the Great Temple. I want to see Apa crowned." Caecilia wondered if she was going to have to weather another tantrum. Her sons were becoming too pampered.

Mastarna had less patience with his oldest than his youngest. "Listen to your mother, Tas."

At the doorway, Larce broke from Cytheris and skipped back to Caecilia. "I want to kiss you, Ati." He reached up to peck her on the cheek. She nuzzled his hair. "I'll give you a thousand kisses," she whispered, "before you go to sleep."

Caecilia watched the maid lead her sons from the chamber with its high ceiling decorated with rosettes and its walls with their horizontal stripes of red, green, and blue skirting the top and bottom. She was still grappling with living in the palace. She missed their family home. Even though they had lived in a mansion, it could not compare to the luxury of the royal residence.

Caecilia moved across to her husband with the bowl of vermilion dye. "You shouldn't make light of the custom, Vel. This is a sacred day for you. Veii's lucumo must color his face red in honor of Tinia, king of the gods."

Mastarna eyed the dish disdainfully. "I'd prefer it if I was only being declared zilath for one year. I'd still be required to wear the paint, but at least I wouldn't feel like a hypocrite. You know I've always protested against electing a king instead of a chief magistrate. And now I'm being crowned one to rule our city until my death."

She sighed and moved a stool to sit close by him, placing the bowl on a repository table. She clasped his hand. "This is what the people want, Vel. They want a ruler to finish this siege without the need for annual elections. They respect you. Why, even your rivals from the Tulumnes clan have placed aside old enmities to support you when the College of Principes voted. And before that, the High Council unanimously decided you were the only candidate. It's unprecedented."

He glanced down at his sling. "And yet I lost my last battle to General Camillus's Romans. More than half my army was massacred. The men of my tribe lost. I don't deserve to be elected Veii's leader after that."

Caecilia squeezed his fingers. "Of course you do. You're Veii's greatest general. Until the Battle of Blood and Hail, you always managed to keep the supply lines free to the north. If King Kurvenas had sent reinforcements instead of shutting the gates against his own troops, I'm sure the result would have been different."

He frowned. "I doubt it. His perfidy caused suffering, but two Roman armies had surrounded us."

"And yet Veii did not fall. The divine Queen Uni sent hail that day to drive our enemies from the battlefield and save you. I pray to the goddess every day to favor our city over Rome." She smiled. "She'll favor you as king also, Vel."

Mastarna scanned her face. "I never thought to hear a Roman condoning a monarch."

Caecilia tensed, withdrawing her fingers from his. "I'm no longer Roman. You know that." She rose and crossed the chamber to walk through the tall bronze doors to the tiled terrace with its fountain and rose garden. The autumn air was crisp, the sky cloudless. She drew her mantle around her as she stopped at the wall that enclosed the terrace, its massive ashlar blocks encircling the high citadel upon which the palace stood.

On the ridge across from her sat the Roman camp, the ravine between them razed of woodland, the stark snaking outline of siege works following the contours of the valleys. She knew such trenches bordered Veii for miles.

For a moment, she recalled her first sight of her new home as she traveled along the road where the Roman camp was now situated: the dizzying heights of the ridge, then the plunge to the valley to the juncture of two rivers, then up again to the plateaued city with its high arx beyond.

There were still sparse pockets of green in places. There should have been a scene of rich autumnal tints crowning the hills, or clothing dense glades, and red-and-gray tufa gorges. And beyond there should have been a patchwork of verdant undulating farmlands with flocks and herds sprinkled across meadows. Instead the Romans had felled most of the woods. The hub of roads that surrounded Veii, which led to places and lands Caecilia still hoped to see, were now deserted. Only Roman armies marched upon those trade routes now. And the rivers were bereft of boats. Trade had dwindled to nothing.

Ten years of war. Ten years of bloodshed. Ten years of conflict with the city of her birth. Rome claimed she had started a war when she'd chosen Vel Mastarna and his people. The truth was not so simple, but one thing was clear. She had never intended to betray Rome. But knowing its generals sought her destruction, she was prepared to welcome the role of traitoress now. After ten years of seeking peace, she had hardened her heart.

Mastarna appeared beside her, encircling her waist with his good arm. She faced him. "I've renounced my city, Vel. I seek its downfall. I am Veientane."

He stroked her cheek. "My warrioress. I named you 'Bellatrix' after Orion's star because I thought you brave, but you've become as fierce as any of my soldiers. I'm glad you are on Veii's side."

She pointed to the enemy camp. "How long before you think assistance will arrive? General Camillus sits on our doorstep. It's been almost two seasons now since fresh supplies have reached the city. I thought our northern commander, Thefarie Ulthes, would've marched from Falerii by now to relieve us."

He frowned. "I don't know what's delaying him. The Roman bastard has squeezed us so tightly that not even spies have made their way through with news. But I will not give up hope. Veii cisterns are full, so we will not die of thirst. And it's clear our wall won't be breached. No enemy has ever done so. Veii is impregnable. This citadel sits astride a high cliff. Two rivers gird us in their embrace."

"Walls can protect us, but without food, what use are stones?" She stared into the distance. "Camillus means to starve us out."

Mastarna also surveyed the Roman camp. "He'll be gone in winter. The Romans elect new consular generals each December. Once he's no longer in office, a different, lesser commander will be in charge. Perhaps that's what Thefarie is waiting for. A chance to attack once Furius Camillus no longer holds command. Wait and see. He'll break through the siege lines in winter. We need to keep our resolve."

"And if Thefarie reaches us? Will you then consider attacking Rome? Unlike Veii, their wall can be easily stormed."

He turned to her. "There's little prospect of that until this siege can be stopped. Let's pray to Nortia, goddess of Fate, this is what she wants for Veii."

Caecilia felt a familiar sense of guilt rise in her but suppressed it. She knew she could not continue keeping secrets from him much longer. "I believe Nortia wants Rome to fall."

He placed his hand on her shoulder. "All I know is that I'm grateful the deity brought us together. I believe she did so for a reason. And one day we'll live in peace together."

Her stubbornness emerged. "Only when Rome bends its knee to Veii."

Mastarna searched her face. "Where's the frightened girl forced to wed me?"

Caecilia straightened her shoulders. "Long transformed. You and Veii have taught me courage."

He smiled. "A warrioress indeed. But you never were such a hawk. I thought you only wanted concord."

She stroked his smooth-shaven cheek, enjoying the scent of sandalwood on his skin. "Remember how you once told me Rome and Veii are like two unrequited lovers? Only twelve miles between them across the Tiber. They're but a god's footstep apart. Both desire to possess the other—only Rome wishes to be the husband and make Veii submit as the wife."

He reached over and cupped her chin between his fingers. His touch was tender. "A Roman wife perhaps but not a Veientane one. You are my equal."

He swept the hair from her neck and kissed the tiny curls at the nape. His mouth was warm, his lips gentle. His hand traced the curve of her spine and buttocks beneath the soft, fine wool of her chiton. She felt herself stir. Even after ten years, her husband could make her knees buckle with desire. "I want you, Bellatrix."

She pressed her forehead to his. "Soon, Vel. The birth of our daughter was hard. I'm not yet healed. Aren't you happy with what I can do for you in the meantime?"

He kissed her brow. "I'm sorry to be impatient." Stepping back, he placed his hand on his sling. "And I want to be able to carry you to bed. We both have wounds that need mending."

Caecilia smiled and clasped his hand. "It's time to get ready to visit the Great Temple." Then she laughed. "No more stalling. I must paint your face."

They moved inside. Semni had finished feeding Thia and was rocking her against her shoulder to burp her. "I'll go now, mistress."

"Wait," said Mastarna. "Let me hold my little princess."

The nursemaid handed the swaddled baby to the warrior who cradled her in the crook of his uninjured arm, careful the child's head was supported. The seven-week-old was tiny against the scarred flesh of his forearm. He bent and kissed both of the child's cheeks, crooning. The tenderness was incongruous in such a hardened man. Caecilia had never seen Vel dote so on his sons.

Thia's mouth curved upward.

"Look, she's smiling, Bellatrix."

Caecilia nodded, glancing to Semni while Mastarna's head was bent over the babe. The women exchanged a smile. Neither would dare tell him it was more likely to be wind.

He touched the silver amulet fastened around the baby's neck by a fine chain with the figure of the huntress Atlenta embossed upon it. It had once been Caecilia's; now her daughter wore the talisman. He kissed Thia's brow. "May this charm always protect you from the evil eye."

"Come, Vel, your daughter needs to sleep."

Reluctantly, he surrendered the infant to Semni. "Take care of my princess." His deep, resonant voice was soft. The baby stared at him, enrapt.

Caecilia led Mastarna to his chair and sat opposite him. Dipping a brush into the red lead, she smoothed the pigment across his face. His features were rugged and scarred. She'd once thought the almond-shaped eyes of the Rasenna people strange; now all of her children except Arnth were graced with them.

She could hear a familiar clicking noise as she tended to him. He was fiddling with the two golden dice he secreted in the sinus fold of his tebenna cloak. They were his talismans. Old and worn and smooth. He would jiggle them when he was worried, the sound marking his tell. She laid the brush aside and placed her hand on his to still his fidgeting. "What troubles you?"

He stared at her for a moment but did not reply. Then he stood and smoothed his tebenna, ensuring its folds were even. "Do I look sufficiently regal?"

She frowned at his evasion. Nevertheless, she surveyed him in his regalia, thinking he was not above vanity. The purple tunic and cloak with their gold embroidery declared he was king. In Rome, a triumphing general wore such garb. The Rasennan kings who had once ruled there had introduced their subjects to the custom, a stately and elegant apparel the Romans adopted readily from the people they called the Etruscans.

Caecilia had been raised on the tales of oppression of those monarchs. How they were ousted as tyrants, and then the Republic was founded. Until she was eighteen and married into Vel's society, she'd despised the Etruscans as her enemy. Now she gladly lived among the Rasenna.

She also rose. Smiling, she smoothed the cloth across Vel's broad shoulders and murmured reassurance. She did not tell him that she was also apprehensive, praying that, one day, he would wear such robes in Rome's Forum. For the goddess Nortia had given her a sign she kept secret from her husband. Her destiny was to return to her birthplace. And the only safe way to do so was as the wife of a conquering hero.

Two

Queen Uni towered ten feet high above Caecilia as she knelt before the goddess she'd once worshiped as the Roman Juno. The sculpted face of the terra-cotta statue was serene in the muted sunlight of the sanctum. There was no indication in the deity's expression she could be ferocious—a warrioress greater than Caecilia could ever be. But the lightning bolt the sky goddess brandished heralded her power. Only the celestial king, Jupiter, wielded a thunderbolt in Rome.

A decade of war had taken its toll. The terra-cotta that clad the columns and roof rafters of the vast temple was cracked, the red-and-black paint fading. Caecilia hoped the immortal would not be displeased the privations of war meant her quarters were no longer pristine.

Despite the neglect of her surroundings the divinity still looked regal. The Veientanes revered her too much to disregard her person. Her goatskin was not tattered, and she wore a diadem and pectoral of gleaming gold. Rings of silver and turquoise bedecked her fingers, and her lapis eyes were deep blue.

Gazing at the divine queen's apparel made Caecilia conscious of her own. Vel was not the only one who was uncomfortable with donning the purple. Yet she could not deny she enjoyed the feel of her fine woolen chiton, its bodice tight, revealing the curve of her breasts and defining her nipples. Its hem was a solid band of cloth of gold. Beads of amethyst and pearl encrusted her heavy purple mantle. She knew her father would hate to see her this way, dressed flagrantly instead of garbed in the modest stola of a Roman matron, wearing a crown instead of covering her head with a palla shawl.

She touched her tiara. It was exquisite. Finely beaten golden leaves overlapped each other with strands looping down beside her cheeks and ears. Its fragile beauty both captivated her and made her nervous. She did not want to be the first Veientane queen to damage it.

"How much longer are you going to pray?" growled Mastarna. "I want to get this service over and done with." She frowned and glanced across to him. He was pacing the cell, impatient, as always, with ceremony and ritual.

Caecilia hoped the goddess would forgive him his irreverence. "We must placate and praise Queen Uni first, Vel. You don't want to incur her disfavor."

Nearby, Lord Tarchon was watching the king with furrowed brow. Mastarna's oldest son was also dressed in royal colors. The prince's good looks were in stark contrast to the craggy features of his adopted father. The bruises suffered in his last battle had healed. His face was unscarred.

In profile, Caecilia could see the straight brow and nose so distinctive of the Rasenna. His dark oval eyes were long lashed, his lips naturally curved upward as though the gods had decreed he should always look contented.

At twenty-seven, Caecilia always thought it odd a man who had just turned thirty could be her stepson. Yet there was a special friendship between them. They were more like brother and sister. And she regretted he and Vel were always at loggerheads. She wished her husband would be more approving of the young cousin he'd taken into his home to raise.

"Caecilia is right, Father. The protectress of our city must be placated before we seek a sign from her."

Mastarna ceased pacing. "Make your devotions, then. But it's Lady Tanchvil who must ensure all necessary invocations are made." He looked toward the portico outside. "Where is she?"

"But I'm here, sire. I was seeing to final preparations."

A woman emerged from the workroom at the rear of the chamber and stood beside the bronze altar table in front of the statue. She bowed to the royal couple. Caecilia rose and joined her husband.

Tall, with broad shoulders, Lady Tanchvil towered over them. Yet despite her strong frame she did not lack femininity. She wore her iron-gray hair loose to her waist, a diadem of garnets across her brow, its ribbons trailing. Her face was white with albumen, almost ghostly. Her lips were deep red with carmine. And the antimony that darkened her lashes made her black almond eyes appear like coals. "I'm sure with Queen Caecilia's piety toward divine Uni, our godly sovereign will think favorably upon the royal family."

The priestess's words were kind but did not stop Caecilia from being daunted by the woman's presence. Tanchvil's confident bearing was born from the heritage of a noble and prestigious family. And unlike the Vestal Virgins in Rome who tended the holy flame, the hatrencu priestess had once been married to a zilath chief magistrate. Now the widow held the most holy of offices. As high priestess of the temple of Veii's principal deity, she was second only in holiness to the king.

The fact the Sacred College had elected a woman to fill such a position astonished Caecilia. Even after living for years with the Veientanes, their ways could surprise her. Rasennan women were held in high esteem compared to their counterparts in Rome.

Caecilia thought of Tanchvil's predecessor and wondered where he was. Artile Mastarna, Vel's younger brother, was the man she hated most in the world. The former chief priest of Uni had tried to abduct Tas. She shivered, thinking how she could have lost her eldest son. The prophet had absconded from the city during the Battle of Blood and Hail. No word had reached them as to his whereabouts. She hoped he'd been set upon by Romans. She hoped he was dead.

The high priestess smoothed the folds of her pleated white chiton with its border of red spirals. Caecilia could smell the faint scent of rose water. The hatrencu was bathed in readiness for the ceremony. "I'm honored to be able to take the auspices today to determine if your reign will be blessed, sire."

"Then let the omen be favorable," muttered Mastarna. "I don't want to start my rule with the populace nervous because the gods decide to be difficult. And I don't like to be called 'sire.' 'My lord' will suffice."

Tanchvil's face registered shock. She was not familiar with the new king's ungodliness. Caecilia rested her hand on Vel's forearm. He was always skeptical of prophecies, a characteristic that made her uneasy.

"You are impious, my lord," said Tanchvil.

Mastarna glowered. "No, I'm practical. You place a heavy onus on the sky goddess. She'll need to provide a miracle to end this siege without assistance from the north. If I can't save my people, then I'm an unworthy king."

"At least there's reassurance our city's sins have been expiated," said the hatrencu. "The last omen Lord Artile presaged was that Veii would remain safe if the traitor among us was punished. The death of King Kurvenas will have pleased our deities, given he engineered the demise of your army, the largest force in Veii."

Mastarna raised his hands, palms outward. "If we're going to speak of portents of doom, Lady Tanchvil, I'd rather you give your opinion about the flooding of Lake Albanus. My priestly brother claimed it was a premonition signifying the gods were unhappy with Rome but gave no reason why. Unless the Romans ascertain the expiation rites to assuage divine displeasure, Veii will never fall." He stared pointedly at the hatrencu. "Artile said he knew what rituals needed to be performed. You're our preeminent seer now that he's no longer here. Have you also deciphered the meaning?"

The priestess seemed undaunted by Vel's challenge. Caecilia was impressed. The rising of the lake in summer when there'd been no rain had posed a mystery. Especially since the brooks and river around it were dry. Lake Albanus lay in the crater of a volcano, fed by no sources other than its own. And then the water had risen to the top of its surrounding mountains and overflowed. Wreckage was left in its wake as it forged a path to the sea.

"Lord Artile stole the Rasennan Discipline when he left. It will be difficult to decipher the meaning without those sacred texts."

"All principes are schooled in that codex. There are many copies of the Holy Books," said Mastarna.

"He stole the only set of special volumes kept by the chief priest of Uni. There are copies in Velzna, the sacred capital. But we're cut off from other Rasennan city-states. I can't send for duplicates."

Caecilia suddenly felt concern Veii no longer had the benefit of Artile's skills. Despite her loathing for the priest, she had to concede his superior powers. He was a mighty haruspex, reading the intentions of the gods in the livers of beasts, and a fulgurator, master of divination of lightning sent from the heavens. Tanchvil had large shoes to fill.

Tarchon must have been sharing her thoughts. "Then we must pray Rome's augurs remain ignorant of the portent's meaning."

Lady Tanchvil touched the gold torque fashioned as an eagle around her neck. "My Lord Mastarna, perhaps you should consider availing yourself of the protection of Tinia, king of the gods, and call down lightning upon Rome as a surety. As a fulgurator, I've the power to summon him."

Goose bumps pimpled Caecilia's arms. The thought of calling down lightning was a potent strategy. The practice was intriguing and terrifying. Unlike Roman Jupiter, Tinia could wield three thunderbolts. When he hurled down his spear of destruction, an enemy city would surely fall.

Tarchon gave a soft whistle. "Such a tactic is rarely employed. It takes great piety and discipline to coax Tinia's approval. One must first induce the Veiled Ones to convince him."

Vel remained silent. He glanced at Caecilia. Despite his disdain for those who sought celestial intervention, he was perturbed by the suggestion. "My time would be better spent planning the practicalities of breaking this siege," he said, "rather than praying to a host of unseen deities. Rome will only fall with strategy and bloodshed. I've no time to rely on holy whim."

Tanchvil's eyes widened. "Again, you're sacrilegious, my lord."

"Perhaps, but I'd rather pray Commander Thefarie Ulthes bring relief to a starving city than hope the king of the gods might choose to strike our enemy's wall."

Tanchvil drew herself erect. Mastarna did not seem fazed at having to look up at a woman.

"Do you also wish to dispense with the auspices for your coronation?"

Caecilia tensed, frightened Vel would continue to act rashly. She squeezed his arm to warn him to temper his words. He frowned at his wife's surreptitious warning.

"No, the people would fret if such a ceremony was not conducted."

Tanchvil pursed her lips. "Then I'll direct my acolytes to prepare. We'll sacrifice six white cows to Uni, and I'll determine the will of the gods."

Tarchon walked across to the altar table and examined the ceremonial paterae dishes and pitchers of wine, the bowls of flour and sharp sacrificial knives. "I'm looking forward to seeing your skill as a haruspex, Lady Tanchvil."

"I don't examine the livers of animals for divination, Lord Tarchon. I'm an augur who reads patterns of flight, or listens to the call of birds."

She clapped her strong sinewy hands. A young cepen priest entered the chamber from the workroom. Caecilia gasped to see an enormous golden eagle on his arm, head hooded, legs tethered. He settled the bird onto a stand. Tanchvil moved across to the creature, murmuring to it and stroking its wings.

"Antar is the instrument of my augury. He's wondrous."

The sight of the raptor, so wild and yet so docile, intrigued Caecilia. She could not wait to see how this woman would predict the future from the journey of this most majestic of birds.

Absorbed in studying the eagle, it took a moment for the queen to notice the female acolyte who had entered the room carrying a shallow patera of oil. There was something familiar about her, with her ringlets of black hair. The girl kept her head lowered, avoiding her gaze. Caecilia blinked as she recognized her. It was Aricia, her maid Cytheris's daughter. She'd tried to help Artile abduct Tas. All believed she'd escaped with the priest. Clearly she'd suffered her own type of betrayal. Caecilia stiffened, anger welling in her, her hands shaking. She was about to accost the girl, but before she could say anything Tanchvil gave the acolyte an order. Aricia limped back into the workroom.

Caecilia wanted to challenge the high priestess about her novice, but Mastarna extended his arm to her, distracting her. "It's time to meet our people."

The queen nodded. There would be time later to make inquiries about Aricia. Swallowing her nerves, she walked to the portico and down into the sanctuary. A crowd had assembled around the podium and altar. A crowd who'd always resented her.

The eagle rested on the gauntlet covering Tanchvil's forearm. Caecilia sensed the creature's power—how his talons gripped the leather, the cruel curved beak, and the potential of his folded wings. It was the bird of Tinia, king of the gods. In Rome, Jupiter held it dear. The raptor could ascend above the storm and carry the soul of the mighty into the presence of the divine. Today, the priestess would send him forth to become the messenger of the gods.

Antar shifted, causing the holy woman to brace herself to bear his weight. The bells on his hood jingled. He was impatient to be free.

Tanchvil carefully removed the hood. The eagle's head and breast were flecked with gold, his dark plumage shiny. If he chose to flap his enormous wings he could break free even before his mistress had loosened the leather restraints. And what was to prevent him from turning and ripping her face with his beak?

The hatrencu lifted her arm to send Antar skyward. Caecilia felt the swish of air as the eagle rose, his pinions extended, seeking the thermals. Holding her breath, she waited to see to which quadrant of the heavens he would fly. His wings stretched in perfect symmetry; the raptor spiraled higher, gliding over the southeast of the city before heading northeast. Then he hovered for a moment before diving and swooping upward again.

Tanchvil raised her arm and called to the eagle. The priestess's cry was piercing, mimicking that of the bird. The winged herald circled, then flew with great arcing flaps to thump down once again upon his mistress's sheathed arm.

"Antar was summoned by Laran, the god of war, but then headed toward Uni's realm. The war will continue, but Veii's mother will continue to protect us."

The throng was quiet. Caecilia knew they'd hoped Uni would decree that Veii would once again be free.

Mastarna's expression was brooding beneath the crimson paint as he considered his response. Tanchvil once again hooded the bird's eyes.

Taking a deep breath, Caecilia stepped forward to the edge of the podium. She hoped her voice would be loud enough. She could feel the eyes of the people studying her as they surrounded her. She was used to their scrutiny—sometimes bearing their suspicion and distrust. Sometimes admiring her for bearing the general so many sons. "My people, do not be disheartened there has been no sign our enemy will yield."

Mastarna encircled her waist with his arm. There was surprise in his voice. "Thank you, Bellatrix, I will speak now."

"No, I haven't finished, Vel." She inhaled deeply again, her nerves settling. People were shifting and jostling to get a better look. Their faces were tired and gaunt.

"Ten years ago the generals of Rome married me to Vel Mastarna against my will. My uncle, Aemilius Mamercus, was numbered among them."

There were no catcalls. Confidence eased through her. She was amazed her voice carried across the sanctuary. She stepped from Vel and pivoted in a circle, ensuring everyone surrounding the podium could see and hear her.

"Ten years ago I was held hostage by King Tulumnes, a wicked tyrant. In fear, I escaped to Rome only to find those same generals were ready to sacrifice me, and war had always been their intention. And just as they forced me to marry, they then forced me to divorce my husband."

Vel touched her forearm. "You need not do this, Bellatrix."

She ignored his warning. "But then a miracle happened." She glanced at him and smiled. "Vel Mastarna rescued me. He gave me a chance to marry him again. He gave me a chance to choose Veii."

She held out her arms. "I've felt your distrust as the daughter of a foe living among you. But know this: I was once Roman, but

I feel no love for that city. I am Veientane and pledge my loyalty to you. And I say now: It's not enough that we defend our city. It's not enough to seek peace. Rome is a wolf who will devour us. It must be killed once and for all." She stepped back and grasped Vel's hand and raised it into the air. "I seek Rome's destruction! Let us conquer the wolf. Let us bring down its wall!"

For a moment she felt sickened at the lack of response. Then she heard clapping, feet stamping in unison, voices joining as one. "Queen Caecilia! King Mastarna! Queen Caecilia! King Mastarna!"

Disbelieving these people were exalting her, tears pricked her eyes. She turned to Vel, smiling. He continued to survey the crowd as he also pivoted on the podium. His look was hard as he gripped her fingers. Above the noise, she heard the anger in his bass voice. "What have you done, Bellatrix?"

She turned back to face the crowd, raising her other hand and waving. She had to shout so Vel could hear her, a current of elation flowing through her. "I've done what I should have done ten years ago. I have declared war on Rome."

THREE

The blood of the white cows had been drained from the runnels into the bolos of the holy altar. There should have been more than a score of beasts sacrificed for the coronation, but in the besieged city there were scant cattle left for such a ceremony. At least the people would feast on the flesh now. The aroma of roast beef filled the air. Those in the sanctuary stood in a circle around the cooking pits, their faces expectant, their mouths watering in anticipation as the carcasses were turned on the spits.

In the city below, sounds of celebration drifted up to the arx. Mastarna had not forgotten the rest of his subjects. An extra grain ration had been offered from the city granary and wine distributed from the private cellars of the palace. His royal predecessors had hoarded the fine vintage for their own use. King Mastarna was more generous, intent on boosting morale.

Mastarna led Caecilia to his chariot. He'd not spoken to her since her declaration. Maintaining his silence, he helped her into the gilded car. The call of their names resounded around them. Aemilia Caeciliana's was being hailed as loudly as the king's. Despite her husband's iciness, she could not help but feel proud.

After so many years of hostility, the adulation was as heady as if she'd drunk strong unwatered wine.

Surrounding the chariot were twenty-four lictors. The royal bodyguards were dressed in black and held ceremonial rods and axes. The head lictor walked abreast of the chariot. Arruns was stocky, half his swarthy face tattooed with a fanged snake, its coils twisting around his neck. She knew the serpent continued to encircle his chest and back. Today, dressed in his uniform, the grotesque pattern was hidden. His hooded eyes always veiled his emotions, his tattooed visage and hooked nose inspiring menace. The Phoenician had been Mastarna's personal protector for fifteen years. Caecilia wondered if he welcomed the presence of twenty-three others. She suspected he doubted they were necessary. If not for him, Vel would have died in the Battle of Blood and Hail. And he'd rescued her from danger more than once. Both of them owed their lives to him.

Smiling to the crowd, Mastarna planted his feet wide, balanced perfectly as he took hold of the reins of the four white horses that pulled the chariot. A retinue of principes followed. These nobles of Veii were richly robed and bejeweled. The women were trying to outdo each other with pectorals of green jasper and lapis and diadems of amber and peridot. The men were no less splendid, dressed in brightly colored tebenna cloaks, their short-cropped hair wreathed.

Vel's smile disappeared as soon as he entered the palace courtyard. "Get a servant boy to bring water. I want to wash off this vermilion," he barked to Arruns as he strode toward the throne room. "I only want to see the high councillors. I'll take audience with the other principes tomorrow."

Caecilia followed Mastarna to the dais with its golden throne. There was a bull's head crest emblazoned upon its back, the symbol of the House of Mastarna. Caecilia took her place beside her husband on her own small throne, conscious of her status at his right hand. Prince Tarchon also ascended the platform and sat on a high-backed chair to the left side of his adopted father. She was pleased Vel had agreed to appoint him to his war council. Maybe Mastarna's coldness toward his son was thawing at last.

The high councillors trailed through the doorway with its tall double bronze doors. General Lusinies approached first. Bald and battered of feature, the warrior knelt to swear fealty. Mastarna acknowledged him with a brief smile.

General Feluske followed. He winced as he bent his knee. Caecilia knew it to be from a worn joint rather than reluctance. He'd long been an ally of her husband.

The last princip to approach was Karcuna Tulumnes.

Caecilia tensed. There was no love between the Houses of Mastarna and Tulumnes. Both kings from Karcuna's bloodline had served Veii badly. His older brother had murdered Mastarna's greatest friend and had terrorized her. And his cousin Kurvenas had shut the gates against her husband and destroyed his army.

As with all of his family, Karcuna was imposing in his height and haughtiness. His cheek would twitch every now and then in a disconcerting tic. She remembered how his brother had towered over her when he was lucumo, intimidating her both physically and mentally, threatening to mutilate and kill and rape her. She wondered why Vel had appointed Karcuna as one of his advisers given such a villainous lineage. And yet the new leader of the Tulumnes clan had not objected to Mastarna's election. Today more was being asked of him—to bend his knee and pay respect to a man who'd opposed his kin for decades.

To her surprise, Vel rose and descended the dais to stand before the princip. "There has long been enmity between our families, Karcuna. Your clan believes in monarchy while mine opposes it. And yet I stand before you as a lucumo because our people demand it. I'm reluctant, but I can't ignore their wishes. For the sake of internal concord, I hope you'll serve me without rancor."

Karcuna squared his shoulders. "I'm not like my brother. Nor my cousin Kurvenas, who I acknowledge betrayed Veii. So I'll not conspire against you, but I won't deny many of my clan have reservations the leader of the House of Mastarna now rules over them."

Mastarna frowned. "Then I ask that you convince them such hostility must end for the sake of Veii. I'm a general with no troops of my own. Now I ask all our warriors to fight for Veii's king. Just as Roman soldiers fight for their state, not their clans."

The princip hesitated. His powers of persuasion would be tested when called upon to convince his tribe to fight under the royal banner. Then, to Caecilia's relief, he knelt before Mastarna and bent his head. "I pledge allegiance to you and to Veii."

Vel's expression was guarded as he reached down and proffered his forearm to Karcuna. "I won't forget this. Veii will only grow stronger now we're allies."

The councillor rose and gripped his forearm.

General Lusinies moved across to the monarch. Caecilia noticed how his hand was raised as though to clap Mastarna on the shoulder, but he dropped it to his side when Vel turned his attention to him. The laurel wreath crown gracing the king's head emphasized the men's newly altered status.

"I hope you now see that agreeing to be lucumo is the best thing for this city, my lord. See how the people welcomed your coronation."

"There's good humor among them today as I'm filling their bellies, but it may not last." Mastarna sat down and accepted a damp cloth from a servant boy to wipe his face clean of the paint. "If I don't manage to bring this city through the siege, their support may wane when hunger stirs discontentment."

"You underestimate yourself, my lord," said Feluske. "And I think Queen Caecilia's call to arms gives hope we might yet attack Rome instead of merely defending our walls."

Caecilia flinched, aware Vel would not welcome being reminded of her declaration. There was an edge of irritation in his voice. "My wife's goal is premature."

At his words, Feluske and Lusinies exchanged glances. Karcuna's eyes narrowed. She could feel his scrutiny before he addressed Mastarna. "My family has always believed Rome should be conquered. Rasennan kings should rule there again."

Vel bristled. "And how do you suggest we do that? Camillus has strengthened the siege lines with stone. And there are few chances for us to engage in skirmishes. The Romans remain secure behind forts and trenches. It's a stalemate."

"So we continue to sit here and do nothing?" pressed Karcuna. "Our warriors grow restless."

Caecilia frowned. The general may have sworn fealty, but he was not above challenging his ruler.

"Camillus will soon relinquish command," said Mastarna. "In the changeover period with his successor, the cordon will slacken, and food will be able to be bartered through the stockades."

Lusinies nodded his head. "And we shouldn't forget Rome has many enemies. Multiple war fronts may well prove too much with their resources stretched thin."

Karcuna crossed his arms. "But that situation has been the same now for years. It doesn't stop the Romans besieging us. They covet Veii's land most. And instead of his usual tactic of razing crops, Camillus is now coercing Veientane farmers to till their land. Daughters and wives are raped if the men resist. The grain grown will feed Rome, not us." The princip turned to Feluske and Lusinies as though expecting them to also challenge the lucumo. "Meanwhile we sit here starving."

The older men avoided his gaze. Caecilia was pleased they still sided with their king. Yet she sensed Vel's anger growing at his strategy being questioned. "We must survive until December. It's time all the principes share their reserves of food just as I do. Let them distribute it to the needier among us."

The three councillors stared at him, saying nothing.

Karcuna turned his attention back to Caecilia. "And what does our queen say? Your wife wants us to march on Rome, my lord. She shows more iron than most."

Caecilia bit the inside of her lip, aware of the princip's implied criticism of Mastarna. It was never her intention to cause Vel embarrassment. She was also surprised Karcuna sought her opinion. She was used to the men of the Tulumnes family spitting venom at her. "My exhortation was to boost morale. I agree with my husband that Veii must be relieved first."

Karcuna smiled slyly. "Then you don't believe Rome should fall as you declared."

This time it was she who bridled. His words echoed his predecessors' distrust for her. In the past, the Tulumnes clan asserted she was a traitor because she wouldn't vow to destroy Rome. She'd often wondered how she could be doubly treasonous when both foes accused her of perfidy.

Having remained quiet throughout the discussion, Tarchon now stood. "I'm sick of Caecilia's loyalty being questioned."

"Enough!" Mastarna cut across his son's defense. "All this talk of conquest is futile. You're forgetting we need the support of the League of the Twelve Rasennan cities. Without extra forces, Veii won't succeed. All the Rasenna must rise. And that's unlikely. Our pleas for support have fallen on deaf ears for a decade now."

Caecilia leaned across to Vel. "Perhaps it's time to adjourn to the banquet," she said loud enough for the others to hear.

He glanced at her, then nodded and rose. "My wife is right. Enough talk of war. Let's enjoy the feast."

The councillors bowed and headed toward the door, but Tarchon called out unexpectedly, "Lord Karcuna, could you stay behind?"

The tall man turned, a look of surprise on his face.

"What's this about, Tarchon?" Mastarna growled.

"I wish to make a formal application to become Sethre Kurvenas's mentor. Lord Karcuna is his guardian now King Kurvenas is dead."

Caecilia took a deep breath, wishing her stepson had not opened himself up for humiliation. This was not the time to make a case to become the lover of the grieving son of the murdered lucumo.

Karcuna stiffened, addressing Mastarna instead of the prince. "King Kurvenas didn't approve of Sethre becoming the beloved of your adopted son. I must honor his wishes as a father."

Caecilia thought Mastarna would concur. Instead, to her surprise, he gave his son his support. "I believe Prince Tarchon's desire to foster links between our Houses has merit."

The councillor cocked his head to the side, his tone less than deferential. "It's enough that I bend my knee to you, my lord. I don't think my young cousin need be tainted by Tarchon's reputation."

"Oh, and what would that be?"

Karcuna's eyes traveled along Tarchon's figure, treating him as though he was some specimen who could neither speak nor feel. "Why hasn't he married? Where are his children? He's a soft one. I can't risk Sethre's reputation."

Mastarna stood. "We've made gains here tonight, Karcuna. Don't lose them by denigrating my son."

The princip's cheek twitched. "I merely speak what all know. You were about to shun him yourself when Lord Artile took him as his beloved. And Tarchon is far from eligible to act as a mentor. He fails to meet the required standards. He's only thirty. He's never held high office. He isn't married. His war record is patchy. And there's no guarantee he would relinquish his role when the boy has grown a beard."

Caecilia's winced to hear Tarchon's shortcomings so brutally listed.

Mastarna tensed beside her at the litany.

Tarchon descended the dais to stand opposite the princip, hands on his hips. "I'm a prince of Veii, and I sit on the king's council. Isn't that status enough?" He placed his hand on his thigh. "And beneath these robes my leg has only just healed from the wound I suffered in the Battle of Blood and Hail. No man has ever questioned my courage."

Karcuna stepped back, running a hand through his hair. He continued to eye Tarchon, unable to control a spasm in his cheek. "Sethre is not fifteen years old as is the usual age for a pupil. He is nineteen."

"I understand Sethre will cease to be my pupil when required," Tarchon added.

The councillor continued to study him, then nodded. "I will think on it, then. But in the meantime you must stay away from my ward."

Tarchon was respectful instead of defiant. "I'll accept any terms you set, Lord Karcuna. I'm grateful to be considered." He cast a look over his shoulder to Caecilia, wanting her to share his success. She smiled at him although she was worried. She knew him too well. It would be hard for him to surrender Sethre when the boy reached full manhood. He was in love with the youth.

Mastarna raised his hand, signaling the end of the matter. "I'm hungry. Let's eat." He placed Caecilia's hand on his forearm to escort her from the chamber.

Lord Karcuna bowed, waiting for the king and queen to walk ahead of him. He deferred to the prince, who followed immediately after the royal couple.

"You surprise me, Vel," whispered Caecilia. "Defending him like that. I'm pleased."

His voice was gruff. "Karcuna's concerns are valid, but I will not have him thinking I condone one of my family being slandered." She squeezed his forearm. "But you'll support Tarchon in this, won't you? It might just be the making of him."

To her dismay, he dropped his forearm from under the pressure of her fingers. The snub startled her.

"I hope Karcuna's final decision is to reject his suit. I doubt Tarchon's ability to be anyone's mentor. He drinks heavily and hasn't stopped chewing Catha leaves to heighten his senses. And he better keep his word to stay away from Sethre until Karcuna makes up his mind. Otherwise there will be trouble."

Caecilia only took in half his words, still concerned with his rebuff. "Are you still angry at me?"

They had reached the entrance to the banquet hall. The guests inside slid from their dining couches and bowed.

Vel clasped her fingertips, leading her to their kline, not responding but nevertheless giving her his answer.

She pursed her lips, irritated at his mood. He was the one who'd always encouraged her independence. Now he was resentful she'd publically dispelled any lingering doubts that she supported Rome.

Vel stepped up from the footstool onto the deep cushioned mattress and lay down, propping his back against the headboard, careful not to jar his injured arm. Caecilia climbed up to sit next to him, choosing not to recline, and fuming he wouldn't speak to her.

Mastarna drained the chalice of wine handed to him by a slave boy. Then he called for another cup and downed it just as quickly. She restrained herself from cautioning him not to drink too much, knowing it would only irk him. And she thought him hypocritical to judge his son for overindulging in wine when he would do the same.

The other diners resumed their positions on their couches. Musicians once again plucked lyres and played their flutes, their melodies an accompaniment to laughter and chatter. Caecilia sipped her wine, enjoying the first mouthful, wondering if she should also welcome inebriation to forget war and politics and duty as well as the moroseness of her husband.

FOUR

Servants were stacking plates on the lower shelves of the repository tables and wheeling them away. A chandelier, its sconces shaped as antlers, was lowered from the ceiling and its many wicks lit. The high ceiling with its supporting single rafter merged into shadow. The feast was over but the drinking continued.

Vel had excused himself from their divan hours ago. Caecilia scanned the chamber. She spied him sitting opposite Lusinies, a gaming table extended across their knees. Mastarna's face was ashen, fatigue shadowing his features. The long day of ceremony had taken its toll. And she knew his arm would be paining him.

His pile of roundels was low compared to his opponent's. He was having no luck with his betting tonight. Caecilia considered whether to join him but was reluctant. She was also tired and didn't have the energy to weather his sullen silence. Losing wagers would do nothing to improve his mood either.

Arruns dogged her steps as she slipped away from the banquet. She gestured for him to remain behind. The Phoenician nodded, but she guessed he would soon be checking she had safely navigated her way to her chamber.

Having only lived a short while in the palace, Caecilia had yet to learn the maze of corridors in the vast building. She soon realized she'd taken a wrong turn when she wandered into an unfamiliar, gloomy hallway. She paused, trying to gain her bearings, when her attention was caught by two figures in a recess between two pillars. Their urgent moans were telltale. She instantly recognized Tarchon's back as he covered the slave boy, his bare, broad shoulders tapered to a narrow waist, his kilt hitched up.

Sensing her presence, he pulled back, startled. The servant straightened and turned. Caecilia's jaw dropped. Sethre Kurvenas bowed his head, face scarlet, as he rearranged his robes.

"Stop gaping, Caecilia," said Tarchon, clasping her elbow and ushering her into a nearby room lit only by a brazier's glow. The youth quickly followed.

Anger surged in her. "By the gods, Tarchon. Are you mad? Does your word mean nothing?"

The prince looped his arm around Sethre's waist in a relaxed manner. She noticed Tarchon's teeth were stained green. He'd been chewing Catha again, the herb that caused his eyes to glaze and the worries of the world to blur.

"It was to be our last time until Karcuna agrees to appoint me as Sethre's mentor." Tarchon placed two fingers under the youth's chin, then stroked his cheek, not at all embarrassed of caressing him in front of the queen. "Tell her, little chick."

Sethre was less confident of displaying affection in front of her. "It's true, my lady," he mumbled.

Caecilia concentrated on her stepson. "Vel said you wouldn't be able to stay away from him. You're just proving Karcuna right in doubting you."

Tarchon shook his head. "The first offer is always rejected before terms are settled." He smiled at Sethre. "I'm a prince of Veii. Karcuna won't refuse me."

Caecilia grabbed his arm. "I wouldn't be so sure. And what of your own self-respect? I thought you'd matured. Why do you need the Catha?"

"Don't worry, Caecilia. Supplies are dwindling. It will cure my addiction."

"That's not an answer."

He peeled her fingers away. "Why do you think I want to dull my senses? I can't touch Sethre after tonight. It causes me anguish." He gazed at the youth. "I love him."

The nineteen-year-old regarded the prince with adoration. Caecilia noticed the down of his sideburns and two spots of high color on his cheeks. She crossed her arms, impatient with their mutual admiration. "I don't understand either of you. I thought Sethre—"

"Hated me. But he's softened his heart toward me again."

Sethre reached for his lover's hand. "My grief blinded me. Father acted dishonorably when he shut the gates. But I was angry and confused after seeing him murdered. And I was wrong to shun Tarchon merely because of the enmity between our Houses. I can't forget how Father threatened to throw him over the wall during the battle." Sethre turned back to her. "You showed your love for Veii today, my lady. I'm sorry I doubted your allegiance. I'm also sorry my father treated you unfairly. "

His words surprised her. As did his deference. She was used to his disdain. She uncrossed her arms. "Then I thank you. But I counsel both of you not to meet again if you wish the chance to act as lover and beloved." She gestured toward the passageway. "I think you should return to the banquet, Sethre. Before someone else finds us."

He bowed, then cast a look toward Tarchon, holding out his palm. Tarchon smoothed his own across it, until all but their fingertips were touching. And then the tall youth slipped into the darkness.

Caecilia studied the prince in the torchlight as he bid his silent farewell. She'd seen how the pampered daughters of the court giggled and simpered in his presence. For a moment she wished he could enjoy both men and women. It would be easier for him to gain credibility if he could sire children. "Do you actually want to go through with this? Even if Karcuna agrees, your time with Sethre will be short. There's no way two freeborn nobles can remain as lovers. You'll both be declared as soft if you continue after Sethre has grown a beard. Do you want that for him? The boy is warrior born. You would condemn him to shame. You escaped such a fate when you spurned Artile. Withdraw your suit and spare yourselves heartache."

"Don't lecture me! My love for Artile was flawed. He was obsessive and sick. I know now it was wrong. I was only eleven when he took me to his bed. It's different with Sethre. I want him to ride into battle with me as much as lie beside me."

Frustrated, she crossed her arms again. "Then prove to your father and Karcuna you're worthy to act as a mentor. Stop drinking so much. And gambling. And chewing Catha! And stick to slaves and freedmen in the meantime."

He snorted. "Next you'll have me married. Only there'll be no children. Would that be fair? Don't you think that would sour relations with my wife's family?"

Caecilia sighed. "I only want what's best for you. I don't want to see you hurt. You know I love you." She placed her hand on his forearm. "You were the first to make me see the Veientanes as my people. To teach me their language, philosophy, and customs."

"When I taught you the differences between Rome and Veii, I never thought you would see your birthplace destroyed. You frighten me, Caecilia."

"You criticize me for seeing the Romans as they truly are? I thought you'd approve."

"I see your stubbornness emerging. Your black-and-white vision."

His words reminded her of Vel's annoyance. She was too tired to discuss it. "I want to go to bed. Show me how to get back to my quarters. These hallways are confusing."

Tarchon placed his hand over hers. "And what about you and your secrets, Caecilia? You chide me for my indiscretion tonight, but have you told your husband how Artile was slowly poisoning you?"

"Not yet," she murmured, not prepared to look him in the eye.

"There's no reason not to speak out now. Artile is gone. Mastarna can't be punished for killing someone he can't lay his hands on."

A sharp pulse throbbed in her temple, the golden tiara now a burden, her head aching. "He has much on his mind. I can never seem to find the right time."

Tarchon frowned. "Confide in him, Caecilia. Otherwise he may not forgive you for keeping such a secret from him."

She nodded. "I will, I will." But her heart was telling her—not yet, not yet.

FIVE

Caecilia closed her eyes, enjoying the long sweep of the comb from the crown of her head to her waist as Cytheris combed her thick brown hair.

Mastarna's deep voice startled her. "You may go now, Cytheris."

Caecilia's eyes flew open. He was leaning against the doorjamb to their bedchamber. His chin was shadowed with stubble, dark circles under his eyes. Even at a distance, she could smell the wine on him.

She murmured to the Greek woman to leave. The handmaid frowned as she edged past the king.

Caecilia stood and extended her hand to him. "Come, my love. You need to rest."

He ignored her, trying to shrug off his tebenna, wincing in pain. She helped him to remove the heavy cloak. Then she eased the sling from his neck, revealing the heavy bandage around his upper arm and elbow. He remained silent, mouth clamped into a tight line. She could see how it galled him not to be able to undress himself even though he welcomed such ministrations when they were both eager.

As she hung the tebenna on a wall hook, the golden dice tumbled from its folds to the floor. She stooped and picked them up, but Mastarna reached across and took them from her without thanks and then dumped them on the table beside the bed.

She started to unpin the amethyst brooch at one shoulder, but he edged back. "What were you thinking, Bellatrix? Exhorting Veii to march on Rome."

"I don't see why you're so annoyed. Last year you wanted to do the same when you rode north to speak to the League. And the people were buoyed by my words. They want to do more than defend Veii."

"Driving the Romans from our lands is different from invading their city. We need the Twelve to unite."

"Do we, Vel? Thefarie is helping our allies, Capena and Falerii, to oust the Romans from their territory. Aule Porsenna is leading the Tarchnans to assist him. Once the Capenates and Faliscans are free of their enemy, we can join forces to march on Rome."

"When did you become a general, Bellatrix? You don't know what you're talking about." He pulled the circlet from his head, tossing it onto the mattress. "Capena and Falerii are also under heavy siege."

His words stung. He never denigrated her. And his coldness made her heart thump against her rib cage. Now it was her turn to be silent, lost for words.

"Your fervor only emphasizes my failure to rout Camillus and feed my people," he continued.

She swallowed hard, realizing the nub of his anger was not just her failure to recognize all obstacles. She'd injured his pride. "That's not true. The people voted you to be lucumo because they believe you will deliver them."

"How? My army was slaughtered. It was the largest in Veii. I'm left rallying generals from different clans. And if we don't get supplies, it's not just food that's denied us. Do you think we can conjure arrows and swords from air?"

"I never thought to hear you sound defeated, Vel."

"And I never thought to hear you want to see Romans slaughtered. Do you understand what you are asking, Bellatrix? Do you want the land of your father put to flame and seeded with salt? For your cousin Marcus to be paraded in my triumph and executed?"

She sucked in her breath. His mention of Marcus cut through her. Only her love for her cousin had restrained her from wanting to see Rome destroyed. But the Battle of Blood and Hail had changed her. Two specters from her past had returned that day seeking to steal Vel's life: Marcus Aemilius Mamercus and Appius Claudius Drusus. One was her kin, the other an admirer who had once claimed he loved her.

It shocked her that her husband might have been slain by her cousin. And she would always remember how Drusus had attacked Vel from behind. At least that coward was now dead, dispatched by Mastarna even when Vel was suffering the agony of a near-mortal wound. "Marcus was ready to kill you when you were on your knees injured. And he told you I was dead to him. I doubt he'd show mercy to us or our children. Why should I feel compassion for him?"

"So you're saying you're disappointed I spared your cousin?"

"He showed no compunction to slay you! I don't know why you stopped Arruns from killing him."

"He wanted to avenge Drusus's death. Besides, the battle was over. I saw no need to send him to his gods. And I thought you would want it that way."

She pointed at his arm. "At least Marcus was prepared to fight you face-to-face. You were lucky to survive Drusus taking you unawares. Do you now regret killing him?"

"No. But the manner in which he attacked me was just the way of war. There are always men who forget honor on the battlefield."

She stood inches from him, her height enabling her to look level with his eyes. She was annoyed by his reasonable attitude toward two men whose hatred was so deadly. Irritated, also, at his reluctance to countenance attacking Rome if given the opportunity. "Do you know how traitors are executed in Rome, Vel? I'll be thrown from the Tarpeian Rock, named for Tarpeia. She opened Rome's gates to the Sabines because of her love for their king. Don't you think the Romans will compare me with her?"

His brow furrowed in puzzlement. "Why do you raise this?"

She reached over and picked up the golden tesserae from the table, fingering their worn surfaces, the numbers inscribed in words that were nearly rubbed away. His talismans. His luck. "You sent Arruns to give these to me after my uncle forced me to divorce you. You gave me the chance to see if the goddess Nortia wished me to return to you."

"Yes, and I've been grateful to her ever since that she signaled she wanted us to be reunited."

Caecilia took a deep breath. "I was fearful on the day. Danger awaited me in Veii. To be suspected as an enemy among your people if I returned, while having my people resolve to punish me as a traitoress . . ." She closed her palm around the tesserae. "I crouched on that dusty road to toss them. How hard my heart was beating, not sure if Roman Fortuna wanted me to choose duty or Rasennan Nortia wished me to forsake all for love."

Vel covered her hand. "I know all this, Bellatrix. Why are you telling me again?"

"Because Fortuna reclaimed me that day, Vel. But I chose you. I gave Camillus and his hawks an excuse to blame us for a war."

He squeezed her hand so hard the edges of the dice dug into her. "You defied the goddess of destiny?"

"No, I believe Fate's intention was that I disobey her. Nortia brought me back for a reason, as you've always claimed."

He broke from her, sinking into the chair. "Bellatrix, you may have doomed us."

"No. I've given us a purpose. For Veii to defeat Rome."

He clenched one armrest. "You've set us an impossible task. You've angered Nortia."

She crouched before him, unfurling her palm so the golden dice tumbled into his lap. "You used to defy the goddess all the time, and you did not come to harm."

"That was when I didn't care if I lived or died. Now I've every reason to live because of you and our children."

She eased herself onto her knees, grasping his hand and kissing it. "I will make offerings to placate Nortia. And I will say prayers to her in her guise as Roman Fortuna. All these years the goddess of destiny has protected Veii. She has spared us from catastrophe. I don't think she wants to punish me."

His shoulders sagged. "I don't believe you can sway her. Fate is fixed. Beseeching her is fruitless. She's the blind goddess, Caecilia."

She was not used to hearing her given name on his lips. She'd always been his Bellatrix. She was used to weathering his ill temper, but his disquiet chilled her. "We're safe, Vel. The traitor has been punished. The Romans don't know the meaning to the portent at Lake Albanus. Queen Uni protects this city. And, in winter, Thefarie will come."

He shook his head. It was as though he hadn't heard her. "What have you done to us?"

She sat back on her heels, frustrated she couldn't convince him. She wanted him to have faith that her decision had been right. And with his gloom, doubt seeped through her. "So would you rather I had never returned to you, Vel? Obeyed Fortuna? Returned to Rome? Married Drusus? Lived a life of regrets and misery? Never borne our sons and daughter?"

"Of course not. But how could you keep it from me all these years?"

"At first, I wanted to ignore what I'd done. And I did not want to burden you with it. Then, as time went by and disaster was not visited on the city, my dread dulled, and I became complacent." She once again sought to clasp his hand. "What purpose would it have served to tell you? Because no matter the result of the dice throw, I always would have chosen you."

He stood, the tesserae hitting the floor and scattering. "What purpose? What purpose! For ten years I concentrated on only defending this city. I could have urged the League of the Twelve to unite when Veii was still strong and Rome was suffering from pestilence and famine. Instead I merely begged for arms to shore up our defense. Now I'm toothless. Trapped behind tufa and masonry."

His deep voice blasted her. She scrambled to her feet. She had sought to rally him; instead, all she'd done was expose his powerlessness. She tried to embrace him, but he shrugged her away, raising his arm in the air as though her touch scalded him. He headed to the doorway.

"Please, Vel . . . where are you going?"

"I need time to think—alone."

She panicked, watching him close down his emotions in a way she'd not seen for years. "Please, Vel, forgive me."

He paused at the door, his gaze stony. "Gather flowers, Caecilia, raid the cellar for wine to make offerings, and get used to the burning smell of incense. You have a lot of praying to do."

She stared after him as she sank into the chair, then turned her attention to the tesserae. Her hand was shaking as she reached down to pick them up. She wished she'd never spoken. That she'd listened to her instincts to hoard her secrets.

After a time, she calmed. She knew her husband. She would not lose him over this. Their love had been tested before. And she thought of her children sleeping in the nursery. They were reason enough for her not to surrender to fear. She may have spurned

Rome but the warrior blood of the Caecilians and Aemilians flowed in her. She was a bellatrix. There was no going back. She would placate Nortia. And Rome would fall.

Six

—

Semni, Veii, Autumn, 397 BC

Semni's palms were sweaty. She wiped them along the sides of her chiton as she walked past the six lictors stationed in the palace courtyard. Then she nodded to two other guards standing on either side of the door to the throne room's antechamber as she ventured inside.

There were only a few petitioners left. Edging into a corner, Semni watched the array of supplicants, noticing how the noble courtiers in their rich robes confidently entered into the throne room one by one, then emerged again, either with satisfied smiles or hunched shoulders. In comparison, the commoners were nervous in their plain garb, toque caps scrunched in their hands, bewildered as to royal protocol.

Arruns had told her to wait until the morning audience had concluded. She stood agog in the antechamber. The bronze double doors to the throne room were imposing with their heavy timber lintel and jambs. The walls were decorated with myths and legends in vivid paint.

After six weeks, Semni was starting to be less in awe of the royal residence, but the immensity and artistry of the tableaux astounded her. She, too, had once painted the Divine in the folly of love or the heroics of war. But she'd done so in miniature with a fine brush on vases, not with broad strokes upon a wall. Her eyes traveled to the large ornamental red-figured vases placed on either side of the doorway, wondering if she would ever have the opportunity to fashion such beautiful objects again.

Despite her attempts to be unobtrusive, the men in the room cast surreptitious glances at her. She showed no cleavage today, but she could not hide full breasts and rounded hips, or the curve of firm buttocks beneath her pleated blue chiton. A little over a year ago, she would have responded with a flutter of eyelashes and the moistening of her lips. And offered more if the man was comely enough. Now Arruns was the only one who filled her thoughts.

Semni crept forward, hovering at the doorway to peep inside the throne room. Garlands of ribbons adorned the walls of the great hall with its high checkered ceiling. And there was an enormous bronze-clad table laden with linen books piled between two candelabras.

The last petitioner had been seen. The high councillors rose from their ivory stools and headed toward the door. Lord Karcuna strode ahead while Lords Lusinies and Feluske sauntered in easy conversation.

Semni ducked back behind the doorjamb to let them pass. A slave followed them, carrying the water clock used to time the duration a petitioner could speak. He regarded her in puzzlement, curious as to why a wet nurse had strayed into such surroundings. To her relief, there were no other lictors present. She did not want the palace abuzz with gossip about the pardon she was asking for today.

Arruns stood next to the dais where the monarchs were seated on golden thrones, their feet resting on lavishly padded footstools. Prince Tarchon stood beside them. Queen Caecilia chatted with Cytheris.

Spying Semni, Arruns beckoned to her, his mien grim. She steeled herself, tucking her thick, wavy hair behind her ears, and smoothed her hands along her chiton again.

The hall was cold compared to the smaller antechamber. Only a few of the braziers were lit. King Mastarna did not waste fuel when his people shivered for lack of firewood.

Semni knelt in front of the podium, but it was not until Arruns knelt beside her that the royal couple noticed there were two more supplicants.

The lucumo's brow creased. "What's this?"

Semni gripped Arruns's hand. She was surprised his palm was as slippery as hers. His apprehension only fueled her own. He always seemed immune to fear. She gulped, doubting she would be able to speak other than in a hoarse whisper. Luckily, he spoke first.

"I seek to marry Semni, my lord. And to claim her son, Nerie, as my own."

"You seek a wife, Arruns?" Lord Mastarna's attention swung to Semni. "And a family? I never thought to see you pursue such responsibilities." Then he chuckled. "It seems you found a pretty benefit when I left you behind while I was on campaign. I hope you're not going to grow soft now you'll always have a warm bed to share."

Semni felt Arruns tense at the king's jest. She knew how much he resented being denied the chance to accompany his master to war.

Lady Caecilia smiled at her husband. "I think you can let them stand now." Her smile broadened as she addressed the couple. "This is wonderful news. But you are both freed; you don't need the king's permission to wed."

Arruns squeezed Semni's hand. His grip was powerful. She doubted he meant to hurt her. "Semni has something to confess to you before I can marry her."

Lord Mastarna gestured the applicants to stand. "What is this revelation?"

Semni's knees buckled a little as she rose. Arruns steadied her. This time the pressure of the Phoenician's grip was bearable, but she could sense his anxiety hadn't lessened. She bowed her head. "My lord and lady, I seek forgiveness. For I said nothing when Aricia took Master Tas to see Lord Artile."

Caecilia frowned. "But you stopped her absconding with our son. I'll always be grateful you saved him. Tas would be in Velzna with the haruspex if not for you."

Perspiration pricked Semni's scalp. She concentrated on addressing her mistress, but she felt the king's gaze boring into her. "No, I mean before the day of the Battle of Blood and Hail. I knew Aricia was taking Tas to see his uncle for many months through a secret passageway to the Great Temple. I didn't help her, but I did nothing to stop her." She let go of Arruns's hand, falling to her knees again. "I did wrong in not telling you. Please forgive me."

Semni heard Cytheris gasp. The queen's face paled, shock in her round hazel eyes.

Lord Mastarna stood and roared. "Forgive you! My priestly brother tried to turn our son against us. Filled his head with dreams of being a great seer. Our seven-year-old son could have been lost to us forever—both in mind and in body."

Semni cringed. The king's mellifluous voice was harsh with rage.

Lady Caecilia gripped the armrests of her chair, her knuckles white. "Why Semni? Why?"

"When Aricia was your sons' nursemaid, she saved me from destitution by bringing me to the House of Mastarna. My husband had divorced me because I'd borne a bastard child. My family had shunned me. She found me starving near the Great Temple on a night when she'd brought Tas through the tunnel from your house. She was kind to me, so I felt obliged to keep her secret. And then, after a time, I was trapped by my own silence. It was too late to speak out without being punished. I didn't want to be cast out again to be homeless. I didn't want Nerie to starve." She steepled her fingers. "I was foolish and selfish, then I realized my mistake. So I stopped her taking Tas. Please, please, forgive me."

Lady Caecilia's voice was full of hurt. Semni had heard the tone before, on the day the princip realized Aricia had betrayed her, the slave she'd freed and protected since the maid was tiny.

"It was I who was kind to you. I heard Aricia's plea to grant you succor. I gave you a job and clothes and food and shelter. And then you repaid me with treachery? Your duty was to Lord Mastarna. To me. To our House. Not to the scheming nursemaid!"

Semni's face burned with shame. "And I'm loyal to you. I'll be loyal to you forever."

"Get up!" The veins in the king's neck were protruding, his ugly scarred face flushed. His eyes that regarded his children so fondly were now hard and black and cold.

Arruns helped Semni to stand. She glanced at him. "Take courage," he whispered in his thick accent, but she noticed there was a sheen of sweat on his tattooed features. She clamped her teeth together, trying to stop them from chattering. She crossed her arms, hugging herself. She was beyond speech.

Lady Caecilia leaned forward. "Did you know that Aricia is a priestess of Uni, Semni? Lord Artile deserted her, but Lady Tanchvil now employs her. If Aricia still plots to steal Tas's mind, then how do I know you won't conspire with her again?"

"She is still here?" Semni cast a look at Arruns, who was also frowning at the news. "Believe me, mistress, I want nothing more to do with her. I am faithful to you."

Prince Tarchon was also studying the wet nurse with a shocked expression before turning to the king. "We should take no chances, Father. The palace is riddled with hidden passageways. We need to seal the entrances. Lord Artile's knowledge of the tunnels under this citadel was expert, and the nursemaid was his avid student."

The prince's interruption only seemed to irritate the king. "I was aware of the secret way to the Great Temple in my own home. I can guess why you have knowledge of those in the palace."

There was a strained silence. Semni understood Lord Mastarna's disapproval. Aricia and she had often giggled at the thought of Lord Tarchon skulking underground to see Sethre Kurvenas when the youth lived in the royal residence. Their affair was a scandal.

Lady Caecilia interrupted, unable to hide her concern. "It's important that Tarchon identifies the palace tunnels now."

The prince crossed to her and placed his hand on her shoulder. "Don't worry, Caecilia. A sphinx symbol is marked on the wall near the hidden entrances. I should be able to find them." He turned to his father. "But there's a reason for their existence. Some provide access to the drainage system, but others are engineered as escape routes. Kings long past have seen them as a guarantee of safety."

Lord Mastarna snorted. "If our enemies ever breach this citadel, I'll face them bearing arms, not scurrying through the dark like a rat."

The prince stiffened. "Then I'll organize a search immediately. I'll ensure they're boarded up by tomorrow." He bowed. "May I be excused?"

Semni saw Lady Caecilia mouth a silent thank-you to her stepson after he'd been dismissed.

The lucumo pointed to a spot in front of him. "Come here, Semni." Her stomach lurched.

"My blood runs cold when I think I might have survived a battle only to find my son had been abducted by evil." He gestured to the empty chair that the prince had vacated. "Did you know Lord Artile corrupted Prince Tarchon when he was only a child? I pray my brother was speaking the truth when he denied tainting Tas in that way."

Semni felt nauseous at the thought she may have been party to the little boy's corruption.

The monarch stood, pushing aside his footrest as he walked to the edge of the dais. Semni shrank back as he towered above her on the platform, anxious he might step down and strike her.

"And so I'll show no clemency toward you today. You'll be taken from here and birched before you are cast into the street. My compassion is saved only for Nerie. Your son will remain under my roof."

A sob rose in her throat. She had hoped her honesty would spare her; instead, the judgment she most feared had been meted.

Lady Caecilia rose and touched her husband's arm. "This is too harsh. She is only seventeen."

The king shrugged her away. Even in her distress, Semni was confused. He always treated his wife with respect. To have him disregard her was ominous—an indication of the depth of his fury. What hope was there of reprieve when even Lady Caecilia could not sway him?

Arruns slipped his arm around Semni's waist. She clung to him, weeping. For a moment she hated him for forcing her to confess. His duty to the master had been greater than his love for her. "Why did you make me do this?" she whispered. "Why couldn't you have let well enough alone?"

"Calm yourself." The certainty in his voice gave her pause. She took a deep breath and ceased her sobbing.

The king fixed his gaze on Arruns. "And what have you to say? Instead of informing us of this woman's treachery, you remained silent. I thought you were trustworthy, Arruns. Now it seems you value a pretty face over fidelity."

The Phoenician tensed at being accused of disloyalty by the man for whom he'd risked his life throughout all those years. His words were deliberate, as though he'd rehearsed them.

"I only heard of Semni's transgression after the battle. I waited until your coronation was over so you weren't distracted from affairs of state. And I made it clear to Semni that I wouldn't wed her unless she admitted her guilt."

Lord Mastarna studied the bodyguard, the anger in his tone lessening. "Then I excuse you for keeping this from me. But this girl is undeserving to be your wife. I'm doing you a favor in expelling her." He offered his arm to Lady Caecilia. "This audience is over. I've nothing more to say."

The queen seemed reluctant to leave. Her hesitation reminded Semni that once the king had left the throne room she'd be led away and whipped. She wondered which of the lictors would exact the sentence. Whether they would let her kiss Nerie before she was ejected. Whether Arruns would be made to watch.

"Master, wait." Arruns's tone was more of a demand than an entreaty. The familiarity of his address was also a reminder that he'd long served the princip.

Lord Mastarna paused. He nodded assent.

"I saved your life in the Battle of Blood and Hail," said the Phoenician, his gaze traveling across to the queen. "And I once stopped bandits murdering Lady Caecilia. I call upon the blood debt both of you owe me. I do not do so lightly." He bent his head, humble again. "I ask that you pardon Semni so that I might take her as my wife."

Amazed at her lover's request, the girl looked expectantly at the king. Nonplussed, the lucumo swiveled around to the queen.

Lady Caecilia nodded. "It's true. We owe Arruns our lives. And he's one of our most faithful servants."

"And what of the girl? She's far from truthful."

"My first thoughts were also to punish her. But Semni proved she saw the error of her ways when she rescued Tas. And I can't have her death on my conscience. For she will perish without a family to harbor her. And I don't want a decent woman to become a whore so that she might eat. Nor a mother to be separated from her baby."

The king's expression softened as he scanned her face. "So you believe in redemption?"

She smiled. "I would not be in Veii if I didn't."

The king's lips curved upward briefly before he turned to his servants. "Very well, Arruns, I'll honor the debt. The girl may stay. And I can't stop you marrying her, but I warn against it. However, if she betrays us again, you'll also be dismissed."

Arruns bowed. "Thank you, my lord. And the birching?"

The queen squeezed the king's forearm. Semni was thankful the noblewoman was prepared to chip away at her husband's judgments. Nevertheless, the lucumo's exasperation was evident. "No thrashing either, then."

The wet nurse sighed in relief. Her gratitude toward the queen was overwhelming. She vowed silently she would spend her days proving she could be trusted. But it was the king she needed to win over. She stepped forward, kneeling and kissing his feet. "Thank you, my lord, thank you. I'll nourish the princess as though she were my own. I'll care for the princes."

Lord Mastarna stepped back at her groveling. "Do you think I would have a woman like you caring for my children? You're not to go near them. You can work in the kitchen again."

Semni leaned back on her heels. Lady Caecilia made a clucking noise and helped the girl to her feet. Her tone was impatient. "Of course she will. Thia is thriving. Semni nurses our daughter with milk and with love. And our sons adore her."

Arruns stood to attention. "I will vouch for her, my lord. Please let her remain as a wet nurse."

The king scowled in frustration at his edicts being undermined. "I see yet again I'm to be overruled by the queen. Very well, Semni may continue to suckle my daughter, but there is one proviso. A wet nurse's milk is soured by lying with a man. I don't want my little princess to take a bitter mouthful." He glared at the Phoenician. "So if you want Semni to continue working in the nursery, you will not lie with her until Thia is weaned." He turned and glared at his wife. "And in this I will *not* be countermanded."

Semni gasped. Having been threatened by a bleak future, she knew the penalty was mild, but it didn't stop her feeling injustice that she was to be denied consummation. She cast a beseeching look at the queen, but Lady Caecilia shook her head, not prepared to champion the maid's case any further.

Arruns remained impassive. "As you wish, my lord."

Not waiting to escort his wife, Lord Mastarna stepped from the dais and strode ahead. Lady Caecilia took her time proceeding through the hall, although she seemed disconcerted the king had left her in his wake.

As soon as the monarchs had left the chamber, Arruns wrapped his arms around Semni. "It's done. I am proud of you."

Exhausted, she laid her head on his shoulder. As she did so, she noticed one person lagging behind. It was Cytheris. The handmaid's pockmarked face was furious. Semni knew that she felt the shame of being the mother of a betrayer. No forgiveness dwelt within her for Aricia. And with the confession today, Semni suspected that she would find no pity from the woman she called the Gorgon.

SEVEN

The kitchen was noisy with the bustle of slaves attending to the preparation of the midday meal. King Mastarna had invited Generals Lusinies and Feluske to dine. There would be no repast that night, though. The time had ended when rich families dined twice a day.

Two naked boys were turning a row of rabbits on a spit over an enormous brazier. A kitchen maid was chopping onions at a table, her eyes streaming. Cook, cheeks still chubby despite less food, was cracking walnuts with a hammer. A flute player was trilling his pipe. In a world at war, the Rasenna could still add melody to their work.

Semni and Arruns entered the kitchen to this scene of industry and aromas. Another maid emerged from the door to the storerooms where the harvest of past years had been preserved: olives and figs, oil and salt. The reserves in the royal cellars were slowly diminishing. The livestock also.

The servants, absorbed in their labor, took no notice of the wet nurse and lictor. Semni searched the room for Nerie, expecting to see the one-year-old sitting on the bench, playing with his favorite ladle with its lion-shaped handle. Her son was nowhere to be seen. Panic seized her at the thought that he'd wandered off into the maze of cellars or ventured as far as the stables at the rear of the palace. Arruns was also scanning the kitchen. "Where's Nerie?"

Cook laughed and nodded toward the corner of the room. "He's discovered the dormice."

The boy was squatting before an earthen pot, his eye pressed to one of the holes that were punched at intervals across the terra-cotta. When Semni lifted him, he protested, leaning his weight forward, arms outstretched.

"Very well." She lifted the lid. "You may look for a moment."

Both mother and son peered inside. Curled asleep on tiers spiraling around the interior was a family of dormice. The furry creatures did not stir despite the light illuminating their den. Seeing them so at peace, Semni felt sorry the offspring of the breeding pair would be roasted and dipped in honey and poppy seeds. Nerie leaned down, determined to touch the animals hibernating within.

Arruns appeared beside them and took the squirming child from his mother. As usual, she was struck by her son's blond hair against the swarthy features of the Phoenician.

Seeing it was the lictor who had wrested him from his fascination, the toddler stood on the guard's broad forearm and jigged up and down as he wrapped his arms around the man's neck. "Roons!"

Arruns smiled and tousled Nerie's hair before grasping Semni's hand and turning to face the others. Her heart raced with anticipation.

"We need witnesses."

The piper ceased his tune. Cook tutted at being delayed in the meal's preparation. The others looked up curiously.

Semni never thought this day would come. One year ago, a bloodied Arruns had helped birth Nerie on the edge of a battlefield. A bond had been formed that night by the light of a flickering bonfire. One that had been tested by misunderstandings and her own foolishness.

Arruns hoisted Nerie with straight arms above his head, making the boy squeal. "All present, bear witness that I claim this child as my son, as though he were from my loins. He will be called Nerie, the son of Barekbaal, also known as Arruns, and Semni Vulca, his mother."

It was the first time Semni had ever heard Arruns's Phoenician name. His first master had given him a Rasennan one. It made her realize how little she knew of his history. He'd always kept her at bay, granting only glimpses to her.

The new father handed their son back to her. Propping Nerie on her hip, she slid her arm around Arruns's waist, expecting him to make another announcement. "Tell them our news."

Without replying, the lictor removed his necklace and slipped the simple bronze pendant over Nerie's head. The charm clicked against the amulet that had been placed around the boy's neck when he was born. "May this bulla protect you forever from the evil eye. May all the great and almighty Rasennan gods and those of Canaan watch over you."

Nerie pulled at the locket, peering at the figure engraved on it, and then showed it to Semni. It depicted a naked woman crowned with a crescent moon and holding a bow.

"Who is she?"

"The divine Astarte. Goddess of love and war, death and rebirth. She is the evening star who watches over us. She is worshiped by the Rasenna on the coast as Queen Uni. Others call her Turan or Aphrodite, goddess of love."

Semni smiled, comforted the foreign deity was so revered. "Then she'll be a mighty protectress for our child."

The servants clapped, calling out their well wishes. Semni nodded, waiting expectantly for Arruns's next declaration. Again he failed to mention there would be a wedding; instead, he thanked those around him and bid them go back to their chores.

Semni squeezed his bicep. "Aren't you going to tell them we are to be married?"

The piper began playing again. Routine returned. Arruns led Semni by the hand into the hallway. Nerie toddled after his parents, sucking his thumb.

The Phoenician halted, standing inches from her. "I'll marry you when we can lie together as man and wife. Until then it's best we live apart."

"Why? I did what you said. I confessed. You said you would wed me. You said you loved me. Or is it because you want another woman now that you can't . . . ?"

Lacing his fingers through her loose knot of hair, he pulled her to him, crushing her against his chest. Then he kissed her, his lips hard against hers. It was the first time he'd embraced her since they'd made love six weeks ago. She stirred with need for him. She echoed his movement, her hands cradling the back of his skull. She felt his heat, wanting to stroke the muscled body beneath his uniform.

"Me!" Nerie tugged at her skirts. The lovers broke apart, staring at each other, Arrun's dark resinous eyes intense under the hooded lids. Ignoring the boy, he leaned his forehead against hers. "Do you really think we could share a bed without breaking our vow to the master? It could be two years until the princess is ready to be weaned."

Semni knew he spoke the truth, but all she could think about was that she'd only lain with him once and wanted more of him. "The king's decree is unfair. I want to bear your baby, Barekbaal."

Arruns smiled at the use of his birth name but shook his head. "Not until this siege is over. It's enough that Nerie was born into war. I want no more of our children to face the threat of death at the hands of the Romans. Perhaps the gods have done us a favor in preventing us from lying together."

"Me! Me!" Nerie's persistence distracted her. She hoisted him onto her hip. "A woman cannot fall pregnant when her milk is flowing."

Arruns's face resumed its somber lines, his feelings once again masked. "Well, we can't test whether that's true without disobeying the master." He stroked Nerie's head and then turned to leave. "It's time for me to return to Lord Mastarna."

Resentment surged as she watched him go, thinking the gods were punishing her for a past wrong that she'd righted. Then she remembered the fury of the king, and what might have been her fate. She hugged her son.

The tightness in her breasts told her she needed to feed Thia. She headed for the nursery, but as Semni rounded the corner into the living quarters, Cytheris barred her way. She could smell the strong scent of aniseed on the maid's breath.

Semni averted her gaze as she tried to pass.

Aricia's betrayal had caused threads of gray to grow in Cytheris's ankle-length plait even though she was only in her thirties. To know her daughter had been faithless to Lady Caecilia had caused her much sorrow. Today she'd learned Semni's act of bravery in thwarting Aricia's plot had been built on deception.

"I need to put Nerie to bed and then feed the princess."

Cytheris placed her hands on her hips. "Thia can wait a little longer. I want you to know the mistress may forgive you, but I never will."

Semni shifted Nerie's weight. The boy was drowsy after all the excitement, his head against her shoulder. "I said I was sorry. What more can I do? I will not make the same mistake again."

"Well, I don't believe you. You've always been selfish and careless. You were early ripe and you'll be early rotten. You cuckolded your old husband and bore him a bastard. Then you drank yourself silly and slept with any manservant who'd have you once you were given a chance of a new life by the mistress."

Semni winced at hearing her sins set out in plain sentences. "Nerie was born from my worship of the wine god at the Winter Feast of Fufluns. It was a sacred union. And I've changed—you know that. I was chaste and sober after I saw Arruns would never have me while I was wanton."

"And now you've snared him."

Semni shoved past her, angry now. Cytheris dogged her heels. "I could scarce believe it when the mistress told me yesterday Aricia had not left the city. Every day I live with the shame of knowing my daughter placed Master Tas in harm's way. And now I learn that you had the chance to stop her and did nothing?"

Semni swiveled around. Cytheris bumped into her at the sudden change in direction.

"I made a mistake. I was scared and stupid. And now I'm being punished. Isn't it enough for you that Arruns and I are to be separated?"

"Forgoing pleasure for a time is a mild punishment compared to what you deserve. You are fortunate the mistress is kind-hearted—and can sway her husband."

"Then be satisfied my admission hasn't made me happy. Arruns won't marry me until Thia is weaned."

Cytheris's eyes narrowed. "He doesn't need to be your husband to bed you."

The Greek woman's lack of sympathy only doubled Semni's annoyance. "Aricia told me that you were also a wet nurse. And you opened your legs for your slave master in Latium. Then fell pregnant with her as proof of your adultery. You were little more than a girl yourself and acted foolishly just like I did. You're a hypocrite and always will be."

Taken aback, the handmaid grew shrill. "My past is irrelevant. You don't deserve clemency. Lord Artile is an evil man. Young

Tas was under his influence for far too long while you could have saved him. Lord Mastarna should have thrown you into the street with the stripes on your back fresh and bleeding. "

"Just like you did to Aricia?"

Cytheris pockmarked face flushed red. "She deserved a beating."

"For her crime, yes. But what about all the other times you whipped her? Your daughter lived with your bad temper. Do you know we used to call you the Gorgon? With your frizzy hair and poisonous stare. With your heart that's made of stone."

"I did what a mother ought to. Discipline only."

"You always loved Lady Caecilia's children more than your own flesh and blood."

Cytheris took a deep breath. "You're wrong. I grieve for the Aricia I lost but despise what she became. I mothered a child who's betrayed all who cared and loved her. And besides, she wants nothing to do with me."

Nerie started grizzling, his lower lip trembling. In the distance, Semni could hear Thia's piercing screams.

"I must go, Cytheris."

The handmaid stepped back. "Yes, go. But I'll be watching you. Aricia has been lucky Lady Tanchvil has taken her in. If I find she's using you to gain access to Tas again . . ."

"Don't worry! I swear by Fufluns I never plan to speak to her."

Cytheris nodded and let her pass. "Then in this one thing we're in agreement. I never wish to set eyes on my daughter again either."

EIGHT

The chiton was white with a bright-blue border. Woolen. Expensive. Semni tied the strings at one shoulder, leaving one breast exposed, white fluid seeping from the dusky pink nipple. She left the sleeves hanging on the peg on the wall. She would fasten them on with fibula brooches after she had finished Thia's feed. She yawned and reached for her shawl, draping it around her shoulders.

In the chilliness of the autumn dawn, she was grateful she'd been spared the fate of shivering in the streets. As wet nurse and chief nursemaid to a king's daughter, she was privileged. She remembered when it was her job to do the laundry for the upper maids, a servant serving a servant. How she used to resent it. Now she was wearing Aricia's clothes.

She lit a taper from the firepot and then the wick of a small terra-cotta lamp. She hoped a slave boy would soon appear to replace the nearly extinguished braziers.

Baby Thia was awake and had squirmed loose from her swaddling. Her head moved from side to side as she sucked her fists. Impatient, the infant searched for the teat as Semni offered her breast, which was tight-packed with milk. She winced as the urgent mouth latched on. Both her nipples were sore and cracked, but at least she had not fallen ill with milk fever. She needed to rub on more castor oil to ease the pain.

For so little a child, Thia had a powerful suck. It was a relief to feel the milk let down after the initial pain of the tug and draw. The little girl was intense, guzzling, and greedy, her eyes closed in concentration, her hands gripping the breast. When Semni shifted in her seat to get comfortable, the infant grew irritable, mewling at having to pause in her feed.

This one will be demanding. She already knows her own mind. Lady Caecilia would have to be careful her husband did not overly pamper his little princess. Having a strong will was one thing. Being a brat was another. Yet it was good to see the babe feeding so easily. Thia's first few weeks of life had been one of constant hunger and fretting. After a difficult birth, Lady Caecilia's milk had dried up. It had taken some effort to convince the mother to relinquish the job of breastfeeding.

Semni glanced across to Nerie as he nestled under the warmth of the bedcovers. He was so different from Thia with his placid and affectionate nature. It worried Semni that she must wean him in order to have enough milk for the princess. Her son had to be satisfied with goat's milk other than one feed per day. She couldn't bring herself to lose that time with him. He didn't complain. Nerie rarely did.

A glow of light from the doorway caught Semni's attention. The curtain was pushed aside, and Lady Caecilia entered, her path illuminated by a slave boy who held a candelabra. Another wheeled in a freshly stoked brazier. Semni tensed at her approach, anxious after yesterday's drama in the throne room.

The queen bent and kissed Thia's head. "Good morning, Semni. How's my little girl today?"

"Hungry, as always, mistress."

She smiled and sat down in her armchair.

Semni breathed a little easier. "Thank you, my lady, for persuading Lord Mastarna to show mercy."

"Thank Arruns. Both of us owe him our lives. It's only right we acknowledge the blood debt."

"I'm sorry for what I did."

Lady Caecilia reached over and stroked Thia's cheek with the back of her hand. "It's forgotten now. We need not speak of it. People shouldn't be condemned for making mistakes for which they atone. You saved Tas. That's what is important."

Semni's shoulders relaxed. "Thank you, mistress."

"Tell me, how long have you and Arruns been lovers?"

The girl blushed. "Only once. After the Battle of Blood and Hail. And I promise we'll wait until Thia is weaned."

Caecilia paused in caressing her child. "Ah yes, Lord Mastarna's edict. I'm sorry, Semni. I'm not sure there is much I can do. When it comes to Thia, he's besotted. Even though I have doubts milk can curdle from lying with a man." She gave a half smile. "If that were true, my sons have swallowed many a sour mouthful and yet flourished."

Semni blinked, surprised at the joke. Lady Caecilia was always reserved with all the servants except Cytheris. It didn't surprise her, though, that Lord Mastarna was ardent. The way he gazed at his wife made it clear he'd not yet tired of her in his bed.

Semni lowered her voice. "Arruns will not marry me until Thia is weaned."

The queen frowned. "But he has claimed your son?"

"Yes. Nerie now belongs to us both."

She patted her hand. "Take heart. Lord Mastarna may yet soften his stance. And Arruns is an honorable man. In time, he will marry you. He will make a good husband, too." She picked up a tortoiseshell lyre from the side table and began plucking the strings with a plectrum, the notes plaintive and sweet.

"My lady, Arruns has never told me in full how he came to save you from the bandits."

The queen ceased strumming the lyre, placing her hand against the strings to stop their vibrations. "Yes, he's a man of few words, isn't he? It happened on the day after I had married Lord Mastarna in Rome. My dowry cattle and goods were being transported to Veii. When the caravan halted outside Fidenae to deal with a lame ox, I wandered down to the river. Gaulish brigands attacked." She shivered. "It was the first time I'd seen a man killed."

Semni murmured. "By Arruns?"

She nodded. "Lord Mastarna had sent him to watch over me. And he's done so ever since." She bent her head toward Semni in a conspiratorial manner. "I think I was almost as afraid of him as the Gaul. His tattoo and his silence were foreboding." She straightened again. "I've since grown very fond of him. I admire him for his loyalty. I'll never forget how he leaped twenty feet from the wall to save his master in the battle. How he hurled a spear to knock down my husband's assailant."

Semni was intrigued to hear more of this woman's past. "Mistress, what did you mean when you said you wouldn't be here if you didn't believe in redemption?"

The princip laid the lyre and plectrum on the table. "I was foolish when I was a bride of eighteen. I hurt my husband. But, like you, I rued my mistakes. Fear can make one do stupid things."

"Mistress, I can't believe you would willingly harm Lord Mastarna."

The queen's brow furrowed. "I wounded his heart but he forgave me. I was so frightened when I came here. Surrounded by my enemies and separated from my people. I believed I might never see Rome again. And then Lord Artile lied in telling me I would bear monsters. I used the Fatales Rites to try and defer my destiny to fall with child."

Semni was shocked at the revelation but not surprised at the priest's malevolence. "You did not want to bear Lord Mastarna's sons?"

"I told you I was unwise. Then I learned how truly evil Artile is. I'm fortunate Uni forgave me for my stupidity and blessed me instead with four healthy children. Fortunate also that I chose Veii and its freedoms."

"What do you mean 'freedoms'?"

She smiled. "Roman women are the possessions of men. There you can be killed with impunity by your father or husband for drinking wine. And sharing a man's dining couch is not even contemplated. The Romans think I am decadent and wicked because I chose to live here willingly after war was declared."

Semni frowned in puzzlement, thinking she would not have lived very long if she'd grown up in Rome. Her father, and her old husband, would have had ample reason to punish her for enjoying a good vintage.

Thia had finished at the breast. Semni shifted her to feed on the other side, but Lady Caecilia placed her hand on the maid's arm. "She is sated. Leave some for your son."

She murmured her thanks and carefully lifted Thia into the queen's arms. The mother placed the infant against her shoulder, rubbing her back, enjoying the feel of the nestling warmth. Semni could not help herself asking more questions. "But why were you married to Lord Mastarna in the first place. Rome and Veii are enemies."

"My Uncle Aemilius and other Roman consular generals arranged the union to seal a truce. I was at their mercy. I left all whom I knew behind. I was separated from the customs and laws and religion of my people."

Semni felt a wave of sympathy. "Why didn't your father protect you, mistress? Why did nobody help you?"

"My father had died. I was my uncle's chattel to do with as he pleased. General Camillus feigned concern, though. Although, in truth, he'd hoped I'd be made a hostage to give Rome an excuse to declare war."

"But why you, mistress? Why did the Romans choose you?"

She gave a little laugh although there was no humor in it. "Ah, that's complicated. My father was a wealthy plebeian and my mother a patrician. After both of them died, my Uncle Aemilius adopted me as his daughter so that I would have status enough to wed Lord Mastarna. And my plebeian roots also satisfied the ordinary people who were always feuding with the rich. I became a symbol of a unified Rome. Aemilia Caeciliana. Half noble, half common. My marriage was to stave off Rome's hunger. It needed Veii's grain after many years of drought. And in return, Veii gained access to the southern trade routes at Fidenae that Rome controlled."

Semni was surprised to hear the elegant woman beside her had the blood of common people running through her veins. She studied her. She was not beautiful with her narrow nose and wide, generous mouth. And without her usual cosmetics, the ugly purple birthmark on her throat was stark against the pallor of her skin, yet the striking hazel color of her eyes drew Semni's attention more than the blemish. Her flowing robes clung to a lithe frame. Semni was conscious of her own curves, feeling her body coarse compared to the noblewoman's.

Noticing the wet nurse's scrutiny, the princip touched her birthmark. "The naevus is ugly, isn't it? But my husband has taught me not to mind it. To him it's a sign of a fortunate marriage, while my father claimed it portended my life would have ups and downs. Both have been right."

Thia let out a burp. Both women smiled.

"Do you miss your Roman family, my lady?"

Lady Caecilia did not reply as she laid Thia in her cradle with its embroidered pillows and kissed her cheek. Semni wondered if she'd heard her. But when the queen straightened, the sour note in her voice returned. "The only person whom I loved in Rome was my cousin Marcus. And *he* tried to kill Lord Mastarna. And said I was dead to him. As for my uncle, he's tried to conquer this city for ten years in order to capture and execute me." She rearranged her thick woolen mantle around her shoulders. "The only regret I have is that I can't lay roses on my father's grave. My prayers for him must be at long distance, although I make sure I honor him steadfastly."

"And your mother, my lady?"

She did not reply; instead, she stepped back from the cradle and walked to the doorway where, pausing, she drew back the heavy curtain. "My patrician mother hated me, Semni. She died when I was eight years old. I only have memories of her cold voice and even icier touch. I don't grieve for her." The brief interlude of shared confidences had ended. "Now it's time to greet my sons."

Nerie stirred, calling out. Semni scooped him into her arms and sat down on the chair, offering him her breast. She pondered Lady Caecilia's story, trying to imagine the terror of being thrust into a threatening world. Their lives were so different and yet there were echoes, too. Semni had also been married against her will. Her father had no qualms about wedding a girl of thirteen to a sixty-year-old man. She also had no links to her family. Her parents were dead, and her siblings had shunned her—although she had brought such exile on herself. And it was clear the folly of youth was not constrained by rank. The queen's confession was equal in weight with her own.

Yet even though she felt compassion for the princip, Semni could not help feeling sorry for herself. The queen had found happiness with her husband, whereas she was being deprived of love. And she was downhearted her own life had departed so far from the dreams she'd once cherished—to be a famous potter, creating beauty from clay, and fashioning fine red-figured vases or shiny black bucchero.

Nerie reached up and touched her cheek, startling her. She bent and kissed the top of his head, chiding herself for her melancholy. There was another dream that might be more possible. That one day Nerie would have a brother or sister with black hair and amber eyes.

NINE

Pinna, Roman Camp Outside Veii, Autumn, 397 BC

Pausing in washing the general's tunic, Pinna lifted her head. Across the ravine loomed the gray-and-red tufa cliff upon which perched the citadel of Veii. She was always aware of it as she went about her work in the camp. When she'd first seen it she'd marveled at its sheerness and the Great Temple atop it with its silhouetted statues on the roof ridge. She'd been surprised to learn the sanctuary was sacred to Juno, although the Etruscans called her by another name—Uni. She'd always imagined the foe would have different gods to protect them.

From her vantage point, Pinna could survey the vast double siege works surrounding the plateaued city. They encircled it for miles. The inner lines faced the enemy trapped within. The outer line protected the Roman forces from the might of the entire Etruscan League. The stone lining the trenches was weathered, and the wood of the stockades was as seasoned as the veterans manning them.

The autumn sun was warm upon her back and hair. Hands dripping, she sat back on her heels and examined them, turning them palms up and then down. She remembered when they were engrained with grave dirt and painful from chilblains when she was a tomb whore. She remembered when they were soft and grimy from the sooty air of a brothel. Here she could put her past behind her. The secret she kept from her lover. One for which he would never forgive her.

Behind her the soldiers were performing drills. The camp was always bustling with activity. She glanced back to the white flag that marked the command tent. Her Wolf, Furius Camillus, would be intent on his paperwork there, or consulting with his officers. The first time she'd met him she'd been overcome with wanting—his favor, his body, to possess a small piece of his power. At that time she'd been frail, but she was a survivor. Now she was strong and confident and content. She closed her eyes and let the sun kiss her skin. For she was no longer a prostitute but a concubine. His concubine. She could not ask for more.

She scanned the citadel again. Inside it dwelt the traitoress, Aemiliana Caeciliana. Rumor told she had four half-breed children now. How could she live with the enemy? How could she choose Veii over Rome? Pinna may have once been a "night moth" streetwalker, but she was pious. She offered gifts to Mater Matuta, goddess of the dawn, every day. Pinna may once have been a registered "lupa," a she wolf in a brothel, but she wasn't as wicked as Caecilia. She never pretended to be a respectable matron and then opened her legs for a foe.

At first Rome believed Vel Mastarna stole her away. That even as war was declared at the border at Fidenae, the Veientane managed to abduct her. That the siege was to right a travesty. Aemilia Caeciliana was to be recovered, dead or living, and retribution exacted for defiling a Roman woman. But soon all knew this wasn't true. No man would be rash enough to steal a bone from under the nose of a Roman guard dog. Mastarna's delegation was outnumbered by an encampment of soldiers. The Veientane had not taken the girl against her will. Caecilia wanted to be with her Etruscan.

"Pinna! Come now. Furius Camillus is asking for you," one of the general's aides called to her.

She rose, dragging the wet cloth from the tub and wringing it before placing it in her basket.

Inside the tent, Camillus was talking to the soothsayer, Artile. The Etruscan's gaze flitted across her in a dismissive manner. She was relieved to be spared his scrutiny. She always found him unnerving. The kohl-rimmed, almond-shaped eyes seemed to read her thoughts. She knew her Wolf had little regard for the priest. He disliked how cagey he was. He also despised Artile as a traitor yet saw him as the key that might bring him fame and glory.

Marcus Aemilius was also in attendance. Seated on a stool, the officer did not acknowledge her other than to scan her, grimace, and look away. It had been the same ever since he'd relinquished her to the general. The rancor between them troubled her. When she'd been Marcus's army wife, they'd shared their secrets and fears.

Camillus beckoned to her. "Massage me while I talk. I have a headache."

Pinna did not look at Marcus as she began kneading the knots between the general's shoulders. It was her skill at massage that had first brought her to her Wolf's attention, which had resulted in her betraying the Aemilian.

Artile was eyeing Marcus surreptitiously. Pinna suspected the Etruscan was a mollis, a soft one who loved only men, never women. She thought how ironic it was that the junior officer also hungered for male touch alone. Yet Marcus had never been caught in the bed of another freeborn soldier. Threat of execution was sanction enough to make him wary.

Camillus thumped his desk. "I'm running out of time, priest! Do you understand? It will soon be winter, and I must resign my command. It's been six weeks since you claimed you could tell me the secret of Lake Albanus. And yet you prevaricate."

Artile remained unruffled. "It takes time to consult the gods on a matter of such importance."

Camillus snorted. "What about those sacred books of yours you hauled away in your wagon? You said you already possessed the key to the correct expiation rites. I think you're a fraud."

The Veientane bristled. "You do well to treat me with respect, Furius Camillus."

"And you do well to remember I can surrender you to a brother who hates you!"

Artile stiffened. "I don't think that's wise."

"Convince me why not. You're little use to me at the moment!" The Roman thumped his desk again, forcing Pinna to stop massaging him.

The priest smoothed his arched eyebrow with one finger. "Because Veii needs to placate the gods by punishing the traitor among them."

Camillus leaned forward, his elbows on the table, his palms flat against its surface. "And you are that traitor."

The priest's shoulders relaxed, his smile arrogant, his tone oily. "Yes, I am that traitor."

"So it's against my interests to hand you back to your brother for execution?"

"Precisely."

The general gestured Pinna to continue her ministrations. "You've yet to tell me why there's enmity between you and Vel Mastarna."

"It's a family matter."

Camillus's eyes narrowed. "I need to understand your motives for deserting Veii. If there's no candor between us, how do I know you won't double-cross me?"

The priest settled himself on a stool. "Believe me, Furius Camillus. I don't take treason lightly. My brother is a hypocrite.

He's been crowned even though he sought the downfall of the last two kings. The Veientane people should be cautious of him."

"Sounds like jealousy is talking."

The haruspex flinched. "I have reasons enough to hate my brother, but it's not because I covet his position."

"Yet the king is the high priest of Veii, isn't he? Godhead, general, and monarch all in one."

"My brother is far from holy."

Camillus smiled. "Or maybe he doubted you were. Did he question your powers as a seer?"

The soothsayer pressed his lips into a straight line. "He's irreligious. And he's high priest in name only. It was I, Artile, the chief priest of the Great Temple of Uni, who was revered. Servant to our city's divine guardian. For that you should be grateful. The goddess is unlikely to favor my brother over me."

"And yet haven't you also deserted Juno? I think that makes your position precarious, don't you?"

The Etruscan fell silent, his arrogance wavering. Camillus continued to press him. "Tell me why you hate Mastarna. And why you're prepared to see your kin and people fall because of your 'family matter.'"

Artile paused, his gaze moving between the general and Marcus before deciding to give his explanation. "My brother accused me of leading his wife astray. And he forbade me to mentor his adopted son to be a priest." His deep voice rose in pitch. "That bitch persuaded Prince Tarchon to alienate me."

Camillus appeared bemused. "You led Aemilia Caeciliana astray? What does that even mean?"

The priest hesitated, fiddling with one of his many rings. "A matter of religious instruction. I discovered that Caecilia is pious albeit misguided. Mastarna didn't approve when he learned she wanted to convert to Rasennan beliefs."

Pinna was shocked, her fingers digging into the general's flesh so he turned to frown at her. She relaxed and continued to stroke his neck. Caecilia was worse than the concubine imagined. She had not only abandoned Rome but forsaken its faith. The woman deserved condemnation.

The general's voice also revealed his disgust. "She'd already been led astray—by a guilty passion. But now it appears her corruption is absolute."

Artile glowered. "You're not the only one who despises her. She's now caught between Rome and Veii. My people are suspicious of her motives."

Camillus signaled Pinna to stop her massage and rose. Marcus also stood in deference. The haruspex remained seated. Pinna wondered how the Etruscan could deign to consider himself of equal or higher status to his captor.

With his coiffed, shoulder-length hair, Artile was a far cry from the bedraggled prisoner hauled into the general's tent after being caught fleeing the battle. Face and lip bruised, he'd been drenched with rain, kohl streaking his face as though he were weeping soot. However, today he was no longer wearing the sheepskin-lined cloak or the peculiar twisted hat she'd learned marked his profession. Nor was he allowed to carry his crooked staff. Camillus insisted the seer be inconspicuous when in sight of Veii. The general did not want Vel Mastarna to know his brother was under Rome's control should any spies manage to infiltrate the blockade. The priest's chin was now covered with a beard instead of clean shaven. And he was dressed in the humble tunic worn by leves, although no Roman light infantryman would be soft skinned and pudgy.

Her Wolf was not impressed at Artile's lack of respect. "Get up! No more wasting time. I want the answer now. It might be imprudent to hand you to Mastarna, but it won't stop me from putting a collar around your neck and making you my slave."

Artile knocked his stool over in his haste to stand. "I need to consult Aplu, the god known to you as Apollo," he stuttered.

Marcus sounded impatient. "General, Rome has already sent a delegation to Delphi to Apollo's oracle. Our own brother Spurius is one of them. This man is wasting our time. It's best to trust our ambassadors rather than him."

"There's a sanctuary only a short distance away from here, Furius Camillus," continued Artile. "It's an oracular place. Aplu dwells there alongside other gods. Let me visit it tomorrow. I'll be able to make the necessary sacrifices there. You'll have the solution faster than waiting for the emissaries to return."

Camillus grabbed the neck of Artile's tunic. "That's what you said six weeks ago!"

The priest rushed his reply. "Tomorrow. You'll have the answer tomorrow. I want to ensure I have not incurred Uni's wrath. To be sure she understands that I betrayed my city but not her. I must seek Aplu's guidance."

Camillus dragged the seer closer so they stood only inches apart. "Are you telling me your qualms have been delaying me, priest?"

"Tomorrow. I promise you. Visit the sanctuary with me. I'll give sacrifice and read the victim's liver to determine Aplu's will."

Marcus once again interrupted. "General, that sanctuary lies flush by the city wall. It's dangerous territory even though we've secured it with a fort. It might be a trap."

Artile shook his head. "It will be worth the risk, you'll see."

Camillus released the haruspex, who stepped back, rubbing his neck where the tunic had cut into his flesh. "Very well, I'll chance it. Marcus, send orders to double the guard along that part of the lines. And make arrangements for the excursion." He sat down again at his desk, rubbing his temple, his headache still present. Pinna placed her hands on his shoulders, knowing he needed her comfort.

The Aemilian saluted, scowling at her before he left. Artile scurried toward the tent flap, halting when he heard the general growl. "This is your last chance, priest."

He bowed his head. "Aplu will reveal all."

Camillus watched him depart, shaking his head. "I don't trust him."

"Then why do you rely on him, my Wolf?"

"Because his reputation as a prophet is widespread. I can't discount it. It's his conscience that is making him reluctant, not his lack of skill." He tapped his gold ring, a nervous habit.

She nodded toward his fingers. "You are granted more protection if you tap it three times."

He sat astride, pulling her to stand between his legs, his hands resting on her hips. "You and your superstitions."

She looped her hands around his neck, lacing her fingers together. She was pleased he hadn't resumed working.

He reached up and tucked her hair behind her ear. "Would you like to come with me to see this sanctuary?"

"Yes. Yes!"

"Then it shall be so."

Pinna felt happiness well. To be asked to accompany him on such a trip was extraordinary. Before the Battle of Blood and Hail, they'd been forced to keep their liaison secret. Her position as his concubine was now taken for granted. All the times of sneaking and subterfuge had ended. "My Wolf, why do you want me to go?"

He shrugged his shoulders. "I thought you'd like to see the temple. As a treat. You needn't come, though, if you're too frightened."

"I won't be frightened. You'll be with me."

He laughed, disentangling her fingers. "Go and finish your chores. I have to work."

She delayed, tracing the scar on his cheek. The needle marks where she'd sewn his wound had almost faded. Surprising her again, he wrapped his arms around her waist and squeezed her, the side of his face against her breasts. She kissed the top of his head.

"Perhaps I want you with me because you've bewitched me," he murmured.

She pulled back. "Don't say that. I don't use spells on you."

He fingered the fascinum and Venus shell around her neck. "Yet you believe in magic. Look at all the charms you wear."

She covered his hand. "All of us need protection, my Wolf. These keep me from the evil eye. You wear no bulla now you're a man, so I need to watch out for you. I can advise you of the precautions needed should an ill omen befall you."

He eased his fingers from under hers. "Enough. As you're a woman, I'm prepared to accept your faith in superstition. But I don't believe in such safeguards, nor should any soldier." He guided her from between his legs and turned back to his desk.

She was sorry she'd spoken and lost the chance to linger with him. Yet as she walked outside to return to her washing, she also touched her amulets. In daylight she made a contract with Mater Matuta, promising that if the goddess convinced Camillus to love her, she would double her gifts. And at night, she used her body, lest pleasure instead of prayer was what was truly needed.

TEN

From the moment she passed under the massive rock archway spanning the road, Pinna's eyes were wide with wonder. She'd been cooped up behind the wooden palisade of the camp for too long. Now she enjoyed the descent into the valley, aware of Veii's citadel above her, looking forward to seeing the fast-flowing water of the river below.

The cart bounced in the grooved wheel ruts of the road. Artile sat sulking beside her, unimpressed he shared his conveyance with a concubine. He clutched one of his sacred books in his arms like an anxious parent.

Pinna concentrated on the sights around her: pine saplings, and holly covering the tufa walls of the ravine. Her Wolf was encouraging new growth after years of harvesting the forests for fuel and forts.

Camillus rode his horse ahead, while Marcus, as head decurion, organized his turma of thirty knights to form an escort around them. The journey today would be perilous. The road and river were companions, running close by the wall of Veii. Too close, at times. The Roman lines were reinforced in such places but were under constant threat from skirmish and arrow fire.

At intervals, they passed large stone domes. After years of neglect, grass covered the massive Etruscan burial mounds. The abandoned tombs were a chilling sight, with their yawning, darkened doorways. Yet despite her trepidation about traversing through the cemeteries, Pinna admired the size of the tumuli. The sturdy columbaria that housed the ashes of the well-to-do in Rome bore no comparison to these splendid sepulchers.

Camillus reined his stallion to walk beside the cart and pointed to a group of statues seated above the doorway of one of the mounds—gods and goddesses on thrones. "Which deities are these?"

Artile studied the images briefly before responding. "They are not gods but ancestors."

"You revere women?" The general's voice echoed Pinna's own surprise.

"The Rasenna venerate both bloodlines. Our male and female forebears protect our families and clans."

Camillus said nothing, steering his horse to walk abreast of Marcus. Pinna was less able to dismiss the sight, turning in wonder to view the sculpture of an Etruscan woman who was considered an eternal guardian. And suddenly she couldn't help wondering about the reputation of Veientane women. How could a mother, daughter, or sister be a heroine as well as depraved?

• • •

The sanctuary was situated near a crossroad where there had once been meetings, markets, and commerce. The area was now deserted. Smithy forges lay abandoned. Shops were derelict. The only activity was that of Roman sentries patrolling the area.

Pinna held her breath when she realized that, to reach the sanctuary's gates, they must pass along a section of the road that ran flush against the city's perimeter. The tufa blocks were enormous, each one as tall as a man and as wide as a giant. There was no mortar between them. Thick, impenetrable, timeless. Panic seized her as she spied the Veientane's own sentinels on watch. The wagon driver urged the donkeys to a trot, while the escort of knights clustered around the cart, shields raised to ward off any arrows. No missiles were fired, though. She exhaled in relief as the party passed through the wide portal into the temple grounds, leaving the horsemen of the turma to station themselves around the boundary.

The serenity inside was a shock. Its greenness. After being surrounded by the wasteland around the camp and the stridency of military life, a place of calm and verdure was difficult to absorb.

A three-cell temple dominated the triangular enclosure. Its pediment was resplendent with the figure of a horse with winged shoes among gods and heroes. Pinna tilted her head to scan the roof decorations with medusa faces backed by fluted shells.

Camillus and Marcus stood some distance from the temple portico studying the complex. They were dressed in armor, hands resting on their sword hilts. She hoped the gods would not be offended by the sight of burnished bronze in a place of peace.

Artile beckoned to the general. His pale face was animated as he pointed to four statues on the roof ridge of the temple. The figures were perched on high pedestals, greater than life size, wondrous. "I'll call the deities by Roman names so you can better recognize them. The sun god, Apollo, stands accosting Herculeus for catching the golden hind of Diana. Mercurius and Latona witness the confrontation. These votives were created by Vulca, the Veientane sculptor who crafted the statue of your Jupiter riding his quadriga atop the Capitoline temple in Rome. On the commission of the Etruscan kings who once ruled you."

Camillus ignored the barb. "Granted, the tyrants were fond of monuments. At least Rome was spared their tyranny when the Republic was formed, even if their buildings remained." He pointed to the pediment. "Who is the god accompanied by the leopard?"

"Fufluns. The Greeks call him Dionysus. The god of wine and regeneration. He is brother to Apollo but is wild and primal compared to the reasoned temper of the god of light and healing."

Pinna marveled again how Rome and Veii shared the same divine rulers. Yet at the mention of Fufluns, she was confused. The god of wine was Liber. She didn't know him as brethren to Apollo.

Marcus gestured toward a large rectangular pool at the side of the temple. "What's the purpose of this basin?"

"The waters have curative qualities. Both Apollo and Minerva are deities who are purifiers and healers."

Camillus fixed his eyes on the pond. Pinna thought of the back pain he hid every day. She wished he would take advantage of the chance to be rid of it.

The priest was studying the general. "Perhaps you should seek its salutary benefits given your constant headaches, Furius Camillus. And the old injury to your leg."

Pinna held her breath. Her Wolf had first gained fame when, as a young warrior, he'd continued to fight a battle with a spear embedded in his thigh. Many remarked on his valor but never his slight limp. He hated to be seen as weak. And he never complained of it aching.

Camillus tensed and swiveled around. "What soldier removes his armor when a foe lurks on the door step?"

Marcus directed attention back to the pantheon, rubbing the scar that puckered the skin at the corner of one eye. "So Minerva is worshipped here also?"

"Yes, this sanctuary is hers, but many divinities share the space in harmony. Apollo is among them. His mantic powers are channeled here. It's a place for prophecies." He turned to the altar at the opposite end of the sanctuary. "Let's ascertain if Aplu concurs with my interpretation. And that I have not incurred Uni's anger."

The men moved toward the wing-shaped altar next to the sacrificial pit that connected the quick with the dead. A soldier emerged from one of the service buildings, restraining a pig by a leash. Pinna did not follow after them. As a woman, she knew better than to expect to be present at a blood sacrifice. She was glad to be spared the sight of the holy butchery.

The sun had burned away the cool edge to the early morning. Ignoring the squeal of the beast as Artile conducted his ceremony, Pinna wandered through the sanctuary, inspecting the large votive statues. She stood in front of Minerva. With an owl perched on one shoulder, the deity held a broad shield. The concubine bowed her head, finding it strange to stand on level ground with a goddess.

The divinity's skirts were almost hidden by overgrown fennel, its yellow flowers bright against the green. Pinna smiled. The herb could season her Wolf's dinner as well as soothe his aches. And it was said a plant growing at the feet of a statue was even more potent as a medicine. As she broke off some branches, her attention was drawn to a trench next to the sanctuary wall. There were hundreds of small votives heaped within. Each was inscribed with a prayer in peculiar writing. Some were broken—shards of spent promises. They must have been dumped there by the priests to make room for new ones to be offered to the gods.

As Apollo was the god of medicine, most of the figurines were formed in the shape of body parts: toes, hands, even a phallus for one who sought to cure his impotence. She noticed a swaddled baby. Had the infant been ill, or was the gift an invocation to bear a healthy one? A strange shape caught Pinna's eye—a replica of a womb. Had this woman been barren? Did she seek succor in childbirth?

Laying aside the fennel, she sat cross-legged on the grass to inspect the grotesque figurine. Her thoughts returned to the brothel. The hollow looks of some lupae were not just because of the misery of their profession. The pimp would force them to abandon their infants on the Esquiline for the crows and dogs. And in the yards of some lupanariae, the vegetables were sustained by a rich compost of dead babies.

When she was a whore, Pinna had been thankful she'd not borne a child. As an emaciated night moth plying her trade outside the city wall, she rarely experienced her courses. Over time her womb pain told her she was barren. But now she wanted to bear her Wolf's son. The yearning to be a mother was a deep ache within her.

Camillus's voice broke through her thoughts. The men had returned to the steps of the temple. "Well, priest, tell us the answer to appeasing the gods, since you claim Apollo has sent a favorable omen."

Pinna rose and crept closer.

The soothsayer walked over to the pool. "Do you know how this basin is full of water when there has been no rain?"

"Get to the point, priest."

"Before you razed our crops, our fields were verdant even in drought. The Rasenna know how to harness the power of water by irrigating dry land or draining swamps."

Camillus sat down on the step of the portico, removing his conical hide helmet and placing it beside him. "Go on."

The Veientane once again drew their attention to the healing pool. "This basin is fed by an underground channel running outside the wall. There are many of these cuniculi that crisscross our fields underground. Our engineers have also carved vast galleries from rock to divert the Cremera River to avoid flooding."

The general leaned forward. "All very enlightening, but what has this to do with the portent at Lake Albanus?"

The haruspex smoothed his eyebrow. "If I tell you, will you let me travel to the holy spring at Velzna? I do not relish being your servant forever."

Camillus laughed. "Don't try and bargain. Tell me now, or those soft hands of yours will soon be caked with dirt and your back striped by a whip."

Artile's voice was thick with resentment. "The waters of the lake have inundated Latium. Where once there were fields, there are only floodplains. Mater Matuta is the Latins' ancient goddess. She has been neglected by Rome. You need to placate her. Draw off the waters and disperse them so that they no longer flow into the sea. You will also please Neptunus, the god of water. The land of Rome's allies will be made arable again. And the goddess of the dawn will give her blessing for Rome to conquer Veii."

Pinna gasped, astounded. Mater Matuta was more powerful than she had ever dreamed.

Camillus tapped his ring. "That's all very well, but how is that to be achieved?"

"The Veientanes are not the only among the Rasenna who know the secret of hydraulics. Knowledge can be bought. And skills taught."

The general shook his head. "It's not so simple. We need to convince the Senate first." He stared beyond the sanctuary to the enemy wall, then studied the soothsayer. "You must satisfy the Curia of your prescience."

The haruspex panicked. "You expect me to go to Rome!"

The general addressed Marcus. "Escort him to your family home. Your father is the current prefect. You must convince him the Senate should listen to the priest. Aemilius, in turn, might manage to persuade my brother Medullinus." He picked up his helmet, then descended the stairs to place his hand on his officer's shoulder. "Draining Latium territory will take many weeks to complete. We can't waste time waiting for the delegation to return from Delphi only to reveal the same solution. If we act now, Mater Matuta will be placated and Veii may yet fall by spring."

"Under the command of another general. It's not fair, sir."

Camillus's expression hardened. "If only I had more time. I would see this finished."

Marcus frowned. "Are you speaking of being made dictator, sir? I don't think . . . it would be difficult for me to argue . . ."

The general squeezed the decurion's shoulder. "I know. There would be howls of protest that there's no crisis for such power to be granted to one man. I only ask for my term to be extended. The Senate may well break with precedent given the circumstances."

The Aemilian's grimace deepened. Such a request was unlikely to be granted.

Camillus did not seem to notice his unease. "You must also break the news that Vel Mastarna is now king. He is no ordinary ruler. We must be wary." He clapped Marcus on the back. "I have faith in your ability to gain your father's support. It's time you thought to your future as well. You're thirty and have served in the army with distinction for ten years. You should stand for election as a military tribune. Your war record rivals mine at your age. And when I add my support and my friends' to those of Aemilius's, you'll be sure to be elected this winter. I will help you canvas votes."

Marcus straightened. Pinna smiled, recognizing his pride. The promise of advancement was seductive. Her Wolf knew how to stroke a man's ego while feeding his ambition.

"And tell no one in camp of what Artile has said. I wish to know the Senate's decision before I raise the men's hopes."

Artile twisted each ring on his fingers in turn. "Please, Furius Camillus. Without you at my side, I might be executed when I set foot in Rome."

Her Wolf adjusted his balteus so the lanyard lay precisely on the diagonal across his chest. Then he placed his helmet on his head, buckling it beneath his bearded chin. "I'll send a message to the Senate that you have ambassadorial status. As such, your presence is safeguarded." He glared at the seer. "I face ridicule for putting my faith and support behind you. Our fates are now joined, priest. You better not be wrong."

ELEVEN

Pinna savored the times she could massage the general, but he was not the only soldier she tended. Every day she would call on Claudius Drusus to change his dressings.

The knight's body had been rent from shoulder to groin by Vel Mastarna in the Battle of Blood and Hail. When Marcus had ridden through the retreating Roman troops to find his best friend, he'd thought Drusus was dead at the feet of the Etruscan. It was a miracle that the Claudian had survived.

She could not forget seeing Marcus return to the camp with Drusus slumped in front of him on his horse. The decurion had been fraught as he begged her to save his friend.

Death hovered over Drusus, ready to steal his breath. Marcus stayed almost as close, visiting him whenever free from his duties. His vigil made him pale and drawn as he also recovered from the injury to his forearm sustained in the conflict.

In truth, the wounded Drusus should have been sent home to be cared for by his family. Instead Marcus insisted a warrior would want to die on a camp cot rather than in a soft bed. "You're the one who has the most to lose if he dies, Pinna," he said. "He lives, or I will tell Camillus that you were a whore."

The wound was gruesome. She thought there wouldn't be honey enough to soothe it or wax enough to seal the bindings. Every day she checked for pus or blackened, dying flesh. The length of the gash was such that it was unlikely some part of it would fail to be infected.

The cut was not the only damage that had been inflicted. His shoulder had been dislocated, his collarbone smashed, and some of his ribs broken. The pain kept him immobile. Drusus's groans were pitiful each time he shifted on his pallet. She hated how he strove to stifle his moans when she wiped away encrusted blood. She would have preferred him to voice his agony. The restraint of sound seemed only to emphasize his torment.

Before the battle, hating him had become a habit. She knew Drusus loathed her, too, for he had once raped her. Although, as a prostitute, she could not assert he'd committed such a crime. That did not mean she didn't have power over him. The knowledge that she could reveal his baseness to her Wolf made him nervous and bitter. There would only be contempt for a man who needed to force himself upon a whore. And Drusus longed for the general's admiration. He couldn't afford for Pinna to provide a reason to Camillus to overlook him for promotion. And so, until the battle, they'd been locked in a tense struggle, each balancing the secret of the other and fearing exposure.

The night in the lupanaria still haunted her—a nightmare from which she would often wake in panic. How Drusus had clamped his hand over her face as he'd abused her, making her feel like nothing, filling her with terror that she might suffocate.

Yet her disgust for the russet-haired Claudian had now receded. His anguish touched her. Where once he'd been menacing, he now was vulnerable.

The fever came on the second night. As evening fell, his temperature rose. His skin burned to the touch, and he groaned with both the hurt of the slashed skin and the soreness in his bones. When she peeled back the bandages, she was dismayed to see the section of the wound on his hip was seeping, the skin around the knots swollen and red. She implored Mater Matuta to save him.

In his delirium, he clasped her hand, his fingers bands of iron, his voice rasping and low. She bent her ear close to his mouth.

"Don't leave me, Caecilia."

She frowned. In his confusion, he thought she was the love of his youth. A love that was dangerous and forbidden.

Drusus's call to the traitoress brought memories flooding back of when she'd first met him. Not the brutal encounter in the lupanaria but a year earlier. Back to a night where ghouls squabbled with ghosts for space in the graveyard of the Campus Martius.

Seeking shelter from a storm, she'd spied Drusus lurking in the sepulcher of his Claudian family. Marcus had been with him. She'd been astonished to watch Drusus engrave a curse onto a defixio lead sheet, then hammer it into the wall. Black magic was the practice of women and the weak minded, not of rich warriors. And when Marcus had read the curse aloud, she'd stifled disbelief to hear it was Vel Mastarna's destruction that Drusus sought.

Pinna's confusion doubled when Marcus departed from the tomb. Alone in the dark, the Claudian was not finished invoking the spirits. Weeping, he'd engraved a love spell on a second defixio. It was an enchantment to regain the love of a girl who'd chosen an enemy.

Pinna's knowledge gave her power. Wasn't the knight also traitorous for loving Aemilia Caeciliana? And a death penalty awaited those who used the dark arts to kill a man. What kind of warrior resorted to magic instead of using a sword? She'd threatened to display both defixios on the speakers' platform in the Forum, but Drusus had paid her to keep silent. Yet when he later stumbled upon her in the brothel, he'd not believed she would continue to keep her promise.

The fevered man's grip tightened around her hand. "Say you love me, Caecilia."

Pinna stared at him, uncertain how to respond. Deciding whether to lie. And in that moment, she no longer hated him but felt only compassion. She could not let a dying man slip into the void without comfort.

"Hush," she whispered, wiping his brow with a cloth. "Rest now. I love you."

"Forever."

She hesitated. "Forever."

He'd closed his eyes.

The fever had continued. She paled to think she would lose him and so also lose Camillus. And her resentment that Marcus should expect her to heal a near-mortal wound tripled—so too her worry that she would fail.

On the fifth day, he woke clear eyed but weakened. He didn't seem to remember seeking a declaration of affection. Instead he scanned her face as she lifted his head so he could sip some water. "Why are you helping me, Pinna? I thought you of all people would leave me to die."

"Thank Marcus Aemilius for that. He convinced me," she said brusquely, then her voice softened. "Whatever spite there is between us, I would not see any man suffer as you have."

• • •

By the time Pinna returned from the sanctuary, it was early afternoon. Drusus was lying on his back on his pallet.

"My lord, wake up."

He opened his eyes, wincing as he eased himself to sitting. The movement started him coughing. "I've been waiting for you. You said you would remove the last of my stitches today." As always she noticed the slight stammer in his voice when he was agitated.

"I was with the general." She knelt beside him and lifted his tunic over his head. There was no modesty between patient and nurse. An intimacy had grown between them. At first he'd resisted being dependent upon her, embarrassed at his helplessness. After a time a familiarity grew between them as she spooned food into his mouth, washed him, and cleaned his ordure. She knew every inch of his body without them being lovers.

His torso was bandaged from chest to groin. She was pleased to see there were no bright spots of fresh blood to indicate the sewn flesh had ruptured. "I'll unpick them now. But you must promise not to try and do too much afterward. It will take you time to regain full strength."

Businesslike, she unwound the strips of cloth, keeping the strapping on his ribs and dislocated shoulder intact. As she leaned across him, her breasts brushed his chest. She edged back, being more careful not to touch him, but as her hands moved down toward his thigh, she noticed he had hardened. He grabbed his tunic and covered himself, face scarlet. It was a curse of his, the unbidden betrayal of emotions by his skin.

Pinna also blushed. "Well, at least we've discovered full strength in one part of your body."

Drusus raised his head. For the first time since they'd met, they shared a smile.

Once the seam along his flesh was exposed, Pinna examined the wound. The bruising had faded to yellow. She was proud her needlework was neat. The scar would not be stretched or deformed. Relieved his erection had calmed, she gently touched the remaining stitches from hip to groin, checking whether she could remove them. She was conscious he was watching her.

"How old are you, Pinna?"

"Twenty."

"The same age as my sister," he murmured. "And tell me, how old were you when you became a night moth?"

She stopped inspecting the wound, unsure as to why he would suddenly seek to know her history. "Eleven."

He winced. She knew it was not from pain.

"How could that be? Where were your parents?"

She sat back on her haunches. "My father was a soldier forced into bondage. My mother and I became whores because we were destitute." She made to rise. "I don't want to talk about it. I need to fetch some tweezers."

Drusus placed his hand on her shoulder. "Wait."

She settled back on her heels. "What is it you want from me? Why do you ask these things now?"

He took her hands. His were large and bony, the knuckles pronounced. This time they were gentle. "I've been thinking. You saved my life as much as Marcus did. Many a warrior dies from infection once the battle has ended. I need to make matters right between us, Pinna. Can you forgive me for what I did to you?"

She stared at him. The hesitancy in his voice revealed his sincerity. "You changed my life, my lord. That night in the graveyard, you gave me bronze enough to allow me to register as a brothel whore. I never planned to expose you. You did not need to fear me." She lowered her voice. "You did not need to rape me."

"I'm sorry, Pinna. Believe me."

She eased her hands from his, aware her Wolf would not want another man touching her.

He must have realized he'd also trespassed. His stutter deepened. "It was because she haunts me."

"I understand, my lord. You were punishing her by punishing me."

Her answer started him coughing. She waited for him to regain his breath.

"When I had that fever, I heard Caecilia saying she loved me. Was that you?"

"Yes."

"You showed kindness. Why so?"

"I thought you were dying."

He frowned at her bluntness. "You have to understand, it's not entirely Caecilia's fault. If my prick of a father had died sooner, I could have married her. Instead, consumed with choler, he ensured I was denied happiness. She was plebeian by birth. Not good enough to marry his patrician son." He paused, then went on. "I liked the laughter in her. But she was too inquisitive about the world of men. More interested in politics than a woman should be."

Pinna was shocked he would attempt to excuse a traitoress. He did not wait for her to respond, though, still dwelling within his memories.

"When Caecilia escaped to Fidenae, I thought it was because she wanted to come back to me. But it was Mastarna she loved." He pounded one fist against his palm, startling her. "She plunged a blade into my heart—stab, stab, stab. Do you know how impotent I feel? Reduced to writing spells to curse him and bewitch Caecilia to love me? And all the time I know that he is holding her in his arms, taking her to *his* bed."

Pinna frowned. "You should have cursed her instead that night. Don't you realize she will never love you? That you need to forget her?"

"Yes, but at least I can kill him. I will not fail next time. I plan for my curse to come true—'I consecrate Vel Mastarna to damnation. May his mind and soul be tormented, his body twisted and shattered, his tongue cut out, and his ears and eyes pierced by hot pokers. And if he has, or shall have, any money or inheritance, may they be lost, and his entire house be stricken with disaster and destruction.'"

She shivered just as when she'd first heard the words read aloud in the tomb. "You condemn her also, you know."

He nodded, eyes pained. "That's my torment."

She rose, uncomfortable with his despair. "I'll get those pincers. And some mint for your cough. You'll need to keep still while I'm unpicking the knots."

Drusus grasped her skirt. "Wait. You comforted me when you thought I was dying. Why are you good to me?"

"I've seen another side of you, my lord."

"So you'll tell no one—about my love spell for Caecilia?"

She eased her hem from his fingers. She understood. If she ever lost her Wolf, the pain would be like a cut no poultice could ever heal. "All I want is to be with the general. To be respected. I was once the daughter of a soldier. That's how he sees me."

Drusus lay back on the pallet. The conversation had exhausted him. "Then we are at peace, Pinna?"

She nodded. "Yes, my lord. We are at peace."

TWELVE

Pinna hesitated at the entrance to Drusus's tent on her return with her supplies. Marcus was crouching beside his friend, his hand on the invalid's shoulder. "How goes it?"

"Pinna will remove the last stitches today. They should have gone weeks ago." Noticing the concubine, Drusus beckoned to her.

Marcus rose and stepped back so she could reach her patient. She acknowledged him without meeting his eyes. Then she knelt next to the pallet, placing her basket and a bowl of warm water beside her.

"I want to get back to duty," Drusus said to Marcus, removing the tunic from his lap so Pinna could reach the stitches. The wounded man showed no embarrassment in the company of the other soldier.

Marcus removed his helmet, dragging his fingers through his cowlick. He concentrated on his friend's face rather than his body. Pinna thought how difficult it must be for him to see Drusus naked when he hankered for him. She hoped Marcus would never cry out in delirium, for it would be the Claudian's name he would call. A secret she alone knew. One he hated that she possessed. One he did not believe she would keep.

"Pinna is right. You must take things slowly. Even with the sutures removed, you'll need to build up power. And your collarbone and ribs need to mend as well."

"I don't like being a cripple."

"It's fortunate the bastard hit bone. At least your spleen, guts, and lungs weren't pierced. You'll be well in no time."

"'Fortunate' is not a word I would use." Drusus winced as Pinna began wiping his skin with garlic juice, shedding his loosened scar tissue and encrusted blood. Then she began the meticulous process of tugging at a knot with the pincers, the flesh resisting before she cut the thread with the honed scalpel, then used the tweezers again to pull it free. As she worked, she was conscious of Marcus's surreptitious glances along the Claudian's lean, rawboned body, which was still muscled despite being bedridden for so long.

Drusus also eyed his friend but not with desire. He was scanning Marcus's thick hide helmet, bronze pectorals, and sword. "You're wearing full armor. Has the general ordered us to ride out to skirmish at last?"

Marcus shook his head. "He forbids it. We're hunkering down and letting the Etruscans starve. He's not wasting time building ramps and towers either. We lose ten men to their one with such tactics." He screwed up his mouth. "Believe me, you've missed no action."

"Where are you going, then?"

"To Rome. I've been ordered to escort the soothsayer there."

"Artile, the brother of the king?"

"Yes, Camillus believes he may well be able to assist the Senate in determining the expiation rites."

"What makes the general think they will listen to a Veientane rat?"

Marcus hesitated. Drusus placed his hand over Pinna's, preventing her from continuing with her ministrations. He raised himself to half sit. "Oh, I see. I'm not worthy to hear the full story. As always, Furius Camillus has chosen you above others." His stutter returned. There was always tension between the men despite their friendship—a rivalry for her Wolf's favor. A contest Marcus always won. Drusus was brave but rash. His present injuries attested to this. Marcus had won an oak-leaf crown in his first battle for saving another's life and returning to the fray. And she knew this galled Drusus—for he was the man who'd needed to be rescued.

Marcus rubbed the scar at the edge of his eye, keeping his tone even. "It's the influence I might exert over my father which he finds useful."

"Even so, the general has marked you out for higher promotion, hasn't he?" Drusus clenched his fists. "While I risk being a civilian forever."

Marcus crouched down again. Pinna edged back to allow him to draw closer to the injured man. He rested his hand on Drusus's shoulder.

"Farewell, my friend. I'll speak to my father about you. If he's elected as a consular general in December, I'll make sure he chooses you from the next levy to fight in his regiment."

Drusus gripped Marcus's arm, his resentment replaced by uncertainty. "You believe I'll fully recover?"

"Yes. Then we'll see Caecilia and her husband destroyed."

Drusus frowned, hesitating. "You want your cousin dead?"

Pinna was nonplussed. Marcus had always declared publically that he would see Caecilia executed. Pinna knew he didn't mean it. Yet something had happened to change him in the Battle of Blood and Hail. Both friends had faced Vel Mastarna and failed to slay him. Drusus's devotion to the traitoress remained, but her kinsman had hardened his heart against her.

Marcus stood and tightened his belt buckle with its horsehead crest. "I saw her that day. She was on the ramparts clad in yellow. Even from a distance I could see its bright color. There she was . . . staring down at me, dressed like some eastern whore. You should forget her."

Drusus reddened, a fit of coughing seizing him. Pinna brushed past Marcus, offering her patient a spoon of honey and mint. "Lie down again, my lord. I need to finish with these stitches." The knight slid down onto the pallet, his spasms easing.

Marcus watched Pinna pick at the knots with the pincers. "That's right, Pinna. Make sure you take *very* good care of him."

She flushed, concentrating on the sutures. "Good-bye, my lord," she murmured. She made sure she kept her head down until the lack of squeaking leather and clanking metal told her that he'd left the tent.

• • •

Pinna grew anxious when she saw Marcus waiting for her in the camp square after she'd finished tending to her patient. He barred her way to the command tent.

"Don't you need to ride to Rome, my lord?" she said, bowing her head. There had been a time when such formalities were unnecessary. He had been simply "Marcus" when she'd shared his tent and his life.

"It's too late in the day to start the journey now. I'll leave early tomorrow." He nodded toward Drusus's tent. "I see that you have duped him into believing you're benign. You no longer circle each other like dogs."

"Being his nurse has changed his feelings toward me. And mine toward him." She lowered her voice. "I never understood your infatuation with him. But in his agony he's revealed the side that makes me realize why you love him."

He glanced around to check if anyone could hear. "It's not infatuation," he hissed. "And don't pretend you wouldn't expose me to the general if you had the chance."

As a reflex, she reached out her hand to touch his arm, then dropped it. "I told you I would never do that. Why won't you believe me?"

"Because you're a conniving lupa. You coerced me into making you my army wife to force me to remain silent about that night in the brothel. I wasn't prepared to let you harm Drusus. We both know Camillus despises soldiers who go with whores. I don't want his chance to rise in the ranks hindered by you crying rape."

His dismissal of her suffering was cruel. She may have forgiven Drusus but she could never forget. And Marcus had been there. He'd watched his friend abuse her and done nothing. And he'd paid for her as well, made potent by imagining it was Drusus, not a woman, he was taking.

She scanned the patrician's face: his pockmarked cheeks, the puckered tissue near his eye, the mark on the bridge of his nose. His brown eyes could be soft. He hadn't made her his concubine because of her threats alone. He'd felt sorry for her, too. And guilty for how he'd treated her in the lupanaria. "Please, my lord, I've done what you asked. I've nursed Drusus to health. Let enmity be finished between us. We were once friends."

"You were no friend."

"You know that's not true. We would talk, you and I, when we shared a bed but not our bodies." She pointed to his forearm. She knew the flesh under his armband was not marred only by his recent wound. The skin was scored with tiny scars—self-inflicted cuts to punish him for his desire for another freeborn. "I understand your torment."

He growled. "Spare me your sympathy, Pinna. You've done well in saving Drusus's life, but your job isn't finished. He needs to be fit enough to fight. You know the way to strengthen men's muscles.

I've seen you massage them and teach them exercises. Although rubbing more than the general's neck has caused you trouble." His eyes narrowed. "Don't think you're safe merely because you warm his bed. I should've told Camillus about you when you became his mistress. If he knew the baseness of your beginnings, he'd clout you hard enough to send you flying back to Rome."

She lowered her basket to the ground and faced him squarely. "But you didn't tell him, did you? And you promised you wouldn't if I helped Drusus. You allowed the general to unwittingly take a she wolf as a concubine. You claim you're prepared to be disgraced by admitting this, but do you really want him to be a laughing stock? And, remember, to confess means you would see your closest friend shamed. Both of you should have spoken up. And now both of you have remained silent. I don't think you'll risk besmirching either of your characters."

He scoffed. "Ah, this is the schemer I recognize. Not the loyal nurse."

She gritted her teeth, wanting to pound his chest and make him understand she was tired of using her wiles. Yet, wasn't she justified to strive to be free of poverty and oppression? Without the web of intrigue she'd woven, she would never have become her Wolf's woman. And she had not actually caused Marcus hurt. She'd wounded his pride, not his heart. Being perceived as a cuckold in the eyes of the camp had humiliated him even if she'd never been his lover. She placed her hands on her hips. "Only because you force me to be. I just want to be left alone with the general. I've healed the Claudian as you asked. When will I stop being beholden to you?"

"When Claudius Drusus can ride into the fray beside me again. When we capture Caecilia and put her husband to the sword."

She shook her head. "What happened in that battle? You didn't hate your cousin before. I sensed you felt sorry for her. Now you're so bitter."

"Are you blind, Pinna? Drusus may never be a warrior again! Mastarna did that to him, but it's Caecilia's fault. Too many men have suffered because of her lust for the Veientane."

He'd grown loud. Her frown caused him to lower his voice. "Caecilia should never have spurned Drusus. Never have forsaken Rome. And it riles me the Etruscan dog sought to sully his name. He claimed Drusus attacked him from behind. But Drusus's scar is on his front. He was facing Mastarna when he was wounded."

Marcus had told her of the accusation. She'd wondered if jealousy had driven the lovesick knight to act dishonorably. Marcus had not seen his friend inscribe the love spell. She alone knew the depth of the Claudian's obsession. Yet she'd dismissed the slur. Why would anyone believe the account of an enemy? Drusus was reckless, but she'd never thought of him as spineless. She picked up her basket, tucking it into the crook of her arm. "May I go, my lord?"

He stared at her, words hovering on his lips, but instead of berating her further, he strode away.

Pinna was relieved. Marcus was angry but she sensed it was bluster. And she must thank unrequited love for her protection: Drusus's for Caecilia, and Marcus's for Drusus. It was cruel to barter in emotions but she had no other choice. No one was going to take her Wolf from her. No man was ever going to reduce her to nothing again.

THIRTEEN

It was twilight by the time she had seen to her chores. Camillus had been fed, relishing the fennel-flavored porridge; although he'd shaken his head when she'd told him it was doubly potent for having been plucked from Minerva's skirts.

She scanned the camp as she unhooked the pot from the cooking tripod to clean it. Spirals of smoke wafted into the air from other campfires. The lowing and bleating of the animals in the enclosure behind the camp reminded her of her childhood, even though her father had never owned more than an ox to pull his plow and one nanny goat to milk.

She could hear the heavy infantrymen warming themselves around the flames, sharing jokes and tales of valor. The hoplites' morale was always buoyed by Camillus. Every morning, the general would inspect his troops, but in the evenings he would often visit his men informally. He knew each of their names and their histories. What battles they'd fought and what scars they bore. And it was this attention that made them love him. They were commoners who were bitter against the patricians, but Camillus was forgiven his class. When he jested with them, his lineage was forgotten. These men would follow him to their deaths if he asked it.

Her Wolf did not look up as she drew back the tent flap. He sat at his desk, a lamp burning beside him. She loved his face with its aquiline nose and high forehead. As always, he was immaculately groomed. His shoulder-length hair was combed, and his short-cropped beard trimmed. His handsome hands were clean. The gold ring encircling his finger was a trophy from the Volscian who'd speared him. Despite the gravity of Camillus's position, and the controlled violence within him, the grooves in his weathered cheeks were etched by good humor, as were the creases around his eyes.

She stood behind him, looping her arms around his neck and placing her cheek against his soft bearded one.

"You're distracting me," he muttered, placing one scroll to the side and unfurling the next. "I need to finish these reports. My visit to the sanctuary has meant I'm behind with my work."

She was not deterred. She was familiar with his moods. If he wanted her gone, she would know it in his voice. She nibbled his earlobe. "I want you, my Wolf."

His tone was firmer. "Don't tempt me."

She drew back and placed her hands on his shoulders, massaging the tendons at the base of his skull while he continued to read. She peered over his shoulder as he took a tablet from the pile. His stylus dug into the wax. His script was neat and sure. She wondered what the words meant. Like most girls, she'd never been taught to read or write. "What do the reports say?"

"Nothing that would interest you. Usual army business. Inventories. Sick lists."

She rested her chin on top of his head. "Everything you do interests me."

He chuckled. "Then you are easily satisfied." He turned around to face her. "Tell me, how is Claudius Drusus?"

She smiled, pleased that he didn't resent her sitting beside the sickbed of another soldier. "His flesh is healing. I removed the final stitches today."

"You're a worthy nurse."

"It will be some time before his shoulder is strong enough to hold a shield."

"It will be hard for him if he can't. He deserved the three silver spears I awarded him."

Pinna knew such accolades would never be enough for Drusus. He wanted a circlet of oak leaves. Or to be rewarded the mural crown—for being the first to scale the wall of the besieged city. "He's jealous of Marcus Aemilius even though they are closer than brothers."

His lips curled in a half smile. "Envy fuels acts of valor."

"So you like to pit them against each other?"

"Competition is healthy. Roman men thrive on it on the battlefield, and in the law courts, and in politics."

"But you're fostering rivalry between two friends."

"You're naïve, Pinna. I want my men to excel. I vie to do better than my older brother, Medullinus. He's resentful that he isn't in office."

"And is it the same with your younger brother?"

"Spurius? Not so much. Although he is ambitious enough." He turned back to his desk.

She was not prepared to let him ignore her. The touch of his skin beneath her fingers had aroused her. Close proximity to him always made her tingle, a shiver of expectation running through her like a breeze caressing water. She slipped off her shoes, then untied the strings of her tunic, stepping from the circle of fabric as it pooled around her feet. Then she loosened the pins from her bun, her fine black hair falling to her waist. She walked around to stand before him, the air chilly on her skin.

He laid his stylus down and pushed back from the desk, his eyes roaming over her tiny frame with its full breasts, rounded hips, and narrow waist. "Come here."

He pulled her to him, his fingers edging around to cup her buttocks. She bent and kissed him, her tongue prying his lips open, her hair shrouding them. She drew away and knelt before him to untie his boots and unfasten his belt buckle. He stood, lifting his tunic over his head, while she unwound his loin cloth. Finally he was naked except for the broad leather girdle that supported his back. He resented having to wear it and was careful to keep it secret. To reveal such a weakness was the real reason why he would never have bathed in the sanctuary's pool. She half rose, ready to unlace it, but he stopped her, sitting down on his chair again.

"Leave it on. I want you here."

Kneeling again, she traced the scar that curved from his shoulder to under his armpit, before trailing her hand along the lump in his clavicle where the bone had never fully mended. She moved downward, running her fingers through his chest hair, feeling the contours of his muscles, the ridges of his abdomen. Then, teasing him, she bent to graze her mouth along the indented scar on his thigh.

He grasped her with strong hands and guided her to stand and then straddle him. Closing her eyes, she enjoyed his hardness. Muscled arms wrapped around her, almost squeezing the breath from her, as he helped her to grind and rock against him.

When they'd finished, he continued to hold her tight, regaining his breath. She laid her cheek on one of his shoulders, her arms encircling his neck. Her own heart was racing. It always amazed her that he would let her mount him. A woman was supposed to be supine, a mere receptacle for a man's semen. His back injury meant he needed her to do more. She welcomed it. He never failed to satisfy her. Or she him.

He rarely admitted their lovemaking caused him discomfort. More than once she wondered if she should offer him relief by other means, but to do so would only shock him. It was also risky. How would she explain she knew whore's tricks without revealing she had been a whore? For that is why lupae were paid—to do what good Roman wives wouldn't. Not that she minded such practices in the brothel or graveyard. Using hand or mouth was better than the thought of a disease that could line her womb.

He stroked her hair. "What am I going to do with you, Pinna? The sun has barely set and you've made me forget my duties. Next you'll have me knowing you in daylight."

She smiled as she swiveled from his lap and stood, extending her hand to him. "Lie down beside me for a time." She nodded to the pile of tablets and scrolls. "All this can wait. You sleep little more than a few hours each day. No man would begrudge you a break."

He hesitated, then, with a small shake of his head, let her lead him to their pallet.

The coolness of the autumn night now intruded after the heat of their lovemaking. She shivered and pulled the wolfskin over them as he slid in beside her. "Let me remove this now," she said, unlacing the belt. He winced in pain but said nothing, settling on his back next to her.

Lying on her side, she laid her head against his shoulder. She relished these times. Somehow, when holding her in the wavering light of a lamp, he was inclined to talk to her. "Were you surprised to learn that it is Mater Matuta who must be placated?"

"Yes. I never thought it would be the dawn goddess who was angry."

She placed her hand on his chest. "She brings the power of the sun. You should worship her fervently. She will bring you victory."

"Are you counseling me in religion and war now, Pinna?"

She chewed her lip, aware she'd been too forward. Then she noticed his smile, his features half hid in shadow, half in light.

"I have family holdings in Latium," he said. "It's in my interest as much as Rome's to see the land drained. I'll be happy to see the goddess appeased."

"My mother came from Satricum," she said. "The town is sacred to Mater Matuta. Mama taught me to revere her."

"Tell me about her."

His query surprised her. She thought of her poor mother, dying of pox and madness. "Why do you ask, my Wolf?"

He stroked her cheek. "Because I wish to know all about you. She's the one who called you 'Pinna,' isn't she?"

"Yes, she called me 'feather, her little wing.'"

"And your father's name?"

"Lollius, Gnaeus Lollius."

"Then your true name is 'Lollia'?"

She inwardly cursed herself. Her given name, and her whore's name, was inscribed on the prostitute's roll. She wished now that she'd given an alias to the cross-eyed city magistrate when he'd registered her. "Yes, but I've not been called that for a long, long time. My father alone used it. 'Pinna' is what I like to be called."

"And your father was forced into bondage when he couldn't satisfy his creditors."

"He couldn't afford to pay the war tax, my Wolf. And most of the year he was away fighting for Rome, so my mother and I tilled the land for him. In the end Father had to sell his animals and small farm. Lastly, his armor. It wasn't enough to pay his debts. When he was bonded, we were forced to travel to the city and find work."

"Little citizen, it pains me that good Romans should fall on such hard times."

She pushed aside her guilt. She didn't deserve to be called a citizen. She'd forfeited that right when she'd become a prostitute. Yet his sympathy stirred her to challenge him. "The common soldiers are paid a salary but the tariff depletes it. Why not let them take plunder instead of giving it all to the treasury?"

"It's not so simple. You know that. The State collects loot for the good of all. The war tax is reduced that way."

"And yet the patricians take their own share of the spoils—treasure and land. It's like cream added to an already sweetened dish, while booty for veterans would go partway to feed their families."

"The nobility are liable for a greater share of the tax."

"Why must soldiers pay anything at all?"

"Because it's used to fund their salaries."

"I don't understand. A tax to pay themselves? They are farmers who must fight all year round. Their women are left to shoulder plows and reap harvests. Debts accrue. And then . . ." Her voice caught in her throat.

He placed his arm around her. "Why do you think I struggle to defeat Veii? You saw the fertile soil of this land. Instead of destroying the crops, I'm forcing the Veientane farmers we've captured to work them. I learned my lesson when I razed Faliscan territory when Rome was in famine. This time I'll feed our people instead of letting them starve." He placed his fingers beneath her chin, making her look at him. "And Veii is filled with riches. There will be plenty to share."

"So you plan to let your troops keep the loot? Be granted plots of land?"

He kissed her on the forehead. "That's not for me to decide. Only the Senate has that power."

His tone told her she should not pester him further. She hugged him, grateful he'd not silenced her.

"Tell me, how did you come to be a servant in the House of Aemilius?"

She tensed, confused again why he was enquiring about her history. She scrambled to remember what lies she'd told him already. "When my mother died, I went from house to house seeking work. Marcus Aemilius took pity on a daughter of a Roman soldier. I was first his maid and then his concubine."

"At least you didn't end up as a slut in a tavern or working in a bakery."

Pinna felt uneasy. Such women were often expected to provide more services than just pouring wine or grinding grain. If he thought they were base, his contempt for a lupa would be even greater.

He did not seem to notice her lack of response, although his next question panicked her. "Tell me the truth, Pinna. How many men have you lain with?"

She'd lost count. But one thing was true; she'd never had a lover before him, never had a man possess her heart. She pondered whether to name a number. How many would he accept before he rejected her? Or should she feign she was a virgin before she met Marcus? She decided not even the general would expect that. "I will not lie, my Wolf. It was not easy after my father was placed into bondage. Men took advantage more than once of a young country girl." Suddenly she was curious, too. "And you, my Wolf. How many women have you had?"

He hesitated. She wondered if she'd pressed too hard.

"There were servant girls in my father's house before I was married, but once I wed I was faithful. My wife bore me two sons of whom I'm proud. By the time she died, my back pained me after I was unseated from my horse in battle." He kissed her hair. "You make me forget that."

"No other army wives, then?"

"My manservant saw to my armor and cooked my meals."

She summoned up greater nerve. "And whores, my Wolf?"

He snorted. "They are for the weak. Better to keep a concubine than visit those poxy prostitutes who follow the regiment."

His disgust made her queasy. At least her admission of lying with others hadn't angered him. "So you don't hate me for my past? That I've known other men?"

He placed his lips against her hair. "My only worry is that you have feelings for Marcus Aemilius."

She gasped. She'd never thought jealousy would eat at him. "He means nothing to me."

"And what of him? Does he still have feelings for you?"

"We speak because I tend to his friend. Other than that, he is cold."

She could tell he was pleased. He sat up, looking down at her as she rolled onto her back and gazed up at him. "I want you to come with me to Rome."

Disbelief and excitement surged. She'd always pushed aside thoughts of what would happen when his campaign ended. "I would be proud to be your servant, my Wolf."

He laughed. "You don't understand. I want you to live as my de facto wife in my house, my official concubine."

She sat up. "In your house?" Then she bowed her head. "I can't give you children, my Wolf."

"I don't want children. I already have two sons."

"They might be displeased, my Wolf. They'll think I'm dishonoring their mother's memory."

He stroked her cheek. "They won't need to deal with that. They live in my country villa. They'll reach fighting age soon. Besides, knowing you, you would try and cosset them."

She pushed aside thoughts that his boys would only be a little younger than she was. Yet her Wolf's age had never worried her. At fifty, Camillus was still virile. And she was attracted to his power. "Didn't your mother cosset you?"

"There was little time for that. I hadn't even lost all my milk teeth before I was chosen to be a camillus altar boy to the chief pontiff. My memories of childhood were of rituals, augury—and politics."

"And that's why you are known as 'Camillus' instead of your family name 'Medullinus' like your brothers?"

He nodded. "But enough of my story. Tell me, do you wish to come to Rome with me?"

She scrambled onto her knees beside him, wrapping her arms around his neck. "Yes! You've made me so happy, my Wolf. I love you."

He broke from her and grasped both her hands, the pressure firm. "You know what I think of 'love,' Pinna. A man is expected to control his emotions. To be in love is to let your soul live inside another's body. It diminishes a man. I want you in my home and my bed, but don't expect me to ever whisper those words to you."

She chided herself. She knew this even though she prayed he might forget his rule. Lifting his hands to her lips, she kissed the back of each of them in turn. "I understand, my Wolf. But I am a woman, and weak, so I can indulge in such an emotion. But I ask nothing more of you than to be your concubine."

She could feel him relax.

"I need to go back to work. No more distractions."

She rose and slipped on her tunic, then helped him to dress—buckling his belt, smoothing the tunic across his back, helping to strap on his boots, rewinding the steps of her seduction. He was right. Love enfeebled a man. She saw this with Marcus and Drusus. It could possess, enrage, and overcome reason. It could drive vengeance and inspire passion and courage. She smiled as she lit another lamp and set up her handloom. For, unlike a man, love gave a woman power. A night moth had become a patrician's mistress. The impossible had been made possible. And in time she felt certain she would hear those three precious words.

FOURTEEN

Marcus, Fidenae, Autumn, 397 BC

Artile was not at ease on the horse. Marcus Aemilius grew impatient with the need to slow down. The soothsayer clung to the gelding's mane, his pudgy body joggled by the trotting motion, his face half grimace, half apprehension. The guard of five knights accompanying him found it difficult to hide their smirks.

Marcus was more irritated than amused. He found it hard to credit that a man did not know how to sit a horse; to grip the bare fleshy sides between his thighs, and guide the steed with rein and bit only. As a cavalry officer at the head of a turma of thirty, he'd forgotten a time when he'd not ridden. It was engrained in him to read the shift in an animal's movements, the eagerness of the beast to charge, the capriciousness of its moods. He leaned down and patted his stallion's neck. The horse responded with a brief shake of his head, stepping high, impatient as well.

Some way behind them, two donkeys pulled the wagon containing Artile's sacred texts and baggage. Two foot soldiers walked beside it. Every now and then the haruspex would risk toppling from his horse to glance over his shoulder to check the Holy Books were still stacked in the tray. He'd insisted on bringing the codex with him in case of further need to consult it.

Marcus had refused to let the priest ride in the cart. If the party was attacked by renegades, he needed to ensure Artile could escape quickly. However, given the soothsayer's incompetent riding skills, the decurion now wondered at his own wisdom. He was keen to sight the Roman garrison at Fidenae and reach the river ferry. It would mark the halfway point to Rome. As always, it struck him how close Veii and Rome were situated. Neighbors and foes, the righteous and the wicked, separated only by a strip of water.

Dark, bruised clouds clustered on the horizon, threatening rain. Marcus hoped some would fall on his city. Artile had revealed how Veii could grow its grain while Rome struggled with drought and famine.

He thought of the last time he'd seen his home: the arid parched land, people scratching for husks, the cattle perishing from thirst. The Romans had borne the harshest of winters and then sweltered under a relentless summer sun. There had been a plague too: the sick dying in the streets, the sky dense with the black smoke of funeral pyres. The Aemilian family had been forced to retreat to the country with other patricians. The escape had been too late for his mother. Marcus pushed aside the memory of her shrunken frame and the pustules on her once-plump face. She could be a bully to others with her sharp slaps and scolding, but never with her only son. Her only child.

In comparison, his relationship with his father was prickly; nevertheless, Marcus would be pleased to see him. Deep down he knew Aemilius was proud of him, although the senator would never show it. It was only when he overheard him with others that Marcus realized his father acknowledged his bravery and achievements. Now he had to convince Aemilius to call a special sitting of the Senate. And to heed the advice of an Etruscan traitor about the meaning of the omen.

As they neared the next bend in the road, the decurion heard the sounds of the Roman outpost near the river: the growling of the sentry dogs, the shouts of a centurion training his hoplites, the hammering of a blacksmith at his anvil, and the grunting of swine in the enclosure. A stockade came into view where civilian traders heckled and bartered with soldiers for fresh vegetables, eggs, and fruit.

Tatius, one of his knights, pointed to the hilltop town rising above them on the far side of the river. Marcus did not plan to waste time scaling the rise. He wanted to reach Rome by midday. And he didn't want to risk Artile being noticed. No knight would struggle to maintain his seat on a horse. No knight had milk-white skin and soft, blistered fingers.

The barge was on the other side of the stream. A line of traffic was banked along the road. Marcus glanced over his shoulder to check how long he'd have to wait for the cart to catch up with his riders. He frowned when he saw how far it was lagging behind. "We'll cross our horses at the ford. I want to get you into Roman territory as soon as possible. The wagon driver can cross later."

"I refuse to risk the sacred texts getting wet. They need to be carried across by boat." Artile waggled his reins in front of him. "Do you think I can control my horse through water? Please, Marcus Aemilius, let me ride the barge."

Marcus scowled, annoyed to be further delayed, but he knew the priest was correct. The Veientane was already having problems keeping upright on dry land. The decurion didn't relish having to fish him out of the river.

Artile dismounted, stumbling a little before regaining his balance. He stepped gingerly as he moved away from the road, before bumping down on his buttocks on the grassy embankment.

Tatius trotted his mount over to his commander. He appeared amused to see the haruspex sitting with his head cradled between his hands, exhausted. Marcus dismounted and handed the knight both horses' reins. "Lead them across the ford and wait for me on the other side."

The ruddy-faced soldier grinned, revealing buckteeth. "Is the fat priest causing you trouble, sir?"

Marcus rolled his eyes. Tatius laughed. They had started as raw recruits together. He did not seek to rival Marcus as did Drusus. He acknowledged the Aemilian as his superior without question.

"May Mars give me strength to get through this day," muttered Marcus, grabbing a goatskin bladder of water from his horse's pack and gesturing Tatius to go. The soldier saluted before he led the animals farther upstream.

On the far side, the ferryman was taking his time to load cargo. It could be a long wait before he would return. Marcus looked across to Artile, reluctant to go near him despite the general's orders. He'd been charged to discover the true nature of the enmity between the Mastarna brothers. It was to Camillus's advantage to understand the motives and passions of all those around him, both friend and foe. Even so, the decurion couldn't comprehend why his commander placed such faith in the seer.

He sat down beside Artile. The soothsayer glanced up when he realized the Roman had joined him. Marcus squirted a stream of water into his mouth from the bladder, then wiped drips from his beard. The priest eyed the liquid, licking dry lips. The Aemilian ignored him, finding it difficult to reconcile how Artile could be so unlike his warrior brother. There was a marked resemblance, but the priest lacked a honed body and battle scars. Yet Marcus couldn't deny both brothers' fame. One was renowned for his valor, the other for his prescience. If in Rome, such a family would be feted.

It was quiet away from the hubbub of the ferry station. The Roman studied the fast-flowing current, wondering how to broach the subject of Vel Mastarna. The water was so clear he could see the pebbles coating the bottom of the stream. It was hard to imagine that these swirling eddies had once been thick with blood. Fidenae was a strategic post over which Veii and Rome had fought for decades. It was the site of massacres and ignominy, triumph and honor. The crossing joined the northern trade routes to the rich salt pans at the mouth of the Tiber. Veii had once controlled all access. Then Rome had thwarted it by capturing the hilltop town nearly thirty years ago. A battle won by his great uncle, Mamercus Aemilius—the dictator.

His thoughts drifted to Caecilia. It was for those trade routes she'd been wed to Vel Mastarna in the first place. There had been concord for twenty years based on a treaty arising after the battle of Fidenae. And it was his father, Aemilius, and other peace-makers, who had sought to continue the pact by offering Cilla in marriage. Marcus had ached for her when he'd heard she was to be sacrificed. He clenched his fists. Cilla. He had to stop thinking of her fondly. Stop using the nickname he'd given her. The glimpse of her on the wall during the Battle of Blood and Hail was enough to convince him she was Veientane now.

"Our pasts are linked more than you can imagine, Marcus Aemilius."

Artile's bass voice startled him.

"My father was killed by your great-uncle at this very place."

Marcus turned to him. He had long felt the burden of living up to the most famous of the Aemilian clan. "Then your father fought for a tyrant. King Laris Tulumnes was a scoundrel who murdered four Roman envoys on the throw of a dice. He deserved to be beheaded when Mamercus Aemilius defeated his army."

Artile's bristled. "The Tulumnes family saw his mutilation as a travesty. And his descendants have fared little better. His son was deposed by Mastarna and his cronies. Then his cousin, King Kurvenas, was assassinated. My brother filled his royal shoes despite bleating how much he loathes monarchs. At least Karcuna Tulumnes is still there to oppose him. There's always been conflict both within and without Veii. Our father would be ashamed of my brother."

Marcus snorted. "What would he think of his traitorous priestly son?"

Artile looked away.

The Roman was pleased he'd pricked the Etruscan's conscience. Yet the seer's declaration that his father had met his death at the hand of Marcus's own famous ancestor only made the decurion wonder what type of man Vel Mastarna really was. "Your brother chose to put such history aside to marry an Aemilian? Why?"

The haruspex's laugh was bitter. "A bone of contention between us. He replaced vengeance with diplomacy—and look how that ended."

"So that's why you hate him? Because you feel he's betrayed your family through the marriage?"

The pasty features hardened. "That's only part of my hatred."

The soldier leaned back, legs outstretched, his weight resting on his elbows. "The ferryman will take some time. I'm listening."

The priest scrutinized him as though hesitating whether to reveal more. "He liked to meddle in my private life. He and that treacherous cousin of yours turned my love against me at the time war was declared."

"Why would they convince your wife to spurn you?"

"I have no use for a wife. It was my beloved, Tarchon, who was persuaded to leave me."

Marcus scrambled to understand, then recalled the priest's conversation with Camillus. How he'd claimed Mastarna's adopted son had shunned him.

He had only met the prince once. Tarchon had accompanied Caecilia to Fidenae when she'd sought to flee Veii ten years ago. He guessed he was the same age as him. Nineteen or twenty. He'd smelled of rose water and worn a turquoise earring and robes of green. Marcus suspected he was a soft one, only having eyes for men. For some time after, he repressed thoughts of kissing those sensual lips; long-lashed eyelids; and the Veientane's taut, honey-colored body.

Had the prince been seduced, or was he willing? Either way, Marcus was disturbed. What kind of world did Caecilia live in? A woman should never be exposed to such behavior. And yet it seemed that she was involved in a drama between two molles. How could she condone an adult aristocrat bedding the son of another noble? Turning a youth destined to be a warrior into a bride. After all, it was a father's duty to teach his son how to be a statesman, knight, and head of his family. For a moment, he felt a twinge of sadness. He'd never sire heirs to whom he could show his battle scars.

He stared at the seer, aware that the odious Etruscan possessed none of the qualities suited to teach a boy how to be a man. Yet he was also intrigued whether Tarchon's relationship with the priest had continued into manhood. Were two equals allowed to be lovers openly in Veii? Imagine such freedom. "I can understand why Mastarna would ensure his son retained his honor. Tarchon was your kin, and was expected to become a soldier, not another man's wife."

"Who are you to judge me? I've seen how you look at Claudius Drusus. You'd bed him without hesitation if he gave you some encouragement."

Marcus felt the blood rush of anger and astonishment and fear. He sat up and seized the priest by the throat.

Artile flailed against him, his hands scrabbling at his. "Camillus . . . wants me . . . alive."

The Roman squeezed the soothsayer's windpipe, ignoring how the man wheezed, his dark cat eyes bulging, his face scarlet.

It was hard to let go.

The haruspex gulped in air, coughing. He slumped back onto the grass, rubbing his fleshy neck, which was now marked with red fingerprints.

Rattled, Marcus stood, glowering at the Veientane. His heart was thudding. All these years he'd kept his love for his friend secret. What had he done to reveal himself? Only Pinna had guessed. Only Pinna knew. "Speak such lies again, and I'll kill you once you've served your purpose."

Artile rose, still rubbing his throat. His voice was hoarse. "Don't worry. You're good at keeping your lust hidden. There's a reason for my fame. I observe and take notice of the smallest of tells. It's the way you avoid looking at Claudius Drusus that made me realize."

"Keep talking, priest, and I might just forget my orders completely."

The haruspex kept his distance, eyeing the officer warily. "Then I'll speak no more. But lost love eats away at your insides. Knowing this, you can understand my bitterness toward my brother. I would see him destroyed along with his bitch. We are as one in that desire."

Marcus spat at his feet, the spittle spraying onto the Etruscan's boots. "Don't ever think we're on the same side."

• • •

Artile fussed over the stolen Holy Books on the trip across the river, ensuring the scrolls were sealed in their cylinders and the folded linen pages were intact and undamaged.

Marcus stood at the railing, barely aware of the shouts of the ferryman as he loaded the other cargo. Balancing on the swaying deck, the decurion stared at the water, watching the wind riffle its surface. His mind was in turmoil. He doubted Artile would be given credit should he voice such gossip. An enemy turned traitor. A member of the House of Mastarna with a long-held enmity with the Aemilians. And Marcus had committed no crime. Yet dung thrown is difficult to clean. Speculation could spread. It would harm his reputation as well as his political and military ambitions. It was this same fear of exposure that drove him to be coerced by Pinna.

When he was younger, he'd often enjoyed one of the servant boys slightly older than him. No one had thought anything of it. It was a master's right. The slave was skilled in the art of pleasure. Marcus remembered the surprise and abandon of the first time, the soft moist warmth of the youth's mouth encasing his hardness. Then how he'd flouted the rules at the promise in the boy's deep gaze; taking turns, gentle strokes quickening into sweet slickened rutting before waking the next morning, lips bruised from kisses, traces of salt upon his skin, confused and guilty that strictures could be broken in passion, and terrified that the servant would not keep his secret that a noble was prepared to act the bride. Yet he was prepared to disobey them again as he rolled his back to the boy, filled with emptiness it was not his schoolmate nestled behind him.

But it was far more dangerous to indulge in an affair with another freeborn in the same way. Even more so with a fellow warrior. Throughout his career, he'd restrained himself from exchanging glances with the soldiers he guessed were soft. It would have only taken a heartbeat to signal he wanted them. Abstinence brought safety.

He readjusted his wristbands. They hid tiny scars. Pinna had warned him that he might poison his blood if he kept slitting his flesh. Now he'd turned to punishing himself with training. Welcoming the pain. He was so fit that there was little flesh on his body, his muscles corded, his face gaunt. His personal penance reminded him that what he was prepared to do in bed was wrong. There was something broken in him in longing to lie with another knight.

His greatest fear was Drusus's disgust. Marcus knew his friend despised freeborns who were molles. And he was not interested in taking slave boys himself. In its way, this was unusual for a man. However, he didn't want to think what Drusus might do to him if he knew he desired him. At least in silence and suppression, Marcus could always be with him. To be denied proximity would be unbearable.

Taking Pinna as his army wife had been a shield. It spared him the pretense of seeking women's company. Before that, he'd endured visiting fleshpots with Drusus, causing him both thrills and frustration. They'd shared their first whore together. He'd balked at the sight of the bored she wolf with her knees raised to her chest. But watching Drusus excited him, especially when his friend met his eyes in boastful mastery of the woman. In that moment he realized that imagining being taken aroused him enough to perform. He'd rushed to thrust into the hot seed his companion left inside the lupa in case his stiffness failed. He thought his revulsion of the harlot was because of the tawdriness of the brothel, but over time he discovered no woman was alluring. He was always reluctant to join in other visits. But there were only so many excuses not to go whoring when on campaign. He needed to prove he was like any other man.

It was rare that Drusus was not rough with a lupa, saying they were paid to endure it. It had shocked Marcus at first. The youth who'd once protected his mother and sister from the beatings of a brutal father carried a legacy of viciousness in him. No Roman should raise his hand to a woman. Behind closed doors, though, the law was flouted. To see his friend abuse whores was disturbing. Yet he never stopped him. Always excused him. Until Pinna.

Drusus had slapped her thigh, then covered her face with his hand as he took her. She'd lain passive and quiet after an initial struggle. It had troubled Marcus but he didn't think of it as rape. She was a prostitute. And then she'd transacted her business with him without complaining. It was only when she sought him out later to coerce him that he understood her despair. Devoid of paint, her heart-shaped face had been pale and drawn, her black hair lank, no longer reddened by henna. Her tears were real. She swore she would kill herself rather than remain a she wolf. Desperation coated her threats. He felt pity for her as well as apprehension for himself. There was shame, too, that he'd been stirred by watching Drusus rather than trying to stop him from subduing her.

Pinna had spoken the truth when she said they'd grown close. It was a relief to be able to talk freely about his feelings without judgment. There was mutual benefit in their arrangement. She pretended she was his woman, while he'd freed her from the brothel. And then she'd humiliated him by making him a cuckold in the eyes of the camp with the general. The sharp point of her ambition had been unsheathed. He didn't believe her declarations that she'd keep his secret. She would destroy him if Furius Camillus were ever taken from her. Another woman whose lust overruled her integrity. Pinna and Caecilia. Was it any wonder he despised them?

Marcus was jolted from his thoughts as the ferry's bottom nudged into the shallows. Sounds intruded again: the thud of the gangplank onto the bank, the chatter of the passengers as they disembarked, the grunts of men as they hefted amphorae of olive oil onto their shoulders.

Artile stood looking back toward the road to Veii. His expression was melancholy. Marcus grabbed his arm, wrenching him around and then prodding him in the small of the back toward the waiting cavalrymen. "A little late for regret, priest. The next time you set foot in your city, Veii better belong to Rome."

FIFTEEN

The Forum was bathed in soft light, shadows pooling with the chill edge of the afternoon. There was a fresh smell of rain, the roads washed clean of muck. Marcus could hardly believe the drought had broken.

The city roiled with people spilling into the Sacred Way and cramming into the side streets. The plebeians were reveling. It was clear many had been drinking steadily. Marcus marveled at their conviviality. The last time he'd been in Rome they were on the brink of insurrection. He navigated through the crowd, making his way to the steps of the Curia Senate House so he could gain a better view. The festival intrigued him. It was not a day proscribed as a religious holiday.

There were three couches draped lavishly with flowing folds of cloth next to the Comitium assembly area. Two wooden statues, their heads molded from wax, were arranged on each divan, leaning their elbows on elaborate cushions. The garlands around their necks drooped from the recent showers. The circlets of laurel leaves on their brows were wilted and turning brown.

The tables in front of them were laden with food—a bounty in a city that lived on rations. Marcus thought it a waste that ants were creeping through the honey cakes, and flies buzzing over fruit. A young acolyte lethargically shooed away sparrows that alighted to peck at crumbs. He seemed defeated by the task.

Marcus edged into the throng again to inspect the effigies, astonished to see there were two women sharing the banquet. He'd never seen such a thing in the flesh or in sculpture. Matrons did not recline next to men when they dined. They sat on chairs and ate after their husbands, fathers, and sons.

A trumpet sounded. The throng parted to allow three magistrates in striped purple tunics make their way to the couches. Prayers were said. Invocations made. The ceremony identified the statues on the divans as deities. Apollo and his mother, Latona, were asked to heal the city; his sister, Diana, to protect the poor and women; Mercurius to stimulate commerce; and Neptunus to provide fresh water. Lastly, the half-god Herculeus was venerated for his strength. Marcus was struck by the presence of the same gods as lived in the sanctuary outside Veii. Both sides sought their protection.

The timekeeper called the dinner hour. The revelers started to drift home. Marcus pulled aside one man who appeared sober. "What are these rituals?"

"A new festival called a lectisternium. The keepers of the Sibylline Books have proclaimed it. It's to appease the six gods who are believed to have sent the plague and inclement weather. There's been a week of devotions. This is the eighth and last day. A banquet has been offered to the gods each afternoon."

"I thought we were in famine."

The man grinned. "No longer. Supplies arrived from the south. And rain has been falling steadily ever since the holiday began. Our cisterns are replenished. Our fields will be fertile again."

"So the rites are not in expiation for Lake Albanus?"

His smile faded. "We still await the delegation from Delphi."

The man moved on. Marcus turned toward his home on the Palatine, but a hand clasped his elbow. He swung around. Icilius Calvus stood before him.

"Marcus Aemilius. What brings you to Rome before the end of the year?"

Marcus shrugged him away. He had little time for the plebeian with the spear-straight back and dour manner. "Furius Camillus ordered me to return." He could see Calvus waiting for further explanation, but he denied him an account. Awkward seconds passed.

The plebeian scowled. "Spare me your patrician arrogance." He gestured around him. "Proclaiming another holiday might please some of my fellow Romans, but I know the true motivation for this lectisternium. And it's only in part to placate the gods."

Marcus frowned. "Why is that?"

"The Senate claims our city has suffered plague and famine because five plebeians were elected as consular generals instead of patricians. The scaremongering is gaining credence. The lectisternium provides an opportunity to pander to the populace with feasting. There's also been a decree that bondsmen are now unencumbered of their debts."

Marcus had heard the complaint about plebeians commanding Rome's armies before. He focused instead on the man's last sentence. "Those in bondage have been freed? I thought you'd be pleased to see veterans enfranchised again."

The grooves around Calvus's mouth settled into grim lines, etched from long years of disapproval. "True, such men regain the citizenship they forfeited. But they'll undoubtedly vote in favor of those who granted them liberty. Six patricians will once again lead Rome."

Marcus was stunned at his cynicism. "I never thought you'd complain that a common soldier could vote."

"The war tax hasn't been lifted. Warrior-farmers still fight all year round. How long do you think it will be before such men fall into debt again? It's the right to keep the spoils they need. And a share of conquered land."

Marcus shook his head at the well-worn grievance. "Booty needs to go to the treasury for the benefit of all."

"Is that what Camillus tells you? He was the only noble elected last year. Many believed he would reward his troops. Instead he denied them Faliscan plunder. And he deprived Rome of grain. I'm standing for the position of consular general again. I will not give up my fight for the rights of common soldiers."

Marcus's impatience changed to irritation. "Look around you. The people are happy. Do you want to incite them to mutiny again? To ensure our State is riven by internal conflict instead of standing as one against our enemies?"

Calvus leaned close, each word deliberate. "I want to see the Senate filled with plebeians. I want to see one elected as consul in the future. So tell your father that if no commoner is chosen as a consular general, there will be ructions. Buying a poor man's favor can only last so long. Discontent will also return unless the omen is solved. If not, the aristocracy's status as intermediaries to the gods may fall into question."

Marcus stepped back, scanning the plebeian's fine woolen toga. Calvus was as rich as any patrician. His concern for paupers was laughable. Not prepared to respond, Marcus nodded curtly, then turned on his heel. Nevertheless, as he pushed his way through the crowd toward his home, he thought of Artile waiting outside the city. Calvus was skeptical about the words of highborn augurs. What would he think about an Etruscan seer? Marcus swallowed hard. What would his father?

• • •

The inner and outer doors of every house Marcus passed on his street were thrown open. Garlands festooned the foyers. Inside he spied people milling around and helping themselves to food piled on tables. He was astounded. It was as if Rome had gone mad with generosity and good will. The rich of the Palatine were sparing no expense. Calvus's words echoed in Marcus's mind. Perhaps there was some weight to his claim the patricians were trying to garner votes through largesse.

The thick wooden portals of the House of Aemilius were closed. Marcus paused for a moment, pleased to be home but wondering why his father was not following the new custom. He banged the door clapper. A young porter he'd not met opened it.

"Come back in an hour; Lord Aemilius will offer refreshments then."

Disconcerted he was not recognized in his own home, Marcus shoved past him, calling for the majordomo. The retainer bustled into view, cuffing the slave boy over the head for his mistake.

"It's good to see you home, master. Let me take your toga. Your father is in his study with his guests."

Marcus let the servant unwind the bulky cloak from around his body. It felt strange to wear one again. He'd grown used to the weight of his armor and his army cape. Inside the city, though, he was required to don the clothes of an ordinary citizen.

As he slipped on indoor sandals, he gazed around the atrium. It seemed smaller than he remembered. There was a forlornness to the room despite the table laden with viands. The familiar scent of herbs drying by the hearth fire was absent. The loom was devoid of yarn and warp weights. Masculinity dominated, his father's panoply displayed on one wall, and the ancestor cupboard containing the death masks of Aemilian warriors opposite. A lump rose in his throat. His mother was dead. He would never see her again.

The sound of male voices floated from the study. Marcus entered the room with its pigeonhole shelves crammed with scrolls. His memories of this chamber were not fond. How many times had he stood here and been birched as a school boy? What would Aemilius do if gossip ever spread that his war-hero son loved another soldier?

The host was seated next to two guests. Marcus was unsurprised to see Scipio, a familiar crony, but the other man was unexpected. Lucius Furius Medullinus sat, leaning to one side on the armrest of his chair. Marcus frowned. His father's relationship with Camillus's older brother waxed and waned. They were often rivals in elections. The Furian was a complex man. He was a patrician and yet could not always be relied to act in the interests of the nobility. He'd supported a measure to grant soldiers a salary.

Marcus concentrated on his father. If anything, his clothes were even more rumpled than usual, another reminder the house lacked both a wife and mother.

Aemilius's bushy gray eyebrows rose in surprise. He stood and placed his cup on the table so he could slap Marcus on the back. "Son! Welcome! But why are you home before winter?"

Medullinus sipped his wine, then drawled, "Don't tell us my brother has made some headway at Veii after failing to take advantage of his win."

Marcus resented the disparaging tone. He knew Medullinus was irked he'd missed out on being elected. It must have been galling to be bested by five plebeians—and his younger brother. "Furius Camillus has tightened the siege in a way no other consular general has done before. The Veientanes will starve soon enough, as long as the next general can maintain constant pressure."

Aemilius glared at him. Marcus realized his mistake. His father had been one of the commanders who'd failed to take Veii in previous years.

Medullinus shifted in his seat, crossing his legs. He was taller and leaner than Camillus, but his hair was thinning. He self-consciously combed strands across his head to hide his bald patch. "You still haven't told us why you're here."

Marcus hesitated, unsure whether to mention Artile in front of the others. "I came to tell you that Vel Mastarna has been made king."

Scipio whistled. "Then we have a formidable foe. I thought he was badly wounded."

"Claudius Drusus slashed and broke Mastarna's sword arm. I doubt he'll be effective in battle again."

Medullinus continued his needling. "It's a pity you did not personally finish him off when you had the chance."

Marcus bristled. It rankled that he'd been made to surrender his spear. Yet if Mastarna had not spared his life, he would never have been able to rescue Drusus.

Aemilius cut in before Marcus could respond to the barb. "My son was among the warriors that nearly annihilated the Veientane army, Medullinus."

Marcus was taken aback at his father standing up for him.

Aemilius gestured him to draw up a chair beside him. "It's strange that Mastarna should have influence without a voting bloc. Stranger still that he was prepared to be crowned. I know he has no love of monarchs."

"What does it matter whether he's their chief magistrate or king," said Medullinus. "We can't assume he'll let Veii fall without a struggle."

"It's Mastarna's general, Thefarie Ulthes, we need to worry about," replied Scipio. "If he and the Faliscans in the north relieve Veii, then all Camillus's efforts will come to naught. And the zilath from Tarquinia on the coast has also bolstered the Etruscan forces."

Marcus was irritated none of them mentioned the plebeian general, Genucius. The decurion admired the commander with the eye patch. "Caius Genucius is containing Thefarie's northern troops, Father. He's an able leader."

Scipio snorted. "He is merely consolidating the gains made by Camillus."

Marcus hid his disgust. The skinny senator had never distinguished himself in battle, although he'd displayed bravery. Marcus glanced at Scipio's arm. There was a triangular indent in the flesh. The tip of a spear point remained embedded deep within. It was rumored the limb was weak. That he suffered constant pain.

"General Genucius proved himself in the Battle of Blood and Hail. After that he swapped commands to enable Furius Camillus to remain at Veii. He thinks of the glory of Rome, not his own."

Aemilius was as withering as Scipio. "Genucius has always been in Camillus's pocket. He was a toady when he was a people's tribune. And he's still a toady. He should have more pride. He leads a regiment of the Legion of the Wolf. He drew the lot to lead at Veii. I would never have handed over such a prize command."

"Perhaps Genucius thinks Rome would be better served if the best commander is in charge instead of six with different strategies. Veii has always had the advantage of having one leader."

Medullinus sat upright, unable to contain his contempt. "Oh, so now we come to the nub of the matter. Is that why Camillus sent you? Is he angling to be appointed dictator?"

Marcus checked himself. He did not want to disclose his superior's reasons. "General Camillus has given me no such direction."

The atmosphere in the room was tense. Aemilius picked up a goblet, dipping it into the krater mixing bowl on the table. "I think we all need another drink." He bent close to Marcus's ear as he handed him the cup. "Have some wine and calm down."

Marcus drained the chalice, annoyed his father wanted to curb him. "I met Icilius Calvus on my way here," he continued. "He claims this lectisternium ritual is a sop to the people. He threatened to stir up trouble again if there are no plebeians elected next time."

Scipio clucked. "He's sacrilegious. The gods are displeased at high office being vulgarized. Only patricians have the skills to conduct the official auspices. We interpreted the Sibylline Books to find the answer for the correct expiation rites. And we were right. Once the lectisternium started, rain fell and supplies reached us. Clearly the gods were punishing Romans for their foolishness in electing commoners in the first place."

"I can't believe Calvus still wants the classes at each other's throats, even though bondsmen have been given their liberty and the right to vote again," said Aemilius.

"Icilius Calvus is dangerous," said Medullinus. "He calls himself a patriot but the Icilian family has long subverted the State."

"The way to counter him and other hostile plebeian politicians is to ensure the most eminent candidates stand," said Scipio. "Citizens want generals who are experienced in leading the Legions of the Boar and the Wolf." He raised his cup to his fellow senators. "To you, my friends. I'm glad we're allies. May we all be successful in the December elections."

Medullinus rose after responding to the toast. "I must leave. I have clients waiting to be entertained." Scipio nodded, also rising. "I must not forget my obligations either."

Marcus watched the men as they grasped each other's forearms in farewell. A tight clique. No doubt there were other such meetings occurring in rich men's homes across the city. And, as he bid good night to the senators, he could not help wondering whether it would be wise for him to be as suspicious as Icilius Calvus.

SIXTEEN

Marcus's palms were sweaty as he retrieved Camillus's letter from his toga. It was time to broach the subject of Artile with his father.

The head of the house appeared fatigued. Marcus noticed how much grayer Aemilius's hair had become since Mother had died. For the first time, he thought his father might be too old to be a general. The responsibility of being a prefect of a city where unrest simmered must be heavy.

He handed Aemilius the scroll sealed with the Furian crest. "This contains the true reason why General Camillus has sent me. He's charged me to present his case. He wants you to arrange a special sitting of the Senate, as they are not due to convene until the Ides."

His father frowned as he read the missive. His face was ashen by the time he'd finished. "Has he gone mad? Why would we listen to a charlatan? A traitor! The brother of the newly elected Veientane king! I know you're enamored of Furius Camillus, son. But I can see why he's sent you to be the laughing stock of Rome instead of himself."

"You are wrong to mock him. Wrong to mock me, Father. I don't trust this priest but his skill as a seer is renowned. I saw him consult Apollo with my own eyes. He has told us how to placate the gods of Latium. We don't need to wait until the delegation returns from Delphi. Camillus wants to see the expiation rites completed as soon as possible. That's why he's asking that his term as consular general be extended. He wants to personally put the precondition for Veii's destruction into effect."

Aemilius was scornful. "Such a request is unprecedented. What Camillus really wants is to be declared dictator with supreme power. But such an appointment is only made if there's an emergency. And that's not the case, even though Rome is threatened by enemies on three points of the compass. Besides, Camillus's youngest brother, Spurius, and his colleagues will return from Delphi soon. They're expected back before winter. Then the newly appointed consular generals can follow the oracle's directions." He scowled. "What this city really needs is to ensure no plebeians are elected again."

"We need to look beyond such squabbles."

Aemilius crossed his arms. "And you would do well to heed me. I'm old enough to have seen too many changes in Rome. I've watched patrician power being eroded like rust eating at iron. Our divine blood has been polluted by intermarriage. Caecilia is an example of that. There were no people's tribunes when I was born. Now they hold this city to ransom by vetoing the levying of troops if they're dissatisfied with our proposals. The rot needs to stop. Nobility must again take control."

Marcus felt like tearing his hair. "We have a chance to conquer Veii, Father! Let's focus on defeating our enemies, not our fellow citizens. We should strike before Mastarna rallies his forces again."

Aemilius leaned back, speaking slowly as though Marcus were a child. It was a familiar lecture—one of expectations and ambition. "You're of an age to set foot onto the Honored Way. I want to see you elected as a city magistrate, a treasurer, and a judge. One day you may even be consul when that office is restored. Certainly, I expect you to be chosen as a consular general."

Marcus sensed his feet being shoved into his father's shoes and the white toga of a magisterial candidate being draped around him. "Camillus thinks I should stand for election as a military tribune first. He's prepared to back me. I want to serve in the army, not be stuck in an office worrying about sanitation, grain supplies, and roads."

His father was irritated at the Furian giving career advice to his son. "You've already gained prestige as a warrior. It's time to become a junior magistrate. Aligning with Camillus is risky. He's a maverick. Even his brother Medullinus views him warily. Your kin, clan, and our friends are more important. It will be Aemilian money and connections that get you elected."

"Medullinus is jealous of his brother."

"He's an eminent politician and soldier."

"So is the general."

Aemilius leaned forward. "I allowed you to pledge your allegiance to Camillus for the last campaign. In winter that service will be over. Don't forget you owe fealty to me."

"Don't deny my serving under Camillus gave you peace of mind, Father," said Marcus, resentful his father didn't want him to seek greater glory on the battlefield. "It galled you to think I might have to salute a commoner like Caius Genucius. As I said, I'm going to stand as a military tribune regardless of who my commander is."

Aemilius's face was now red with choler. "Show me respect! I would never have spoken to my elders as you do."

Marcus knew he should restrain his insolence, but he was tired of being submissive. Of being the dutiful son. "And I want you to start seeing me as more than a boy who should bow his head and always accept your opinion as my own."

Aemilius leaned across and gripped his son's arm. His grip was like iron, reminding Marcus that this man might look gray and old and tired, but he still possessed strength and a strong will.

"Do you know how hard I've worked to overcome the stigma of being the uncle and adopted father of a traitoress? Remember that Medullinus and I brokered the peace treaty that saw Caecilia married. But politics change. And war changes politics most of all. He and I both had to grow talons and sharp beaks after our misjudgment. The House of Aemilius can't afford to make any more mistakes." He squeezed harder. "Now you support Camillus in this lunatic scheme to bring an enemy priest before the Senate. What if Artile Mastarna is perfidious? What if the rites he proposes are intended to bring about calamity? Our family will be ruined, as will Rome. Do you want that?"

Marcus eased his arm from under Aemilius's hand. "What am I supposed to do, Father? I'm honor bound to obey my general. My oath to Camillus does not expire until he leaves office. And he has the right as a consular general to call a meeting of the Senate, even if you don't agree with the decision he seeks."

Aemilius slumped in his chair, hand to his brow, fingers pinching the bridge of his nose. "It's true. He has that power." Then he dropped his hand, meeting his son's gaze. "Where's the Etruscan now?"

"Waiting on the Campus with my men."

"Very well. I'll order the official messenger to call the senators to meet at the Temple of Apollo Medicus. As a foreigner from an enemy city, Artile can't speak before the Curia inside Rome's sacred boundary."

"Thank you, Father."

Aemilius grimaced, shaking his head. "I will make it clear I don't agree with Camillus's plan. Do you understand?" He stood with a slowness that hinted at creaking bones and age-weary muscles. Marcus rose in deference. To his surprise, his father patted his shoulder. "On second thought, a military tribune is a useful first step. We will lobby for votes together, you and I. And when I'm made consular general, I'll be proud to have you under my command. Father and son. Two Aemilian warriors together."

SEVENTEEN

Dawn's light was muted. Gray. A soft rain was falling, the drizzle enough to slowly saturate clothing. There was a breath of winter in the air.

The senators ascended the steps to the portico of the Temple of Apollo Medicus. The god may have been all seeing, but as a foreign Greek deity he was denied residence within the city wall. Nevertheless, the Senate chose his sanctum on the Campus Martius to give audience to enemy emissaries. Rome had claimed the divinity as its own.

The procession took some time. Marcus stood to the side and watched three hundred men pass. The effect was impressive, a moving mass of white and purple.

The doors of the temple remained open once the politicians had taken up their positions inside. The space in front of the doorway was reserved for the ten people's tribunes. Icilius Calvus stood on the portico sharing the same curious expression as his colleagues—who was the ambassador who was seeking an audience?

There were murmurs when Tatius escorted Artile onto the portico. The priest was wearing a cloak, the hood drawn forward to hide his face.

Inside, Aemilius was making his welcome address. Marcus clenched and unclenched his fists as he listened to the announcement that Furius Camillus had called an extraordinary sitting. He wondered if the deliberations would be thrashed out by nightfall. The Senate could only sit from sunrise to sunset.

His name was called. Taking a deep breath, Marcus signaled Artile to follow him inside. The priest kept his head bowed, his face hidden. Tatius remained beside the doorjamb.

Sunlight had not yet infiltrated the chamber. The gloom was splintered by torchlight from sconces on the walls. Three large braziers were burning but did little to heat or illuminate the room. A huge statue of Apollo stood inside the entrance, holding a laurel branch in one hand, a lyre in the other. Marcus bowed his head to both the entity and the assembled elders.

Makeshift wooden rows had been erected around three sides of the chamber to mirror the arrangement of the Curia inside Rome. Those who were more notable sat on stools on the lowest level; those lesser in status craned their necks as they stood on the elevated rear tiers.

Aemilius beckoned to his son to speak, then sat down.

Marcus cleared his throat. His voice caught at first, but as he unfurled and read the scroll, his nerves settled.

"I, Marcus Furius Camillus, Consular General, call the Senate of Rome to heed the advice of Artile Mastarna, high priest of the Temple of Uni, the great haruspex and fulgurator of Veii, in the matter of the prodigy of Lake Albanus. This is for the benefit of all Romans, and to ensure the destruction of our foe. It is a matter of urgency. As such, I seek to have my term of office extended until all expiation rites have been conducted."

A babble of angry voices erupted. Marcus glanced across to Aemilius, who shook his head, the gesture reminiscent of his paternal warning the night before.

Protocol was forgotten. Scipio called out, "How dare you bring an enemy into our midst."

Artile stepped forward. The senators fell silent. Drawing back his hood, the seer let his cloak slip from his shoulders and fall to the floor. He lifted a tall conical hat he'd been hiding beneath the folds and placed it on his head. He had exchanged ill-fitting armor for the garb of his profession. And with the change of clothes, his confidence had been restored. His long tunic and sheepskin-lined coat protected him more than any breastplate. His soft leather ankle boots seemed hardier than hobnails. And when he tied the straps of the hat, it was as though he was buckling his helmet. He straightened his back and thrust out his chin. Marcus noticed how his shoulder-length locks were now oiled. His face was shaven clean. His eyes rimmed with kohl, his lashes blackened. His hypnotic stare focused on the wisest men in the city.

Medullinus was first to break the silence. His chair grated against the tiled floor as he stood. "My brother insults us in sending this charlatan. It's timely his term is coming to an end."

Scipio added, "All of us here possess skills of augury. Why listen to a treacherous priest?"

Artile's mellifluous voice echoed in the high vaulted chamber: "I am no fraud." The effect of his perfect Latin was marked. Medullinus sat down again. The senators remained quiet. "I can read messages from the gods in the livers of sacrificial beasts. I can read the future in the spark and flare of red, white, or black lightning. I spent a decade at the Sacred College at Velzna learning my craft. Roman augurs ask questions to which the gods merely answer yes or no. Rasennan soothsayers listen to complex answers to interpret divine will. If you fail to heed Furius Camillus's request and ignore my counsel, then you do so at your peril."

Marcus winced, thinking Artile unwise to denigrate these sages. Yet he could not deny Artile communicated directly with deities in a way that made Roman attempts seem clumsy.

A senator called Titinius called from the second row, "The Sibylline Books are silent on the issue. On what authority do you claim you have greater knowledge?"

"Because Rome only possesses three of the nine Sibylline Books, which only contain obscure Greek verses from Apollo's oracle regarding certain proscribed rites. My people, on the other hand, possess the Etruscan Discipline, which includes all the branches of our religion in intricate detail: the Book of Thunderbolts reveals the meaning of lightning, and the Book of Acheron instructs how to ensure passage to our Afterlife." He paused, ensuring he had the attention of all. "And the Book of Fate gives insight on how to prophesy destiny, or even defer it."

Whispering and rustling filled the chamber. Postumius, a man known for his bluster, called, "This is a trick! Why would we trust an Etruscan? The reason Rome doesn't possess all nine Sibylline Books is because of one of his race. The tyrant, Tarquinius Superbus, tried to cheat the sibyl and ended up paying full price for only three. She destroyed the other six."

Artile was unfazed. He smoothed one eyebrow with one black-painted fingernail. "Don't judge my people by King Tarquinius's hubris. I'm not lying when I say I know the expiation rites required."

"And what guarantee do we have you'll not steer us to disaster?" asked Medullinus. "I prefer to hear what my brother Spurius says. His delegation seeks communion with Apollo at Delphi. They'll return soon."

The priest remained condescending. "The journey to Delphi is perilous. It could be months before you are given your answer."

"Our representatives sailed in summer," said Scipio. "We expect them to arrive back any time now."

"You're naïve if you think your emissaries will be granted an audience immediately. The crone, Pythia, can only be consulted on the seventh day of each month. The Delphians take precedence, and their leaders choose the representatives of the next city who are to be given the opportunity to speak. They favor their own countrymen before foreigners. Those remaining must draw lots to determine the order. And if the sun sets before a question is put, those unheard must wait until the next month and start the procedure again." His gaze traveled across the tiers of listeners. "The days are growing shorter. Apollo does not reside in Delphi during winter, and so Pythia retires for the season. If Rome has not queried her by December, your ambassadors must sojourn in her land." He pointed to the statue of Apollo. "I, on the other hand, have spoken directly to the god of prophecy, and he has confirmed the answer I ascertained from my sacred books."

More murmurs, more shuffling of feet of those standing. Medullinus leaned across to whisper in Aemilius's ear. The prefect nodded, his voice rising above the undertones. "So why did Lake Albanus rise in time of drought? What does it signify?"

The seer closed his eyes as though listening to a celestial voice. "Rome has neglected Mater Matuta, the ancient goddess of your allies. It has also offended Neptunus who caused the waters to inundate the fields and flow into the sea. Apollo advises that the Romans must drain the floodplains and divert the torrent so that the ash-pale soil of Latium will be fertile again. He states that Mater Matuta once again must be honored. Only then will Veii's gods desert its walls."

Artile opened his eyes. They were dark and gleaming. Marcus saw the others were enthralled, drawn to the aura of authority the haruspex exuded.

Medullinus was less spellbound. "The fact remains Furius Camillus is asking us to accept the word of a traitor." He pointed to the Veientane. "If you are the faithful servant to your gods, why do you now wish to reveal secrets that would lead to the destruction of your own people?"

The Etruscan bowed his head. When he raised it, he appeared humble. "I've grappled with my conscience. But who am I to keep secret the will of the divine? It may well be as great a sin to conceal what the deities wish to be known as to speak what should remain concealed. My duty is to the gods, not to men—not even to my own kin and kind."

Marcus winced at hearing how shifty the seer sounded. His hopes that Camillus's submission might be considered favorably faded. Artile may have been speaking the truth but his sophistry was suspect.

"I think we've heard enough," said Aemilius, standing and facing the assembly. "Let the debate begin. Shall we grant Camillus's request?"

There was no discussion. Every senator voted with his feet, moving to the left of the chamber for the negative. Marcus was glad Furius Camillus was not there to see such utter rejection.

The session had concluded. Marcus was ordered from the chamber. He nudged Artile to follow, warning him not to speak again. The priest scowled as he collected his cloak from the floor.

Tatius was waiting at the doorway. Marcus gestured him aside, away from the ears of the people's tribunes on the portico. "Take him to the general's country villa. And post a guard. I'll take no chances others might ignore the haruspex's diplomatic protection."

Artile's voice was choked with anger. "Wisdom is wasted on fools. They'll regret giving time to allow the Twelve to come to Mastarna's aid. The expiation rites should be conducted now."

"Shut up," barked Marcus, shoving him. "Your arrogance has cost Camillus an opportunity to secure a victory."

The three men threaded their way through the plebeians. Marcus felt a tap on his shoulder. Calvus's lips were pressed into a straight line. "Camillus should be ashamed—letting an Etruscan lecture Romans on piety. The Senate made the correct decision."

Marcus repeated his order to Tatius, denying Calvus access to Artile. Then he brushed past the plebeian, not prepared to engage. All he could think about was Camillus's reaction to the news. He'd failed the general. There was a twinge of cowardice in his relief that he wasn't expected to return to camp. Pinna would need all her skills to calm her lover's rage when the messenger told him Rome had given him a resounding no.

SIEGE

Eighteen

Caecilia, Veii, Winter, 397 BC

Winter had arrived. With the braziers stoked high, the bedchamber was warm once the heavy curtains had been drawn across the doorway. Returned from kissing her children good night, Caecilia drew back the drapes a fraction, hesitating before entering, drawn to watch Vel in his nightly routine.

In the flickering light of the lamps, he stood at a pedestal table of waist height. His movements were ordered and precise. He removed the gold torque from his neck and dropped it into a bronze cista, closing the canister's lid. Pouring warm water from a pitcher into a ewer, he added a few drops of perfume from a flask. Then he stripped off his heavy woolen chiton. The broad purple scar that sliced his chest in a diagonal was dark against the smoothness of his olive skin. He wrung a cloth and wiped himself down.

Even after long years of marriage, Caecilia never tired of admiring the broadness of his shoulders and chest. There were strands of gray in his dark, curly, cropped hair, but his body showed few signs of aging. It was honed, his buttocks and thighs sturdy and taut, the muscles of chest and abdomen defined. And she loved grazing her lips over the battered contours of his face, the scar from nose to lip, and the dark stubble that stippled his chin.

His brooding anger at her revelation about the dice throw had lessened as the winds from the north grew colder, rattling the pig-skin membranes of the windows and whistling through the drafty halls of the palace.

His forgiveness was a blessing. Until then he'd been distant despite holding her before they fell asleep and kissing her lips upon waking. Then the tension had eased. He'd become devout, joining her in appeasing Nortia. His piety should have been reas-suring, yet she fretted. Was it because the fragility of their life had been accentuated? After all, she'd defied a goddess.

He did not carry the golden dice any longer. She did not men-tion them, not wanting to blow upon the coals of an argument that had already cooled.

Caecilia pulled the curtains aside and entered the chamber. Vel glanced past her. "Where's Cytheris and your hot water?"

She placed her mantle onto a wall hook, untied her snood, and shook out her hair. "I had a bath instead." Stepping close, she trailed her finger in a line down his chest to his navel. "I thought you could help me undress."

A smile curled on his lips. "With pleasure." He tried to unfasten one fibula brooch on her shoulder with fumbling soldier's fingers.

"Do you need some help?"

"Yes." He concentrated on the easier task of untying the sash at her waist. The blue chiton slid to the floor, revealing a fine woolen slip beneath. He kissed the base of her throat. "Too many layers in winter."

She hunched her neck, his breath tickling her. "Finish the task." She laughed, urging him to unlace the shoulder strings so the shift also fell.

Naked, goose bumps rose on her flesh after the warmth of the clothes. She tried to press against him, but he stopped her, turning her around so her back leaned against him. She murmured, "What do you want?"

He covered her hands with his and placed them over her bosom. She felt her nipples harden beneath her touch. A tremor ran through her as he kept her palm steady against one breast and guided the other hand down, caressing the curve of her hips and her belly. "This is what I want," he said. "Soft skin, firm flesh."

She sighed, arching her head back against his shoulder, absorbed in the sensation of feeling her own body. He continued to move her hand down until her fingers reached her smooth-shaven mound. She was wet, ready as he was, his erection hard against the small of her back and her buttocks.

"This is what excites me," he whispered as together they stroked her. She relaxed against him, responding, the anticipation unbearable, until he lifted her in his arms and laid her on the mattress. He edged off her slippers, nuzzling her toes and insoles, then rested her ankles on his shoulders.

"This way first?" he said, leaning forward and easing into her. She stretched her arms over her head, her hair a nimbus around her, not needing to reply.

• • •

She loved the time afterward. Once the lamps had been extinguished and there was only the glow of the braziers, she would snuggle next to him under the weight of the plaid blankets. Lying on her side, she would rest her head on his chest. She felt secure, loving how he made her believe she was beautiful even after the birth of four children. And with the rush of the day behind them, they could find comfort in sharing concerns: politics and the people, court intrigues and family dramas, and, of course, the ever-present pressure of an enemy entrenched beyond the perimeter of the city.

Tonight, Mastarna was quiet and pensive. She raised herself on her elbow to look at him. "What is it, Vel? Is your arm aching?"

"It's nothing."

She was dubious. The flesh had healed, but she was not so sure the bone had knitted properly. "You can tell me if your arm is hurting. I will not think you less of a man for such an admission."

He smiled. "It's strong enough to bear your weight when I carry you to bed."

She studied the dark circles beneath his eyes. "I'm serious. Do you need some valerian to help you sleep? You barely rest for more than a few hours each night."

"Don't fuss. It's not the physical pain that keeps me from sleeping."

Caecilia searched his face. "Then what worries you?"

"Do you remember when I once told you that every warrior drags a host of dead men in his wake? In my case, it's not just my enemies. I dream of my men lying wounded and dead."

"You must stop blaming yourself for the defeat."

He sat up, leaning against the beech headboard. "Who else is to blame, Bellatrix? Camillus and Genucius used a strategy that I once used on Roman generals. Luring me to fight head-on against one army while another attacked from the rear."

She also sat up, slipping her arms around his waist. "You survived, Vel. You will have another chance to square the score."

He wrapped his arms around her and sighed. "I should never have been made king. We still sit here surrounded. If supplies of food don't reach us soon, I fear we might be starved into surrender." His hug tightened. "It's been months since we've been able to conduct funeral rites in the necropolis. The dead are trapped with us. What if I cannot deliver this city? What if there are more ghosts clamoring for vengeance against me for my failures?"

"What do you mean 'more ghosts'?"

"The men I led into a massacre. Their souls wander tormented on a battlefield that now lies covered in snow. The maimed would have been stabbed by spears and mutilated by sword, limbs and genitals hacked from them, and heads cut off and spiked on lances to be paraded in mockery. Why wouldn't my troops haunt me? A commander who survived while they were denied the honor of a funeral, their bodies left to rot instead of being cremated, their path to the world of the Beyond barred. Forever made phantoms."

Caecilia was stunned. He'd never given her a glimpse into his anguish. She was ashamed she'd not considered he would be assailed by such guilt, thinking him inured.

Until the Battle of Blood and Hail, she'd never witnessed carnage. On that day, she stood on the heights of the wall and watched Vel attacked. As hail rained down, she'd experienced the sight and smells and sounds of warfare. And most horrific of all, the stack of corpses heaped at the double gates, men denied refuge by a king who wanted Mastarna and his tribe massacred. The horror had been vivid and visceral. For weeks she'd constantly relived what she'd witnessed until she'd taught herself to stow the visions in the back of her mind. "I'm so sorry, Vel. I did not realize."

He lay down again, guiding her to join him, drawing the covers around them. "My fear is not only of death, Bellatrix. It is that I'll be defeated and disfigured. To be made a specter that never finds peace."

She stroked his stubbled cheek. It was rare for him to talk of his fears and doubts. "Why are you speaking of this now? It's not like you to be preoccupied with death."

He covered her hand. "You defied Nortia. I can't conquer Rome while confined in this city. What if she punishes us? What if you and our children die because of me?"

The sick feeling returned. The fear she'd caused her family to be doomed had beset her as autumn faded and there was no sign of the siege lifting. She made offerings to Nortia every day: sweet gifts of flowers and honey to woo her. But after a time, she decided not to surrender to melancholy that Fate would not forgive her. She gripped Vel's fingers. "Nortia will be placated. Uni will protect us. Thefarie will break through enemy lines. You'll march on Rome. I refuse to give up hope."

Vel kissed her fingers. "My warrioress."

She nestled beside him again. "Remember the Atlenta pendant that Thia now wears? You first gave it to me and told me the huntress and her husband were turned into lions by the goddess of love? We will be lions, Vel, together forever."

He pressed his lips to her hair. "That's only a story. And those lovers were transformed because they offended the deity. I'd rather hold you for eternity as you are. To believe we will meet again in Acheron is a consolation. And Fufluns will protect us there."

At his mention of the wine god, a sharp pulse started in her temple, echoing her heartbeat. She was afraid of the violent and wanton ways required to secure Fufluns's protection. And Artile had taught her a judgment day awaited her in the Rasennan Beyond, where demons and monsters hindered the journey, a peril that threatened a promised haven. She believed in a simpler ending, a merging of her soul with the Good Ones. She whispered, "Do you want me to desert my father's religion?"

"No, Bellatrix. I promised you I would never do that."

She placed his hand on her breast, her own upon his chest. "Because I will love you until my heart ceases beating."

His tone was wistful. "And my love for you will continue after I have taken my last breath."

His words hung heavy between them.

Vel turned on his side away from her, drawing her arm across him. "Let's go to sleep."

After a time she heard the shallow rise and fall of his breath as he slept. But peace was denied her. She lay on her back to stare at the ceiling, the laurel leaf pattern distorted in the wavering light of the braziers. The gloomy talk had reminded her of another ghost, and a danger in not believing in the Afterworld.

Slipping from under the bedclothes, she stepped down from the footstool, feeling the chill floor beneath her feet. She grabbed her mantle from the wall hook and wrapped it around her, padding across to the pedestal table. She lifted the handled lid from the ornate bronze cista and rummaged inside. Her fingers touched the golden dice. She pushed guilt aside and continued searching. At the bottom of the container, she found what she sought: a gold-and-onyx ring. Vel had not worn it for years. It was a gift from Seianta, his first wife.

Her thoughts turned to the Mastarna family tomb outside the sacred boundary. In it lay a sarcophagus with a sculpture of man and wife locked in an everlasting embrace. Mastarna and Seianta. Their terra-cotta image impervious to time. No such casket existed for Vel and herself. The war had prevented the commissioning of such a memorial.

Was Seianta waiting for her husband in Acheron even now? Was the Rasennan couple destined to be reunited?

When Caecilia had first married Vel, she'd shared him with Seianta while the dead girl haunted him. She'd felt her presence in their bed as surely as flesh and blood had lain between them. He claimed his love had ended long before Seianta died. Their affection challenged when their little girl, sickly and weak, had been granted only one year of life—their union broken after the death of their deformed son. The Tarchnan girl hated Vel for denying her what she believed was the chance for their children to become lesser gods through the Calu Death Cult. For each to become one of the Blessed.

Caecilia placed the ring into the cista, covering it with his other jewelry. Shivering, she climbed back into bed, molding herself against him. In reflex, he rolled over, encircling her in his arms without waking.

Caecilia willed sleep to come as the heat of his body transferred to hers. There was one more secret she vowed she would never tell him. Her reticence was fed by a selfish dread. She could not bear to think he might slip the gold-and-onyx ring on his finger, praying he could again embrace Seianta. For if Vel knew what Caecilia kept silent, he might again seek the love of the wife who'd been so cruelly wronged.

NINETEEN

Caecilia opened her eyes to muted light, her head fuzzy from lack of sleep. She reached for Vel, but the bed was empty. He always rose at dawn to train with Arruns.

Reluctant to attend to the beckoning duties of the day, she once again contemplated what had denied her slumber. Vel wanted to meet her in Acheron. But the pathways there frightened her.

As a naïve bride, she'd found the Rasennan religion seductive, promising life after death. And Artile had been adept at persuading her to worship Aita, god of the dead. The reward was tantalizing—to be one of the Blessed. Then he'd chained her to the rigors of the Calu Cult until she'd discovered the price of reanimating the dead—human sacrifice.

The image of the Phersu setting his hound on a blindfolded man at the funeral games horrified her. Those who followed Aita claimed the Masked One performed a holy rite. To Caecilia, he was merely an executioner. Vel didn't worship the death god, but he wanted her to gain entry to Acheron. His way to achieve this was no less disturbing. The orgiastic rites of the Pacha Cult, honoring

Fufluns, scared her. Tears welled. She rested the back of her hand against her eyes.

Cytheris bustled into the room with the laundry basket. "Goodness, what's the matter, my lady?"

Caecilia wiped her eyes and sat up. The maid hastened to her side, arranging the coverlet around her mistress's nakedness.

"Vel spoke to me about the Beyond last night. I don't want to be initiated into the Mysteries. I don't want to become a maenad. I can't worship Fufluns if I'm expected to be one of the raving women during the rites."

The handmaid climbed next to the princip, encircling her shoulders. How many times had Cytheris comforted her? She was like an older sister despite divisions of rank. Caecilia always found comfort in the warmth of the maid's cushioned embrace.

"I keep telling you, mistress, the Spring Festival is meant to be a celebration of Fufluns's journey from Acheron. After his sojourn there throughout winter, we thank him for breathing new life into bud and vine. There's a procession and games and revels. It's not meant to be frightening."

"How can you say that? You were there the night I stumbled into the rites. I was drugged by the Divine Milk. There was pandemonium, the noise of the bullroarers deafening, the double pipes shrill. The maenad used whips. They ate the raw flesh of fawns! Are you telling me you worship Fufluns after what happened?"

"Yes, I still follow the Pacha Cult. But you must remember the Athenians attended the festival that year. Their god has a darker side than our Fufluns. He is Dionysus the Wanderer. It was they who brought the Divine Milk, which is far more powerful than the strong unwatered wine that usually sets the senses reeling." She withdrew her arm from around her mistress. "It's cold in here. The braziers need to be stoked. And it's time I helped you dress."

She gathered up Caecilia's chitons from the night before and dropped them into the laundry basket. There was no comment as to why they were in a tangle on the floor, but the maid couldn't hide a half smile. Then she opened the cedarwood chest that contained a rainbow of robes and drew out one of deep yellow with a blue border. "Your favorite, my lady."

Caecilia's nerves still thrummed as she dressed. "I've heard that Dionysus drove the first maenads to insanity because they refused to give up the role of devoted wives and mothers. It's said they tore their own children apart in frenzy before becoming his devotees. I'm faithful to Uni, the mother goddess. She's the enemy of Fufluns. If I bowed to him, she would punish me."

Cytheris picked up a comb from the side table. "You worry too much. You always have. All are equal when seeking communion with the wine god. Such myths are spread because Greek men don't like women drinking and acting in abandon. They would deny their wives and daughters the chance to celebrate the power of regeneration."

Caecilia sat down so the handmaid could tend to her hair. "You mean the chance to sleep with another woman's husband."

Cytheris pursed her lips. "It is an ecstatic union. A way for your spirit to merge with the divine. Our bodies are just instruments to achieve this."

"I don't want to lie with another man. I don't want Vel to take another woman either. I couldn't bear it." Tears welled again. "And I don't want Seianta to reclaim him."

The maid stopped brushing and walked around to face her. "The master doesn't love his first wife. He stopped loving her well before he met you."

"Seianta suffered so much. All those dead babies." She touched Cytheris's hand. "I think she might punish me if she had the chance."

"For what, mistress? What could you possibly have done wrong?"

"Kept her secret from Vel."

"What secret?"

"One I swore I would take to the grave. Yet if I don't believe in the Beyond, Vel will return to Seianta. Because if he knew what Artile did to her—"

Intent on the conversation, the sound of the curtain being drawn aside startled the women. Vel stood in the doorway.

His cold expression was enough to convey to Cytheris that she should leave. The maid curtsied, collecting the basket and hurrying to the door. She cast a worried look toward her mistress as she scurried past the king.

Still wearing his bronze cuirass, Mastarna's hair was plastered to his head with sweat. "Another secret, Bellatrix? How many more surprises do you have in store for me?"

Caecilia ran to him, but when she tried to embrace him, he held her at bay. She dropped her arms to her sides.

"What did Artile do to Seianta?"

She hesitated. Vel gripped her upper arms. "Tell me!"

"Poisoned her so that your children would be weak and deformed."

He let go and took a faltering step backward. She tried to clasp his hands. He snatched them from her.

"How do you know this? Why didn't you tell me?"

"Artile told me on the night I escaped to Fidenae. The Zeri poppy juice he gave Seianta contained a drug which ensured she wouldn't conceive."

He stared at her. "Why?"

"He wanted Tarchon to be your only heir, thinking he could manipulate him. But instead of merely preventing Seianta falling with child, it made her miscarry or bear—"

"Cripples like my daughter." His voice cracked. "Or misshapen like my son. No eyes. His mouth cleaved in two. As small as my hand. Only two hours alive."

The rawness of his grief made Caecilia twist inside. The last time she'd seen him so vulnerable was when he'd first told her the story of his children. How Artile lured Seianta into believing she could defer the death of her daughter by the Fatales Rites. Then, when the child had died, the seer convinced her to follow the Calu Cult to ensure the little girl became one of the Blessed. And all the while feeding Seianta poppy juice and poison that would lead to the birth of a grotesque little boy.

"I'm so sorry, Vel."

He turned, gripping the edge of the footboard of the bed, his arms straight and head bowed. "Seianta blamed me for our daughter's death because I wouldn't let her continue the Fatales Rites. I saw her sinking into addiction to Artile's potion. I forced her to stop. But in the end I relented because I wanted an heir. She could not bear lying with me without the Zeri." He shook his head in disbelief. "And all the while, she was being poisoned."

Caecilia took a deep breath. She'd trodden in Seianta's footsteps when she'd first come to Veii. Artile had fed her fears, then uttered soft promises to quell them. He'd also slipped Zeri into the sacramental wine for the Calu Rites. Under its spell there was respite from apprehension as well as enslavement to a cycle of bliss, withdrawal, and wanting. She remembered Artile's spiteful triumph when he'd declared the elixir had ensured any seed planted within her would be cursed.

Vel straightened as though reading her thoughts. "You also drank my brother's potion when you were gulled by him. Was it contaminated? Is that why you didn't conceive for a year?"

"My fate was to be either barren or sorrowing."

With a guttural roar he shoved the pedestal washstand crashing to the floor. His cista bounced and rolled against the wall, the jewelry spilling from it. He walked to her table, sweeping aside the silver boxes with nail files and hairpins. Her glass flask of perfume shattered as it hit the floor, the floral scent exploding into the air. Pastes of carmine, albumen, and khol streaked the floor.

"Please, Vel. You're frightening me."

He halted, his fingers clenched. "I will find him and kill him."

Caecilia crossed to him, her palm covering his balled fist. "Can't you see why I never told you about this? I knew you wouldn't be able to control your rage. I didn't want to see you executed for murder."

He pulled away, cradling the elbow of his injured arm. "Any judge would say I was justified."

"Perhaps, but I didn't want to risk it. I'm glad your brother is no longer in Veii."

"You should have told me. First the dice throw, and now this. How can I trust you, Bellatrix?"

Blood drained from her face. "Please don't say that. There was another reason I didn't speak."

"What?" he growled. "What excuse is there this time?"

"Because . . . because I knew that if you discovered Artile had caused Seianta's pain, you would forgive her. Maybe even yearn for her again."

His expression softened as he cupped her face in his hands. "Have you so little faith in me? My love for Seianta lies in ashes; it can't be rekindled."

She pressed herself against him, the cold metal of his armor hard against her.

He wrapped his arms around her, his cheek resting on her hair. "Promise me there are no more secrets."

"None," she murmured. "Never again."

They held each other, smashed glass and cosmetics scattered around them, the scent of lilies heavy in the air. Caecilia's heartbeat slowed, relief flooding through her. Every bittersweet lie at last exposed.

TWENTY

Semni, Veii, Winter, 397 BC

Clasping Nerie's hand and cradling Thia in the crook of one arm, Semni smiled as she headed to the family chamber. Given the princes' high-pitched squeals, she suspected the king was visiting them. Her mouth dropped open as she passed through the doorway. Aricia sat on a chair, Larce and Arnth capering around her. Semni scanned the room to find the junior nursemaid, Perca. Timid as always, the thirteen-year-old was standing to the side, whistling softly with a worried look.

Tas was perched on a stool beside the visitor, enrapt. Goose bumps prickled Semni's skin as she remembered how Aricia had stoked the boy's fervor before. She didn't understand why he would be so eager to meet her again; the last time he'd seen his former nursemaid, he'd been scared by her urgent pleas to flee while a battle was raging. The patterns of affection forged from birth under her care must have been hard to erase.

"What are you doing here?" Semni let go of Nerie's hand and strode over to the boys, pushing Larce behind her to a howl of protest. Then she grasped Arnth's elbow and dragged him beside her.

"Perca, get over here!" She handed the baby to the maid. "Take the children to the nursery." She glared at Tas. "You, too."

The boy stuck out his chin. "No."

His insolence stung. She thought they had formed a special bond. Now with the appearance of Aricia, such affinity had taken second place.

The cepen rose, wobbling. "Don't worry, Semni. I don't plan to snatch him. I just wanted to see him." She looked across to the younger boys. "I miss all of them."

Larce tugged at Semni's chiton. "Why are you so angry? Please let us stay."

She patted his curls. "Do as I say, young master. I need to talk to Aricia alone."

The prince's shoulders slumped, but obedient, he followed Perca as she gripped the hand of the squirming Arnth.

Semni swung Nerie onto her hip. He clung to her, alarmed by the stridency in her voice. She glared at the seven-year-old prince. "Do as I say, Tas. Go with the others."

Again he made no attempt to move. Aricia crouched down and stroked the boy's cheek. "Listen to her, my pet. You can tell me more about your dream another time."

The endearment grated. She felt a knot in her stomach at how quickly the two had fallen into intimacy. "What dream?"

"The wolf and the bull that are fighting underground. Queen Uni is watching them."

Semni wasn't prepared to interrogate him further about his vision in front of the novice priestess. "Why aren't you with your tutor? Have you run away from him again?"

"No, he has a stomachache and is lying in bed. He told me to practice my writing by myself." He pointed to a wooden and wax tablet on the table.

"Go and find your brothers. Now!"

Tas hesitated, looking at Aricia. She smiled and nodded assurance. "Go, my pet. Do as Semni says."

The boy submitted with reluctant footsteps. At the doorway, he turned, avoiding the wet nurse to gaze directly at Aricia. He smiled, showing his new front teeth. "So I'll be the greatest fulgurator in Veii one day? I'll understand the gods' wishes in lightning and thunder."

"Yes, my pet. And a haruspex skilled in reading the livers of beasts."

"Even though Apa says I must be a warrior?"

Semni sensed she was losing control. "Go!"

Once the boy had disappeared, she rounded on Aricia. "How dare you fill his head with nonsense again! How dare you cross the threshold of the House of Mastarna after what you did!"

"I came with Lady Tanchvil. She's visiting the king and queen. I thought I could ask for their pardon, but they refused to see me."

"So you decided to defy them again and find Tas."

"It was you I wanted to find. I want your forgiveness. I want to seek my mother's, too. There are so many whom I've wronged."

Semni was disarmed by the girl's candor. An image surfaced of the uncertain nursemaid who'd shared shy confidences and sought Semni's love: an innocent with a crush on a rebel.

She glanced toward the doorway, aware that proximity to Aricia would unfairly condemn her if she were seen. Yet she was curious how this girl had survived after being evicted by Lady Caecilia, then deserted by the manipulative priest. "What happened with Lord Artile?"

"He betrayed me. He promised me he would make me his acolyte. He promised to teach me how to read so I might study the Holy Books. But he never planned to take me to Velzna to see the sacred spring. He used me to get to Tas. When I failed to bring the prince to him, he absconded, carrying the codex with him."

"How did he escape?"

"There's a shaft beneath the statue of Queen Uni in her temple. It leads to the bottom of the citadel cliff. And Artile knows the tunnels that snake through the ravines and hills that lead out of the city." Tears pricked her eyes, the memory raw. "I hope the Romans caught him."

Semni shivered, recalling the seer's spellbinding eyes and voice, how he could cajole and flatter, or instill dread. Aricia had been enticed by him as easily as Semni had once seduced men with fluttering eyelashes and coy smiles. She pressed Nerie's head to her shoulder, rocking him. He nestled close, sucking his thumb.

Aricia lifted the hem of her red-bordered chiton to reveal one leg. The flesh on the shin was marred by a long scar. "He was so angry when I failed to bring Tas to him." She brushed the tears from her eyes. "The blows of his rod broke my bone."

Sympathy welled at the sight of the injury. Semni was aware of others as well—the weals left by Cytheris's whipping. Aricia had truly been punished for her transgression, both in body and in mind.

The girl reached for Semni's hand, lifting it and laying her cheek against the palm. "I've been so foolish."

Semni knew she should pull away, but her friend's anguish stopped her. "Yet your dream has come true. How did you come to be Lady Tanchvil's acolyte?"

Aricia's smile was radiant. For a moment Semni wondered if the pain of betrayal had been replaced by a fresh infatuation.

"The cepens at the temple found me after Artile had beaten me. They tended to my wounds and let me stay in their workroom. Then Lady Tanchvil was appointed as the high priestess." She picked up Tas's writing tablet. "She took pity on me. She's training me to join the College of Priestesses who serve Queen Uni." Digging the stylus into the wax surface, she added some lettering. "I can read and write now." She held out the tablet to her. "See, I've written your name."

A pang of jealousy hit Semni. A new world was opening to Aricia while her own was shrinking.

Aricia reached over and stroked Nerie's fair hair. "I hear Arruns has claimed Nerie as his son. You must be pleased."

Her words brought the wet nurse to her senses. The conversation must end. Once again, Aricia was compromising her. "You need to leave. Do you want me to be punished again because of you?"

"What do you mean?"

"I confessed to the king and queen that I remained silent about your secret visits with Tas and Lord Artile. And now Arruns refuses to marry me because Lord Mastarna has forbidden us to lie together until Thia is weaned. I'm denied happiness because I placed loyalty to you above this House. I won't risk breaching that duty again. I will be telling Lady Caecilia you visited here to see the princes. And you must promise me you won't try to do so again."

Aricia was aghast. "I'm so sorry. I want so much for you to pardon me. Can you find compassion in your heart?"

"What are *you* doing here?"

Both girls swiveled around. Cytheris stood in the doorway. The older woman glared at Semni. "Did you let her see Tas again? Touch the children?"

The wooden tablet thudded to the floor as Aricia limped to Cytheris, kneeling with difficulty before her. "Mother, I've come to beg forgiveness." She reached up to take her hand, but Cytheris placed her arms behind her back. Her pockmarked face was rigid with disapproval, her eyes stony. The Gorgon had returned. She ignored her daughter, addressing Semni again. "Did she see Tas?"

The nurse raised her hands in protest. "I sent the princes away as soon as I saw her."

Cytheris seized a handful of Aricia's black ringlets and tugged them. "Get up and get out. You are not welcome here—ever."

The girl lurched to her feet. "Please. I have changed. I want to make amends."

Cytheris released her hair. "You're the one who wanted no more of me. Who spat out words of hatred. Who betrayed a mistress who'd only ever shown you kindness."

"You disowned me, too. Beat me. But now I'm contrite."

Cytheris tutted. "I don't believe you. I can never trust you again." She turned to Semni. "I thought you'd learned your lesson. Wait until the mistress hears you've let her sneak in here."

Semni was indignant. "I didn't let her in! And I told her to leave as soon as I saw her. Ask Perca."

Aricia collected her red shawl from the chair and wrapped it around her before covering her head. There was sadness in her slumped shoulders as she headed toward the hallway. "Don't blame Semni, mother. She asked me to go as soon as she saw me. Do not fear. You will not see me here again."

When her daughter had gone, Cytheris walked to a chair, gripping its back, her eyes closed as though in pain.

Semni walked to her. She didn't believe Cytheris hated Aricia. She'd seen her distress after Lady Caecilia cast the girl into the street. Yet the show of emotion had been fleeting. Cytheris was expert at hiding her feelings, a hard veneer protecting them from view. Today, though, Semni wondered if there would come a time when the lacquer would erode and Cytheris's regret and hurt would be on display.

Nerie reached out and touched the handmaid's frizzy hair. She opened her eyes, catching hold of the boy's fingers and kissing them. Had she ever done the same to her own daughter?

"Why can't you forgive her?"

"And you can? After Aricia caused you and Arruns heartache?"

Semni hesitated, thinking carefully. Hating Aricia was not as simple as Cytheris thought. "Yes. I think I can. I know what it's like to be remorseful and yet unforgiven because of my own foolishness. And now I'm grateful I've been given another chance. I don't begrudge your daughter the same. Not when she was the first person to overlook my faults."

Cytheris grew less adamant. "How can I forgive her unless Lady Caecilia finds it in her heart to grant mercy? Aricia must first convince the mistress that she is worthy."

Semni doubted the queen would ever forgive Aricia. "I'll go and tell her what happened."

"Wait."

Cytheris crouched and picked up Tas's tablet, her long ankle-length plait snaking along the floor. "Why was she holding this?"

"She was showing me she could write. Lady Tanchvil is teaching her."

Cytheris raised her eyebrows. "Then she is still full of dreams and nonsense. The College of Priestesses of Uni is not going to accept a half-blood freedwoman into its ranks." She rose, placing the tablet on the chair.

Semni shrugged her shoulders. "She might surprise us." She walked to the doorway with Nerie, expecting the Greek woman to follow. Instead Cytheris lingered, tracing the letters in the wax, smiling. Her pride was plain to see.

TWENTY-ONE

Semni walked along the barracks' corridor until she found Arruns's cell. Crouching in the doorway, she held Nerie around the waist. In the flickering line of wall torches, his blond hair seemed like gold.

Inside the room, Arruns was naked to the waist, wearing an ankle-length kilt. The faint, acrid smell of pitch filled the air. Even with his swarthiness, she could see his untattoed skin was tinged pink. A barber must have stripped the hair from his body only a short time ago. It was as though he wore a cuirass of flesh, the muscles of his pectorals and abdomen defined. As always, the writhing serpent intrigued her as it wrapped around his torso and neck, the jaw open and eating half of his smooth-shaven skull, the forked tongue licking his cheek. Her longing for him was so deep that it hurt.

He frowned when he noticed her. "You shouldn't be here."

"I brought your son to see you." She crouched and gave Nerie a nudge as she released him. The boy tottered, arms outstretched.

Arruns smiled and lifted the tot over his head and onto his shoulders. "Perhaps you can stay a little while." Nerie giggled, unconcerned by the gruesome scales marking the man's skin.

Semni drew the door curtain shut and sat down on the pallet. Arruns lowered himself to sit beside her, taking care to ensure Nerie did not wobble and fall. Usually so inscrutable, Arruns could never hide his delight when in the company of his son. For a moment she felt jealous that his eyes did not light up at the sight of her in the same way.

"I also came to tell you that Aricia visited here today."

His smile vanished. He lifted Nerie onto his lap.

"Who let her in?"

"She came with Lady Tanchvil. When the mistress wouldn't see her, she crept into the princes' chamber."

"Without being stopped! I'll see that the lictor who was on shift is punished."

"Don't blame him. That witless Perca let her in."

"What did Aricia want?"

"Forgiveness."

He grunted. "Then she will be disappointed."

"She's repentant. She realizes her mistake."

He glared at her. "And you would err in giving her consolation. Promise me you won't try to see her again."

She nodded, anxious not to displease him. "I promise. And I made it clear she was not welcome to return."

"And the mistress? You told her?"

"Yes, I told her straightaway. Are you not proud of me?"

He encircled her shoulders. "Yes, I'm proud."

She shivered, his contact arousing her, surprised the force of her desire could be so strong with a simple gesture.

Mistaking the cause of her trembling, Arruns looked across to the small brazier burning in the corner. "Are you cold?"

"No, it's you who makes me quake."

He slid his arm from around her, making her regret that she'd spoken.

"Perhaps you should go."

Semni slipped off her shoes. "It's late. Your men are occupied in their quarters. The princes and Thia are abed. Can't we lie beside each other for a while?" She drew aside the blanket and lay on her side on the pallet. Nerie crawled across and snuggled next to her. "Our son will be the guardian of our chastity."

Arruns stared at her, temptation grappling with duty. She extended her hand to him. Nerie giggled and copied her, thinking it a game.

He glanced at the door, then back again. "For a short time."

The cot creaked as he eased his bulk onto the narrow breadth, lying on his side so he would not squash the toddler. He propped his weight on his elbow, his palm against the side of his face. The boy lay on his back, turning his head from one side to the other, regarding his parents and this strange new arrangement. Semni reached into her purse, retrieving a tiny wooden carving of a rabbit. Nerie smiled and fingered his favorite plaything.

She wanted to walk her fingers down the muscles of Arruns's abdomen, pull aside his kilt, and check whether the markings on his body reached to his groin. She resisted, knowing that to touch him would end this time together. "One day I'll see if the snake is two headed. We were so rushed that night, we didn't even take off our clothes."

"Don't worry, it will be worth the wait." Arruns smiled with a flash of chipped teeth, surprising her. It was not like him to joke.

"We'll need a bigger bed when we're married," she continued, unable to rid herself of the image of them lying naked.

"That will take some getting used to. Until I was promoted to head lictor, I slept on a bedroll outside the master's room."

"Then this bed is luxury. As is my own."

He sighed. "I'd prefer a hard floor if it meant I could be a lone bodyguard again."

"Aren't you proud to be in charge?"

He pointed to the bundle of rods tied with red bindings that stood propped against the wall. A double axe was strapped to them. "Carrying the ceremonial fasces and wearing a uniform? I'm a simple man, Semni. I liked it best when the master did not need twenty-four men to watch over him. He does not like all the fuss either."

She stroked Nerie's cheek as the boy sang to his toy. "And being a warrior? Do you miss that, too?"

Arruns remained silent, listening to Nerie's garbled tune. She did not press him for an answer, already knowing this man hated war yet longed for battle.

She studied his hooked nose and hooded lids. So close to him, she could see the ink in his pores. "It must have hurt to be tattooed."

His response distracted him from the child. As always, she was struck by the resinous color of his eyes, the dark rings around the irises. "It was agony."

"Who did it to you?"

"A Veientane trainer. He liked to gamble. He'd win wagers on me when he pitted me against other wrestlers. Decorating me with a serpent instilled fear into my opponents." He ran his hand over the coils. "He had the artist work on the pattern over many weeks because the task was so great. Six slaves held me down as the pigment was tapped into my skin by a bone nail. Over and over. Pinpricks of blood welling, then smeared away. They would wash it with saltwater to stop it from being infected. I would recover, and then the hammer and needle would be wielded again. First on my back and then my front, slowly moving upward."

Semni was surprised at his flood of words. The brooding man who usually spoke little, and observed others silently, was at last speaking.

Arruns touched his neck and ran his hand over his skull and cheek. "The face was the worst. It became so swollen that I couldn't eat. They fed me liquid through a reed. I kept hoping the ink would wash away. That I would not be marked as some monster. That my mother would not shy from me should I ever see her again. Over time, though, I've come to believe the serpent protects me. I've lived with him so long. We've become old friends."

Semni traced the line of each scale. She'd always thought Arruns had been the one to seek the tattoo. To hear he had been forced was horrifying.

At her touch, he tensed. He covered her hand with his, his palm engulfing hers. "Don't. It's hard enough to have you lying so close to me."

She removed her hand. "How did the Veientane come to own you?"

"You don't need to know my past."

"You're Nerie's father. And I'm to be your wife. I want to know all about you, Barekbaal."

Arruns scanned her face. "I'm no longer that man, Semni. There's pain in the memories. Sometimes it's better to forget than try to remember loved ones whom I'll never see again."

"Or perhaps it will give you peace to speak of those you've lost to one who loves you now."

"You will not like all that I tell you."

"I've promised to no longer keep secrets from you, Arruns. You must do the same."

She rested her hand on his chest again. This time he did not stop her. She could smell his maleness. How his stripped skin was smooth beneath her fingers. "Tell me about your family."

"My father was a trader in purple in Sidon. I grew up with the stink of crushed murex shells. He planned for me to follow him in the business just like my three brothers. He was prosperous, owning a fleet of biremes that plied the crescent coast of Canaan, the land the Greeks call Phoenicia, up to the rich city of Byblos and down to Tyre.

Again she was surprised. She'd always thought Arruns to be from as humble origins as herself. "Biremes?"

"Shallow draft ships with two banks of oars. I made my first voyage when I was sixteen. Soon I was undertaking longer journeys, venturing farther as my father's business thrived. Rosetta and Alexandria, Cyrene and Carthage, where nobles and kings sought the purple, its rich color denoting power. But I was always restless. Dissatisfied with being a trader's son."

He paused. Nerie had fallen asleep, thumb in his mouth, a tiny slumbering barrier between them.

"At times our ship would encounter galleys with three banks of rowers," he continued. "These triremes boasted bronze battering rams on their prows. They were the warships of the royal navies of the city-states in which we docked. I admired the armor of the warriors who manned them. I wanted to share their glory. The last memory of my father was his anger when I refused to sail with him. Instead I joined the king of Sidon's navy."

"How exciting."

"No, it was the action of a rash youth who deserted his family and obligations. I believe the goddess Astarte punished me. I haven't seen my family for fifteen years."

The pain in his voice was difficult to hear. "I'm sorry, Arruns."

"I fought sea battles for two years. I learned what it was to kill instead of barter. To be cruel when called upon to do so. And then one day we were attacked by a Syracusan war ship and defeated. I was taken prisoner. And my world changed forever."

He placed his hand over hers, checking her from caressing their son. "You will not like the rest of my story."

She whispered, "Trust me."

He held her gaze. "The Syracusans sold me to a Rasennan slaver from Tarchna. The son of a trader became goods to be bought and sold. I struggled against my bonds, so they doubled them and placed a yoke on me. The restraints didn't constrain me. My strength attracted the attention of a trainer from Veii. He bought me to pit against others in fights."

"And he was the one who tattooed you?"

"Yes. And that is why I strangled him when I got the chance."

Semni gasped. "You murdered your master?"

"You wanted to hear my story. I've told you before that I was condemned as a criminal. My job was to kill." The heat in his voice worried her. She was used to a chilling silence when he was angered.

"I killed men in sea battles, and I killed or crippled those whom I wrestled. And I killed that bastard trainer after he'd tortured me and then tried to beat me once too often."

His revelation disturbed her. Yet why? She'd always known his job required him to be brutal. It did not scare her he'd been the Phersu. "And that is when you became the Masked One?"

"Yes, I was condemned to be sacrificed at the funeral games. Only Lord Mastarna heard I'd been a proud warrior brought to misery. He gave me the choice to be the Phersu and wear the mask of a holy executioner or be a victim blinded by a sack over his head. To either be the instrument of the gods or die like an animal. Your people demand a hooded man's throat be ripped apart by a hound in an arena so that his blood will reanimate the dead. At least in Canaan, a man is treated with reverence when he's gifted to the gods. His body is purified and his fear quelled by potions before the priests offer his life to divine Ba'al."

"Your gods seek human flesh, too?"

"When Ba'al demands it. He's the lord of the rain, bringer of crops, bringer of life."

Nerie woke, disturbed by his father's voice. Arruns patted the boy's back in awkward strokes. As always, she was struck with his tenderness when it came to his son. The hands that could strangle a man to death could be gentle. He handed Nerie the toy rabbit again and looked across to Semni. "Lord Mastarna used to let me fight in the light infantry but now he only sees me as a lictor."

"I know. It's your duty to him that keeps us apart."

"But I'm still required to be a murderer. Why would you want me?"

Reaching over to touch his cheek, her fingers traced the tattoo to comfort a long-ago hurt. "Because I love you, Barekbaal. You are a warrior to me."

TWENTY-TWO

Pinna, Rome, Winter, 397 BC

The scent of the violets was sweet, the roses fragrant. Pinna pressed the winter blooms to her nose, then her lips. She crouched beside her mother's gravestone, laying the flowers upon it. "Forgive me for neglecting you while I was in camp, Mama. Don't be angry. See, I've brought food for you." She sprinkled some salt and grain, then fed wine and oil through a pipe to the urn below.

Rising, she scanned the cemetery of the Campus, the Tiber curving around it. The river was running fast, no stinking mud today building up around the island of the two bridges. The cattle grazed, finding patches of grass where the snow had melted. They chewed their cud, then dipped their heads to tear up more blades.

The early morning was icy, the winter sun weak. The thick wool of her two tunics kept her warm. Her Wolf ensured that she was well dressed. Pinna rearranged her shawl over her head. The chance to cover herself modestly had been forbidden to her as a lupa, but now an aura of respectability clothed her. As Camillus's concubine she went unnoticed. Just another woman citizen in appearance. There was no requirement to wear a toga to mark her profession. No hissing or looks of contempt as she walked the streets.

She glanced across to the nearby Claudian tomb adorned with its boar's head crest. The chance meeting of Drusus there had changed her life. The bronze weights she'd extorted from him paid for Mama's body to be cremated instead of decaying on the Esquiline Hill. The urn that was now placed underground had been the last luxury Pinna could afford, though. She'd returned home from the funeral to discover she'd been robbed by a pimp. Her life as a whore in his brothel began.

She doubted she would ever forget those times. Fractured images of her mother as a lupa surfaced—body abused, mind lost, not knowing her own daughter at the end. Pinna closed her eyes, willing herself to conjure different glimpses of her—her tar-black hair twisted into a knot, her rough farmwife's hands, her weathered face, and the softness of her smile. She longed to see her, to feel her embrace. It was hard to think of her milling below the ground with a thousand other Shades indistinguishable from each other. Pinna looked down at the grave. "May your ashes turn to fragrant flowers, Mama. May you forever be at peace among the Good Ones."

Pinna delved into her basket again. She planned to remember Gnaeus Lollius today, too. Her fingers closed around a handful of black beans, food to appease a malevolent spirit—food for her father.

Winter always reminded her of him. Before Rome required men to fight all year, the change in season meant the return of Lollius to dwindling resources and hardship. His cold mood would mirror the weather. Yet, although he was a man of little affection, Pinna knew he loved her.

She and Mama never saw him again after he'd been forced into bondage. Pinna was anguished, wondering how he'd died. Had he been beaten to death when bound in chains? Had he suffered

illness? Where had he been buried? In a trench among other paupers? Or had his body been burned and his ashes scattered to the
wind? Had anyone kissed his lips to catch his last breath and so
release his soul? She feared he was a wandering, vengeful spirit
that she must always dread. For a ghost had one purpose—to punish those who'd wronged them or failed to grant succor after death.
And so, as she laid the beans next to the flowers, she hoped her
piety and prayers were enough to assuage him.

Conscious she still had much to do, she headed to the Aventine,
hastening along the road to the fruit market, the night's snowfall
sullied by the ruts of cartwheels and animal droppings.

Someone grasped the edge of her basket. She halted and
turned. Cauis Genucius stood there. It was the first time she'd been
alone with him for two years. She'd been spared his presence in
camp after he'd agreed to lead his army north to Falerii. And when
he visited Camillus in Rome, she made sure to keep clear of him.

"What's your hurry, Lollia?"

She'd forgotten how hairy and florid and heavy he was. His
beard was bushy, covering the skin of his neck as well. She tried to
dispel an image of him naked, covered with a thick black pelt. She
glanced around to see if anyone was listening. "I'm called Pinna
now."

He directed her to the side of the road. "It worries me you've
duped Furius Camillus into making you his de facto wife. It shows
that even a clever man can be made a fool."

She tried to pull the hamper away, but he held it fast. "I have
not fooled him, my lord." Yet again she tried to break free but he
gripped the basket with both hands.

"When I chanced upon you naked in Camillus's tent before the
Battle of Blood and Hail, I was prepared to ignore a passing dalli-
ance. But I respect him too much to let a whore run his household."

She bridled. "I'm a citizen. Daughter of a soldier. There's no
disgrace in a nobleman having a concubine who once was poor."

"You forfeited your citizenship the day you opened your legs for money. I'm going to find your name on the prostitutes' roll and show it to him."

Her pulse quickened. "Please, don't tell him. Poverty led me to that life. There was no other choice."

"Destitution is never an excuse for a freeborn woman to taint herself."

His lack of sympathy sparked anger. "If you expose me, I'll tell Lord Camillus the type of services you paid me for."

He fixed his one eye on her, the socket of the other hidden by his eye patch. "I know he has little time for whoring, but he's not going to worry about another soldier sleeping with a harlot. Besides, I'm sure he enjoys the fact you're experienced. Why else would he keep you?"

She flinched. "It's not the fact you had to pay that will disgust him. He's nothing like you, *my lord*. I don't knead his prick with my feet to excite him. And he would never use his tongue like you did—slobbering over me down there." She lowered her gaze to her crotch, then raised her eyes to meet his. "He might overlook a man fucking a lupa, but a pervert? What kind of man . . . what kind of *soldier* does that to a woman?"

His cheeks flushed red above his beard. He let go of the basket, but thrust his disfigured face close to hers. "Ah, now that's more like it. The slut from the gutter." He pulled her shawl from her head. "No use pretending you're decent, Pinna, with your hair covered and shoes on your feet. You should be bareheaded and barefoot in that lupanaria again."

She gasped, astounded he would treat her so in public. She glanced around, worried who might see them but passersby seemed uninterested.

"Tell me, what about Appius Claudius Drusus and Marcus Aemilius Mamercus? What fetishes do they have that they keep hidden?"

She pressed her lips together.

Genucius dug his fingers into her forearm. "Tell me!"

She winced. His ability to expose the others alarmed her. She'd promised both officers she would remain silent. And now Marcus had been chosen as a military tribune at the recent elections. She did not want his reputation harmed. Genucius, too, had been successful. He was now one of the ten people's tribunes. Mud would stick to him also. "All three of you have been tacit about me," she said. "If you speak out, you'll not only humiliate yourself but also discredit them. Do you want that on your conscience, my lord?"

He thrust her away. "You will never escape your past, Lollia. I wasn't your only customer. There might be others who'll recognize you, even though you no longer paint your face and your nipples."

She tensed. It was true; she'd been fortunate not to have been detected since returning to Rome. Yet she now resided among the rich. Her customers had mainly been the lowlifes of the city. "We all must hope that doesn't happen, musn't we?"

Pinna lifted her shawl to cover her head again. Genucius did not move. "You think me weak. But some believe it's best to satisfy bodily cravings with a whore. One thing I'll never do is fall in love with a lupa." He glanced around him, his voice taking on a different tone. "Furius Camillus is my friend. If you love him, Lollia, spare him. He's destined for greatness—he can't risk a scandal."

She froze. His pleading distressed her more than his bullying.

He strode away, not waiting for her to reply.

Pinna stared after him. His concern for Camillus shamed her. Genucius had once been one of her favorites, a good-natured talker who liked to complain about his wife after his lust had been satisfied. Now she had made him hate her. As she had Marcus. And once done to Drusus. She was like poison in a well.

She pressed her hand to her breast, her heartbeat so strong she could feel it through her bones. Would her Wolf hate her one day as well? Was it better to hurt his feelings and leave him now than expose him to public humiliation later?

Yet where would she go if not to his home? Retrace her steps to the brothel? Return to degradation? The thought of losing him terrified her. She could not live without him. She drew the shawl across to shield her face and continued to the Aventine Hill.

• • •

Her Wolf's atrium was spacious and warm. No wind whistled through cracks in its timbers. At night, the roof hole's cover was bound tight against the cold. The cistern was filled with clean water. She'd never lived in such comfort. Her father's hut was humble with its earthen floors, thatch roof, and mud walls.

Camillus had bestowed all the duties of a wife upon her. She stoked the hearth fire until it burned brightly and placed the boyish statuette of the Lar on the table at meal times. Yet Pinna worried she was committing sacrilege every time she touched the effigy of the spirit who guarded her Wolf's home. She did not wish to bring misfortune on her lover. And so she baked more salt cakes than necessary to throw into the fire to thank the Lar and the goddess of the hearth. She also did not forget honey cakes and wine for the other many household spirits. As a further precaution she hid amulets in crevices. She even hung bells in the garden to ward off evil influences.

Camillus grew impatient with her. "You know how I feel about your superstitions. The spirits are not displeased at me taking you as my concubine."

At least she was spared living with his sons. They remained in his country villa. She'd met them briefly on the journey back to Rome. Two youths on the verge of war. It was clear they doted on their father, basking in the radiance of his smile while darting looks at her behind his back. Their hostility toward the usurper of their mother's memory was palpable.

The majordomo and housemaid would eye her when she asked them to attend to tasks. Even the porter was snobbish. Yet she told herself she'd never been a slave. Her rough peasant vowels may have jarred after their mistress's refined accent, but if their widower master did not look down on her, why should they?

Most disturbing, she sensed his wife all around her. The matron's touch was present in the furnishings of the house and the routine to which her servants adhered. She could not stop herself imagining her Wolf lying with the patrician woman. And she was jealous of the pride in his voice whenever he mentioned the mother of his sons.

Still shaken by her meeting with Genucius, Pinna tried to calm herself by burnishing Camillus's armor, polishing the bronze and leather with oil and beeswax. His prowess as a warrior was always on display. His panoply dominated one side of the atrium, together with the array of silver spears, wreaths, and enemy trophies.

Today she was nervous about making a good impression. It was the first dinner party that Camillus had held since returning to the city. There had been plenty of consultations in his study at the beginning of winter. Nobles and commoners canvassed for his vote before the elections. Pinna suspected that, beneath their pure white togas, some candidates hid dirty tactics. In the end, the aristocracy succeeded. Six patricians had been elected as consular generals, among them Medullinus and Aemilius. Her Wolf's headaches lasted for days at hearing the result.

Taught to cook simple fare by her mother, Pinna was daunted by the prospect of organizing a banquet. She'd chosen the best cuts of meat herself and scoured the market to find fresh winter fruit. She'd also directed the porter to scrub soot from the walls, and the maid to clean the hearthstone.

A blast of chill air swept through the hall, making the flames flare. Pinna heard the porter greet his master. She hastened to meet Camillus, who smiled when he saw her. Yet as he stepped into the atrium, he stumbled.

Pinna gasped, reaching to steady him. He straightened, looking down to check what he had tripped over. Pinna could not see anything that might have caused his misstep.

"My Wolf," she urged, "it's an ill omen to stagger on the threshold."

A look of irritation crossed his face. "Nonsense."

She touched her Venus shell, uneasy that he should dismiss her. "You must go outside again and reenter. You must utter a prayer to the god of safe passage. There are evil spirits that dwell in doorways."

Seeing her agitation, he softened his stance. "Very well, I will indulge you this time."

"And you must step into the room with your right foot."

He turned and retraced his steps. Pinna only relaxed once he'd safely entered the atrium. She brushed the snow from his shoulders before helping him remove his toga. "Thank you, my Wolf," she said as she knelt and swapped his boots for indoor sandals.

Rubbing his hands, Camillus scanned the room. "You make me proud, Pinna, but you don't need to scrub away the paint. My guests will not notice a little dust."

She smiled but thought him wrong. His guests would judge her for everything tonight. To them, she was masquerading as the mistress of his house: a housekeeper, not a matron, a bed warmer, but not the mother of heirs. She was nervous about meeting his brother Medullinus. And Genucius would be there, disapproving and resentful. As for Scipio, she would grit her teeth to cope with his surreptitious ogling.

Her Wolf stood next to the fire and warmed his hands. "Where's Artile? In his room as usual?"

She nodded. She hated the sly, creeping creature. Ever since he'd been dismissed by the Curia, he had sulked in the house. She thought the Senate would order him to be expelled. Instead Camillus persuaded them to allow the priest to reside with him. He saw the haruspex as valuable even if his peers did not. "Is Lord Artile to attend the dinner party?"

"No. I doubt any of my guests would welcome him sharing their couch. However, I wish him to address them. I doubt they'll like what he has to say either."

She ventured. "What is it?"

He smiled and headed for Artile's room. "Curious as always, Pinna. But it's not for your ears. Tell me when the others arrive."

TWENTY-THREE

Pinna wiped her palms down the sides of her best tunic as the majordomo ushered Scipio into the atrium. The senator was careful to hide his interest in front of his host. She helped him remove his toga, trying to keep at arms' length to avoid inhaling his bad breath. The patrician's liking for fermented fish garum sauce was obvious.

When Lucius Furius Medullinus arrived, she was not spared. He scrutinized her, starting with her feet, then moved upward to linger on her breasts before studying her face. "So this is the concubine I've heard about, Brother. I'm surprised. There must be a decent Roman matron you could make your wife. After all, you're the one who introduced the bachelor tax to encourage men to marry our war widows."

The ugly way he spoke was galling. Her Wolf was curt. "I haven't brought you here to talk about my domestic life. Let's go into the dining room. Pinna, bring Caius Genucius through when he arrives."

The door knocker clanged not long after. Pinna noticed the fineness of Genucius's clothes as he entered. They were of better quality than the senators', despite the absence of purple stripes. The half-blind plebeian was not restricted to being a landowner as members of the Curia were. He could line his pockets with bronze earned in trade.

He removed his brown boots and placed them beside the senatorial red ones. The difference in footwear no doubt rankled. He then pushed his swollen feet into his thong sandals. Thick veins snaked under the skin of his legs, and the inside of his ankles were blue from tiny burst blood vessels. Pinna knew how his feet ached and was glad she did not have to rub them anymore.

"Good evening, my lord. I'll show you through to the others."

"Still here, Lollia? Still thinking of yourself?" He leaned closer. "Let's hope he doesn't ask you to marry him. I'll have to speak up then. No matter the consequences."

She was determined not to feel ashamed at her selfishness. She said pointedly, "My name is Pinna, my lord."

He sniffed and headed to the dining room.

Pinna hastened to the griddle to check the pork and directed the maid to carry the tray of eggs through to the guests. It was the first of the courses she planned to serve that night.

By the time she entered the dining chamber, the majordomo had lined up the men's sandals along one wall. The four diners now reclined on three couches set at right angles to each other. Medullinus lay in the place of honor, Scipio in the middle, while Genucius and Camillus shared the third divan. The serving table sat in front of them, plates stacked ready for use.

Every time Pinna delivered a new dish and removed the scraps, she was aware of Scipio's furtive glances and Medullinus's judgmental stare. Only Genucius ignored her.

Despite the liberal helpings of honeyed wine, the mood was far from jovial. The apples and dates served for dessert didn't sweeten the atmosphere either.

By the time of the drinking session, the air was stuffy from the heat and hazy from the smoke of the braziers and torchlights. Pinna served olives stuffed with goat's cheese. Given the guests' moroseness, she wondered if it was wise to encourage their thirst with the salty food.

She chose to stay and pour the wine herself rather than ask the majordomo. She was keen to listen to the conversation, hoping the men would forget her if she stood in the corner. She was pleased Camillus didn't dismiss her until it struck her that he might consider her just a servant after all.

The alcohol increased the tension between the brothers. Her Wolf rarely mentioned Medullinus when he was in camp. It was almost as though he wished to deny his sibling's existence. There was envy, too. The elder Furian had twice been a consul, while Camillus had yet to gain such power. Nevertheless, the newly elected consular general could not match her Wolf's fame as a warrior.

"There are still five war fronts." Camillus counted them on his fingers. "Veii, Capena, and Falerii in the north. The Volscians and Aequians in the south and east. And we need to maintain home defense. The Wolf and Boar Legions are stretched thin."

Medullinus belched before responding. "And your point, Brother? We have faced such resistance before. That's why Rome elects six consular generals to lead its armies instead of two consuls."

Genucius spluttered, "You know that's only half true, Medullinus. Splitting the legions into six regiments wasn't the only reason why consular generals were introduced. As soon as the law enabled commoners to progress on the Honored Way, another bill was passed to elect consular generals instead of consuls. It's no wonder Calvus and the other people's tribunes are resentful."

Scipio and Medullinus glared at Camillus in silent admonishment that he'd invited the commoner to dine with them. The host ignored them, signaling to Pinna to pour them all another drink.

Medullinus was not prepared to be distracted. "So you admit Calvus is willing to encourage mutiny, Genucius?"

With the conversation growing heated, Camillus kept his voice even. "Let's all calm down. The fact of the matter is that all our fine patrician generals have their work cut out for them. Aemilius and Titinius face bolstered forces at Falerii and Capena. And Postumius has neither the brains nor mettle to make headway at Veii. In the south, the Volscians have attacked the garrison at Anxur again, while the Aequians harry our colony at Labicum in the east. Our two legions are splintered and are making no gains. We need more men to fight."

Scipio scoffed. "Calvus will veto any levy to raise more troops. He doesn't care if Romans are dying at our enemies' hands. I, for one, would shed no tears if some accident should mysteriously befall him."

There was a heavy pause. Scipio picked up a toothpick and fiddled with it, aware he should not have spoken his thoughts. Pinna was shocked. The body of a people's tribune was sacrosanct. A death penalty awaited those who harmed such a representative.

Genucius sat up and glowered at the skinny senator. "So you'd think of murder now, Scipio? To use a sword in the back to counter resistance?"

The senator also sat up. "How dare you accuse me of conspiracy."

Still reclining with his weight on his elbow, Medullinus drawled, "Scipio meant nothing drastic, Genucius. I'm sure he only meant it would be advantageous if Calvus was waylaid from attending the Comitium when a law is being proposed . . . perhaps by a fellow tribune."

Genucius flushed beet red. "I'm no man's puppet! Don't expect me to assist you. I'm as incensed as any other commoner that patricians profit from plunder while the plebeians are denied it."

Scipio laughed. "You've helped Camillus often enough by vetoing your colleagues when it suited his aims."

Swinging his legs over the side of the couch, Genucius stood. "I'm not staying to listen to this."

Camillus sat up and reached across to grab his elbow. "Stay, my friend. It's important you hear what else I have to say. There is a reason I've invited you all to dinner." He called to Pinna. "Fetch Artile Mastarna. Then you may go."

She hastened from the room, leaving behind the sound of protests from the patricians about taking audience with the Etruscan. By the time she returned with two pitchers of wine, Genucius had sat down again on the edge of the couch. Artile sauntered to the divans, looking far from a man forced to swallow his pride.

Pinna loitered in the hallway outside, curiosity overcoming caution.

Camillus rose and stood beside the haruspex. "Tell my guests what you have discovered, Artile. How our consular generals have failed in religious matters."

Medullinus sat up so that the three guests now reminded Pinna of crows perched on a fence. "What nonsense is this?"

Genucius raised his palm. "Let the priest speak. I don't think we should dismiss him."

To Pinna's surprise, Scipio agreed with the plebeian instead of Medullinus. "I'd also like to hear what the seer has to say."

Artile adjusted his crescent fibula on his cloak. "The rising of Lake Albanus was not just because the sacred rites of Mater Matuta were neglected. The current consular generals omitted including the Votive Games of Latium in the religious calendar this year. It is no wonder your allies are prepared to break the Latin Pact. You have disrespected their gods more than once. Then you refused to drain the floodwaters that have destroyed their farmlands."

Scipio frowned, glancing across to Medullinus before returning to the priest. "More expiation rites are required?"

Artile fixed his dark oval eyes on the senator. "The error of those currently in office must be rectified. A duly consecrated date for the Votive Games must now be declared by new leaders."

Medullinus stood, pushing the serving table aside. He ignored Artile and stepped in front of Camillus. "Are you saying there need to be fresh elections?"

"Precisely. You're the consular general who drew the lot to govern Rome while the others wage war. Declare an interregnum. Vacate all offices. Conduct new elections that observe due formalities, and renew the auspices so the correct date for the games can be set."

Medullinus spluttered, "This is outrageous! What makes you think I'd listen to this priest? What is his authority for such a declaration?"

Artile was unconcerned at being challenged. "I have scrutinized your religious practices while living here. I have also consulted our Holy Books. Mater Matuta's temple lies in ruins in Rome. Your allies need to be placated."

Medullinus refused to respond to the priest; instead he sneered at Camillus. "Tell me, Brother, has this traitor cast a spell over you as has your concubine? You are becoming feebleminded."

Camillus bristled. "Your hubris will cause Rome to suffer. Admit that you've failed in your duty to interpret the sacred calendar."

"I'm going to wait for the delegation from Delphi. Once the oracle has spoken, we'll know what needs to be done."

Scipio was pensive as he studied the Etruscan. "Let's not be rash. Perhaps the priest speaks the truth. It could take months for the envoys to return. I think we should act now."

Medullinus rounded on him. "So you can be elected instead of me, Scipio? You missed out this time."

The senator also stood, hackles raised. "I only think of the good of all Romans!"

Camillus kept cool in the face of rising tempers. "Listen to me. The Latin tribes are obliged to provide us with troops under the pact. But they're distracted by the damage caused by the floods. If we alleviate the Latin crisis, the soldiers of Latium will be freed to supplement our forces in the south, and we can concentrate on Veii."

Genucius smiled. "Ah, now I see. There'll be no need to raise a levy. The concerns about Calvus would be solved."

Medullinus stopped glowering at Scipio and swiveled around to face Camillus. "'Crisis'? Oh, so that's what you want, Brother, to exaggerate calamity by using this fraudulent priest, then claim the means to avert it. You don't want to be appointed an interrex. You want to be made dictator!"

Genucius spoke before Camillus could respond. "Perhaps six months under your brother's direction might help Rome to victory. He is our most accomplished general—"

Medullinus erupted. "I'm not listening to any more of this!"

Camillus's tone remained reasonable. "At least let me travel to Satricum where the great sanctuary of Mater Matuta stands. That city is no longer in Volscian hands. I'll assure Latium that Rome is aware of its plight. Measures can start to be put in place. Time will not be wasted."

"No!" Medullinus sat down on the couch and pointed to his bare feet. "Call that woman of yours and tell her to bring me my sandals!"

Pinna retreated, anxious not to be discovered listening. She'd only gone a few steps, though, when her Wolf stepped into the corridor. "Eavesdropping as usual. You heard him; he wants to leave."

She stooped and picked up the sandals from the row beside the doorway. Medullinus snatched the pair from her, his spite turning to her as he slipped on the thongs. "You do yourself no favors, Brother, by consorting with this peasant girl."

Pinna tensed, uncomfortable at becoming the center of attention.

Camillus tensed. "She's the daughter of a veteran who was sold into bondage due to this city's failure to support its soldiers."

The consular general rolled his eyes. "Don't say you've become a bleeding heart as well. At least promise me you have no plans to wed her. You'll be a laughing stock if you do. And threaten your sons' inheritance if she bears more children."

Pinna flushed scarlet. She felt trapped, paralyzed by humiliation.

"There's no law forbidding a senator marrying his concubine. And Pinna is unable to bear children."

Medullinus's gaze raked over her again. "Whether you're plowing a fertile or barren field, you're still seen as weak to fall for a pretty face and some juicy cunni."

The consular general headed for the doorway. Camillus grabbed his shoulder and wrenched him around. "I could always best you in a fight when we were young. I'll do so again if you insult her."

Medullinus shrugged him away, then gestured toward the Veientane. "You're bringing our House into disrepute. People are already questioning your judgment." Not waiting for a response, he stormed into the corridor.

Embarrassed by the siblings' argument, Scipio followed, his head down. Pinna heard the clip-clop of his sandals on the tiled floor as he hurried toward the atrium.

Artile smoothed one eyebrow as he observed the descent of the dinner party into disaster. He seemed vexed rather than amused, though. Once again, his counsel had been ignored. He flinched but said nothing when Camillus barked at him to go to his room.

Genucius glared at Pinna, lips pursed. She turned her head, unable to deal with his silent censure.

Her Wolf placed his hand on the plebeian's back. "I will not forget your loyalty, Genucius. Together we reduced Mastarna's army at the Battle of Blood and Hail. I believe there'll come a time when I'll be dictator. And when I am, I'll ensure you're made a knight."

Genucius was taken aback. "A knight?"

Camillus smiled. "A dictator can bypass Senate and Assembly. I see no reason why wealthy plebeians who provide their own horses can't be equestrians. I'll make sure you lead a regiment."

The men grasped each other's forearms. Genucius nodded. "Patrician and plebeian, shoulder to shoulder."

Camillus pulled his friend close. "And you'll do what you can to keep Calvus in check? Our alliance remains firm?"

Genucius nodded again. "Yes. Our friendship remains strong. If necessary, I will not let Calvus succeed in vetoing any troops— provided you support my ambitions to once again hold power."

Pinna was astonished. Was it bribery or loyalty she was witnessing? Either way, both men had strengthened their bond. She stooped and handed Genucius his sandals. He regarded her and then Camillus. For a fleeting fraction, she sensed he was going to speak out; instead he thanked her for his shoes.

When the men left, Pinna called to the maid to help her tidy the room. Thoughts spun in her mind about the night's revelations and altercations. And then, in the clatter of clearing dishes and wine cups, she felt a surge of happiness. Her Wolf had defended her to his brother. And he'd not derided the suggestion that he take her as his lawful wife.

TWENTY-FOUR

Marcus, Falerii, Winter, 397 BC

The icy burn bit into Marcus's flesh as he dived under the water and resurfaced. He swam with strong, energetic breaststrokes to ward off the cold.

Around him, the men of his brigade griped as they waded into the river, shivering and crossing their arms before they submerged and joined their commander in the exercise.

Drusus dived after his friend, yelling at him to set up a race to the far bank into deeper waters. Marcus eased up to let his competitor draw even. Furious splashing and kicking ensued until both glided to the edge, Marcus's fingertips touching first. Drusus laughed and cursed, then challenged him again, turning to give himself a head start. He streaked away. Marcus yelled in protest, and a new contest began.

Drusus reached the shallows first and stood, waist deep. Marcus caught up, also standing, and gave him a thump on the back, calling him a cheat. His companion smiled and shrugged, then dived into the river, doing another lap. Marcus noticed Drusus did not seem hampered by his weak shoulder when buoyed by the current. However, the joint was a latent concern. It had been dislocated so many times that another knock could wrench it from its socket. Marcus doubted the knight had strength to wield a shield as a bludgeon if forced into hand-to-hand fighting. Aemilius must have thought the same. He'd promoted Tatius to head decurion instead of the Claudian.

Marcus hated to see his friend's frustration at being passed over. Pinna claimed Drusus was jealous of him. But it was a friendly rivalry, not based on spite. She did not understand that nobles jockeyed for position. If anything, Drusus had greater chances than he did in the future: His father and uncles were dead. He was the head of an extremely wealthy house. He held the potential to broker deals and buy favors if he could manage to control his moods and temper.

Marcus watched the decurion continue swimming. If Drusus still felt pain from his injuries, he did not show it. Yet even though he strived to keep up in training, his face had been pinched and white at the end of the run this morning. He appeared relieved to rest his shield on the ground and strip off his armor for the swim.

The other knights were less enthusiastic. They hastened to finish, then splashed from the river. Marcus headed for the bank, his feet stirring the mud as he strode from the water.

"You're a bastard, sir," called Tatius, his lips tinged blue. "We're going to ride, not swim, into battle."

Marcus grinned at him as he drew on his tunic. Despite feeling sorry Drusus had been overlooked for promotion, he was happy for Tatius. "Show some respect, or I'll make you run up that hill again in full kit."

"Better than freezing my balls off." Tatius hacked up a gob of spit, then reached down to pick up his breastplate and buckle it on together with his heavy linen kilt.

"You mean 'better than freezing my balls off, *sir*.'" The tribune's tone grew serious. "You'll thank me for ensuring your fitness when you find yourself unseated from your horse. You'll need to stand your ground against some hoplite hefting a huge battle shield."

Tatius saluted, his bucktoothed smile vanishing. "Yes, sir."

Marcus dismissed him, then signaled the others to return to camp also. He enjoyed training with the knights of his old turma, not wanting to lose a connection with them. However, he knew he shouldn't encourage overfamiliarity. In time, gaining higher rank would lead to loneliness. The length of an arm raised in salute was not the only distance that existed between a commander and those who must obey him.

Donning their heavy leather capes, the men trudged back across the field to the rough-hewn timber palisade, its sharp honed pickets standing like a spiky row of teeth. Their gruff voices traveled across the open space between the river and the camp perimeter with its wide ditch. General Aemilius had ordered the woods to be cleared, but the area was still heavily patrolled. He was taking no chances of a surprise Faliscan raid when so deep within enemy territory.

Marcus nodded to the two sentries as they made their pass. He was in no hurry to return to his duties, waiting for Drusus to finish his swim. He surveyed the landscape around him. The yellow-and-red tufa escarpment on the other side of the river rose high above, with the mouths of tombs carved into the rock face. Below was a forest thick with beech and ash. For a moment he envied Falerii its countryside. One day, he hoped he could admire it without assessing it as terrain to be conquered or scenery where danger prowled.

He gazed at a leaf held by the current, sometimes swirling in an eddy, then sailing free. It amazed him that the stream in which they were swimming was the Tiber. Not the sluggish brown river that girded Rome into which the Great Drain emptied shit and piss, but a pure current that was clean and fast flowing, carving its way through peaks and ravines. This waterway was the enemy's lifeblood as much as Rome's. His people would not be satisfied until they controlled every township from the lake at its source to the salt pans at its mouth.

Marcus wondered if such a feat would ever be achieved. For months now their regiment had suffered the drudgery of camp life as they lay siege to the fortified hilltop town. Falerii could not boast the size or wealth of Veii, but its fortifications were just as secure and its inhabitants just as stubborn. The Faliscans may have been hemmed in behind their wall, but the Romans were locked outside in the wind and weather, while their foe lay cozy in their beds.

Blockading the trade routes was no less difficult. Inches, feet, and yards were gained and then lost as Veii's northern troops harried the Roman regiments. At least Thefarie Ulthes had yet to relieve Veii, although some supplies were trickling through.

Marcus now believed it was time for the Romans to abandon a frontal assault on Falerii and Capena. Instead they should concentrate on the Etruscan citadel of Nepete to the west. Nepete was said to be the gateway to all Etruria. Conquering it would give Rome a foothold in the territory. He'd suggested such a strategy to his father, but Aemilius had merely said he'd think on it.

He glanced across to Drusus, who waded toward him, the water dragging against his waist, then his thighs. Water streamed off his back and down his body, his skin stung pink from the cold. He shook his head, droplets flying from his russet hair, then rubbed his beard, flicking water away. Marcus felt his prick stiffen and hurried to don his leather cape, bending his head to hide the flush of embarrassment at failing to control himself.

Drusus sauntered across to his clothes, reaching down and drying himself, taking his time, impervious to the chill air. Marcus looked up again, unable to stop himself from scanning the long scar running along the side of his friend's chest to his groin. Livid against his pale skin, it would take some time before it faded. He doubted, though, that Drusus would ever forget his flesh being sliced—or who had caused the wound. He imagined trailing his finger along the seam, exploring it and more with his tongue—storing the images for later use to fuel the rhythm of his hand.

"What are you looking at?"

Caught out, Marcus was relieved he didn't feel his face burn again, although his loins ached. "Your scar. Pinna did a good job."

Drusus peered down, running his hand along part of the cicatrix. "I have to admit I would have perished if not for her." He pulled on his tunic and cape, then sat down next to Marcus.

"Then you don't hate her anymore?"

"No. I am past that."

"Still, I wouldn't trust her if I were you. Do you believe she wouldn't reveal your secret if it suited her?"

Drusus stammered, "What do you know about my secret?"

Marcus was confused by his friend's apprehension. "I was there that night, remember? The lupanaria."

Drusus's speech returned to normal. "Yes, yes, of course. The night in the brothel. I treated her badly. I've tried to make amends."

Marcus frowned. "Is there something else she holds over you? She has a talent for extortion."

The decurion straightened, dragging his fingers through his wet hair, his voice terse. "She holds the rape over me, that's all. What I want to know is what she holds over you? You've never said why you really made her your concubine."

"I told you, I took pity on her for what we did."

"But you did nothing wrong. Just fucked a prostitute. Why worry about that? Camillus disdains those who use whores, but it's hardly something he'd punish you for."

"True, but I'd gain no respect from him either."

Drusus scowled. "I agree. Needing to force a whore who's paid to open her legs seems cowardly. He'd think less of me. He'd probably pass me over for promotion." His tone was bitter. "Unlike you, who seems to do no wrong in Camillus's eyes."

Marcus ignored his resentment. "I took her as my army wife to protect you. I didn't want to see the little bitch maligning you to the general."

Drusus scanned Marcus's face. "That's it? You let her share your bed because of me? There was no threat to you personally?"

Marcus was perspiring, as though deceit was oozing from his pores. To his relief, Drusus did not press his query but instead slapped him on the back. "You're a true friend. And I owe my life to you twice over. First against the Volscians and then outside Veii." He surveyed the river. "Maybe one day I will return the favor."

There was sincerity in his voice. Wistfulness, too. Marcus knew it worried his friend that he must always be seen as the victim, not the hero. He placed Drusus's neck in a playful headlock. "You're the one who cut down Vel Mastarna. I surrendered my spear. How do you think I feel knowing that I owe my life to an enemy?"

Drusus ducked his head from Marcus's hold. "One day we'll get the chance to slay that smooth-skinned bastard. Do you remember the defixio?"

"It's hard not to forget a night spent in a sepulcher in a storm."

Drusus picked up a pebble and lobbed it into the water. "I recite the curse in my dreams."

Marcus was glad that he alone knew of his friend's use of black magic. "The death penalty awaits those who use a defixio to condemn a man."

The decurion threw another stone with greater force. "I told you, I seek an enemy's downfall, not another citizen's."

The tribune frowned. There may well be a loophole in the law, but it troubled him that his companion placed such store in superstition. Marcus rose, extending his hand. Drusus grasped it and swung himself to standing.

"We won't need evil spirits to destroy Mastarna," said Marcus. "One day, we'll bring him and my cousin home to face judgment."

Drusus hesitated. "I know we declare such things about Caecilia to Camillus. But do you truly seek her execution?"

"Of course I do. We've been through this before."

"I know, but sometimes I'd like to think . . . I hope . . ."

Marcus was astounded. "Oh, for goodness sake! Do you really believe Mastarna absconded with her? And has forced himself on her all these years to sire their four children? You did not see them on the day my father compelled him to divorce her. They stood apart, but their bodies leaned toward each other as flowers turn their faces to the sun. They whispered together in Etruscan, keeping secrets from us in plain view, while their eyes traced lines of adoration from eyes to cheeks and lips." He reached across and placed his hand on Drusus's shoulder, knowing he needed to be harsh. "They were speaking words of love. Believe me, my friend. She's not pining for you. So why do you persist with this fantasy?"

Drusus flushed scarlet and shrugged him away. His hands balled into fists. "Because she makes me strong! Imagining Caecilia lying with Mastarna gives me the surge that rips through my chest whenever I kill a man in battle. The blood rage. To kill or be killed. No rules to hold me. It's as great as the flow of pleasure when my seed spurts into a whore. She gives me a reason to fight."

Marcus stared at him, stunned at the vehemence. Drusus's aggression was well known. He could be foolhardy in his bravery. But Mastarna's accusation niggled. Had Drusus attacked the Veientane when his back was turned? Marcus never dared to repeat the slur to him, but now his doubt deepened. Was Drusus's warped love for Caecilia enough to impel him to cowardice? He pushed the thought aside, ashamed at questioning his friend's honor. "I'm sorry. I didn't know the depth of your pain."

Drusus said nothing as he bent to pick up his corselet, retreating from the intimacy of confidences. "My groom needs to polish this."

Marcus heard a shout. To his surprise, he saw Tatius striding toward them from the direction of the palisade. He instinctively scanned the horizon but saw no sign of an attack. "What is it, Tatius? Why your haste?"

"General Aemilius wants you to return immediately, sir. He's ordered an execution. He wants everyone to be assembled."

"An execution?" Marcus was shocked. Capital punishment was an extreme measure. As far as he was aware, there'd been no instances of cowardice that would warrant such a measure.

"Who, and what for?" Drusus also sounded stunned.

Tatius could not hide his contempt. "One of the hoplites has been caught taking it from another one."

Marcus managed to keep his voice neutral as he acknowledged the news. The thought of what he was about to witness made him feel sick. As he dressed and collected his weapons, he avoided looking at Drusus. He'd already heard him grunt in disgust. He could not bear to see the scorn in his friend's eyes for a warrior who enjoyed what Marcus himself had with a slave so many years ago.

TWENTY-FIVE

At the fifth blow to his shoulders, the young soldier fell forward to the ground. A centurion dragged him upright onto his knees again and handed the cudgel to the next hoplite.

The infantryman hesitated, glancing at the naked man kneeling in front of him. The victim's skin was webbed with huge red welts. The reluctant soldier struck a blow, then handed the bludgeon on to another from his unit. The next man had less compunction, striking the victim's head with a vicious blow. "Pathicus!" He hissed the epithet, spitting on him.

The youth slumped forward again.

"Pick him up!"

Sempronius, Aemilius's other military tribune, barked the order. The guilty hoplite was one of his men. Marcus suspected the superior officer savored the cruelty.

The centurion righted the convicted soldier and handed the club to the next man.

Marcus watched, his bowels cramping. He did not avert his eyes, knowing he must not show weakness, but he felt sweat trickling down his sides and back. He glanced over to the hoplite who had plowed the miscreant. He was not much older than the beaten man. His face was white, the apple in his throat working. He kept his eyes glued to the punishment, flinching at each blow. He'd been called upon to make the first hit to prove that he knew his duty. His arm had been shaking, but his aim and force was enough for the centurion to pass the cudgel to the next. As the penetrator, he would be spared a clubbing, but Marcus wondered if he'd been lucky not to be the one facing execution. Maybe they took turns. Maybe, like him, neither of them cared who submitted to be the pathicus bride as long as they could share each other. One thing was certain: the lover better choose a different male partner next time—a slave or freedman, not a warrior. He'd have to prove himself with a woman, too, unless he wanted to be shunned as a mollis.

Clenching his fists, Marcus wished the torture of the passive hoplite who had let his masculinity be degraded would end. To his credit the offender did not scream or even whimper. He was brave when facing his penalty.

General Aemilius watched aloofly. His cloak had slipped from one shoulder, his breastplate buckles loose. Marcus wondered whether he feigned dishevelment to catch people off guard. There was nothing messy about Aemilius's mind. He was sharp and wily and ruthless. No one was going to question his toughness when it came to showing how he treated a pathicus under his command. Yet the condemned man was probably little older than the stable boy Aemilius had brought from Rome for his own pleasure.

What would Marcus's father do if his son was discovered with another soldier? Deal the death blow in private as a patriarch, or endure the disgrace of his son being publically executed? As an officer, Marcus would be killed for corrupting a subordinate, even if he was the one to act as husband.

He restrained himself from glancing at Drusus. Dreams were one thing but reality was another. And yet he would risk doing whatever was asked if the russet-haired warrior reached out one day to stroke his cheek and tell him that he loved him.

Another thwack. Marcus focused on the beaten soldier again. All the comrades in the unit had taken their turn. The victim lay prostrate, unconscious. The centurion raised his vine-wood staff high and brought it down with practiced force, staving in the victim's skull. Then he kicked the dead man over onto his back. The youth lay with vacant eyes, blood gushing from his mouth, his tongue bitten in half.

The assembled troops were dismissed. The soldiers were quiet as they scattered to resume their duties. It would not take long, though, before talk of the execution would be on everybody's lips.

Marcus needed to be alone. He headed toward the animal enclosure to spend time with his stallion. Drusus caught up with him, clapping his hand on his shoulder as he fell into stride with him. His tone was jovial. "The pathicus got what he deserved. One of them should have rammed his gob as well. He was probably a cocksucker, too."

Marcus walked on. Drusus grabbed his arm. "What's the matter with you?"

He shrugged him away. "We just saw someone clubbed to death. I don't think it's a joking matter."

Drusus raised his eyebrows. "You feel sorry for him?"

"I think watching a soldier die dishonorably is a miserable thing. He was twenty and made a mistake."

"A mistake? He was a warrior. Who wants to fight beside a man who lets himself be conquered like a girl? To let his body be abused? If he has no self-control, then how could his men trust him in a battle? A man who can't govern his own desires is incapable of governing others."

Marcus walked on, angry at a world of rules and duty. No man could question his valor, but at heart his cravings made him no better than the man who'd been bludgeoned. Would Drusus relish the chance to be the first to raise the cudgel against him? Shout loudest to ridicule him? Spit on his corpse? He stopped, turning around. "So speaks the man who declared his love for my cousin in front of his superiors and was hauled away for his troubles. Did you control yourself when you smeared the ceremonial spear with your blood and hurled it at Mastarna at Fidenae?"

"I was young and foolish," he stammered.

"You were twenty, just like that hoplite."

"Don't you *ever* compare me to that pathicus."

Marcus stabbed his finger into Drusus's chest. "I don't. But you still hunger for Caecilia. Until you can rid yourself of sentiment, I don't think you should stand in judgment of anyone."

"You throw that in my face? After I confided in you?"

Marcus's spark of fury dampened as swiftly as it had ignited. "I'm sorry, my friend. It's just that I hate watching executions."

Drusus nodded, draping his arm around Marcus's neck as they fell in step toward the horse yard. Marcus was aware of his touch and height, how he leaned his head close to his. It was an agony of nearness, a reminder of futility.

"How long has it been since you've had a good fuck, Marcus? That's your problem. Pinna may have been trouble, but at least your mood was better when she shared your bed. Let's find one of those Faliscan whores who follow the camp tonight."

Marcus tensed. The last thing he needed was to pretend he lusted after women. He could not live a false life again. "I don't think so. Look what happened last time we shared a whore."

Drusus chuckled. "True. But this time I'll hold my liquor and not be rough."

Marcus shook his head. "No, I don't want the pox."

"That's always your excuse." Drusus slipped his arm from around Marcus's neck. "Maybe you should find another concubine, then."

The tribune forced himself to sound light hearted. "Look what happened the last time I did that."

Drusus laughed. "Then you'd better find a boy."

Marcus opened the gate to walk into the yard, calling to his horse before replying. "Perhaps. Father always says his does the job but without all the nagging."

"Well, whoever you decide to screw, just make sure it isn't another soldier."

Marcus clenched his teeth. He did not plan to bed anyone again. He'd disciplined himself to control his urges. Self-denial was ingrained in him.

The stallion trotted to him. Marcus raised his hand to pat it and noticed his wristband. The crisscross of tiny scars on his inner wrist had long healed, leaving fine white lines on his skin. He had told himself he did not need to inflict them any longer. He'd convinced himself that grueling exercise and abstinence were atonement enough. But tonight, in solitude, he would take up his dagger and enjoy the sharp, satisfying pain of iron pricking flesh.

TWENTY-SIX

Caecilia, Veii, Winter, 397 BC

Caecilia was keyed up with anticipation. A messenger had arrived from Thefarie. Vel insisted she attend his war council to listen to the envoy. "If we're to hear the worst, then let's do so together, Bellatrix."

There was no doubting that the High Council chamber was the preserve of men. Caecilia felt as though she were an interloper in this room with its masculine aura and symbols of power. An oak table extended the entire length of the room, its legs carved into the shape of claw-foot lions. As son of the king, Tarchon sat at the right-hand side of the monarch's chair. Caecilia was pleased to see he was clear eyed and alert. The days of drinking, gambling, and chewing Catha were over. He was committed to proving to Karcuna Tulumnes he could be a suitable mentor to Sethre.

The three generals were already present. Karcuna was seated on the opposite side of the table from Tarchon, drumming his fingers on its surface. He did not acknowledge the prince but instead watched Lusinies. The bald general was pacing, his brow wrinkled below the smoothness of his pate. Joints creaking, Feluske winced as he eased himself onto the armchair next to Karcuna.

Caecilia hesitated, not knowing where she should sit. Vel murmured reassurance and escorted her to the far end of the table facing him. She wished she could sit next to Tarchon instead of being flanked by Feluske and Karcuna. The former acknowledged her with a wave of one crooked forefinger; the latter ignored her.

Dressed in purple, his mantle edged in black spirals, Mastarna was the last to take his place. Caecilia sensed he was uneasy, but she felt a rush of excitement to see the messenger. Thefarie must be close at hand. This siege may yet be ended.

Mastarna hunched forward. "Is Thefarie Ulthes sending troops to relieve Veii?"

The herald bowed. "No, my lord. The general's forces are fully engaged in the north at Falerii and Capena against two regiments of the Legion of the Wolf. There are no reserves to march south."

Having expected to hear good tidings, Caecilia's spirits plummeted. There would be no rescue. She looked across to Vel. His eagerness had also vanished, his face resuming somber lines.

The others exchanged worried glances. "What of the Tarchnans?" said Lusinies. "Have they not helped to swell our numbers?"

The courier shook his head again. "Aule Porsenna is dead, my lord. As are all his men."

Mastarna straightened in his chair. "How did an entire contingent come to be killed?"

"A unit of Romans hiked cross-country and waylaid the Tarchnan zilath and his men as they traveled home. Lord Porsenna did not expect the enemy to intercept his troops in Rasennan territory. They were slaughtered, and all the plunder they'd seized from battles was retrieved by the foe."

Shocked, Mastarna leaned back, shoulders slumped. He and Porsenna had been more than friends. The Tarchnan was his former father-in-law. Mutual grief over his daughter Seianta's death had cemented their bond. And it was in Porsenna's navy Vel had fought as a mercenary when he was just a youth. The scar that crossed his chest was the price paid for fighting the Syracusans on the zilath's behalf. Now his Tarchnan friend was dead because he'd come to Veii's aid.

Seeing the king speechless, Lusinies continued the interrogation. "But why had Porsenna withdrawn support from Thefarie? Was there some falling out between the two?"

"Rumor reached us that General Aemilius has plans for the Romans to take Nepete. As a result, Porsenna considered Veii's conflict no longer his priority. He was concerned to return to Tarchna to strengthen its battlements should the gateway to the Rasennan cities fall."

Caecilia glanced across to Tarchon. His siblings lived in Tarchna. And Vel would also be worried that the House of Atelinas, his mother's family, would be endangered.

"And you, soldier. How did you come to break through the Roman siege lines?" asked Karcuna.

"Via the cuniculi tunnel network under cover of darkness."

Feluske scrutinized the travel-worn messenger. "Have you come alone?"

"No, sir. There are ten of us camped outside the outer siege lines beyond the road to the Capena Gates. If I do not return within three days, they have orders to return to Falerii without me."

To Caecilia's relief, Vel recovered his composure. "And what is the state of the Roman defenses?"

"The earthworks around the northwest bridge are still strongly reinforced, but farther to the east, the trenches are in disrepair. Postumius's soldiers are ill disciplined. Some of the forts and stockades are undermanned. You could smell the stink of their shit from the latrines even upwind. There's been an outbreak of bowel fever. Their manpower is diminished with so many sick."

Mastarna leaned back in his chair. "Go and clean yourself up, soldier. Eat. Await my orders."

After the herald left the chamber, the generals erupted into a chorus of concern. Mastarna raised his hands. "One at a time."

Lusinies sat down. "This is dire news. The only zilath from the Twelve who came to our aid has perished. And Rome threatens Nepete. No other city is going to help us now."

Feluske shifted his weight on his seat as though to relieve pressure on his hip. "I dread saying this, my lord, but we may have to sue for peace. Supplies are diminishing. If we cede some of our farmland to the Romans, it may well appease them."

Lusinies nodded. "Feluske is right. Both cities have suffered. A plague ravaged Rome last year. Their soldiers are weary of fighting all year round. I'm sure they would be happy to be home on their farms rather than camping under tents with a griping belly."

A sharp pulse beat in Caecilia's temple; she was disturbed to hear talk of capitulation. Didn't these men know that land alone would not satisfy the Romans? The enemy would expect a reckoning, too. Would these principes require Vel to hand her over in return for supplies? "Do you think Rome would be satisfied with a scrap thrown to them like some morsel fed to a pet dog? We are dealing with a wolf that'll tear out the throat of its prey and devour its carcass!"

Lusinies halted and stared at her, while Feluske and Karcuna swiveled their heads toward the king. Caecilia realized she'd overstepped herself in voicing her opinion. She'd grown used to independence, but in this room she had no standing. Her presence in the war chamber was on the indulgence of her husband.

Vel ignored their indignation. "You all know Caecilia speaks the truth. A few parcels of land won't be enough for Rome. Veii would be required to bend its knee. Is that what you want? To be governed by our enemy after all we've endured?"

Feluske's voice hardened in a way Caecilia had never heard before. "Will you let your pride prevent you from providing sustenance to your people, my lord? A truce could be arranged on mutual terms. After all, there was peace for twenty years until you . . ." He faltered.

Karcuna Tulumnes thumped the table. "Say it, Feluske. Until Mastarna married *her*. The descendant of Mamercus Aemilius, who paraded the head of my father on a spear at the battle of Fidenae."

"Be careful how you refer to your queen, Karcuna," growled Mastarna. "And Mamercus Aemilius killed my father, too. Veii was forced into a precarious peace after the defeat. I wedded Caecilia to maintain the truce."

The tic in Karcuna's cheek flickered. Despite Vel's admonishment, he thumped the wood again. "But then you married her a second time! This war would never have begun if she'd returned to her people."

Mastarna stood, his arms straight, his palms flat against the table. "So what do you propose? For me to surrender my wife to her executioners? You know the seeds of conflict were sown long before she escaped. And she would never have fled at all if your brother had not threatened to have her murdered and raped!"

Caecilia tried to remain calm. "Lord Tulumnes, you pledged allegiance to my husband to heal the rift between your Houses. Is your word worth so little? Would you see Veii weakened again by internal strife when it's facing its greatest crisis?"

Karcuna opened his mouth to speak, but Lusinies strode across to him and placed his hand on the princip's shoulder. "We can't begin fighting among ourselves again. Caecilia has declared her fealty. It's time for the Tulumnes clan to stop threatening her."

Feluske nodded. "She's our queen and should be shown respect. There's no way I would ever condone her being harmed."

The words of support sent a rush of gratitude through her.

"Show me the vow you swore to me was not false," said Mastarna. "Apologize!"

Hands balled, Karcuna bowed his head with unwilling deference. The rancor of two generations was engrained in him. "I seek your pardon, my lady."

Despite the princip's grudging tone, Caecilia decided to be gracious. "Your apology is accepted."

Seconds passed as though time was dragging its heels. The belligerent mood eased. Mastarna sat down, gesturing Karcuna and Lusinies to do the same. Feluske turned to the king. "Then what are we to do, my lord? If you will not treat, what are our alternatives? We cannot sit here trapped and starving."

Mastarna hunched forward. "Postumius is unpopular with his troops. Unhappy soldiers lack self-restraint and determination. The security of the fortifications to the northeast of the city has grown lax. There may yet be an opportunity for us."

Tarchon found the nerve to speak after listening to his elders arguing. "An opportunity to do what, Father? Force a breach?"

"Not a frontal assault but a night attack. I want to break through the northeast siege lines. The unit waiting for Thefarie's messenger outside the Capena Gate can set the stockades and forts to the flame as a distraction while we launch an assault. Take the Romans by surprise while they're sleeping and their sentinels are bored and dozing."

Caecilia was pleased to hear his fervor, seeing the energy rise in him. And yet there was a nub of anxiety within her at the danger Vel craved.

Lusinies smiled. "After that, our troops will ensure no blockade is reinstated by continuing to ride out and skirmish."

Mastarna raised his hand. "Yes, the armies stationed in the city can do that. But the force that breaches the Roman lines will march to defend Nepete. From there we rally the Twelve to attack Rome when the League meets at the sacred fountain at Velzna in mid spring."

Lusinies scratched one of his thickened earlobes. His laugh was nervous. "My lord, I hardly think we can launch an invasion. And the Brotherhood will be concerned with shoring up its own defenses if General Aemilius does attack Nepete."

"That's the very reason why the League must take a stand," said Mastarna. "Nepete is the key. It opens the way for Rome to stalk the northern cities as well. We need to destroy the wolves' den, not just pursue the packs that raid our territories." He rose, opening his palm and extending it toward his wife. "We need to heed Aemilia Caeciliana's call to conquer Rome."

Karcuna's attention fixed on the queen. She felt the heaviness of his stare. He'd sworn fealty to Vel, but was there a residue of rebellion? The keenness in his voice took her by surprise. "There is risk in the scheme, my lord, but perhaps it's what is required. We can't remain defensive any longer. And I have always wanted to see Rome occupied. Which of us do you propose should march north to put the plan in train?"

"I will lead the force. Their leaders trust me."

Caecilia stifled the impulse to cry out. Vel could die in her quest to destroy Rome.

"But your army has been decimated, my lord," said Feluske. "Surely it's more prudent for you to remain here."

Vel did not respond, instead walked the length of the table to stand between Karcuna and Caecilia. The princip rose, towering over both king and queen.

"I have said before that it's time for all Veientane soldiers to marshal under the royal banner," said the lucumo. "Those remaining men of my clan will join with Tulumnes's tribe. Karcuna and I will fight as one for Veii, not with our own armies. We will forge a true allegiance when we ride into battle together."

Karcuna hesitated, then bowed his head. "I'm honored to be given the opportunity to bring the fight to the Romans." He glanced at Tarchon and back to Mastarna. "My ward, Sethre, is yet to be blooded. I ask that you take him with you as your aide, my lord. It will guarantee there'll be no temptation on the part of the prince in my absence."

Tarchon stood, about to object, but Vel's glare stopped him.

"Very well. Sethre will ride with me to learn the skills of war. He has proved himself to be a talented horseman. Let's see if he can keep his seat in a battle."

Tarchon frowned. "Why are you depriving me of the chance to be a warrior again, Father?"

"Because I wish to give you a greater opportunity. You'll govern Veii in my stead. Lusinies and Feluske will act as your advisers."

"You trust me to act as regent?" Tarchon was incredulous.

"A man from the House of Mastarna must stand in my place. You've proven you can restrain yourself from excesses over the last few months. Now everyone can judge if you have the ability to be a statesman."

The prince glanced around to Caecilia and grinned before bowing to the king. "I won't fail you, Father."

Rising, Caecilia smiled at her husband. She never thought the day would come when he would put such faith in his adopted son. "I will leave you men to your strategy and tactics."

Mastarna placed his hand on her arm. "Stay." He addressed the principes. "I expect my wife to sit on the inner council from now on. As queen, she must have a say in all decisions."

To her relief, the councillors made no protest, not even Karcuna. She swallowed hard, unsure what to say. She'd come so far from the Roman girl who hungered to be privy to the world of men. She'd once thought that, if she had the chance to wield a sword, she might save herself from the fate of wedding an enemy. Now that foe was placing a city into her hands.

Twenty-Seven

Freed of her swaddling clothes, Thia lay on her back with her legs raised, trying to grab her toes. Caecilia sat on cushions on the floor beside her. Semni stood nearby, smiling. Cytheris, too, seemed content as she sat winding thread onto an amber spool.

The winter was mild, the bitter iciness of the past years forgotten. The palace was drafty, though. Caecilia was homesick for their old house, its atrium and garden made cozy by the warmth of family life. At least she'd found a smaller room within the private chambers. She had made it the family haven deep inside the palace.

She bent over and nuzzled Thia's tummy. Her daughter's giggles always raised her spirits. But tonight Vel would leave. Dread would again hover on the threshold of her mind. Yet she'd learned to hide heartbreak. Her tears only made their partings more difficult.

With shrill squeals, Larce and Arnth ran into the family quarters, their chase echoing through the chamber. Clad in full armor, Mastarna followed with mock ferocity, striding with enormous steps toward one and then the other, lunging to miss deliberately by inches before sweeping Arnth into his arms. Larce pounced on his back. Tas looked up from the scroll he was reading. He frowned at being distracted from his studies.

From the corner of her eye, Caecilia noticed Arruns propping his master's shield and sword against the heavy timber doorjamb. He was inscrutable as always. Nevertheless, she knew he was hiding his disappointment the king was not taking him to war.

Noticing his lictor, Mastarna rose, shaking off his two sons, although each one latched onto his legs to hinder his movement. "I will be a little while longer, Arruns. I wish to bid farewell to my family."

Tas studied his father's armor and walked across. "Are you leaving us, Apa?"

Vel stroked the boy's hair. "Yes. I'm going to ask the League of the Twelve for assistance. You must be the man of the family while I'm gone."

Tas ducked his head away, reluctant as always to be touched. He appeared nervous at being issued with such a responsibility. "But I haven't grown a beard yet. I can't be a man."

Vel glanced at Caecilia, bemused at how his firstborn always interpreted words so literally. She smiled and crouched before her son. "Don't worry. Tarchon will look after all of us."

"Come. I have something to give each of you," Vel said, extracting Arnth and Larce from his legs and depositing them onto the nearest kline. "You, too, Tas."

Disdainful of his younger brothers, the eldest prince climbed onto the divan next to them, keeping a small space apart, his tawny eyes solemn. The other two boys settled onto the plush mattress, their legs dangling, eyes wide, and shoulders straight, like two fledglings waiting for their mother to feed them.

Vel offered Caecilia his hand. "Ati and Thia also." Intrigued, the queen lifted the baby into her arms and let him help her sit next to her sons. Larce shuffled on his bottom over to her and kissed Thia's cheek. The baby grabbed at his nose. Caecilia put her arm around him.

The king beckoned to a servant boy who approached carrying a bronze cista by its handle. Mastarna delved into it, pulling from it three golden amulets.

"For my firstborn, Vel Mastarna Junior." He looped the necklace over Tas's head to nestle beside his birth charm.

The boy fingered the tiny carving. "It's a bull like the boss on your shield." He pointed to the pendant hanging from his father's neck. "And your bulla."

"Yes, the symbol of our House. And Fufluns was known to show himself as such a great beast."

Larce leaned forward, peering at the other totems in his father's palm. "What about me?"

"A dolphin for you. It's sacred to Fufluns, too. After all, we need to journey over sea to reach our ancestors in Acheron."

Keen for his turn, Arnth grabbed the bulla from his brother's hand. "I want the dolphin!"

To avoid a squabble, Mastarna prized the talisman away and gave it back to Larce, then handed Arnth the last amulet. "For you, little soldier, I have a leopard. Its lithe grace belies the savagery within."

Their youngest son showed it to his mother and growled like the beast. Larce eyed it. "It's like the big cat in your bedchamber in our old house, Apa."

"The leopard is Fufluns's companion. It will protect us in the Beyond after we die."

Caecilia frowned, disturbed at her husband's choice of presents. Vel had not mentioned worshipping Fufluns to her since she'd expressed her qualms to him. Why then was he granting his sons symbols of the wine god's protection?

"You once sailed upon the sea, didn't you, Apa?" said Tas.

"Yes, I was a mercenary for the zilath of Tarchna. I helped him to fight the Syracusans."

"And you saw dolphins?"

"Yes, carving a path through water."

"I have dreams about a bull," Tas said, unexpectedly. "A wolf springs from a cave to attack it. The bull pierces the wolf with its horn, but then the wolf leaps onto its back and sinks its fangs into its hindquarters. Queen Uni watches them."

Mastarna looked at Caecilia, his brow creasing. He turned back to Tas. "And tell us. Who wins this battle?"

"I don't know. I always wake before I see which animal wins."

Caecilia frowned. The boy often had nightmares. There was a darkness that existed within him, fears that could not be tamed. His brooding silence gave credence to his nickname, Tas, "the Silent One." Hearing he was suffering from this nightmare in the isolation of his room, she felt a pang of guilt. "Why didn't you tell me about this?"

To her surprise, Tas clenched his fists and glared at her. "Because I wasn't scared! Even though I saw the blood upon the horns, the flesh beneath the claws. I'm not a baby anymore, Ati."

His father patted him on the shoulder. "That's right. Dreams can't hurt you. And men should never be afraid of a little gore."

Tas stared at him. "But demons can harm you after you die, Apa. That's why we must sacrifice to Aita, the god who rules Acheron."

"And did Uncle Artile tell you that?" The boy nodded. "Yes, Apa. When Aricia used to take me to see him."

Caecilia felt a stab of concern. What legacy had the priest left? He had molded their son's mind for almost a year. Could the lessons taught him ever be unlearned? The Calu Death Cult was fearful and oppressive. Tas had been tutored in dread while being fed on dreams of being a seer—a tug-of-war between the perils of the Beyond and the heady elation of communing with the gods.

"Forget what your uncle told you," said Vel. "Fufluns protects us. You need not follow the Calu Cult."

Behind them, Arruns coughed to gain attention. "Master, it will soon be sunset; you need to prepare to leave for the Capena Gates."

"Tell Lord Karcuna I'll join him presently. I want to bid farewell to the queen and princess first."

The guard bowed. Caecilia could see his concern at the length of the king's farewells. The attack was scheduled to take place in the dead hours of the night, but this required organization and commands to be issued first.

Mastarna took Thia from Caecilia, lifting her above his head with straight arms. The little girl's body went rigid.

Larce laughed. "She looks as though she's flying."

Vel swooped the baby down again to Caecilia's lap. "Remove the Atlenta pendant, Bellatrix. The amulet is rightly yours. I've had something special made for our daughter to replace it."

He drew a necklace from the cista. Three tiny gold bees were strung upon a chain. An insect sacred to Fufluns. "Honey brings sweetness to our lives." He kissed Thia's fingers as she reached up to touch the shiny gift. "And you are the sweetest of all, my princess."

Caecilia unclasped the silver Atlenta pendant, then fastened the bee amulet around her daughter's neck. Now all four children had gained the wine god's protection against the evil eye.

Mastarna returned his attention to the boys. "It's time for me to say good-bye to you, my sons."

There were howls of protest from the younger boys. Tas stepped down from the kline. Arnth scrambled to his feet on the couch and launched himself across to his father.

Vel laughed, catching him. "Be good, little soldier."

Larce opened his arms. "I will miss you, Apa."

"I, also, small one." He squeezed both until they giggled. Tas hung back, saluting him instead.

"No hug for me, then, Tas?"

"I'm too old."

"But I'm not." The father grabbed him so that Tas was pressed against the others, a jumble of squirming bodies against muscled biceps.

Quieting, Mastarna let them go and touched each of the bullas around their necks in turn. "Make me proud. Protect your mother and sister."

"Like the dolphin," said Larce, raising his bulla.

"Leopard," shouted Arnth.

"No, like the bull," said Tas, gaze intense. "Because it is the strongest of all."

TWENTY-EIGHT

Once the boys had gone, Vel sat down on the couch beside Caecilia and delved into the cista again. "I have something for you, too, Bellatrix."

"So many treasures today," she said, sensing the gift would also be a totem of the wine god.

The boon was a silver mirror of exquisite beauty. Two figures were engraved on its back. Two lovers embracing, gazing into each other's eyes, lips almost touching. The names etched beside them were "Fufluns" and "Areatha." She was torn between gratitude and disquiet as she kissed him a thank-you.

"The divine couple are devoted to each other," he said, stroking her cheek. "As are we."

"So the god who inspires infidelity is faithful to his wife?"

Vel slipped his arm around her waist. "Yes. He is a paradox. A dying god."

She scanned his face. "Why do you now turn to him instead of Nortia?"

His expression was as serious as Tas's. "Because I have changed ever since you told me of the dice throw, Bellatrix. You've set me a challenge. I can't save Veii until I first conquer Rome."

Once again, Caecilia regretted telling him her secret. She hated the pressure she'd placed on him. Yet the thought of worshiping Fufluns troubled her. "Vel, I've seen what's required to submit to the wine god. I can't follow him. Please don't ask that of me."

He cupped her chin in his hand. "The rites of the Spring Festival you attended were not the way of the Rasenna."

"People were beyond drunk. They were possessed, screaming out the god's name, beseeching him to reveal himself as they rutted."

"The divinity offers contact with him through elation. He is a communicant between the living and dead." He brought her fingers to his lips. "He also has the power to enchant and bring joy through the bounty of the vine. You know that well enough. I've seen you merry on wine and no sign that you don't welcome it."

"There is a difference between good humor and frenzy."

"Wine is Fufluns's gift, Bellatrix. Granted, it can fuel deeds of violence and lust, but it can also make a poor man feel rich, a slave free, and the weak powerful. Under its sway you are no longer fearful. There is candor, too, and forgetfulness of woe."

Listening to him filled her with growing unease. She remembered how her pulse had quickened when he declared he was planning to conquer Rome. Now her heartbeat raced at his defense of the deity. Had he always felt this way and kept it from her? Had he always resented her depriving him of ecstatic union?

"So what are you saying, Vel? Do you want me to forsake my belief in Uni so I can worship him? The goddess stands for all that Fufluns isn't. I revere her as the protectress of married women. She has sheltered me through the birth of each of our children. She saved Veii, and you, in the Battle of Blood and Hail."

"Of course not," he said, his impatience evident. "But don't you understand? There is good and evil in all of us, even the gods. They have loves and wants and hatreds as intense as any mortal. And you know there is violence within me just as there is love for you and our children. Even Uni has her darker side. She can be vengeful and hostile."

He tried to draw her closer, but she placed one hand against his cuirass. "Why, Vel? Why your fervor for this god?"

He grasped her shoulders. "Because I've been thinking more of death. Not just mine, but yours. And our children's. I want the comfort of knowing we'll meet again in the Beyond. I want you to believe in my afterlife, not in the cheerless existence of your Roman dead."

Stunned by his desperate tone, Caecilia slipped from the kline, a flush of heat spreading through her. Mastarna had never asked her to forsake her religion, the last and only link to her birthplace. A Roman death required no reckoning or retribution. She would merge with the mass of ancestral spirits, no longer an individual, but one with many: freed from emotions, devoid of bliss or woe, love or hatred. "At least there are no perils awaiting me when I become a Shade."

He shook her. "But our children and I will need to appease you once you join such a host. There is a reason why the Roman dead are called the Good Ones. It's a name to placate them from rising to torment the living."

Caecilia steadied herself. She felt as though she were treading a pathway to a past where there had only been differences between them. He was asking her to make a choice she thought he'd never demand. "Have I held you back from your worship all these years?"

"No. I promised to respect your beliefs. I also lacked piety myself, but now . . ."

"But now you seek to conquer Rome."

"Yes, the stakes are higher. Either Veii succeeds or it is destroyed." He lowered his voice. "We are destroyed."

She was truly frightened now. Mastarna seldom admitted he was afraid. His bravado was reassuring even if she teased him for being vain. The fact that he always survived, always returned, kept her hope alive. "You've taunted Nortia so many times, Vel. I didn't think you feared death."

He rubbed his brow with his fist, the gesture sharp. "Of course I feel my stomach tighten every time I lower my helmet and raise my shield. And pray for courage like every other man. But this is different." He hugged her. "Don't you understand? I never know if I'll return to find you or our children taken by plague—or that Rome has breached our wall. Not only do I fear losing you while I'm alive but also after I'm slain. To believe we will meet again in the Beyond is a consolation, even if our bodies may never lie together in a grave."

She rested her head against his chest, the bronze of his corselet denying her the warmth of his body. "I don't know what to do."

He kissed her hair. "Bellatrix, I can't force you to follow Fufluns, but please consider giving libation to him and kneeling before his shrine while I'm away. Remember there were many things here that repelled you that you now enjoy. Perhaps you can accept this, too. And then," he whispered, "at the next festival after I return, we might seek communion together under the stars."

Caecilia froze. She did not want to meet his eyes, to let him see her doubt that she could ever surrender to his faith. For even if for divine purpose, how could she watch him climax with others at Fufluns's feasts? How could she welcome lying with another man behind a mask?

Outside, the timekeeper called the hour, startling them. The inevitable melancholy of farewell stole over her. She picked up the Atlenta pendant from the divan and showed it to him. "I'll wear this to protect me while you're gone. Atlenta has long kept me safe. And, remember, we will be lions after we die."

Mastarna hesitated, his request hanging between them, then he smiled and kissed her a sad, deep, sweet good-bye. "Yes, Bellatrix, we will dwell in paradise together."

TWENTY-NINE

Semni, Veii, Spring, 396 BC

The massive pithoi jars stood in the shadows of the storeroom like a phalanx of headless soldiers, shoulder to shoulder. If they had not been half sunk into the floor, they would stand as high as a man.

Semni held Nerie's hand as she entered the cellar, Perca following on her heels.

"Ssh," she whispered, placing her finger to her lips. "Be very quiet so we can hear if the princes are in here." The one-and-a-half-year-old giggled, unable to suppress his excitement at being included in the game with the three older boys.

Spring had arrived, but its warmth had yet to infiltrate the deep interior of the palace. The air smelled of dry earth, although a faint smell of barley pervaded it. Coated with dust, most of the pots were empty, their contents gone to feed the palace household.

Lord Tarchon had ordered grain supplies to be further rationed. And Lady Caecilia had decreed the palace stores should be distributed equally among the families of both servants and courtiers. The principes expressed their discontent at such largesse, but the queen dismissed their griping, determined to show her fairness.

Semni knew she was lucky to eat one meal per day when those in the city struggled. Denied a healthy diet, though, she was aware her milk was drying up. Only two weeks ago, she'd had her first flux since Nerie was born.

Tired of the princes complaining their tummies ached, Semni thought a game would distract them. The cool confines of the network of cellars were a perfect setting for hide-and-seek. She signaled Perca to search the far end of the chamber. Whistling, the girl crept between the pithoi, trying to flush out a prince. Semni followed suit, peering around the contoured sides of the earthenware containers decorated with wavy lines and spirals. Nerie dogged her steps.

A stifled noise caught her attention as she reached a wooden bench where a pile of large terra-cotta buckets was stacked. It was then she spied a round wooden lid propped against the side of one of the pithoi. As she drew closer, she heard the sound of a whimpering child.

"Quick, Perca, come and help."

Semni gripped one of the container's clay handles and leaned over to peer inside. Down in the gloomy interior, Larce stared up at her, eyes brimming with tears. Arnth stood beside him, grinning.

"How did you two get in there?"

"Tas helped us, but now we're stuck," wailed Larce.

Semni rolled her eyes and leaned over the edge as far as she could, extending her hands to them. They were too far belowground to reach. Larce started blubbering.

"Calm down," she urged. "I'll try something different." Scanning the room, she noticed a ladder. "Help me with that, Perca."

The two girls managed to heft the ladder up and over the side to drop it down next to Larce. "Stop crying and climb up. Be careful. It might wobble."

The four-year-old was beyond taking direction, though, continuing to sob. Arnth pushed his brother out of the way and clambered up nimbly, laughing as Semni hoisted him over the top.

"Baby," he taunted Larce, confident now he was on safe ground.

"Am not!" Seeing his brother had escaped successfully, Larce was determined not to be bested.

The rescue accomplished, Semni sat down with a sigh of relief and rested against the pithos, pulling a boy down on each side of her, an arm around them. "You are never to do that again, do you hear me?"

Larce gave an exaggerated nod. Arnth's cheeky grin was less than reassuring.

Semni glanced around, realizing she had yet to find the last brother. She scanned the rows of pithoi. There was no telltale lid propped against any of them. "Do you know where he is hiding?"

Larce shook his head. "He said he was going to see the gorgon."

She frowned, wondering if he meant Cytheris. She knew the boy had overheard her and Aricia use that name. Yet she doubted he would refer to the handmaid as such. She looked across to Perca. "Do you know what he's talking about?"

The girl shook her head.

Semni pushed Nerie off her lap and stood up, dusting down her chiton and helping the boys to their feet. "Larce? Do you know who Tas was talking about?"

The boy shrugged. "He said Medusa lived down here."

Semni frowned, irritated the child had wandered away. "Take the princes back to the nursery, Perca. I'll find Tas." She handed her son to the girl. "And ask Cook to keep an eye on Nerie."

After the group had left, Semni weaved her way through the pots, puzzled the oldest boy had not revealed himself. "Master Tas, you can come out now."

She rounded the last row only to reel back in fright. A gorgon glared at her from the gloom with locks of wild hair and a stony stare. She gulped, resisting the urge to run away. Then she remembered Medusa gave protection against the evil eye. What was she guarding?

The circular bas-relief was broad, the width of a large window. Why would a cellar boast such a decoration? The paint on the features was peeling. It must have been there for years. She crept closer, wondering why it was at an angle. Then she noticed the hinges and realized it was a portal to another room. She surveyed the wall beside it and gasped. There was an emblem of a sphinx etched into the brick. A sign that a tunnel must lie beyond. She scanned the floor. Small footprints were outlined in the dust. Her stomach lurched. Tas must have ventured into the hidden passageway.

Semni took a deep breath, then swung open the Medusa hatch. It was pitch black inside. She felt as though hands would grab and yank her into the darkness if she thrust her head inside. "Tas! Come out this minute!"

She heard the scuttling of mice in the blackness. Panic rose at the thought that he might be trapped inside. She turned and ran out of the room to the corridor, scanning the row of torches on the wall. One was already missing. She wrenched another from its bracket.

She balked once again when she returned to face the mythical creature, but the knowledge the boy could be hurt gave her courage enough to push the torch through the opening. She peered inside to find there was another storeroom beyond.

Edging her way through, she stepped down onto an earthen floor. The air was warmer in the chamber, protected from drafts, the smell fusty. The flames of the torch steadied, becoming smooth and sculpted in the stillness. She raised it high. The room was empty, its corners dark beyond the halo of light. As her eyes grew accustomed to the gloom, she noticed there was a heap of bricks scored with scorch marks piled against one wall.

The hair on the back of her neck stood on end at the strong sense she was being watched. She swiveled, illuminating each wall. A shadowy figure loomed. A scream stuck in her throat, terror turning her hoarse. She closed her eyes, hoping blindness would protect her. She waited for a hand to seize her.

When nothing happened, she opened one eye nervously. In the flickering light, she saw that a woman was painted on the wall with high arched wings fanned out behind her. Vanth. Dressed in hunting boots and a short chiton, the spirit held a torch to guide the dead to Acheron. Her face was serene with beauty, belying her danger. Semni's teeth chattered. A benign demoness guarded this chamber. There was evil here.

Tearing her eyes from the painting, she swung around, vainly trying to see if the boy was huddled in a corner. She paced the line of the walls, and in the wavering light, she saw another Medusa hatch slung open with a sphinx painted beside it. This time when she thrust the brand into the space beyond, she shuddered. There was a low narrow passageway leading into the blackness.

Blood thumped against her temple. She found it hard to breathe, not sure what to do. She'd managed to force herself into the first hidden chamber, but she doubted she could enter the tunnel. The very walls might close in on her and crush her.

Minutes dragged. Where had Tas gone? An image of his secret trysts with Lord Artile returned. And how the prince managed to access the temple where they used to meet.

Scrambling back through the hatchway to the cellar, Semni dropped the torch in her haste as she sped through the maze of corridors to the service lane. Picking up the sides of her chiton, her shoes slipping on mud and slush, she knocked people aside as she rushed toward the sanctuary next door. A place where she knew Prince Tas would find Aricia, the priestess who had once again lured him there.

THIRTY

Semni halted when she reached the sanctuary, surprised to see a long line of worshipers snaking up the steps and across the temple portico. Each was waiting their turn to enter and lay votives before Uni.

Knowing she could waste no time in finding the prince, Semni edged past. "Excuse me, I'm on a royal errand," she repeated. "Excuse me, let me pass." A pathway was forged despite grumbles until she reached the doorway to the chamber where Queen Uni resided.

There was a hush to the room, the air dense with incense fumes. Acolytes were marshaling people to ensure the business of devotion was efficient, directing supplicants to move forward to deposit their gift on the altar table, kneel to pray, and then move on. Semni was amazed to see the floor littered with statuettes as well.

Two cepens cleared away the excess figurines, piling them to the side, discarded prayers jumbled in a heap once they had served their purpose.

One woman knelt before Uni, pulling her son down beside her. The child looked fatigued and was coughing, his eyes red and face flushed.

Semni hurried to the workshop at the back of the sanctum. She'd once hidden and watched Artile speak to Tas of the firmament and thunderbolts and portents there. Before she crossed the threshold, though, Lady Tanchvil emerged from the workroom holding Tas by the hand. Aricia followed.

The boy examined his feet rather than look at Semni.

"Thank the gods," she murmured, then curtsied before the high priestess.

"You have come for the prince? Aricia was about to deliver him home."

Semni was relieved the hatrencu was honorable. "I'm glad, my lady. Thank you." Then she waggled her finger at Tas. "You've been very naughty. You shouldn't have run away like that."

"I came to tell Aricia about my dream."

Semni glowered at the acolyte. "How dare you tell him to find you again?"

Aricia reddened. "I didn't. He came of his own accord."

"Silence!" The augur pivoted and walked back into the workroom. "Let's speak in here. The whole of Veii need not know of this matter."

Semni glanced over her shoulder to see the inquisitive expressions of the people in the queue.

The table in the workroom was cluttered with paterae dishes and boxes of incense—not the heady scent of expensive myrrh but cheap ground pine and juniper bark. In the corner, the great eagle perched on its stand. It swiveled its head to fix the women with its cold eyes. The sacred geese of Uni were corralled in a covered pen, scrawny and subdued. Usually they were plump and vocal, allowed to roam free in the sanctuary. Perhaps Lady Tanchvil thought it too great a temptation for the hungry to commit sacrilege and add them to a pot.

Semni was daunted at being in close proximity with the high priestess, who towered over her in statuesque elegance. Her white chiton was plain, decorated only with a broad border of scarlet. A single crimson tassel hung from one shoulder, a symbol of the princip's status. As the augur took her seat on a stool, Semni caught a glimpse of short red laced boots on broad feet.

The hatrencu beckoned Tas to stand in front of her. "I found Vel Mastarna Junior creeping into my temple. I've spoken to him severely. I did not realize there was a secret passageway." Her tone was stern. "Don't try to come here again, Tas. I will not have my temple infiltrated even by so small an intruder."

He nodded, voice solemn. "Yes, Lady Tanchvil."

"Good boy." The priestess's eyes met the wet nurse's. "You should take better care of your charge."

Semni bristled at the admonishment, feeling it unfair. How was she to know Prince Tarchon had not identified all the passages? And she'd no idea Tas would be so disobedient. She grasped his hand, shaking it. "What were you thinking going through the tunnel?"

He stuck out his chin. "I wasn't afraid. Uncle Artile and Aricia showed me how to use the passages safely. Once I reached the Great Gallery, I found the tunnel from our old house to the temple."

"Great Gallery?"

"There's a cave where various tunnels beneath the citadel intersect," said Aricia. She crouched beside the boy. "My pet. What you did was very dangerous. It's a warren down there. You could've become lost. What if your torch had blown out?"

Lady Tanchvil clapped her hands to gain attention. "Enough. It's time the prince was taken home." She leaned over the table, selecting a fresh sheet of papyrus from a pile, and then picked up her stylus to write a missive. "You must give this letter to the queen, Semni. I must explain that Aricia had no part in this."

Semni curtsied and took the scroll. "Come with me," she said, taking Tas's hand. To her annoyance, the boy twisted away, remaining next to the hatrencu. "Please, what about my dream?"

The seer frowned and placed her hand on his shoulder. "What you've told me about the bull and wolf was just a nightmare, my prince. Such visions aren't delivered by the deities. The Veiled Ones speak to the gods, who then send omens by lightning and thunder, or reveal celestial will in the livers of beasts or the flight of birds."

"But I want to be a soothsayer."

She smiled. "Perhaps one day. But for now you must heed your mother and father and not run away from your nurse." She gestured to Semni. "Take him. I have work to do." She flipped open the fold of a linen book lying on the table. "I still hope to solve the mystery of Lake Albanus."

Aricia stepped forward. "May I accompany them to the palace, my lady?"

Absorbed in her study, Lady Tanchvil did not look up. "Very well," she muttered. "But don't linger, Aricia. The evening rites need to be performed."

Semni was unimpressed, still suspicious of Aricia's intentions. She pulled Tas behind her as she walked into Queen Uni's chamber. Aricia picked up her pace and grabbed Semni's elbow, leading her into a corner away from the statue and worshipers. "Please understand," she whispered. "I didn't know Tas would come here."

The wet nurse glanced around her, conscious she did not want to be overheard. "I don't believe you. Did you encourage him when you visited the palace that day?"

"No!"

Tas tugged Semni's chiton. "I found the tunnel myself. I've been searching the house for months for symbols of the sphinx. Tarchon didn't find the one in the storeroom." He smiled at his former nursemaid. "I missed Aricia. She's the only one who understands I want to be a seer."

Aricia patted his head. "Nevertheless, you should not have tried to find me, my pet."

Semni kept her voice low. "Tas entered a cursed room because of his need to tell you of his vision."

"What do you mean a cursed room?"

"One with an entry hatch decorated with a gorgon's face. Inside there was a vanth guarding a pile of burned bricks."

Aricia blanched. "Mother told me about this. Before the war began, a thunderbolt hit the palace. Because it was an ill omen, the lightning was buried and the place where it struck sealed. Expiation rites were conducted, but the demoness must still stand guard." She crouched in front of Tas. "Weren't you frightened by the vanth?"

His composure was unnerving. "I was scared at first, but then she let me pass unharmed."

Aricia stroked his hair. "But you were treading where evil had been interred, my pet."

The expression in his gold-flecked cat eyes was calm. "A fulgurator should not be afraid to view the prodigy of a god."

Semni shook his hand. "But you're not a fulgurator. You're a little boy!"

Placing the prince in front of her, she guided him toward the doorway. Now that her panic had lessened, she took more notice of the supplicants. A few were coughing, sweat beading their brows. A man was holding a little girl in his arms. She lay limp, her face and arms covered with bright-red splotches. Semni scanned the chamber. Children stood with swollen bellies and stick limbs. Their parents were also thin, clothes loose on gaunt frames. Her gaze traveled to the votives. Effigies of swaddled babies and the busts of children abounded. Semni felt her gut tighten. These people were not just seeking divine intervention to end this siege. They sought to save their children.

Desperate to escape from the disease, she gripped Tas's hand and raced across the portico and down the stairs. She was frantic to reach the forum and the safety of the palace. She heard Aricia limping after her, calling for her to stop.

Tas struggled to keep pace. "Not so fast, Semni." She didn't heed him until he tripped, falling onto his knees. She halted, helping him to his feet, aghast his flesh was skinned raw from the cobblestones.

"I'm sorry," she said, lifting him into her arms. He wrapped his legs around her waist, his arms around her neck, and rested his head upon her shoulder. He was heavy compared to Nerie. She placed her hands under his bottom, bearing his weight.

Aricia caught up, catching her breath.

Semni glanced back to the crowd in the sanctuary. "That child has the red scourge. I suffered from it when I was young. One of my brothers died from the same. Do you think there will be a plague?"

Aricia grimaced. "You've been spoiled living within the palace. The sickness is everywhere. Why do you think there's a crush to seek divine protection? If it's not to cure the pestilence, it's to make offerings for those who have died. Here on the citadel where the rich live, you can't see the heartbreak. But go below into the streets and marketplaces of the city, and you'll see only despair and desolation."

She pointed to the huge cistern in the square. "Look around you. We've water but no food. The enemy blockades were tightened after the king's army broke through them. And those supplies that were bartered through the stockades for a time weren't enough to feed a city. Veii is teeming with people. Peasants from the countryside have fled behind its walls to seek protection from the Romans who ravage their farms. The grain ration is too scant to sate hunger. The cattle have long ago been eaten. Now dogs and cats and even rodents have become food. Any bird that flies over the city is shot down. Some citizens are reduced to boiling nettles and eating snails and insects. If the king does not deliver us soon, the only rites recited will be those for funerals."

Semni stared at her in horror, then surveyed the double gates of Uni at the end of the forum. A line of people was queued on the single road from the city. More of the ill, more of the anxious, more of those seeking hope.

She eased Tas to the ground, aware their conversation would be frightening him. He clutched her skirt, observing the crowd, eyes troubled. "Come on," she urged. "I need to get you home."

Reaching the steps of the palace, Semni could see Aricia's confidence fading. The novice gazed with apprehension at the huge bronze-studded doors at the entrance. Semni was filled with sympathy for the girl. Tas had embroiled her in a predicament that was none of her doing. "I don't think it's wise for you to be seen. Let's go around to the service lane."

Aricia bit her lip. "No. I should make it clear to Lady Caecilia that I had no part in the prince's outing."

Semni wished that Cytheris could see how earnest her daughter was to prove she'd mended her ways. She rested her hand on her arm. "This is not the best time to press your case. I'll give Lady Tanchvil's letter to the queen and also tell her you were not at fault."

"But don't you want me to assure Lady Caecilia that you weren't involved?"

Semni hesitated. She'd not thought that she might be seen as complicit. Yet the high priestess's letter should also absolve her of being a conspirator. "No, it's best you go."

Aricia bent down and gave Tas a hug.

He clung to her neck. "I didn't mean to get you in trouble."

"Promise me you'll never try and see me again, my pet."

Semni felt pity for the girl again. She reached across and pecked Aricia's cheek after she extracted the prince. "Good-bye, my friend."

Aricia smiled. "It means much that you think of me fondly."

The sudden shouts of male voices drowned out further conversation. Semni turned. Foreboding in their black uniforms, Arruns and two lictors raced down the palace steps. The Phoenician glowered at the two girls. Under his scrutiny, Aricia backed away and then limped as fast as she could toward the sanctuary.

Trembling at the approach of the guards, Tas gripped Semni's hand. "I think I've made a big mistake."

THIRTY-ONE

Semni was fuming as she settled Thia into her cot. Arruns had refused to speak to her. Instead he'd turned on his heel, not waiting for her to catch up as he strode into the palace.

Cytheris was similarly unimpressed when she sighted Semni and Tas. She snatched the boy's hand away from her. "Where have you been? Half the palace guard has been looking for you and the prince!"

At least Lady Caecilia had not judged Semni without hearing the full tale. The queen's relief at seeing her eldest son safely home had soon been replaced with shock when she heard where he'd been. She had scanned Lady Tanchvil's missive, her brow creasing in realization that the prince had once again been drawn to Aricia like iron filings to a lodestone. The dismay in her round hazel eyes was painful to watch.

After hugging her son, Lady Caecilia had then berated him and decreed his punishment. The boy was sent to bed with a sore bottom after Arruns dispensed a spanking. Despite showing bravery enough to traverse a forbidden room and the pitch black of a tunnel, the child's courage failed him at the hard edge of the lictor's hand. At each slap he'd sobbed. His mother had sat white faced and tense but did not rescind her sentence.

Semni patted and rubbed Thia's back until the baby closed her eyes and was ready to be placed in her cradle. Then she lay down beside Nerie, who was fast asleep on her bed. He'd been fretful tonight. Usually content to have his place usurped by the princess at his mother's breast, he'd been possessive, trying to push Thia away and sit on Semni's lap alone.

Sleep eluded her. She was seething that Arruns had assumed her guilty. Even when he'd heard Tas's admission, he'd not apologized.

She drew on her chiton and shoved her feet into slippers. Crossing pools of light and shadow in the torchlit hallways, she navigated her way to the barracks. She dragged the curtain open to Arruns's cell door, then swept it closed behind her.

He was sharpening his dagger in the lamplight, the metal scraping rhythmically against whetstone. He stood when he saw her, frowning.

Semni launched herself at him, shoving him. "Why do you always think the worst of me?"

He staggered back a step, caught off balance by the surprise of her attack. Not waiting for a reply, she pummeled him on the chest with puny fists. "I went to retrieve Tas. I didn't take him to the temple!"

The knife and whetstone clattered to the floor. He caught hold of both her wrists. She struggled against him but could do little but flail her elbows as she tried to free herself to hit him.

"What more can I do to convince you to trust me?" she hissed. "I stopped lying with other men to prove I could be faithful. I became a better mother to Nerie when you told me I was neglectful. I confessed to the master and mistress and risked being expelled for you." His calm silence was infuriating. She wriggled her hands, resisting again. "Why don't you answer me?"

He was gruff. "I believe you had no part in what happened today. That's not why I'm angry with you. I saw you kissing Aricia's cheek. I told you not to befriend her again. She means more to you than me if you choose to ignore my wish. She deserves no forgiveness."

She gasped in frustration, the injustice scalding her. He was condemning her for a moment's affection for a girl who was contrite. "No one should be blamed forever. And don't tell me what I can and can't do."

He held her fast, his fingers manacles. "If you are to be my wife, then you should obey me."

"And I don't want to be your wife if you don't trust me!" She thrashed against him, then, maddened he would not let her go, she bent her head and sank her teeth into his hand.

Grunting in surprise, he released her, examining the bite mark. Semni ran to one end of the bench and grabbed the pitcher and threw it at him. He deftly caught it and placed it on the worktable. Infuriated, she reached for the ewer, ready to launch the next missile, but before she could grab it, he lunged and enveloped her in a bear hug, restraining her arms against her sides.

Her cheek pressed against the cloth of his uniform as she struggled against his strength. She was incensed he could so easily control her, conscious also that he could crush her ribs with the merest increase of pressure. "Let me go!"

He continued to pin her against him. "Are you going to stop trying to hurt me?"

She squirmed, but resisting his iron embrace was tiring. She relaxed. She could hear his heart thudding, the beat slow and calming. "You can let me go. I promise to stop."

He dropped his arms from around her, but as he shifted back, she clasped his forearms, a different emotion rising. "Hold me."

He hesitated, but she encircled his neck. "Hold me," she whispered into his ear, nipping the lobe. "I want you." He inhaled and closed his eyes, his body tense, but he did not move away. She grazed her mouth across his, her teeth tugging at his lower lip. At her teasing, he groaned and wrapped his arms around her waist, lifting her to sit on the bench. She gasped at the force and speed of his embrace but as he slid his hands along her thighs under her chiton, she gripped his wrists. "Not yet. I want to see all of you," she said, releasing him to unbuckle his belt and tug at the sides of his uniform. Impatient, he pulled his tunic over his head, throwing it to the floor in one fluid movement, then reached for her again, but she still held him at bay, her arm straight, one hand pressed against his chest.

Her eyes followed the coil of the serpent. It was narrow as it twisted around his massive neck, then gradually thickened as the scales wrapped around the musculature of his chest, waist, and abdomen, before tapering again around his hips down to his groin to disappear into his thatch. She smiled. His penis was erect and ready. The snake was not two headed but it had a tail.

"Don't make me wait," he growled, seizing the shoulder of her dress, ripping it in his haste. She smiled, wriggling out of the shift, her hair tumbling down her naked back and breasts. Then she wrapped her legs around his waist. As he pushed into her, her nails dug into the flesh of his back, and she dragged them downward, raking the scales of the snake. Arruns arched for a moment, then pumped harder. Semni tightened her legs around him, locking her ankles across each other, determined not to let him go until they had both finished, wanting his power and heat, waiting for the moment when his seed would flow into her.

• • •

His breathing was ragged. Hers also. Semni laid her head against his shoulder, his sweat coating her cheek. They said nothing, their body heat cooling. After a time, he carried her to the pallet so they could hold each other.

"I have heard of fighting tooth and nail," he murmured. "I did not think making love would be the same."

"Well, you promised me it would be worth waiting to see the other end of the snake. I wasn't disappointed."

He didn't comment, but in the failing light of the oil lamp, she noticed him smile.

Thoughts of what she'd seen at the temple surfaced. If the red scourge spread, not even palace walls would protect those inside. And the prospect of starving now seemed real. She didn't think she could bear to watch Nerie dying of either plague or famine: his little body skeletal, his belly bloated, his eyes dull. She couldn't bear to lose Arruns either. "It was frightening to walk through the citadel tonight. The sickness is coming. Are you afraid of dying?"

Solemn, he turned on his side, observing her. "I try not to dwell on it. Instead I'm determined no man will kill me. I would prevent others taking you and Nerie, too. And the royal family."

"Fists and daggers cannot battle hunger and disease. You could perish from a rash instead of a wound. Hunger may deprive you of the strength to defend yourself."

His eyes flickered. "I have faith in the master."

"Why do you believe in him so much? He's a man like any other."

"Perhaps, but his courage is without limit, and he's wily. If anyone is to find a way to rescue this city, then it will be him. I owe him my life."

"And he owes his life to you! The debt has been repaid." She thought of how Arruns suppressed his frustration at his master not taking him to war. "Don't you resent him for leaving you behind?"

He pressed his lips into a hard line. "He expects me to protect the queen and children. It's not my place to question his decision. And now I've breached my promise to him by lying with you."

His retreat into duty irritated her. "I don't regret what we did. We should enjoy life while we can." She ran her fingers along one corded vein on his forearm. "My milk is drying up. I don't know how much longer I'll be able to nurse Thia. I don't think Lord Mastarna would be angry now. I know Lady Caecilia would understand."

He engulfed her hand with his palm. "And what if you fall with child? You should've let me pull out of you like I did the first time. You know I don't believe that another son should be born into war. What awaits him? A lingering death by starvation? A fevered ending by the scourge?"

"I want your child, Arruns. I don't care if there is a war."

He sat up. "We must not do this again. We must wait until you're released from your duties as a wet nurse. And that will only happen when Lord Mastarna returns. I don't want to betray his trust."

She frowned, frustrated he should retreat back to observing an unfair vow. Determined to persuade him to change his mind, she rose and kneeled on the pallet, bending and running her tongue along the channel between the muscles of his chest and abdomen to his groin. She heard his sharp intake of breath as she grasped the snake's tail, his body responding as she planned. "And this serpent? What does he want?"

"You are wicked."

"No, I'm hungry. And so is the snake."

CRISIS

THIRTY-TWO

Caecilia, Veii, Spring, 396 BC

The stench hovered in a pall, death and ordure and smoke intertwined with the sadness of weird keening desolation. Caecilia gagged and pressed a kerchief saturated with her lily perfume to her nose as she sat beside Tarchon in the royal carriage.

Bodies were piled in the street, ready to be fed into pyres. The cadavers were stacked high, a grotesque fuel for fires that otherwise used dung for combustion. A city of the living was being turned into one of the dead. Exhausted, survivors tended the sick and dying, wondering if they would be next. Caecilia's eyes pricked with tears to see how many of the corpses were those of children. The red scourge marked the young as its favorite victims.

People trudging along the pavement stopped when they saw their queen, bowing their heads as she passed. Some were emaciated, death's heads instead of faces, their lips cracked, eyes bloodshot. All wore dark mourning clothes. The rainbow of blue and green and brown denoting class distinctions had disappeared. Everyone was equal now, unified by grief.

Caecilia signaled the driver to stop and called to Arruns to lift her down. He shook his head. "No, mistress." She pursed her lips at his disobedience, but before she could insist, Tarchon restrained her. "He's right, Caecilia. Even with twelve lictors, your safety can't be assured."

She shrugged him away. Since she'd declared her own war on Rome, there'd been no hostility toward her from the people. She only wished their acceptance did not go hand in hand with defeat. "I want to speak to them."

"What are you going to say that will make a difference? There is no more food to give, no medicines to offer, no wood to provide. You come with empty hands. What use is royal sympathy?"

"At least they'll see that I have not forgotten them or fear them. Unlike Feluske, who locks himself away. He may be a general, but he is spineless."

"There's good reason to fear the red scourge. I suffered from it and survived when I was a child in Tarchna. Can you claim the same protection?"

Caecilia shook her head. The thought she might contract the disease terrified her, but she couldn't let fear keep her from her duty. And she believed Vel would feel the same. "Palace walls will not protect any of us from the sickness. Many are already stricken within. All I can do is hope that Queen Uni does not wish me to die just yet." She extended her hand to Arruns. "Help me to the pavement."

Tarchon grasped her shoulder. "I said no."

His vehemence surprised her. She hesitated, debating whether to let her own obstinacy challenge his, but then she decided to heed him, her courage failing as she heard the hacking coughs among those standing nearby.

"Move on," she ordered the driver. Once again, she pressed the kerchief to her nose. Raw sewage ran along the gutters, and she glimpsed side streets piled with human waste, flies hovering and rats scampering over it, while scabrous dogs, too diseased to be eaten by humans, slunk into alleyways. Caecilia prayed the cisterns would not be contaminated. If so, there would be thirst as well as hunger.

With the influx of peasants who'd fled from the brutality of the Romans, the city teemed with people. All sought accommodation now they were bereft of their land and their livelihood. Those without relatives were sleeping in the open, their makeshift shelters forming slums.

Caecilia felt helpless. There was a pull toward futility, only her belief in Uni sustaining her. And yet, why was the deity so cruel? Why had she seemingly forsaken her people? It had been over a month since Vel had left. At least with the arrival of spring, she knew he would be in Velzna at the congress. She tried not to think what would happen if he failed.

In the forum, Caecilia noticed a scaffold with four bodies dangling from nooses, flies crawling over sightless eyes and protruding tongues.

"They're thieves who stockpiled food and then sold it at extortionate prices in the black market," said Tarchon. "I'm trying to see justice is served even though our world is disintegrating around us."

Caecilia turned her head rather than view the criminals, always queasy at such sights. A crowd had collected. The people held out their hands, beseeching, their voices plaintive. This time she did not heed the prince's restraining hand on her shoulder. She ordered the driver to stop and shrugged Tarchon away. Stepping down into the street, she walked to the platform where the town crier would normally stand to make proclamations. Arruns hurried after, signaling the lictors to form a cordon at its base. With a scowl, Tarchon joined her. "Mastarna will kill me if you're harmed."

Ignoring him, she held up her hands. She was surprised at how obediently the people ceased their pleading. A quiet descended, the only sound that of a flapping awning that had come loose on a deserted shop.

Caecilia scanned the host of the wretched who were now her subjects. "Veientanes, I see your suffering, and my heart bleeds for you. I see your children dying. I have faith, though, that King Vel Mastarna will relieve this city."

A man, eyes hollow, called out, "But when? When will he come?"

"Only the gods know for sure, but I believe in my husband."

A woman pushed through to the front. "The gods have forsaken us, Aemilia Caeciliana. And what offerings do we have to appease them? There are no animals to sacrifice, no wine to pour libations."

"Then we must promise them a reward if they answer our prayers. And when the lucumo returns, and supplies once again flow, we will lavish gifts upon them."

There was a silence again. The flapping of the awning seemed even louder. She scanned the weary faces, praying blank stares would not turn into glares, that skin and bone would not rise up and attack her. Then she remembered the ambition and cruelty of the enemy generals. "Do you wish to surrender?" she called. "Do you wish to relinquish Veientane land and kneel to the Romans? If so, then speak, but consider whether it's better to die a citizen of Veii than a slave of Rome. Is it not better to live in hope of rescue than exist in despair forever?"

Tarchon leaned close. "Enough. There's no point to this."

She ignored him. "Tell me. Let me know your will. And if it's to cede defeat, then I'll ask Prince Tarchon to yield his spear to the enemy on behalf of Veii."

There was a murmur, glances exchanged, bewilderment that they were being offered a choice. A man with skull-like features raised his fist into the air. "No surrender." His call was repeated: "No surrender." The phrase echoed, filling the air where only minutes before there'd been silence. The chanting continued. Caecilia felt relief sweep through her as fiercely as the elation on the day she'd declared war on Rome. Tarchon stood incredulous, surveying the mob before him. Again he spoke to her, but she could not hear his words above the noise. Smiling, she turned to him, expecting him to be buoyant, but instead he was glowering. He offered his forearm, leaning closer than before. "No argument. It's time to go."

• • •

Caecilia gulped in fresh air, staring down from the ramparts of the arx to the city below. Usually she found peace here, remembering a time when she would study the flight of hawks gliding on the updrafts. Now even the birds did not hover over Veii. Instead she gazed down on the sight of hundreds of black puffs wafting from funeral pyres, grim evidence of the despairing world beneath the vast, cloudless blue realm of the gods.

Tarchon stood beside her, his back to the city below. "You had no right to let them decide. Only the war council can determine whether we should capitulate. What would have happened if the people wanted to yield?"

"But they didn't. I sensed it would be so."

He sighed. "What has happened to you, Caecilia? No wonder Mastarna is exasperated with you. You've become reckless, whereas before you used to seek to control your fate. You encourage feats that have no surety, first wanting to march on Rome and now asking the people to believe Mastarna will save us."

"Vel will succeed. This time he will convince the Twelve to bear arms."

"Wishing won't make it so."

"So what do you want to do, Tarchon? Vel appointed you as regent. Are you going to lead Veii into submission?"

His hesitation was alarming. "Lusinies and Feluske are thinking of asking for a truce. We did not foresee a plague. We have no idea how long before help will arrive—or if it will come at all. At this rate, the Romans may force entry into a city full of weakened soldiers and citizens riddled with disease."

She balled her fists. "You know Rome is not going to treat. Peace will come with subjugation." Her voice rose. "Vel directed that I sit on any war council. Why wasn't I consulted? Are you and the generals excluding me?"

He reddened, indignant. "We have not gone behind your back. The matter was raised informally."

She regretted her accusation. "I'm sorry. Forgive me. It's just that I'm so fearful. Don't you think I worry that Vel might already be dead? That I must watch my children waste away? Or that our people will perish? Sometimes I wonder if it might be best that I surrender myself to Rome . . . but I am too much of a coward."

Tarchon put his arm around her. "You have always been brave, Caecilia. Foolish sometimes, and too stubborn, but definitely brave."

She pulled away. If anything, his sculpted features were even more beautiful in their gauntness. "And who would have thought you would grow sensible. So sober and wise."

"It's easy to be temperate when there's not enough wine to get drunk, nor Catha leaves to take the edge off my worries."

"You joke, but what I say is true. Vel would be proud of you. And you are seeing to your duties diligently."

"There is little work to do. It's no use trying to extract taxes from a populace who is destitute. And what use is a treasury full of gold and jewels that cannot be eaten?"

"Vel will come. Then the coin in those coffers will once again prove useful."

"What we need is more grain to ration." He pointed toward the countryside beyond the plateaued city. "We need our farmland to be harvested."

Caecilia also studied the greening furrowed fields beyond. It made her bitter knowing the crops that would burgeon there were destined for Roman bellies. They reminded her, too, that the stone walls of Veii had become her prison. One day she'd hoped to visit the sea in Tarchna to understand the life Vel had once led. She'd wished to meet his kin, the Atelinas family of his mother, who were also Tarchon's cousins. "Do you miss your relatives in Tarchna?"

Tarchon appeared quizzical at the sudden change of topic. "I barely remember my brothers, Caecilia, and my mother and father are dead. Veii has been my home for nearly twenty years. And who wouldn't welcome living in the house of the richest man in Veii compared to struggling on a meager inheritance as the youngest of seven brothers? Even now Mastarna is earning wealth although he has no way to receive the money. His Tarchnan captains still sail his fleet of ships to trade with Carthage and Athens. And he owns interests in tin and iron mines in the Tolfa Hills. Mastarna adopted me to give me a better life. I don't regret moving here despite Veii being under siege."

"He also adopted you to place a barrier between you and Artile. As your uncle, he should never have touched you."

Tarchon reddened. She regretted speaking. Neither of them wanted to remember the priest who'd manipulated them.

"I don't want to think about that part of my life. Artile broke all the rules when he took me to his bed when I was a child. I should've become the beloved of a warrior statesman when I was fifteen or sixteen." Tarchon clasped her hand. "Do you think Karcuna might actually agree to let me be Sethre's mentor?"

She nodded. "I think so. When he sees how you have taken your responsibilities seriously."

"You once disapproved of such arrangements. What has changed your mind?"

Caecilia smiled. When she'd first come to Veii, she'd been blinkered and ignorant, seeing only faults in its society. Roman virtues were all she knew. But now she understood Vel's own mentor had taught him to be a great soldier, patron, and statesman. If Tarchon could prove his worth, then he was entitled to the same chance with Sethre. And he was an able teacher. She spoke and read the Rasennan language because of him. And he'd opened her eyes to her own unfounded prejudices. Protected her, too. Rome would demand she despise him but she'd said farewell to that legacy of intolerance. She squeezed his hand and kissed his cheek. "You."

THIRTY-THREE

The rash appeared on the third day. The inflammation stained Larce's skin, first behind his ears, then, within hours, spreading over his face and neck, his chest and tummy, until his little body was scarlet.

When the child was not burning, he would shiver, his teeth chattering, the fever gripping him in a violent chill. He lay with his eyes half closed, his breathing labored as he coughed. The spasms denied him sleep.

Caecilia felt powerless. There was no cure. There were not even herbs to assist him. No mint or marshmallow to soothe the cough, no borage or hyssop to bring down the fever. All she could do was offer comfort. Propped against the bed's headboard, she helped Larce to sip honeyed water as she held him. The sight of his rib cage protruding beneath stretched flesh was piteous.

She would not leave him. She was not prepared to risk others in the house being infected. She alone bathed his body, changed the bedclothes, and peeled damp nightgowns from him. Even the task of dressing him seemed to exhaust him.

Her guilt gnawed at her. Why had she gone into the city? Why had she placed duty to the people above her own children? She'd brought the scourge home with her. Would Vel forgive her for such recklessness?

Cytheris would visit, pleading to take over the vigil to give her mistress respite. She had suffered and survived the scourge when she was young. The fact others had lasted gave Caecilia hope Larce would also be spared. Doubt pricked her, though. She could not forget that the majority of bodies burned in pyres were those of children, a horrific kindling.

She coaxed Larce from his lassitude to take nourishment, holding the palmette-shaped spoon of porridge to his mouth so he could eat, tipping a spouted cup to his lips so he could drink. She longed to see the sweet gleam in his brown eyes instead of a dull, pained expression.

When he managed to gain relief from the coughing and fall asleep, she would lie on her side next to him, studying him as he slumbered, pushing his lank hair from his brow, stroking his flushed cheeks. She was reluctant to sleep herself, keeping watch that he was breathing. She was terrified she might miss his passing, aware there was only one second between this world and the next. She needed to be awake, desperate to kiss his lips and breathe in his soul so that she could release him to the Good Ones.

At times she would hear Thia crying in the nursery, sobbing for her mother's attention. And Tas and Arnth's voices were often heard in the hallway, pleading with Semni or Cytheris to allow them to enter. Each time, she fought back the urge to go to them, determined the scourge be contained within her chamber.

In the back of her mind she heard Artile's voice. How he had predicted that she and Vel would have a son who would bear a son. Would only one of her boys survive to manhood?

She exhorted Uni to save them all. Then Aplu, the god of light and healing, who also cherished children. She wrestled with the thought of which child the gods might spare. She loved each of her children in different ways.

She remembered her relief when she realized she was pregnant with Tas. Thrilled that Uni had pardoned her for her foolish and frightened attempts to defer a child. Her pride in bearing her firstborn still remained. The wonder of holding a new babe to her breast for the very first time could never be repeated. The joy of finally handing a son to Vel had been overwhelming. Yet Tas was solitary and perplexing, reluctant to display affection. She found it difficult to understand him. She worried there would always be distance between them.

When Larce was born, she'd feared she would have no more love to give. But she'd soon discovered that love was not finite. It expanded each time she bore another child.

Arnth had been Vel's from the start. His little soldier. A small replica of his father, with his sturdy limbs and curls, despite possessing the round eyes of his mother. He'd inherited Vel's wildness and quick temper as well. She knew he was born to lead. She imagined him kissing her good-bye as a young warrior, his love for her restricted to one small corner of his mind while he sought lovers and adventures.

Death had lurked in the birthing room as she labored with Thia. Caecilia was proud she had fought to free the babe from the womb. And there was a selfish contentment that a girl could be kept close compared to the boys. A daughter could be coddled, while sons needed to be toughened for war. Vel clearly felt the same. To see the seasoned soldier coo and dandle his little princess always made her smile.

Caecilia loved all her children, but she could not deny Larce was her dearest. And this caused her shame, knowing she should not choose a favorite. Yet she had a special bond with him that transcended her feelings for the others. There was a beauty within him, the symmetry of his features an echo of Tarchon's. As a baby, he would purr as she nuzzled his neck, a smile always ready upon his lips. As he grew older, he liked to run his finger over the birthmark on her throat, laughing when she teased him that it was a paint splash made by the gods. Even after he had learned to walk on steady feet, he would seek her hand, swinging arms as they walked along. There was little jealousy in him either. He held out his arms to cuddle Arnth and Thia when they were born.

Now, watching him lying limp on her bed, a tiny figure on the broad expanse of linen, Caecilia wondered how she would function if he died. She lived with the constant worry of the loss of her warrior husband, a dull ache that flared to sharp panic in the small hours of the morning. But she never expected to face the same anguish over a child, that she might bury one of her children instead of them chanting the death rites over her.

"Ati, Ati!" Larce struggled to sit.

"Hush," she crooned, drawing him onto her lap. "Hush. I'm here."

"I saw the blue demon," he sobbed. "He was laughing and holding a hammer. He was going to hit me on the head to make sure I was dead."

She rocked him. "Ssh, it was just a dream. There are no monsters here."

"But the blue demon will be there when I die." He clutched her. "I don't want to be alone in Acheron. I want you to be there."

His pleading tore at her. She crushed him against her. Suddenly the Roman spirit world of the Good Ones seemed one of terror and nothingness. How could she tell him he was destined to dissolve and merge with the Shades? Larce needed solace, not dread. She wished Vel were here to hold them. He hadn't been present at the birth of any of their children. How would he feel to be absent when one died?

She felt the bulla pendant on Larce's necklace hard against her breast. Calming herself, she eased his arms from her neck and drew the coverlet around them for warmth. She slipped the chain over his head, showing him the tiny gold figurine.

"See Fufluns's dolphin? Apa gave it to you to protect you from the evil eye. The dolphin will guide you across the Great Sea in Acheron."

The boy stroked the amulet with his forefinger. "So I will be safe in the Beyond even when I die?"

She brushed the hair from his brow and kissed him. "When you journey to the Afterworld, you will meet all your family at a banquet. Grandmother and grandfather are already there."

"So we will be together again?"

She replaced the bulla around his neck, patting the dolphin. Suddenly, acknowledging the power of the wine god's creature gave her hope. If Larce was going to be taken from her, then she wanted to believe she'd see him again. "Yes, Apa and Tas and Arnth and Thia. All of us, forever."

Larce encircled her waist with his arms, laying his head on her chest. She noticed the rash behind his ears was turning brown. His skin was cool against hers. His fever had broken. Relieved, she murmured a prayer of thanks to both Uni and Fufluns.

"Why are you are shivering, Ati, when your skin is hot?"

She realized she could not stop trembling, her muscles contracting, the rigors uncontrollable. Her teeth chattered as she spoke. "It's nothing, my love."

"My lady!"

Cytheris stood at the doorway holding Arnth by the hand. When the servant saw how her mistress was shaking, she hurried to her, lifting the boy to sit on the edge of the bed. He was listless and coughing, his eyes leaden.

Larce crawled over to sit next to his brother. "Ati, Arnth has a paint splash just like yours behind his ear."

Caecilia closed her eyes, hoping when she reopened them the evidence of the telltale rash on Arnth's skin would have vanished.

Instead the scarlet flush remained. Head aching, limbs achy, she lay down, holding out her arms. "Bring him to me."

The handmaid helped Arnth lie beside his mother. Even with her own fever, Caecilia could feel his temperature was high. He nestled against her, whimpering. The sound cut like a knife. Her youngest was not one to whine. "Cytheris, why didn't you tell me sooner?"

"I'm sorry, mistress. His fever has been mild and only worsened today. The rash has visited him quicker than I've seen before." She pressed her palm against Caecilia's forehead. "You're ill, too."

"Don't worry about me. What of Tas and Thia?"

"Semni's milk protects the princess. And Tas is yet untouched."

Caecilia nodded, reassured. Larce sidled back to lie beside Arnth, his brief spurt of energy sapped.

Caecilia coughed, then coughed again. "And the others?"

"Perca and Cook are gravely ill. Semni forced Arruns to go to bed. He refused for a time, but now the sweats have gripped him."

Caecilia's guilt worsened. The red scourge was finding other victims she may have infected. Another rigor seized her.

Cytheris drew the quilt over the mother and sons. "Rest," she murmured. "I'll watch over you all."

Caecilia tried to demur, shivering, needing sleep but fearful once again. What if Arnth died before she awoke? What if she was the one to perish? And in that moment, she knew she must worship Fufluns. She needed to ensure she and her family would remain together forever.

The chair scraped across the tiles as Cytheris drew it next to the bed. "Sleep, mistress. I will wake you should Arnth worsen."

Eyelids heavy, Caecilia murmured her thanks. She was overcome with a yearning for Vel, needing him to be with her. She drifted into a fevered sleep, trying to conjure an image of him in the blackness between closed lid and tired eye.

Caecilia woke. Her mouth was dry. For a moment she was disoriented, wondering why she was sleeping in daytime.

She dug the heels of her hands into the mattress, pushing herself to sit, anxious to find Larce and Arnth. "Cytheris! Where are they?"

Dozing in a chair, the handmaid's eyes flew open at her mistress's croaky voice. "They're fine, my lady." She hastened to the bedside and reached for Caecilia's hand. "Larce is playing with Semni. And Arnth is sleeping in his room. The rash has almost faded. I thought it best to give you some peace. The fever has gripped you for days."

Caecilia was not ready to finish the roll call. "Tas and Thia?"

"The gods have spared them."

She found herself. Cytheris placed her arm around her. "There, there, mistress. The worst is over."

Caecilia broke from the maid's embrace and rested the back of her head against the headboard. "Bring them to me."

Cytheris hesitated. "Soon, but first let me bathe you and change your clothes. It's better you greet them with untangled hair and smelling clean." She bustled to the doorway, beckoning to the slave boy who was stationed outside to fetch hot water and fresh sheets.

"Come, my lady, let me help you to stand."

Too long in bed, Caecilia let the servant assist her to step onto the footstool and then the floor. The brief exercise tired her. She closed her eyes to let giddiness pass, then, with unsteady steps, walked to the armchair and sat down.

The slave boy returned with a pitcher. Cytheris dismissed him, then poured some hot water into the ewer, steam curling from the surface of the fluid. The handmaid's face was lined with fatigue. Her vigil had been lengthy.

"Cytheris, do you remember that day in the family sanctuary with Artile? When he predicted my future as a mother?"

The Greek woman paused in helping her mistress from her sweat-stained nightdress. "Yes. But why do you speak of the rogue now?"

"Because of what he said. That I would bear a son who would bear a son."

"And you have born three."

"But what if it means only one will survive to be a man? I kept dwelling on it as I lay watching my boys suffering with fever."

"You always worry too much, my lady. One may never marry, or sire only daughters. And one might be like Prince Tarchon, not interested in women at all."

Caecilia blinked, aware yet again how she could take a kernel of concern and let it swell into calamity. She hugged the maid, taking Cytheris off guard. "What is that for, my lady?"

"For being a good friend."

Nonplussed at the declaration, the servant eased herself from the embrace and then dipped the cloth into the bowl. "Lift your arms so I can wash you."

Caecilia felt childlike as she stood and held on to the chair for balance. Cytheris wiped her clean from armpit to hand, and between each finger. Then, sweeping the princip's loosely plaited hair to one side, she pressed the cloth along neck, shoulders, and spine before bathing breasts and belly. Caecilia closed her eyes as the handmaid smoothed the cloth along the swell of hips and buttocks, mound and inner thighs, before bending to wash the queen's long legs.

What had happened to the prudish girl who wore her ugly woolen stola as a shield? The Roman virtue of modesty had been instilled in Caecilia from childhood. She'd shied from intimacy, reluctant to stand naked before either man or woman. Yet Cytheris had encouraged her to welcome Vel's embrace. And he'd taught her there was no shame in sensuality or being greedy for sensation. To seek the touch and scents and tastes of passion. To forget Roman strictures and custom, and accept pleasure was not a sin.

She glanced down at her body. The rash was no longer livid but brown and fading in places. Cytheris fetched a fresh gown from the linen chest. The sheer fabric glided over Caecilia's skin, fine and soft and lovely.

"Tell me, is the rest of the household well?"

The Greek woman bowed her head, voice cracking. "Arruns has recovered, as has Perca, but Cook . . ."

It was the queen's turn to murmur solace, but at her touch Cytheris stiffened, composing herself, always mindful of keeping her emotions under control.

"I'll help you back to bed and fetch the children."

"No, wait." Caecilia pointed to the cista on the side table. "Bring me my paste and spatula. I can't greet them with a red-tipped nose and puffy face. The remnants of the rash will only frighten them."

As the servant covered tearstains with albumen and pale lips with carmine, Caecilia realized there was one more person who might not have survived. She turned her head. "And what of Aricia?"

Cytheris stopped combing. "I heard she's well, mistress."

Seeing the happiness on the maid's face, Caecilia knew the time had come to cast aside distrust. She guessed Cytheris's loyalty had stopped her from reconciling with her daughter. "You must visit her. Make peace. The plague has shown me that we must ensure words of love are not hoarded. Aricia has shown she is contrite. I've been stubborn in not forgiving her. And selfish in expecting you to do the same."

Cytheris beamed, her missing dogtooth revealed, not hiding her feelings this time. "Thank you, mistress. Thank you!"

She returned her smile, then bade her bring the children to her. Settling back onto the bed, Caecilia listened to her sons' piping,

eager voices drawing closer along the corridor, and murmured a
prayer of thanks to Uni for saving them.

THIRTY-FOUR

Semni, Veii, Spring, 396 BC

Cheeks flushed, eyes bright, Semni tugged at Arruns's hand, urging him to follow her to the stairs to the upper story. He refused to budge. "Why are you leading me to the loggia?"

"I've something to tell you, and I don't want anyone to hear."

He frowned. "I don't like the sound of that."

She tugged at him again. "Come on. I won't keep you long."

He hesitated, then let her lead him up the narrow stone steps.

At the top, she let go of his hand, walking to one of the caryatid columns sculpted in the shape of a woman. Grasping the pillar with one hand, she swung in a half circle, breathing in the fresh spring air.

Arruns moved across to her, studying her with a quizzical expression. "What is it? Why are you so happy?"

She clasped his hand, placing it on her belly. Her smile was wide. "I'm with child."

He pulled away as though scalded. "Are you sure?"

His appalled look spoiled her delight. It wasn't what she'd expected. "Yes, I'm sure. My flux has not come for two months."

She placed her hands against his chest, searching his face. "Aren't you pleased? I'm going to give you another son."

"I told you I want no child to be born into this war." He turned and leaned against the balustrade, staring down at the ashes of a funeral pyre smoldering in the square. "The worst of the plague is over, but we're still starving." His hooded eyes were hard. "I told you that you should not have let me come inside you."

Her temper flared; she didn't want to acknowledge she'd been reckless. Instead of using vinegar and brine to wash away his seed, she'd prayed he had planted a child within her. "I didn't think I could fall pregnant while I was breastfeeding . . . and what about the second time? And the third? You were careless, too."

"You made me forget myself. We should never have broken our vow to the master."

She placed her hands on her hips. "I've told you before, I have no more milk. We're no longer bound by his rules."

"That was not so when we defied him."

She glowered at him. "So this is my fault?"

"No, it's mine. I was weak." He resumed his scrutiny of the forum.

Semni strode to the end of the loggia, unable to bear being near him. She'd thought his reluctance to father a child would be forgotten with the joy of the news. Instead his first thought, as always, was his duty to Lord Mastarna. She rested her forehead against a caryatid, stifling the urge to cry. In the grim world of disease and famine, the discovery she carried new life had thrilled her. For a brief moment there had been hope instead of despair; now Arruns had reminded her she was deluded. What he said was true. She would bear a child who may well have no future.

She'd been disbelieving at first, wondering how she could vomit when deprived of food. She worried she was suffering from a different symptom of the red scourge, but there was no fever or cough. Then morning after morning she woke to nausea, and remembered how she'd felt when carrying Nerie. Only this time, the queasiness stirred excitement instead of apprehension.

Absorbed in her misery, she was startled when Arruns touched her shoulder. "I'm sorry, Semni. It's just that you surprised me."

She shrugged him away, leaning back against the pillar. "So what do you want me to do? Take a hot bath and try to massage him away? Climb up and down those stairs a hundred times to try to dislodge him? And if that doesn't work, use a rod to risk my life as well as his? Because there are no herbs left in this city to purge him from me."

He crushed her to him. "Stop it. Don't say such things."

She encircled his waist. "I thought you would be pleased."

He drew away. He was gaunt, his hook nose more prominent, dark circles beneath his eyes. His muscled body had shrunk with lack of food and exercise. He'd refused to let her nurse him at first, too proud to admit he needed help until the rigors felled him. The rash had marred his swarthy skin, even discoloring the blue tattooed snake.

"Don't you see, Semni? Loving you and Nerie has complicated my life. It was easy before. I didn't think about dying. I was invisible. Alone. No one to live for and no one to mourn my passing. Now I fear losing you and Nerie"—he placed his hand on her belly—"and the child of my flesh growing within you."

She covered his hand with hers. "Don't you think I feel the same? I thought you would die of the scourge."

He grimaced. "We may yet all die of starvation if Lord Mastarna doesn't arrive soon. You might not bear our son to term. Nerie may waste away."

She wasn't used to hearing bleakness in him. He was always so confident the king would return. But he was right. How could she nourish the baby within her if she could not feed herself? And her breasts were dry. Both Nerie and Thia had to make do with gruel. Her thoughts flickered to her son. The child who used to smile so readily was now solemn and lethargic. "Don't say that. Tell me you still believe in the lucumo."

Arruns turned once again to view the forum and the sanctuary of Uni beyond. "The gap in time where the king might relieve this city is closing. Falling ill to the red scourge has sown doubt in me." He placed his hand on her stomach again. His touch was tentative. "Can I feel him stir within you?"

She smiled. "It's too early. But he's in there growing. And we must believe the king will return."

"To see the proof of our disobedience as your belly swells."

Semni was frustrated with his gloom. "I'll speak to the queen. I know she thinks her husband's edict unfair. And I've seen how she can cajole Lord Mastarna from ill temper. I don't think he will be displeased for long."

He clasped her hand, leading her back to the stairs. "Perhaps, but we must wait to see what he says before we marry."

She pulled up short, twisting from him. "But you said you would wed me once Princess Thia was weaned!"

He sighed. "It's not so simple. You know that."

"Yes, it is. Lord Mastarna might never come. If so, I want to spend my last days as your wife. I want to live with you and Nerie as a family. I want the child inside me to feel the warmth of both his parents as they embrace in bed."

He closed his eyes. She could sense the struggle within him. To keep her distant would maintain his belief in Lord Mastarna.

She traced the serpent's forked tongue and fangs on his cheek. He opened his eyes again.

"Let's ask the queen for her permission, then." He kissed her. "Let's tell her about the baby and that I want to take you as my wife."

Thirty-Five

The strains of the lyre were poignant. Semni hesitated to interrupt the queen while she was playing. She knew she welcomed her solitude after attending to her daily duties and bidding her children good night.

Lady Caecilia sat in a wicker chair on the terrace in the fading light of the spring evening. She paused in her melody, resting the instrument on the claw-foot table beside her. She picked up the mirror with an ivory handle instead, examining its ornate back rather than gazing at her reflection.

Semni was nervous as she hovered at the door. Talk of a confession had slipped easily from her tongue when speaking to Arruns, but now she faltered. She'd broken faith once again with her mistress. She wished to speak to her alone first to ask forgiveness.

The princip sensed the nursemaid's presence. She turned from her scrutiny of the mirror. "Semni, is something wrong? Is Thia ill?"

Semni waved her hands, palms outward in reassurance. "No, my lady. Don't worry. The princess is sleeping."

The queen sighed. "I wish it were not hunger that feeds her exhaustion."

Semni felt a pang of guilt. "I'm sorry I have no more milk to give her."

It was the noblewoman's turn to gesture away concern. "You mustn't apologize. Your milk saved her from the scourge. It's not your fault you can no longer nourish her or your own son." She pointed to an empty chair nearby. "Come and sit down, and tell me why you're here."

Semni perched on the edge of the chair, her hands clasped. "I have come to beg forgiveness yet again, mistress."

Lady Caecilia's body tensed, her voice rising in alarm. "Is this about Tas?"

"No. It's about Arruns."

"But he has recovered from the pestilence, hasn't he?"

"Yes, my lady. He's well."

"I don't understand, then. Why are you speaking of compassion?"

Semni bowed her head. "We have broken our promise to Lord Mastarna."

The queen frowned in puzzlement, laying the mirror in her lap.

"He forbade us to lie as man and wife," prompted Semni.

The princip's shoulders relaxed. "Oh, I see. Well, I'm sure there will be more important issues to concern the king when he returns." She gave a small smile. "Besides, what my husband doesn't know won't hurt him."

"I fear he'll know soon enough, mistress."

Lady Caecilia reached forward and covered the girl's hands with her own. "Oh, Semni. You're with child? Aren't you delighted?"

She nodded, beaming. "Yes, yes. I'm very happy. But Arruns is upset we disobeyed Lord Mastarna."

The queen cocked her head to one side. "Then tell him not to fret. I know my husband. He once told me the Rasenna knew better than others how death stalks us. That in time Aita will deny us wine to drink, food to eat, and lips to kiss in this world. We are already deprived of the first two. As for the third—the king would not begrudge a man and woman snatching pleasure before they may be robbed of life."

"So you would have no objection to Arruns marrying me now that I can no longer act as a wet nurse? Do you think Lord Tarchon will give us permission in the lucumo's stead?"

Lady Caecilia squeezed her fingers. "Of course. And a wedding will cheer everyone's spirits."

The knot of apprehension in Semni's stomach dissolved. She slipped to her knees, kissing the queen's fingers. "Thank you, my lady. Thank you!"

Smiling, the princip withdrew her hand, knocking the mirror from her lap. Semni picked it up and stood, glancing at the engraving on its back. She recognized Areatha and Fufluns at once. Absorbed in each other, husband and wife were embracing, their lips a fraction from a kiss. The lovers' youthful features were beautiful as they stood surrounded by intertwined ivy and vines leaves. She handed the looking glass back to the queen. "May I go now, mistress?"

To her surprise, Lady Caecilia gestured the maidservant to resume her seat. "You worship Fufluns, don't you?"

Nonplussed, Semni sank into the chair. "Why, yes, mistress. I believe in the wine god."

"So you have been initiated in the Mysteries?"

"Yes, I'm a follower. I wish I could attend a Spring Festival, though. But none have been conducted since the war began. The people haven't been able to escape the city to revel under the stars."

The queen looked startled. "Then I was at the last one held."

"You were? I envy you, mistress."

Lady Caecilia frowned, then leaned forward. "But you have celebrated the Winter Feast, haven't you?"

The nursemaid nodded. "Before the Romans campaigned all year round, we could celebrate when the enemy returned home in winter. We would bid farewell to Fufluns, knowing he would sojourn in the Beyond until spring. In times past, the festival marked the laying down of the vintage."

"I remember it well. The people set light to the abandoned siege engines. Our foe's war machines became fuel for bonfires. And then the merrymaking would begin."

Semni was wistful. "I wish I could merge my spirit again. There has been no Winter Feast for two years."

The queen glanced at the mirror and then back to the girl.

"Tell me, what is it like to take communion with Fufluns?"

"Rapture, my lady, bliss."

Her answer did not appear to please the princip. She rubbed her temple as though soothing away pain. "But you were married then, weren't you? To the pottery workshop foreman. What did he think about you lying with other men?"

Semni was taken aback, unnerved at what had become an interrogation. "He was not a believer. He didn't approve but he didn't stop me."

"Didn't it worry you that you were being unfaithful?"

She reddened, thinking that she was ready to cuckold her old husband without the need for religion. "For believers, coupling with others in worship of Fufluns is a sacred union. You feel the god within you as your heart responds to the beat of the drum. The wine courses through you, strong and unwatered. You're dizzy as you dance. Filled with elation."

"You're intoxicated."

"You're possessed by the god's spirit through the wine's magic. It's like being in a trance."

Again Lady Caecilia paused, digesting each morsel of information. She glanced around her as though checking for eavesdroppers. "So you weren't whipped?"

Stunned by the question, Semni shook her head. Her father used to thrash her often enough. And it helped her sixty-year-old husband to harden if he birched her. But she'd never suffered pain at a Winter Feast. "No, my lady."

"And the possibility you might fall with child. Was that not a concern?"

Again the girl was surprised. Surely Lady Caecilia knew Nerie's blond father was a fellow worshiper? "It was a risk I took. The resin and alum plug failed when I lay with the man with the ram's head mask." She smiled. "But I don't regret bearing a son conceived on the night of the Winter Feast."

The princip's eyes widened. "I didn't realize . . . I always thought Nerie was a result of one of your many . . ."

"You mean from sleeping with any man who wanted me."

This time it was Lady Caecilia's turn to blush.

"Don't be embarrassed, mistress. I know I was a slattern before I met Arruns."

"And if you ever get the chance to reach ecstasy again, won't he be jealous?"

Her words gave Semni pause. She'd not thought about this. Yet Arruns had never complained that she followed the Pacha Cult.

"Fufluns is not his god, but I believe he sees the feast as part of a holy rite."

"And what about you? Would you be happy for him to seek epiphany with another woman?"

"You must understand, mistress, it's different under the mask. You are liberated from fear and care, jealousy and duty. There's just heat and madness. I'm no longer Semni. And he would no longer be Arruns. If he wished to follow Fufluns, I wouldn't deny him the chance to ward off death through seeking ecstasy."

She pointed to the decoration of entwined leaves on the edges of the mirror. "See the ivy? It's sacred to the wine god. It blooms in autumn and fruits in spring. It grows green in winter when the grape vine is dry and lifeless." She traced the grape leaves. "Vines give us the fruit of life. They are sunlight and warmth. Ivy is shadow and night. So too is Fufluns. You must accept light and dark when you worship him. And then you can forget mortal bonds for that brief moment in time."

"You speak with such passion, Semni. You make me understand a little more."

"May I ask why you ask all these questions, my lady?"

"Because I wish to follow the Pacha Cult as the king has asked. I want Fufluns's protection for me and my family in the Afterworld. But I revere Uni. I fear she wouldn't approve of me worshiping Fufluns."

"Veientane women have long worshiped both deities without being punished. We honor the divine queen as the guardian of our city, but all the Rasenna revere Fufluns. We turn to Uni to protect us in childbirth and give succor to our children, but it is the god of fertility who promises us resurrection." She pointed to the couple on mirror again. "Do you remember the day you came to the pottery and saw the last vase I ever painted? It depicted Fufluns and Areatha as well."

"Yes, I do. You were a skilled artisan."

"Thank you, mistress. I remember how you and Lord Mastarna held each other when he came to say good-bye before the battle." She ran her finger over the immortal pair etched into the silver. "Just like them, you had eyes for no other."

The queen bowed her head, examining the mirror again. "Yes, I love Vel very much."

Her mention of Lord Mastarna's first name surprised Semni. The queen never directly referred to him as such to any servant other than Cytheris. "Fufluns and Areatha were the most devoted of couples. The god fell in love with her when he found her asleep after the slayer of the Minotaur deserted her. But after such betrayal came a happy marriage. And Areatha bore many sons."

"You know the myth well."

"I know all the legends, my lady. They were the inspiration for my vases. I enjoyed learning of divine love and passion, bickering and heartbreak."

"So what, then, is the rest of Areatha's story?"

"I won't lie. Her life was one of melancholy as well as joy. For there is the pain in loving Fufluns. He's a suffering god, and those who love him can suffer, too. Some say Areatha was killed by one who hated the freedom Fufluns granted to women. Others speak of her hanging herself because she had angered the goddess of the hunt. But Fufluns descended into Acheron and saved her from Aita. Thereafter she became immortal." Semni pointed to Areatha's wedding tiara. "See her diadem? Fufluns tossed it into the sky to create the Northern Crown in her honor. At night you can view the starry corona and remember her."

"Lord Mastarna calls me 'Bellatrix' after a tiny star in the constellation of Orion." The queen placed the mirror on the table and took up the tortoiseshell lyre again. "But I don't want to be likened to this sad goddess, Semni. Or my husband to Fufluns. I just want him to return so I can embrace him again."

The queen averted her head, and Semni realized she was holding back tears. The girl hesitated, not sure what to do. Yet she sensed offering words of comfort would only cause the noblewoman to weep.

She thought of Arruns. How she would hate it if they were parted. Lady Caecilia had spent years as the wife of a warrior, never knowing if a farewell kiss might be the last ever shared. She stood and curtsied. "Thank you, mistress, for allowing us to wed."

Lady Caecilia brushed her fingers across her eyes. "I'll pray for your baby. And that your life with Arruns will be blessed."

The nursemaid headed to the doorway, but before she reached it, the queen called, "And I'll also pray you'll have the opportunity to render other myths in terra-cotta one day. Then I'll be able to fill this palace with red figured vases with your initials etched into their bases."

Semni curtsied again, tears pricking her own eyes. In this beleaguered city, such a world seemed a lifetime ago and a lifetime away.

THIRTY-SIX

The perfume of the roses in Semni's bridal wreath was heady. Veii was not devoid of spring blossoms even though deprived of food. Cytheris and Perca had filled dozens of vases with grape hyacinths and lilies to add an air of gaiety to the day.

The bride and groom sat on bronze stools opposite each other in the palace courtyard. The sumptuous surroundings were fit for the nuptials of the nobility, not the union of a maidservant and lictor. Nevertheless, there was a familial atmosphere. Dressed in their best clothes, the staff had been allowed to attend. Semni could not help a fleeting moment of sadness that Cook was not there. She missed the woman with flour-dusted hands who was always ready to gossip.

The witnesses were not the group of servants before whom Arruns had claimed Nerie. Instead ten royal lictors acted as the official observers. Semni always felt intimidated by these burly men with their weathered faces. Now they were relaxed and grinning, pleased to participate in the marriage of the Phoenician who led them.

Although used to royalty, Semni was daunted at the presence of the aristocratic guests. Lady Caecilia and Lord Tarchon stood resplendent in purple. The queen had insisted the regent preside over the ceremony. Semni was overwhelmed. She never imagined there would come a time when a ruler would officiate at her marriage.

Cytheris and the other handmaids chattered as they waited for the ceremony to begin. The Greek woman held Nerie on her lap. Cross-legged on the floor next to Perca, the three princes also watched the preparation for the rites. Semni noticed the lethargy of the children. She hoped the wedding would distract them from their hunger for a little while.

She touched a brooch fastened to her bodice. Cytheris had given it to her that afternoon when she'd helped her to dress her hair. A tiny Medusa's head was engraved on it. The frizzy-haired maid had smiled when she'd placed it in Semni's palm and folded the girl's fingers around it. "A gorgon from the Gorgon," she'd said, then patted Semni's knee. "I give it to you with no malice. She will protect you from the evil eye."

Semni had kissed Cytheris on both cheeks. "You love Nerie as would a grandmother. The baby I carry will be yours to cherish as well."

Rearranging the mantle slipping from one shoulder, Semni was grateful Lady Caecilia had given her a chiton of fine linen bordered with blue spirals from her own collection. The gown was cinched at the waist with a girdle studded with tiny glass beads. The girl lacked the elegance of the queen, but she gained the attention of the men around her. Some of the lictors' glances lingered. But her dimpled smile was reserved for her groom alone.

Her first wedding gown had been of rough weave, homespun on her mother's loom. How she'd hated her father for marrying her to an old man. She'd dared not complain. She'd been expected to bear many sons to further both bloodlines. And so it was perplexing when her mother gave her a posy of lupins and laurel on her wedding eve. "Here's the secret to ridding a babe seeded within you. Use flowers like these until you're fifteen. I don't want to see another of my daughters die in labor due to narrow hips and too small a womb. I was lucky to survive bearing your brother when I was twelve."

Semni placed her hand on her stomach, glad Arruns's baby lay cocooned within. Nevertheless, the shadow of her mother's fate was sobering. The matron had died in child bed with her eighth. Yet if Lord Mastarna did not send help, Semni might not need a birthing chair. There were six long months remaining for her son to grow within her. Nerie had been born in autumn. Would this child also have the chance to first open his eyes to the season of turning leaves and the harvest moon?

Arruns was dressed in his uniform. He was also wearing a wreath on his brow. The blooms were incongruous above the bared fangs and forked tongue of a serpent. The bodyguard scowled as he fiddled with the garland. Semni smiled at him, but he was too nervous to acknowledge her. A faint sheen of sweat covered his shaven skull. Used to being unobtrusive, he did not like being the center of attention.

Lord Tarchon called all to gather and began the rites. Arruns offered Semni a gilded wooden pomegranate. She, too, offered him the fruit, the symbol of fertility, life, and marriage. Saying a prayer, the prince lifted a sheer wedding mantle and placed it over the couple's heads. Semni felt the fabric settle upon her hair.

Enveloped together under the filmy material, there was no sign of the ruthless killer when Arruns smiled. The pair clasped each other's hands, exchanging their vows. The veil was lifted, the intimacy broken by the applause around them. Barekbaal and Semni were now joined as one.

Husband and wife rose. Semni leaned across to kiss her husband, but aware of an audience, he avoided her mouth and gave her a quick peck on the cheek. Lord Tarchon clamped the body-guard's shoulder with his hand. "Is that the best you can do? By the gods, kiss her properly!"

Issued the challenge, Arruns handed the prince the pomegranate and grabbed his bride by the hips. Pressing Semni hard against him, he planted his lips on hers for long moments, until, releasing her, she gasped and then caught her breath.

Lord Tarchon called, "That's better. Now she might have something to look forward to in the nuptial bed!"

The room erupted into good-natured laughter, the awkwardness of rank forgotten. Others in the room became bolder, their suggestions growing more ribald. Semni laughed, hugging her husband.

One of the court musicians played his flute, the melody trilling above the hubbub of conversation. The castanet player added percussion, the lyre player strummed in harmony. After hearing only paeans, the jauntiness of the tune reminded Semni of a time when such entertainment was commonplace. Tonight there might be scant provisions for a feast, but at least cares could be forgotten with music.

"May your life together be blessed." Lady Caecilia stepped across to the couple and kissed Semni on the cheek. She hesitated to extend the same affection to Arruns, her reserve maintained, but her gaze was fond.

After raising a toast to the union of their loyal servants, the prince and queen led the royal children from the courtyard. Arruns sat beside Semni dandling Nerie on his knee in time to the rhythm of the music. He'd removed his wreath and looped it around the boy's neck. As Nerie plucked the petals, his father pressed his lips to his son's fair head. The lonely man had been made whole.

The celebration lacked wine to fuel merriment, but soon most of the guests were singing raucously. Some of the lictors even coaxed the maids to dance. One grabbed Semni, giving her bottom a pinch. Glaring, Arruns slipped Nerie from his lap and placed his hand against the man's chest in warning. The guard backed off, grinning. "You can't help me for trying."

Cytheris saw the exchange. She scooped Nerie onto her hip and cleared her throat. "I think it's time for the bedding. Let bride and groom join as one. We can celebrate well enough without them!"

Taking his wife's hand, the Phoenician said in his gruff voice, "I have a job to do."

Laughter followed as he led her away. Semni's heart was beating fast. Tonight she would lie with him as his wife. Even though she was familiar with his roughness, and the heat and power of his flesh, she wanted their new life together to start with slow caresses and tender embrace.

To her surprise, he did not lead her to the barracks but pulled her toward the stairway to the loggia.

"Why are you taking me here?"

"Because I want to begin afresh."

Intrigued, she ascended to the gallery and stood beside him next to the caryatid column.

He placed his hand on her stomach. "I'm sorry I didn't greet the news of our child with joy. I want this baby whether born into peace or war."

"So you have hope, Arruns?"

"Better to have faith than to surrender to despair." He looked down at her belly and then met her gaze. "Can you feel him stir within you yet?"

She smiled at his eagerness to touch his child. "No, I have not quickened."

"Then you must tell me as soon as he moves."

She slipped her arm around his waist. "The minute he does."

Both stood quietly, gazing at the forum. Twilight was nearly over, night encroaching in hues of deep blue. The houses and buildings around the forum were dark shapes with pinpricks of candlelight in open windows. She gave him a squeeze. "Do you wish your family could have been here today?"

"I try to rid myself of such ideas. Although it's harder to ignore them now I have you and Nerie, and the baby." He gazed at the evening star twinkling beside a thick sliver of moon. "Astarte is gazing down on us. It comforts me she's also observing my kin across the Great Sea."

Semni pressed her hand to his chest. "What's the sea like?"

"An endless stretch of water. It changes color depending on the sea god's moods—from blue and light green in the sunlight to dark green or black with storms." He swiveled his head to look at her. "If we survive this war, I might be able to take you and our children to the coast. Lord Mastarna may choose to visit his mother's people in Tarchna."

She liked that he spoke with confidence. "We are freed, Arruns. We can leave the House of Mastarna if we wish. We could travel to Canaan. And along the way I could see the cities where my vases used to be exported: Rhodes and Athens, even Carthage."

His expression clouded. "Leave the House of Mastarna?"

"Yes. We aren't bound to the king and queen forever."

He shook his head. "My past can't be recovered, no matter what you say. I would feel a foreigner in my own birthplace. Do you think I could become a trader in purple again when the red of those I've killed stains my hands?"

"Your duty is to your family now. Just as there is new life growing within me, there can be a fresh beginning for us if we can survive."

Brooding, Arruns fell silent, staring across the forum.

She regretted speaking. She didn't want the happiness of the wedding to dissolve. "I'm sorry. It's enough that you love me. It's enough that we'll be a family together living in peace in Veii."

He swung around, hugging her like a drowning man grasping for something to keep him afloat. Speaking of possibilities had only heightened the fragility of their existence. It was time to hold each other and defy death through passion. Semni placed her cheek against his untattooed cheek, touching the unmarked skin of Barekbaal, the man from Sidon, who loved the sea. "Husband, let's go to bed. You have a job to do."

THIRTY-SEVEN

Pinna, Rome, Spring, 396 BC

Pinna settled beside the hearth fire and threaded the needle to begin her mending. The atrium was filled with the mellow light of the afternoon. She enjoyed the spring warmth and the routine of the task, her fingers busy but her mind at rest.

When she heard the sound of the outer street door opening, she took no notice. Her Wolf was due to return from his day at the law courts. The majordomo duly hurried to greet the master.

Raised voices caught her attention. Camillus and Medullinus emerged with a third man, whom they supported around the waist. The visitor's toga was thick with dust, his face sunburned and gaunt as he hobbled between them. Camillus called to her, "Where's Artile?"

The question was answered as the Etruscan emerged from his cubicle. He hovered in the doorway, curiosity plain upon his features.

Camillus rapped out orders from over his shoulder. "Come into the study. My brother Spurius has returned from Delphi." Then to the majordomo and Pinna each in turn, "Get some wine," and, "Bring water to wash his feet."

For a moment resentment spiked at being commanded as though she were a servant. As his concubine, she'd not expected to tend to another man. Surely the maid was more suitable for such a job. Would Camillus ever have ordered his wife to kneel before any other than him?

By the time she entered the study, she'd suppressed her indignation. At least she had an opportunity to once again listen to the senators in plain view.

Spurius was slumped in an armchair, his toga heaped on the floor. Dark rings of perspiration stained his tunic under his armpits. His face was lined with exhaustion. Medullinus drew up a stool beside him. Camillus also appeared troubled to see his younger brother in such a condition. He poured a goblet of wine to the brim. The traveler drank it in one long gulp, then gave it back to be refilled.

The family resemblance of the three siblings was striking with their aristocratic profiles and compact, lean physiques. Even in his tiredness, Pinna could tell Spurius had the military bearing of a man accustomed to issuing orders and having them obeyed.

Artile lurked next to the bookshelves, scrutinizing the Romans. His expression was apprehensive. His future lay in the hands of the weakened Spurius. Had Apollo given the same advice to the Roman delegation?

Pinna placed the ewer and jug at the guest's feet. Then she kneeled to unlace his boots which were caked with grime. She wrinkled her nose at his stink but took her time, wanting to linger as long as possible.

Guiding one of Spurius's feet onto her lap, she wiped his soles and callused heels, then his dirt-spattered calves and ankles. The skin was scratched and bruised. As she wrung out the cloth, the water turned murky.

"We were shipwrecked on our return," he said. "We're lucky to be alive. It's taken over a month to secure passage to Rome."

Camillus clamped his hand on his brother's shoulder. "Then we must give thanks for your safe return. We were worried when you were away for so long."

"Our case was not dealt with immediately. We had to wait throughout winter until Apollo returned to Delphi." Spurius rubbed the back of his neck and winced.

Camillus sat down in a chair opposite him. "What's the matter?"

Spurius grimaced at another spasm of pain. "It's nothing. I was thrown when the ship struck ground. My neck was jarred."

"Then Pinna will help you. She's skilled at massage."

The guest glanced down at her, as though first noticing her.

Medullinus snorted. "Yes, I can imagine just how skilled she is."

Spurius looked first at one brother and then the other, confused at their exchange.

She waited for her Wolf to introduce her as his concubine. Or at least put Medullinus in his place. Instead he ignored the jibe and signaled to her to attend to Spurius. "Rub his neck."

Hurt that he would ask her to perform so intimate a task, Pinna sat back on her heels. Medullinus smirked. Determined not to show she was humiliated, she rose, keeping her expression blank, and stepped behind the emissary. Pressing her fingers into the base of his neck, she tested whether it was bone as well as muscle that was damaged. He tensed as she touched a sore spot, then his shoulders relaxed as she eased into the massage. He said nothing to her, prepared to accept the ministrations without further acknowledging her.

Camillus dragged his armchair closer. He sat with legs apart, hands on each knee, leaning forward. "What did the oracle say about Lake Albanus?"

"As always, the Pythia spoke in a trance, the fumes of the great chasm enveloping her. But Apollo's priests interpreted her words. They said that the dawn goddess, Mater Matuta, had been neglected. That Rome had offended the gods of Latium by the wrongful observance of the rites."

Astounded, Pinna twisted her head to look at Artile. The smile on his face was triumphant. Camillus also grinned, beckoning to him to come forward. The priest sauntered across.

Medullinus couldn't hide his shock. He also leaned forward, gripping Spurius's forearms. "And the expiation rites? What were prescribed?"

"That the waters of Lake Albanus must be dispersed so they no longer mingle with the sea. Only then will the gods be appeased, and Rome will conquer Veii."

The consular general leaned back as though he'd received a blow.

Camillus cocked his head to one side and laughed. "Well, it seems Artile has been right all along, Medullinus."

Spurius scanned the soothsayer from head to toe, taking in the features of the foe with his unbearded chin, oval eyes, and long ankle-length tunic. "You're Artile Mastarna? The Veientane seer?"

Unperturbed at such scrutiny, the Etruscan met the Roman's gaze.

Medullinus smoothed his hair over his bald patch. "There's much for you to catch up on, Spurius. Our brother here decided to value the word of a traitor."

Camillus crossed his arms. "One who has proved his reputation was not exaggerated."

Pinna stopped massaging Spurius's neck as he swiveled to look at his older brothers in turn, then turned his gaze back to the haruspex. "What's going on here?"

Camillus stood. "I'll tell you what's happening. I captured Artile back in late summer after the Battle of Blood and Hail. It's now spring, almost a year later. The answer to Lake Albanus has been known all this time. Instead of heeding me, the Senate shunned the seer and ignored my advice. The precondition for victory over Veii could have been fulfilled by now."

Medullinus pressed his lips into a straight line and muttered, "He was a traitor."

"That's right. He was betraying *Veii*. Why not take advantage of it?"

"You think Veii would be conquered by now? You think you should've been made dictator? There was no crisis to demand such an appointment. Only your ambition."

"I warned you the date of the Votive Games had been wrongly proclaimed. I advised you to court our allies and drain the floodplains." He thumped the desk beside him. "It's time someone competent was governing Rome."

Medullinus stood, balling his hands. "Be careful who you call incompetent, Brother. The Senate and I acted prudently. I make no apologies for that."

"Will you concede now that new elections must be held? That those in power who declared the wrong date for the games must stand down?"

"We don't need to vacate office. We can make reparations to Latium and begin the irrigation of Lake Albanus."

Spurius gingerly rose and pushed between them, a hand against each of their chests. "Stop it. The Furian brothers should stand shoulder to shoulder, not pitted against each other like dogs. Let us look ahead now. Rome has the chance to grasp victory at last."

Pinna stared at the peacemaker. Had it always been thus? Had he pulled apart his squabbling siblings in a time of skinned knees and tree climbing? He could not claim the same glory as his older brothers, but he was both an esteemed augur and politician.

Artile broke through their argument. "Tell me, Spurius Furius Medullinus, did the oracle give the delegation any more advice?"

Spurius stared at him. "Why, yes."

"A tithe for Apollo, perhaps."

The ambassador's jaw dropped. "You're right, one tenth of the spoils taken at Veii must be sent back to Delphi in tribute."

Once again, Medullinus appeared startled, then his expression changed. There was grudging respect in his voice. "You are indeed prescient, Artile Mastarna."

The haruspex caressed the crescent fibula at his throat. His despondency and resentment had vanished. "I think the Curia should acknowledge my powers."

Medullinus grimaced as though tasting gall. "Don't expect us to grovel to you."

Camillus picked up a fresh scroll and stylus from his desk. "I think Artile should be afforded due respect once Spurius and the other envoys formally confirm that he was correct." He offered the papyrus sheet to Medullinus. "Call a special meeting of the Senate. And this time, I will address it with the greatest seer that Rome has ever known at my side. I plan to propose that an interregnum be established so that fresh elections can be held. I will ask that the irrigation of Lake Albanus be commissioned without delay."

Medullinus stared at the scroll. "The other consular generals will be incensed when they are recalled from the field. Especially Aemilius, given his success in ambushing Aule Porsenna. He's poised to attack Nepete. We'll lose momentum in the north."

"Better to weather the displeasure of six men than the wrath of the divine," murmured Artile. "And General Aemilius may well have roused a sleeping giant. The Twelve will not be pleased the gateway to Etruria is being menaced. It would be unwise to launch an attack until the religious issue has been resolved."

Pinna glimpsed Medullinus's uncertainty at the priest's warning about Nepete. Was it yet another example of Artile's prescience? Spirits had been buoyed when word came that Aemilius's men had ambushed Porsenna's troops. The zilath had deserted Thefarie

Ulthes's forces as swiftly as he'd come to their aid once he feared Tarquinia might be threatened.

"Better not to court disaster, then," said Camillus, turning to face his brothers. "I trust you'll both agree to nominate me as one of the three interreges? And support my candidature for consular general."

Spurius sank into his chair again, fatigue overcoming him. "Of course, I'll support you." He turned to Medullinus. "I know this is a blow to you, but at least we'll have one of our family in power."

Pinna saw loathing in the oldest brother's gaze as he glared at her Wolf. He had been bested. Pinna doubted he would either forgive or forget. He snatched the scroll from Camillus's fingers. "You will only be interrex for five days, remember, and then you must pass on authority to the next of the two interreges until the elections are held." He remained sullen. "But know I'll never support you being made a dictator."

Spurius rubbed his neck. "Why do you carp on this? Camillus knows there's no crisis, only a way forward."

Medullinus bent and placed the papyrus on the table, dipping the stylus into the inkwell. For a time, the only sound in the room was the scratching of his pen. Pinna thought the point might break with the force of his strokes. He handed it to Camillus who waved it at Pinna. "Get this delivered."

She bridled, stung by his peremptory manner. Walking across to him, she curtsied in an exaggerated way. "Yes, master." At her obeisance, he paused, finally aware how he was treating her. He clasped her wrist before she could move away. She waited, thinking that at last he would introduce her to Spurius as his de facto wife. Instead he smiled and let go of her. "Thank you, Pinna. That will be all."

Swallowing hard, she hastened into the atrium to find the majordomo. She had thought her Wolf was proud of her. She'd heard him challenge Medullinus for insulting her before. Tonight he'd made her feel worthless. No more than a maid who had a talent for soothing a man's pain. She had grown prideful. She was deluded to think the society in which her Wolf lived would ever accept her. Boundaries of rank were set in stone. Peasant and patrician. Concubine and master.

THIRTY-EIGHT

Lying awake, staring into blackness, Pinna could not forget her Wolf's brusqueness. She worried he was tiring of her.

After dinner, he'd accompanied the travel-weary Spurius to his home. As yet he'd not returned. He'd been keyed up when he'd left the house, his discontent dispelled now that his faith in Artile had been vindicated. The prospect of holding high office again was within his grasp. He was one step closer to achieving his quest to conquer Veii.

Restless, she rose and lit a lamp and crept through the slumbering household to the storeroom next to the garden. The chickens were settled on their roost, the air redolent with the smell of soil and herbs.

The linen chest was squeezed between amphorae of oil and grain sacks. In the lamplight, Pinna delved inside the box, drawing a palla shawl and stola overdress from it. The garments were the symbols of a female married citizen.

Jealousy surfaced even though Pinna knew it was a dead woman she feared. Camilllus's wife had been a univira. Honorable. Untainted. She'd lain with only one man, her husband. And if he'd died before her, she may well have shunned marriage for the rest of her life, devoted to him beyond the grave.

Placing the palla shawl on a crate, she donned the stola. The fine wheaten-colored cloth slid over her night shift. The material billowed around her tiny frame and pooled around her feet.

She tied the ribbons at her shoulders, then peered inside the chest again. There was a tunic with a flounce sewn into its hem, emphasizing the patrician's respectability as well as her flair for fashion. She selected two sashes, cinching the first tight under her breasts and the other around her waist before arranging them so the fabric draped in folds.

Was his wife beautiful? Was she young? Kind or haughty? Her Wolf said theirs had been an arranged marriage. He claimed there was no passion between them.

Again Pinna inspected the contents of the chest, noticing the woolen fillets to braid into her hair. Yet another privilege of a matron. Were her locks lank or lustrous? Thick or thinning? Did he run his fingers through them as he did through hers?

The sound of the door creaking startled her. Camillus stood on the threshold. In the cold of early morning, wisps of his warm breath lingered in the air. "What are you doing, Pinna? I returned to find you missing from our bed." He stepped inside, raising his lamp higher. His quizzical expression turned to surprise as the light revealed her red-handed in his wife's clothes.

She froze as he examined her. He placed his lamp next to hers. "She was taller than you. She lacked your curves."

Stricken with guilt, Pinna fumbled with the drawstrings, but he reached across and stayed her hand.

"Is this what you want? To be able to wear a stola and palla?"

She bowed her head, humiliated to be exposed in her fancy. She waited for his anger but instead his touch was gentle. He brushed her lips with his fingers, his other hand smoothing the pleats of the dress until he rested it on her waist. "Because that is what I want also. I want you to be my wife."

She was unsure if she'd heard him correctly. Her stunned silence provoked laughter. "Well, what do you say?"

She wanted to forget the sin that stained her. She wanted to say yes. Then she remembered Genucius, the sour aftertaste of his threat spoiling the sweetness of the moment. "I can't, my Wolf. It wouldn't be wise. What would your family say? Your sons? Your friends?"

He wrapped his arms around her. "I don't care what they think."

She shook her head, drawing back within the circle of his embrace. "Yet you were reluctant to introduce me to your younger brother yesterday."

He frowned. "Was I? It was not deliberate. I was excited to hear his news. Don't you see? I will be a general again. No longer powerless."

She felt ashamed she'd doubted him. She could feel the energy within him even though he'd been awake all night. She was touched that his first thought on returning home was to find her. His request that she tend to Spurius now seemed trivial. He had things of greater import than her feelings on his mind. Nevertheless, the same qualms about the differences in their rank assailed her. "My Wolf, I'm a farmer's daughter. You're a nobleman."

"No, you are Lollia, daughter of Gnaeus Lollius, a soldier of Rome. And now you will be the wife of Marcus Furius Camillus."

She bowed her head, unable to face him, but he hooked his finger under her chin, guiding her to look at him. "Pinna, don't be afraid. It's not against the law for patrician and plebeian to marry anymore."

She covered his hand with his. Genucius was right. She loved Camillus too much to let him be ridiculed, the great general ruled by his cock instead of his brain. "Please, my Wolf. How could I ask

Juno for her blessing? She may grow angry that I dare to wed you. A concubine is impure."

"Nonsense. You will loosen your hair and sacrifice a lamb to cleanse yourself before her altar. And then, when I wed you, such a rite will never be needed again. You'll no longer be tainted as an unmarried woman who has lain with me."

Pinna wished it were true. She reached up and touched the scar on his cheek, tracing the line of the grooves that defined his mouth, the laughter creases around his eyes. "I must say no, my Wolf. I will not be the one to weaken you."

Camillus stepped back, grappling with rejection. Confused as to why she would refuse his proposal when it was clear that was what she hungered for. "No one will dare challenge my strength." He turned toward the door. "But I can't command you."

She grabbed his arm. "Wait! Please don't be angry."

He turned back to her.

She untied the ribbons and sashes so that the stola rippled to the floor, then she stepped from the crumpled circle of cloth, shivering in her night shift. "I'm content to be your concubine, my Wolf. I already have all that I could wish for."

The loud, boastful crow of a rooster was piercing. They glanced around. A shaft of light, rosy and bright, shone through the doorway. Pinna smiled. Her goddess had once again fought back the night to ride her chariot across the sky. She held out her hand to him. "See, my Wolf, Mater Matuta is pleased with us. We can witness the start of a new day together."

He locked his fingers through hers, watching the room fill with light.

"You're like the sun to me, my Wolf. Fierce and bright and hot. You should worship the dawn goddess. She will bring you victory."

"I will take all steps to placate her and the Latins."

She looped her arms around his neck. "Her temple is derelict in Rome, my Wolf."

He laughed, stroking her hair. "You're persistent on her behalf."

"I want her to protect you."

"Perhaps she already has. My victory against the Volscians was at daybreak. It gave us an advantage of surprise. They didn't expect the enemy to spring from the verge of darkness."

She lowered one hand, stroking his thigh. "When you received this wound? When you fought with a spear still embedded in your flesh?"

He grasped her hand. "There is no time for that. It's daylight."

Pinna blocked the thought that even whores end their shift at sunrise. She walked across the room and shut the door, once again plunging them into a gloom lit only by the wavering flames of the oil lamps. She was prepared to break taboos, prepared to risk offending her deity.

Even in the half shadows, she could see his surprise as she shut the chest's lid, then clutched two handfuls of his tunic, pulling him around. Yet he didn't resist, smiling as she pushed him down to sit. She straddled him, knowing her influence over him would always be as a lover, not a wife.

Camillus rested his forehead against hers. "I don't know what to do with you, Pinna. You're stealing my soul from me."

Her heartbeat spiked, her voice catching. He may not have said the words, but she knew he loved her. "My Wolf, you have already stolen mine."

THIRTY-NINE

Marcus, Nepete, Spring, 396 BC

A wind was blowing, whipping up swirls of dust from the ditch that surrounded the Roman encampment. The young sentry was nervous as he approached Marcus. "Sir, there is an Etruscan delegation that wants to see the general."

The tribune frowned and hurried to the gate. Three horsemen were surveying the stakes of the palisade. One dismounted, removing his crested horsehair helmet and tucking it under his arm. He had a satisfied smile upon his lips—far too confident for a man seeking to enter an enemy fort. Marcus ordered the gates to be opened.

"I bring a message from King Vel Mastarna," the messenger said in crude Latin.

Marcus remained impassive, forcing himself to control both his surprise and curiosity. "You may enter, but the others must remain outside." He rapped out an order to the sentries to close the gate again, then turned on his heel, striding toward the command tent. The Etruscan took his time to follow despite being confronted by hostile stares.

Marcus was impatient to hear what Mastarna had to say. The last word they'd received about the king's movements was that he'd traveled to the Etruscan congress. Marcus found it intriguing that Karcuna Tulumnes rode with him. He knew there was ill will between their Houses. Now the descendant of a tyrant and Veii's new king were allies.

Reaching the command tent, Marcus told the Veientane to remain outside while he informed his father of his arrival.

Aemilius was sitting at his desk, a hunk of cheese and a bowl of figs before him. He held a goblet of watered wine in his hand. The rigors of being on campaign had reduced the senator's waistline, but he was never one to go without food.

"An emissary from Vel Mastarna seeks to speak to you, Father."

The general cocked one bushy eyebrow. "Strange."

Marcus shrugged. "He's a smug bastard."

The envoy gave a curt half bow once granted permission to enter. He offered the Roman general a scroll. "From King Mastarna. I've been ordered to wait for your reply."

Aemilius took another swig of wine, then wiped his mouth with the back of his hand. He gestured to the man to place the letter on his desk. "You can wait outside the gates. I'll give you my answer after I have finished my meal."

The Etruscan seemed unperturbed at the abrupt dismissal. "Very well, but it may well give you indigestion."

When the herald had gone, Aemilius pushed his half-eaten meal aside and broke the seal. Color drained from his face as he scanned the words. Marcus had never seen his father so unnerved. "What does it say?"

"The entreaties of the Capenate and Faliscan delegations swayed the confederation. The Etruscan cities have pledged assistance. Their armies will bolster the Veientane forces."

Marcus was stunned. All Etruria planned to rise. Rome's greatest fear. "But the League has always left Veii and its allies to fend for themselves. Why the change of heart?"

"Our recent incursion into Nepetan territory must have made them nervous. They fear we may venture farther north and west."

Marcus pointed to the letter. "What answer does Mastarna seek?"

Aemilius focused on the scroll again as though double-checking its contents. "A similar ultimatum has been sent to Titinius at Capena. He and I either agree to retreat permanently or the combined forces of Etruria will commence their march on Rome— starting with battles tomorrow on the plains outside Nepete and Capena. Karcuna Tulumes and Thefarie Ulthes have united forces with the other Etruscans as well."

Marcus stared at him, grappling with the enormity of the threat. "What are you going to do?"

Aemilius stood and paced, consumed in thought as his son watched on. There was no time to seek the advice of the Senate. And time was limited to consult with Titinius, too.

Finally the consular general sat down and picked up his stylus. "The northern regiments of the Wolf Legion are the first lines of defense."

"Do you mean we are to fight? What chance do we have? We'll face thousands."

Aemilius's eyes hardened. "I've fought this war for ten years. We've gained ground here. I'm not about to run. Mastarna will have his answer. My army fights tomorrow while we send word to Rome. It will gain time for the Senate to decide whether to sue for peace or send reinforcements."

Marcus took a deep breath, knowing his father had just condemned his regiment to death—nigh on fifteen hundred men. And how would Rome meet the challenge of the Twelve? There were no reserves. Rome risked falling to a sleeping enemy that had woken.

"But Rome's fortifications can't withstand an assault, Father. Isn't it better to surrender and seek the best terms in a treaty?"

"Fearing death is for women, Marcus. I never thought to hear you lack courage."

He bridled, infuriated his father could accuse him of being gutless. "Maybe prudence is what is needed here. Slaughtering one third of the Wolf Legion for the sake of pride deprives Rome of manpower to fight another day."

The general scratched an answer on the bottom of Mastarna's missive. "Do you think we Aemilians have any choice but to stand fast given Caecilia has disgraced our clan? Others might choose to relent, but we must prove we'll never resile from seeking her destruction."

"But circumstances have changed. No one in Rome would condemn us for accepting we can't succeed against the League."

Aemilius shook his head. "My mind is made up. Let the Senate decide our city's fate. I'll face mine tomorrow. Smaller forces than ours have fought against greater odds and succeeded."

Marcus's stomach churned. Every time he rode into battle, he knew, with one spear thrust, he could die. He summoned valor every time he did so. To charge into battle with no hope of survival would take a different type of bravery. Yet he'd sworn an oath to his general and to the Roman people. If his father wished to die for the glory of Rome, then he must accept such a destiny, too. He stood to attention. "What are your orders, sir?"

Aemilius handed him the scroll. "Give this to the Etruscan prick, then call Sempronius to me. Claudius Drusus as well. He's a skilled horseman. I'll need him to ride to Rome. And choose another to send word to Tititinus of my decision. A third must inform Postumius at Veii."

Marcus saluted. He was relieved Drusus would be spared from the massacre. As he walked from the tent, he studied the missive. There was a blotch of ink from the force of the stylus, but the handwriting was legible. For a moment he wondered if "No sur-render" would be the last two words he'd ever read.

• • •

Drusus stormed toward his tent. Marcus shouted to him to wait. The decurion ignored him, instead barked at his groom to pack his kit and ready his horse.

Marcus tried to place his hand on his friend's shoulder. He batted it away, the blow far from friendly. The tribune stepped back, surprised. "By the gods. What's the matter with you?"

"What's the matter? I thought your father wanted to promote me to head decurion. I thought I would lead a turma in combat. Instead, I'm reduced to being a courier."

Marcus frowned. "He's asking you to brave enemy territory. It will be a dangerous ride to Rome."

Drusus flung open the flap to his tent. "No, he thinks I'm not yet battle ready. I can tell." He ducked inside, letting the flap shut behind him.

Marcus stared at the goatskin, aware there was a grain of truth in what Drusus said. Aemilius often questioned him as to whether he thought the Claudian had regained full strength. Steeling himself, he entered the tent. "You're the best horseman the regiment has. You'll need to ride through ravines and thick forest in the dark."

Head bowed in the low-ceilinged tent, the knight drew on his balteus, checking the attached scabbard and sword were secure. "The best horseman? No, that honor goes to you. Together with all the promotions. It sickens me to see the favor granted to you. Great nephew of the mighty Mamercus Aemilius. Son of a con-sular general."

Marcus spoke through gritted teeth. "The Claudians are also an esteemed patrician clan. You lack no opportunity for advancement. You're the head of your House."

"What chance do I have to be elected as a tribune or magistrate? I've spent ten years fighting away from Rome. You need backers working for you while you're on campaign. Aemilius pushes your interests every chance he can get. He milks friends for their influence on your behalf. And now you're one of his senior officers."

"I've earned my rank! And I've gained fame through my valor, not my connections."

"Oh yes, the oak-leaf crown. Won when a lowly cavalryman. You saved your poor friend, Claudius Drusus. Don't you think I'm fed up with living in your shadow?"

Marcus was incensed. "I thought there would be more gratitude than resentment for saving your life."

Drusus grabbed his helmet. "I was the man who wounded the great General Mastarna, and yet it's you who is lauded. My heroism goes unnoticed."

"Great Mars, Drusus. Camillus awarded you three silver spears for the Battle of Blood and Hail. He reprimanded me for disobeying the call for retreat even though it meant I—"

"Saved my life again. I don't need to be reminded." He collected his shield. "And here you are—a military tribune commanding a brigade of knights and a battalion of infantry while I'm still a decurion. Worse, a mere messenger."

Marcus was stunned. Was this how Drusus always felt? Bitter? Jealous? Had boyhood friendship eroded without him realizing? Had envy hardened into hate? Would Drusus care if he died? "Well, you'll have a better chance to realize your ambitions after tomorrow. I doubt I'll survive against a horde of Etruscans. You won't have to live in my shadow when I become a Shade."

Drusus's face suffused red. He lowered his shield to the ground. "I'm so sorry, my friend." He gripped the tribune's shoulders. "I'm a fool. Forgive me."

Both men fell silent. Death had always stalked them, but the moment it would arrive was unknown. Now Marcus knew his allotted time. At least he'd be spared the pain of living without Drusus had their destinies been reversed. He willed himself to speak his feelings but faltered. He didn't want the last memory of his friend to be Drusus's disgust.

Suddenly the red-haired soldier hugged him, the metal medallions on their corselets clanging. The embrace was momentary, that of a comrade. "Know that I love you like a brother. I'm proud to have served under you. I'm thankful you saved my life twice over."

Marcus's voice caught. "Go, then, Brother. Warn Rome."

Drusus picked up his shield and spear. "I'll ride swiftly. I'll bring reinforcements. Better Rome fights than concede to Etruria."

Marcus placed his hand on his friend's leather armband. "No, I hope the Senate decides this conflict with Veii must end. Ten years is enough. Better to swallow pride than let Mastarna rule Rome. And with peace, Caecilia will be spared. Isn't that what you want?"

"What I want is for *him* to die! I want his head on a spear. I want him to suffer."

"Then pray I meet him tomorrow. Pray he may yet fall, even if his army wins."

"And I'll pray that the smaller can defeat the greater. But if not, know I'll not let your death go unavenged."

After Drusus had left, Marcus took a moment to compose himself. He could hear the shouts of the centurions outside as they marshaled their companies. He knew that, as soon as he emerged, he would be swept into the turmoil of preparation. He breathed deeply, rueful he'd resisted the urge to pull his friend close and bid farewell with a kiss. He had courage to kill a foe but was too cowardly to declare his love to a man he would never see again.

FORTY

Snowcapped Mount Soracte loomed dark and lonely above the plain, its serrated mass blued by distance, the gray chain of mountains beyond billowing along the horizon. The clouds hid the sun. The battle that day would be fought under bleak skies.

As Marcus prepared to inspect his troops, he wished he could recall each hoplite as could Furius Camillus. The general knew the battles in which his soldiers had fought and how they'd received their scars. It was a knack of his to recognize each warrior, inspiring their loyalty. Marcus remembered the first time he'd been acknowledged in such a way, firing him to pledge allegiance to both the Furian and to Rome.

Riding along the lines, Marcus took care to ask the names of the men he didn't know. It was the least he could do before urging them into an onslaught that might see them dead by the end of the day. Wind-burned veterans in the rear and middle rows of the phalanxes grunted approval as they saluted. Marcus called to one. "How many times have you shown courage?"

The infantryman thrust out his chest. "Only my foes can tell you that, sir."

He smiled. "Then I must watch you today, given I can't hear the words of those you slay." His response provoked a grin from the ranks.

The younger soldiers in the front lines also saluted. Marcus felt sad these inexperienced youths may never fight another battle. They would be the least likely to survive. One young hoplite's face was white, unable to hide the tremor in his spear hand.

"Your first fight?"

"Yes, sir."

Marcus remembered waiting for his initial encounter with a foe. How hard it had been not to vomit out his fear. How he'd prayed his bowels would not turn to water. He leaned down toward the soldier. "Believe me, nerves will give birth to courage."

The youth's eyes met his, back straightening. He saluted again. "Yes sir!"

His review of the phalanxes ended, Marcus directed his bay to inspect the companies of leves. These light infantrymen could not afford the panoply of a hoplite but were just as brave. Armed with only four javelins and their shields, they would be the first to engage the foe together with the slingers and axemen. He murmured encouragement to all the skirmishers. They showed surprise, then smiled at gaining the attention of a military tribune for one brief moment.

Marcus raised his lance to the assembled battalion, bellowing, "Today you are Rome. You fight for our State, not for personal glory. Every man must hold his ground to help each other. We will be outnumbered, but while there is breath in our bodies we may yet drive back the multitude!"

The troops roared in response. No ragged shouts. No feeble yells. Pride swelled within Marcus, feeling Furius Camillus would be proud of him as well.

• • •

Early morning birdsong was drowned by the clash and scrape of metal as a thousand hoplites took their position. Buckles on corselet straps were tightened, swords adjusted in their scabbards, boots laced fast.

Marcus waited on a rise at the head of the brigade of two turmae he would lead. Behind him, Aemilius viewed the entire battlefield, the standard-bearer beside him holding aloft the wolf insignia. The general would remain at the rear, but his troops did not doubt his daring or resolve. He would make the decisions that day as to whether to advance or retreat, regroup, and advance again. For the first time Marcus could remember, Aemilius had embraced him. The moment of affection was both startling and upsetting.

Twelve men across and eight men deep, the ten phalanxes of the regiment stood in one long battlefront. Their heavy armor declared their wealth and status. Each warrior's shield overlapped, protecting the man to the left with wood, leather, and bronze. Marcus noticed how the emblems emblazoned on the shields identified each soldier. The varied decorations formed a motley pattern but the weapons were uniform in one respect. Round and heavy and curved outward, they covered the hoplite from chest to groin.

Each company was a bristling beast, a death machine. Long javelins in their right hands, the first three ranks held theirs horizontal, the spear points poking through the gaps in the rows in front. The next two lines held their lances at a slant, ready to be brought down to take the place of fallen comrades. The veterans at the rear stood with their javelins upright, the last line of attack. Together, these serried hoplites were the backbone of the army, and its awesome blade.

As Marcus faced the enemy, he tried to blot out all around him, listening only to his heartbeat and his breathing. He inhaled and exhaled evenly, remembering his advice to the young hoplite.

Nerves give birth to courage. Great Mars, let it also be true for him today.

He concentrated on the Etruscan armies opposite. Their phalanxes also stood with spears leveled. Compared to the conical, leather helmets of the Romans, the enemy's bronze headwear boasted crests of horsehair or feathers.

He counted the depth of their ranks. Ten phalanxes were lined up to match the Romans, but instead of standing eight deep there were twenty rows of hoplites in each company. And behind each phalanx was another phalanx. And another. A seemingly inexhaustible reserve of men.

Marcus checked their standards. He could see the bull insignia of the Veientane king and the badges of Falerii and Nepete. There were also standards of three northern Etruscan armies. Marcus frowned, expecting to count more. Those of the far northern League cities were missing. The Roman army would not meet the titan it expected.

Marcus waited with his brigade on one side of the regiment, Sempronius's knights on the other. The tribune felt reassured that Tatius's squadron flanked him, confident of its prowess.

The horses were skittish, pawing the line, impatient to engage. He studied the opposing cavalry. The manes of the Etruscans's long-legged steeds were plaited, their collars and body armor studded with terra-cotta medallions. The cured bull hide pectorals on the Roman horses were plain in comparison. Again he assessed the numbers. The contingents of enemy knights were in the hundreds, and protected the weak left flank of their phalanxes. He swallowed hard at the thought of the charge. Given the depth of the opposing force, it would be a long, frightening ride. Any hope that his brigade might reach the rear to force a rout seemed impossible.

The war horns sounded. Blasting and strident. Mastarna was impatient.

Marcus's horse snorted and tossed its head. The tribune steadied it as he called to his knights above the baying of the war hounds. "Wait for my command."

The din of war erupted. Thousands of men on either side thumped their spears against the front of their shields or banged the clappers on the bosses. The bombardment of sound was as much a weapon of terror as any sword or spear.

The Aemilian braced himself for the Etruscan war cry. The last time he'd heard it was at the Battle of Blood and Hail. The hairs on the back of his neck stood on end as the shrieking ululation bore into his brain. Around him, the horses whinnied and shifted at the screeching. The Roman regiment roared a response, but there was wavering morale in their reply.

Javelins sailed through the air. The Etruscans had begun their attack. Marcus signaled the leves and skirmishers forward to fill the space between the opposing phalanxes. A salvo of spears and slingshot exploded, the air thick with wood and stone. The dogs bounded into the fray, bringing down prey and savaging them, yelping in pain when they were stabbed.

Hurling their slings twice around their heads, the slingers let loose shot that stove in skulls and sent bone splinters and brains flying. Then a volley of arrows blackened the sky. Marcus grimaced, regretful Rome disdained using bowmen. The Etruscans did not consider it beneath them to employ any means to soften up their foe. He gritted his teeth, waiting for the foe to run out of ammunition.

Above the tumult, an Etruscan tuba blasted a series of short, sharp notes. Suddenly the fusillade ended. All the skirmishers and leves retreated, taking their places at the sides of the field. Bodies of axemen, spearmen, and slingers littered the ground, the wounded groaning. Marcus winced to think those who could not crawl out of the way were destined to be trampled.

He scanned the line of Roman phalanxes. Only a few young hoplites had been killed, their bodies dragged to the side, and the men behind them taking their place. The smell of shit wafted on the breeze, a combination of fear and waiting in formation.

The Etruscan trumpet call ascended in pitch. To Marcus's surprise, the cavalrymen opposing his brigade wheeled their horses around and rode to the far side to join the knights facing Sempronius. The vulnerable left side of the Etruscan phalanxes at the edge of the battlefront was now exposed to attack. Marcus scanned the companies immediately in front of him. The standard of the Veientane bull was prominent. His battalion would face Vel Mastarna's troops. The king's taunt was clear. He did not fear the puny attempts of Marcus's cavalry would make an impact.

Tatius shouted to the tribune, "What are your orders, sir? Do we help Sempronius?"

"No, there would only be confusion if we tried to change our formation. Concentrate on attacking their hoplites from the side, or head to the rear. Kill any who are separated from their companies. Cut down those who are fleeing. Tell your men not to stop until I order them. No man must fail to steep his spear in blood."

Roman trumpets sounded. General Aemilius had signaled to advance. Marcus barked at Tatius to return to his turma, then rode to the head of the battle line to encourage his hoplites. He shouted, "Death to Mastarna! Death to Mastarna!" His troops took up the war chant. He returned to the rise to view the battle, buoyed by the barrage of Roman voices.

With a slow, steady pace, the enemy phalanxes advanced toward each other: a clanking, thudding march of two monsters. The stomping pace quickened. The foes drew closer and closer.

The collision of the line of opposing metal-clad beasts was monumental. Marcus steadied his stallion at the booming clash. And then there was only fury and effort and gore. Each hoplite aimed his spear at his rival, stabbing through the gaps in the wall of shields to pierce gullet or neck, armpit or groin. No room to duck behind shields. Only a small chance to move the head to the side. Men fell and were flattened, the man behind stepping up, then the third. The two sides pressed forward, a scrum of enormous power, as each vied to push the other back and break the pack.

Marcus watched the nearest phalanx. The Romans strained to resist the force of the Etruscans' extra ranks. Some young hoplites were suffocating, caught between the pressure of the enemy's weight and the force of their own veterans shoving them forward. Chests were pressed against their own spears and shields, backs crushed by the shields of those behind. Trapped by their own momentum, there was not enough space for the dead to fall, their comrades holding the corpses upright. A ghastly host of living and dead were now locked in combat.

The impetus of the Etruscans was too great. With a roar, the enemy gained the advantage. Those on the vulnerable left side of the Roman phalanx, which was already drifting backward, floundered. Marcus could see the heads of the hoplites turning in bewilderment and alarm. The phalanx collapsed. Isolated groups merged and then parted.

The men of the splintered companies now faced hand-to-hand combat as personal duels ensued. Marcus watched as, down the length of the battlefield, he saw other phalanxes also break apart.

The time had come to charge.

Armed with fresh lances, his contingent of leves stood ready to attack. The cavalry and light infantry might yet be able to forge channels through the foe's lines and harry the Etruscan hoplites: the swift against the slow, the light against the unwieldy.

The warhorses tossed their heads, shifting and rearing, champing at the bit. The knights shortened the reins, controlling the equine warriors by heel and hand.

Marcus held his lance aloft, kicking his stallion's sides to gee him. His throat tore as he screamed a fresh war cry, his yell spurring the cavalry and leves as they rushed forward into battle.

Time and distance expanded. Marcus felt like his horse pounded for miles toward the foe, each hoofbeat competing with the thumping of his heart.

Time shifted again. Shortening. He made his first kill, thrusting through the neck of a man with his spear. He had no time to savor it. Instead he began a rotation of slaughtering. Sweat streamed down his face. He didn't attempt to wipe it away, shaking his head instead, flicking it from his eyes.

An Etruscan tuba blasted three times. Suddenly a nearby group of Veientane hoplites created a small phalanx again and faced Marcus's men. The horses whinnied and reared backward, terrified by the wall of spears. The tribune turned to scan the rise for his father, but Aemilius was nowhere in sight. No war horn sounded a retreat. He must continue to lead his men into a bloodbath.

Knowing that remaining on horseback was of no use, he called to the brigade, "Dismount and beat them back with shield and sword."

He vaulted from his horse. The other knights did the same, discarding spears and drawing swords from scabbards as they formed a line. Marcus counted heads. Only twenty cavalrymen remained.

The enemy tuba sounded another tune. An airborne message far more complex than any Roman call sign. To Marcus's horror, another group of Veientanes formed a phalanx behind his horsemen. Mastarna had closed a net around them.

In the distance, he heard the legion trumpeter's frenzied notes. Aemilius was ordering all to retreat.

Pandemonium erupted. Turning on their heels, the Roman hoplites lumbered toward camp, but the heavy armor that protected them in the scrum now hampered their speed.

Marcus surveyed the battlefield. Horses were squealing, struggling to rise on broken legs or lying on their sides. The grass was torn up by hundreds of boots and hooves. And everywhere lay a gruesome expanse of the wounded, body parts, and corpses.

Hemmed in by the two Veientane phalanxes, Marcus cursed. The call had come too late.

Next to him, Tatius spat a great gob onto the ground. "No surrender then, sir?"

"No surrender. Let's take as many as possible to the grave before we're killed." Then he yelled. "Form a circle!"

In a paltry imitation of their hoplite brothers, the knights shuffled together to stand shoulder to shoulder. Small, round shields overlapping, their palms slippery with sweat, they gripped the hilts of their weapons. The enemy warriors leveled their spears, ready for the final kill.

Another tuba sounded. He braced himself for the assault. In his last moments, he would understand what it was to be an infantryman, crushed and impaled by a barrage of spears. "Stand fast. Die well. Rome will remember us."

The enemy remained poised.

There was no advance.

The phalanx in front of Marcus parted to reveal two riders. The Etruscan horsemen trotted toward the circle of Romans with the confident gait of the triumphant. One knight sat astride a great gray horse. A spiral decorated the man's cuirass, a bull's head boss upon his shield. He wore a purple tunic and cloak, a blue horsehair crest atop his helmet. His young comrade, one side of his face bleeding, held aloft the standard of the Legion of the Wolf. Marcus felt sick to see the proof of his regiment's defeat. He clamped his jaw, determined more than ever he would never surrender to Vel Mastarna.

FORTY-ONE

The Veientane king ordered his hoplites to lower their weapons as he guided his horse to stand in front of the Roman tribune. He said nothing, scrutinizing the circle of men from the height of his stallion, his hard coal-black eyes staring from between the hinged cheek pieces of his helmet.

"We meet again, Marcus Aemilius Mamercus," Mastarna said in his accented Latin. "Only this time my troops hold the advantage. What do you suggest I do with you?"

Marcus kept his eyes level, not prepared to look up to a foe as he stood shoulder to shoulder with Tatius and the soldier on the other side of him. "We're prepared to fight until none remain standing." His throat was hoarse from yelling.

Mastarna's horse shifted on the spot. "I don't think it need come to that, tribune. You and your men have fought bravely. I'm prepared to spare you."

Tatius grunted, glancing sideways at his officer. Marcus ignored him, still refusing to meet the king's eyes. "I don't plan on surrendering my spear to you again, Mastarna."

"It looks like you've already dropped your spear." He smirked. "However, I want neither it nor your sword. It's enough that I've dented your pride." He turned to his aide. "Sethre, show our Roman captives what we have seized."

The arrogance of the young horseman grated as he dangled the pole with the wolf's head banner upside down. Marcus scowled, angered by the disrespect shown. Yet he noticed the youth's skill in handling his high-stepping stallion with the pressure of his thighs alone. The crest emblazoned on his corselet also caught his eye: the winged lion of the Tulumnes clan. There truly must have been a reconciliation if Vel Mastarna kept a rival at his side.

Mastarna took the ensign from his aide and righted it. "I have your legion's standard, Marcus Aemilius. Your father was kind enough to abandon it before he and his army turned tail and fled."

Marcus flinched, hating his derision. He believed Aemilius had beaten a strategic retreat, not run away.

Mastarna handed the standard back to Sethre, then walked his horse around the circle of knights. He returned to stand in front of Marcus. "From the look on your soldiers' faces, tribune, I think they prefer my offer to being hacked to pieces."

Tatius murmured from the corner of his mouth. "Don't believe him, sir. We'll fight if you give the order."

Marcus was grateful for his loyalty. But even though he hated ceding, he didn't see the point in sacrificing men who could fight again in the future. "You'll let us retain our weapons? You won't take us prisoner?"

Mastarna barked an order to the phalanx to open a way for the Romans. "We'll keep your horses. By the time you return to Rome all you'll have suffered will be sore feet and hurt pride."

Marcus was reluctant to express gratitude. "Agreed, then." He sheathed his sword and slung his shield over his shoulder. Then he ordered his cavalrymen to form a line to march back to the camp.

The tumult had subsided. Instead of war chants there were groans and whimpers or the boasts and laughter of Etruscan soldiers. They were stripping armor from the Roman dead. Marcus knew worse awaited—mutilation. Vengeance would be exacted for past defeats.

Mastarna must have read his thoughts. "Are you worried for your fallen and maimed? Camillus didn't let me bury my clansmen after the Battle of Blood and Hail. Instead he allowed his troops to desecrate their bodies, then leave their flesh to rot and bones to molder."

Marcus wasn't about to admit mercy should have been shown to Mastarna's tribe. And Camillus's ruthlessness was no different to any other general's. "You Etruscans do the same."

"Never under my command."

Marcus didn't respond. He couldn't deny Vel Mastarna was an honorable man. After victory in one battle at Veii years before, he'd burned the enemy dead with due respect.

At his silence, Mastarna leaned forward. "You've nothing to say? Well, tell your father this. Tell Camillus, too. I can't speak for my allied commanders, but I'll have your slain cremated. I'll not send them to the afterlife as tortured souls. I believe the valiant in life should remain valiant in death. And I'll let you retrieve your wounded—that is, of course, if your comrades have not abandoned your camp already."

Marcus fumed, hating the insinuation that Aemilius was heading a stampede of panicked fugitives.

Mastarna shouted a command. Ten hoplites formed a detail around the equestrians. "These men will escort yours from the field. There's still danger in traversing a battleground with men wild with blood rage."

His continued fair treatment rankled. Marcus was determined not to feel appreciation. Nevertheless, he managed a begrudging nod, then gestured his men to move.

"Wait," called Mastarna. "You stay, Marcus Aemilius."

The tribune frowned, unable to suppress a tremor of apprehension, even though he doubted the king was likely to double-cross him.

Tatius halted and swung around, not prepared to leave his leader with his foe. "I'll stay, too, sir."

Marcus rested a bloodied hand on the decurion's shoulder. "No, leave. He's given his word to free me."

The bucktoothed soldier spat on the ground near the king's horse. "I don't trust any of the slant-eyed bastards."

Vel Mastarna remained cool at the insult. "I see you inspire allegiance in your men. Rest assured I don't plan to keep you long."

Tatius joined the others, casting glances over his shoulder as he headed across the field. The squadron plodded with heads bowed, dejection in each step.

When the Romans were out of earshot, Marcus was surprised when Mastarna swung down from his horse to stand beside him. The king handed the reins to his young aide, who also appeared disconcerted at his general's action.

Up close, Marcus could see the ugly scar marring the Veientane's face. Unbidden thoughts of Caecilia surfaced. Did she shut her eyes when she lay with her husband to avoid viewing such disfigurement? Or were the power of his physique and the timbre of his voice enough to distract her?

"What do you want, Mastarna?"

"To remind you that you owe me a blood debt twice over. I spared your life at the Battle of Blood and Hail. So, too, today. I expect you to repay me should ever the opportunity arise."

Marcus bristled, resentful of being reminded he was doubly beholden to a foe. "I'd rather you execute me. I've sworn an oath to Rome to kill you. It takes precedence over personal vows. If I ever have the chance to meet you in combat, I will not hesitate to follow my orders."

Mastarna growled. "I understand that. The obligation you owe will be to my wife should she ever demand it."

Marcus was shocked. "What you ask of me is impossible. I would have no say in her fate. Rome will exact its punishment on her."

Mastarna's voice was cold. "So Caecilia is truly dead to you."

"Yes. She's a traitoress."

"She no longer bears any love for you either."

Marcus felt as though he'd been struck. Then he chided himself at being irrational, disturbed he should care whether splinters of fondness remained in her. "I presumed nothing more."

"Nevertheless, I expect you to do your utmost to repay the blood debt in whatever way my wife determines."

Marcus's eyes narrowed, trying to understand Mastarna's plea. "Do you fear Rome will prevail in the end? We heard all Etruria was rising, but I didn't see every pennant of the Twelve."

The monarch stepped closer. The tribune forced himself not to step back, assessing his own chance of survival if forced to fight hand to hand.

"Such bravado from a man who will return home with his tail between his legs. Believe me, Marcus Aemilius, there are enough Rasenna committed to ruling Rome again. This battle is only the beginning." He paused, eyeing his captive up and down. "At least I know if we do ever meet again, you'll attack me head on—unlike Claudius Drusus. I hope no awards were bestowed on him in death."

"He did not need burial. You failed to kill him. And you're a liar. He is no coward."

The king's eyes widened. "He survived? I thought I'd given him due retribution." Then his expression hardened. He turned and raised his sword arm. "Here is proof of his spinelessness. See this scar? It's on the back of my arm. I either received it running away like your hoplites did today, or it was a blow from a man who took unfair advantage."

Marcus stared at the seam of stitched flesh, how it arced around the back of Mastarna's bicep and elbow. Doubt flickered. What had happened that day? Was Mastarna speaking the truth? It would not be the first time his friend had acted rashly. Yet how could he accept the word of an enemy? Perhaps Mastarna spewed false accusations to cover his humiliation at being felled. "I have nothing to say."

Mastarna grunted and walked to his stallion. Sethre slipped from his horse, crossing to his commander and lacing his hands together so the monarch could step up to mount. Marcus watched with interest. Mastarna couldn't vault onto his horse. He smiled, glad Drusus had weakened their enemy.

The king gathered the reins of the gray, once again staring down at Marcus.

"Tell me. My lictor rendered you harmless that day outside Veii's walls. But if he hadn't, would you have killed me when I was on my knees?"

Marcus straightened his shoulders, remembering Drusus mired in the mud, his body ripped open by his enemy's curved blade. "Yes. I would have shown no mercy."

Mastarna grimaced. "Then this is where we differ. I spared you today because I won't kill my wife's kin. I will not have your blood on my hands. For Caecilia's heart is tender, even though she claims she has toughened it against you."

Marcus stared at him, nonplussed. This foe was calling upon familial obligations that no longer prevailed. In war, there could only be black or white, love or hate. Yet Mastarna was forcing him to feel grudging respect for his integrity. He was not about to acknowledge it, though. "My answer remains the same."

The ruler dug his heels into his horse's blood-splattered flanks, turning its head and leading it toward his soldiers, stopping to congratulate them.

Flanked by two Etruscan hoplites, Marcus picked up his abandoned spear and then trudged across the battlefield. The clouds parted, the sun shining directly above him. Between sunrise and noon, hundreds of Romans had died. He murmured a prayer to Mars in gratitude for sparing him. Once again, his lips had brushed death's mouth and survived.

FORTY-TWO

Pinna, Rome, Spring, 396 BC

The market was congested, its air laden with aromas of basil, chives, and dill. Barrows were bright with the colors of asparagus and radish. An array of geese and partridges hung from their feet, heads dangling, while salted fish lay heaped in baskets.

Pinna walked through streets clogged with traffic. The calls of vendors were noisy and insistent. There was a feeling of good humor among the shoppers. News that the riddle of Lake Albanus had been answered was on everyone's lips. The key to placating the gods was known. Veii was destined to fall.

She listened to snippets of conversations that made her swell with pride.

"With Camillus now an interrex, Rome will soon be back on course."

"Why didn't the Senate listen to him before?"

"We need him to be a consular general again."

There was also talk of the wondrous Etruscan soothsayer. Artile was no longer hidden. He'd taken his place beside Camillus this morning as both men traveled in an open carriage to the Forum.

The seer preened, superior again. The senators had declared he was correct to have advised Rome to irrigate the Latium floodplains.

There was another reason for the buzz of excitement. A debate was to be held in the Comitium even though the calendar did not prescribe the holding of an assembly. The Forum teemed with male citizens gathered to listen to the speakers.

Yesterday, after the long spring evening ended, Camillus had returned home from the Curia elated. He'd taken her breath away as he'd hugged her, his exultation infectious. Pinna shared a sense of his power. It was as potent as a drug, as thrilling as a surge of desire. "Elections are to be called, Pinna. I'll stand as a candidate. I'll lead an army again."

He'd ripped the joint of pork kept aside for him. He drank no wine, wanting to keep clearheaded. And then he'd taken her, voracious and urgent, before falling into a dead sleep. Three hours later he'd risen to plan his address to the citizens of Rome. She knew he wished he could be declared dictator. But there was no emergency, only good tidings. With the secret of Lake Albanus revealed, the steps Rome needed to defeat its enemy were clear.

She glanced up to the looming heights of the Capitoline Hill. Having been privy to the discussions of the Furian brothers, Pinna was keen to watch Camillus in the Comitium today. And so she decided to scale the Hundred Steps to see if she could spy him from above as he addressed the convention. She would not be able to hear him, but there would be satisfaction in seeing her lover on the speakers' platform.

Threading her way through the hustle and bustle, she reached the bottom of the stairs. She looked upward, daunted at climbing them with a heavy basket. She was puffing by the time she reached the top.

She gazed beyond the sanctuary's wall to study the portico of the Great Temple and its pediment. At the apex, Jupiter rode his quadriga with its four white horses. An image of the red-and-black-columned temple of Uni skimmed her memory. In Veii, Queen Juno challenged Rome's divine ruler in magnificence. Would the Veientane counterpart submit to being Jupiter's consort when her city was captured?

Pinna glanced sideways to the Tarpeian Rock. She shivered at the sight of the barren ground at the cliff's edge. She imagined Aemilia Caeciliana sobbing for mercy as she struggled not to be thrown off. It would be a horrible death. A flight of terror, then the pain of hitting the ground, back and neck broken.

Curbing her thoughts, she concentrated on looking beyond the place of execution. On the twin peak opposite, the fortified citadel on the Arx Capitolina was lit by full sun. Pinna saw sentinels at the guard posts keeping an eye on the city below, while others scanned the horizon beyond the outer wall, ever wary of external threat.

She scanned the vista of the seven hills. Her own past could be plotted here in the swells and dips of land: the dank caves of the Esquiline where she and Mama huddled in destitution, the lupanaria on the Aventine, and Camillus's house on the Palatine. The history of her degradation and salvation lay side by side.

She surveyed the swarm of people below. The market produce was bright with color, but otherwise Rome was shrouded in somber hues. Constant war had taken its toll. She recognized the dark togas of grieving fathers, sons, and brothers. And widows could be identified wearing double-folded cloaks, one end thrown over their shoulders. A symbol of mourning. An emblem of pride. Their husbands had died for Rome.

The Comitium was packed. Each tier of the circular arena was crammed with citizens, while senators congregated on the Curia steps, shuffling to make space to view the orators. The Republic on display.

A number of politicians had mounted the speakers' platform. Even from a distance she could recognize her Wolf. Medullinus stood together with Scipio and Spurius, the two other interreges who would govern until the elections were called. The tall, straight-spined Calvus was also there. Pinna could not see his expression, but his manner conveyed his usual contempt of patricians. He stood apart from the four others.

Suddenly, a horseman galloped toward the platform. There was something familiar about him. From the wide, angular shoulders and length of his body, she thought it was Drusus. The crowd parted to let him through lest they be trampled. The politicians moved to the edge of the podium and bent to listen to him.

A trumpet sounded in the distance. A short succession of urgent blasts. Pinna frowned, looking toward the source of the sound. It was a siren from the watchman on the Janiculum Hill across the Tiber. Pinna's heartbeat quickened as the sentry on the Arx echoed the frenzied alarm. It was a warning signal. Rome was under attack.

Panic exploded. Women screamed as the crowd in the Forum shoved each other to head toward the citadel. Pinna glanced toward the markets. Stalls were pushed over, awnings pitching sideways, feet tripping on tangled ropes, barrows of vegetables sent flying.

Like a mice plague, people emerged from pot-holed alleyways, offices, shops, and houses. All possessed the same intent: to reach the safety of the three-sided Capitoline cliffs and the fortress on the Arx. Pinna watched in horror as the throng converged on the Sacred Way, jostling and elbowing each other, jamming the Clivus Capitolinus, the single dusty road from the Forum.

Pinna searched for her Wolf. He'd commanded Drusus to dismount and was now sitting astride the steed's back. Managing the reins, he controlled the beast in the roiling crowd, digging his heels to urge the animal to charge toward the Aventine's vulnerable gates. He was shouting at people to stand aside, not attempting to avoid anyone in the stallion's path. There was much for him to organize. Makeshift wooden bridges across the Tiber needed to be dismantled. The gates around the perimeter locked. The ramparts manned.

And then she heard: "Etruria is rising! Etruria is rising!"

Her heart thumped, disbelieving her city was being invaded. A voice within her told her to avoid the turmoil of the throng, but she knew safety lay behind the citadel on the Arx. Leaving her basket, she merged into the press of people entering the Capitoline precinct. Ululating, women clambered up the steps of the Great Temple to beseech protection from Jupiter, clutching their children.

Pinna sought the shelter of thick masonry instead. She continued running through the sacred enclosure until she reached the rise to the citadel.

Siren blasts rent the air, fueling the chaos. The crush thickened as the crowd from the Forum now converged with the others on Clivus Capitolinus. Pinna panted with the exertion of keeping pace as the crowd ascended to the other peak. A woman next to her fell. Pinna tried to reach her but was pushed forward before she could help her. The victim's cries were muffled by the din of the stampede.

On the citadel, soldiers herded people through the gates, shouting at them to hurry, their anxiety adding to the hysteria.

Once inside the Arx's wall, the mob spread into the fortress's environs. The injured sat holding bleeding foreheads or cradling broken limbs. Others called out the names of loved ones from whom they'd been separated. Women wept. Children wailed. The horns continued.

Pinna climbed higher up the hill, driven by a need to escape as one would from rising floodwaters. She knew there was no possibility of the entire population crowding into the Arx. The high walls of the Palatine would have to serve as a refuge, too.

The troops of the home guard were busy checking the breastwork. The thought of relying on these scarred veterans made her nervous. Over forty-five years of age, they could no longer serve in the front lines. Yet were there enough of them to defend the city from the might of Etruria? Rome was not impregnable. It could not survive a siege.

Trembling, she listened for the sound of an earsplitting battle yell and the thunder of hooves. But no battle horns sounded. No drums. No barking from the dogs of war. If the Etruscans were launching an offense, it was a silent one.

More soldiers appeared, yelling at everyone to cease their lament. They gave reassurance that Camillus had doubled the guard around the city walls. And there was now a cordon of troops protecting the Forum. The Palatine was also secure. No enemy had yet been sighted.

Intent on facing her fears, Pinna picked her way through the seated groups to the highest point of the Arx. Another trumpet sounded. This time the notes were familiar. They declared the return of a Roman army. At the sound, others in the citadel started to head for the ramparts. Pinna asked permission from a sentinel to stand at the wall.

An army was assembling on the Field of Mars. To her relief, their helmets were plain and conical, not bronze and crested. She scanned the ranks. There were no spears raised, no shields held in battle readiness. Then she spied the wolf standard.

A soldier hurried past. Pinna called after him. "Why have those troops returned?"

"General Postumius ordered a retreat from Veii. There has been a massacre at Nepete. The League of the Twelve has joined Vel Mastarna in the north. Even with the outer siege lines manned, there is no way the regiment at Veii could withstand an assault."

Pinna's nerves jangled. There was no foe at the gates but there was one on the march. And if an entire Roman army had deserted in terror, then what chance had Rome?

She peered down, hoping to catch a sight of Camillus riding out to meet Postumius. And as dread gnawed at her, she wondered if her Wolf would be thrilled or daunted that he finally had his crisis.

FORTY-THREE

Caecilia, Veii, Spring, 396 BC

Caecilia shivered as she stood in the deserted Roman camp. Many of the tents had been knocked over in the panic of retreat, leaving a jumble of guy ropes, pegs, and hides. Cooking pots hung on tripods over campfires that were burning low, plumes of smoke wafting lazily above them. Chickens strutted amid the mess, pecking at cold porridge in the bowls.

Other tents remained intact, pegged in precise rows waiting for their occupants to return. Inside were hand mills, camp ovens, plates, cups, and spoons. Only the rumpled blankets strewn across pallets were evidence of the Romans waking to terror.

Lusinies's troops were moving through the detritus, collecting abandoned weapons. A shield lay on the ground, one half burnished, the other dull, indicating its owner had been disturbed midtask. Caecilia was incredulous, knowing each piece of armor was a prized possession. She thought of the shame that awaited the fugitives who had left them behind.

She had woken to the insistent blasts of Roman war horns. Hurrying to the terrace wall, she was astonished to see hoplites running from the main camp to join a swarming exodus on the Via Veientana.

What had struck fear into the foe? She had closed her eyes, listening for a countermelody to herald the approach of a Veientane army, but she heard no tune from Rasennan tubas.

Tarchon's grin had been broad as he joined her on the terrace. "The Romans are retreating."

"I can see. What has happened? Is it Vel?"

"There is no sign of his troops, but our scouts report the enemy are fleeing from the forts around the entire perimeter of the city. Both the outer and inner siege lines have been deserted. It's as though they believe demons are nipping at their heels."

She was stunned. What had tipped the balance?

The white flag of the command tent fluttered in the breeze. Inside, the general's desk was covered with scrolls listing inventory in the quartermaster's store. The tedium of the siege had reduced a warrior to an office clerk. After two years, this camp had become a permanent township.

She walked outside to join Tarchon. Cows with full udders lowed in the enclosure. To her dismay, she saw Veientane peasants tethered there as well, yokes around their necks and shackles on their ankles. As Lusinies's soldiers freed them from their bonds, they wept at the sight of their liberators. She hurried to them, murmuring words of reassurance. The freed captives acknowledged their queen with feeble smiles as they were lifted into wagons to return to the city.

Tarchon clasped her hand. "Come with me."

He led her to the ridge opposite the arx. It was strange to look at the citadel from this perspective. She felt satisfaction. The jewel in the crown of Etruria was safe.

Singing drifted from the city. The voices of the Veientanes, so long subdued, now filled the air. The townsfolk could make their pilgrimages to lay the ashes of their loved ones outside the sacred boundary. No longer would urns be the only full containers in otherwise empty pantries.

The regent pointed to the patchwork of fields. "Just think, Caecilia, the harvest will no longer be claimed by Rome. Our granaries will be full."

She smiled, glad that balance had been restored.

A wagon train manned by Lusinies's men passed them. One cart was laden with produce and barrels of wine. Caecilia was overwhelmed by the rich scents of fruit and vegetables. Tarchon pinched two apples and handed her one. The flavor exploded in her mouth. She never thought a simple fruit would taste like ambrosia.

The prince finished his apple, eating the core and spitting out the pips. "I've placed a guard on the Roman camps while I arrange for supplies to be distributed. The wooden forts will be hacked down to provide fuel, too. I don't want a riot when the people try to recover what they can in a frenzy. There must be some order to our recovery."

She studied him, impressed with his foresight. The city could not afford to descend into its own type of chaos. "Your father would be proud of you."

"Do you think so?"

She nodded, looking around her again. "Why do you think the Romans fled?"

"We will know soon enough. In the meantime, let's enjoy freedom. And if Mastarna has succeeded in the north, trade will once again flow. We'll be able to feed our people."

She slipped her arm around his waist. "I pray he and Sethre are safe."

He grew serious. "I worry for him. He is untested in war . . ."

She squeezed him, forgetting her own fears for her husband. "Let's not dwell on shadows that are yet to show substance."

The effort of happiness was tiring. Dizzy, she sagged against him. Tarchon called to one of the wagons to halt and lifted her onto it. She felt better when seated. Gazing across the valley, she breathed in freedom. Above the citadel a flock of starlings swooped and dipped, the formation merging and parting, a winged revel. It had been months since birds had flown over the citadel. It was as though they sensed the danger was over. Caecilia smiled. She did not need Tanchvil's skill at divination to know it was indeed a good omen.

FORTY-FOUR

Marcus, Rome, Spring, 396 BC

The sight of the sharp-bladed axes bound in the fasces was a reminder of Camillus's absolute power. The fact his twenty-four lictors carried them within the city also cautioned that the dictator could order executions without trial.

The deserters from Veii were divided into groups of ten. Each soldier cast lots. One was chosen to die. The remaining nine stoned him to death. The decimation was a purification ceremony to purge the regiment of disgrace as much as a terrifying penance.

Grim faced, Camillus watched the sentence carried out in the Forum instead of the Campus. Only a week after the massacres at Nepete and Falerii, the populace of Rome was still reduced to living behind fortified walls. The dictator knew the names of each warrior who was killed, but he didn't hail them as he would before a battle. No appeal against his verdict could be made either. His declaration to those assembled was chilling. It was a warning to all who served in the legions. "I'll lead you to victory if you follow me. But no soldier should forget to fear me more than the enemy."

After the decimation, Marcus followed Camillus into the Curia. The three hundred senators of Rome were absent. Given the state of emergency, the general was using the building as his headquarters.

Slanted shafts of light from slatted windows stippled the gloom of the rectangular chamber. Assured and confident, the dictator sat on a curule chair. The distinctive hinged ivory stool with its crisscrossed legs denoted his supreme authority. His frustration at being denied the chance to lead Rome had disappeared. Clad in breastplate and purple cloak, he was an impressive figure.

As usual, Marcus noticed the tension between the politicians around him. Medullinus was disgruntled. As the presiding consular general in Rome, he'd been required to appoint Camillus once the Senate recommended a dictator be appointed. How maddening it must have been to relinquish power to his fraternal rival. Camillus had never been elected consul, but as sole governor, he trumped him.

Aemilius was injured, his leg heavily bandaged, crutches resting on the floor as he sat on a stool. Before he'd ordered the retreat from Nepete, he'd plunged into the fray. A chunk of his thigh had been sliced away. His face was tinged as gray as his hair and eyebrows. He'd been shaken at the loss of so many of his hoplites. And Sempronius and his brigade had not survived. To add to his woes, Aemilius was mortified to find the error he'd made with the sacred calendar meant he'd been required to stand down from office.

Scipio was in a good mood. Camillus had declared him Master of the Horse. The honor of being appointed as second-in-command was immense. Backing the Furian in the past had proved fruitful.

Spurius was pensive, tapping his upper lip. Marcus had been surprised when Camillus had chosen Scipio over him. The tribune suspected sibling rivalry simmered below the surface after all.

Genucius was hearty, pleased Camillus was in charge. He had a chance for advancement again.

Medullinus's voice broke through Marcus's thoughts. "Brother, I don't relish treating with Veii, but I think you should consider consulting the Senate about the possibility."

"You want peace with Veii? Why? Rome isn't on its knees. I don't plan to grovel to Mastarna."

"Our people huddle behind our walls," said Spurius. "We sit in trepidation of being overrun. I'm sure we could broker reasonable terms."

"I don't believe there'll be an invasion. Our spies report that the Etruscans aren't on the warpath. I think Mastarna was exaggerating. The Veientanes were only bolstered with armies from three Rasennan cities."

"Nevertheless, three additional city-states are enough to conquer us," said Aemilius. "We should not be hasty about considering a truce."

"Are you turning into a dove again? I never thought to hear you give up this conflict. Your son and his men showed extraordinary courage at Nepete. I'm sure Marcus still has the appetite to fight, even if you don't."

At the jibe, Aemilius's beetling eyebrows formed a solid line, but he refrained from replying. Marcus knew his father's bitterness in losing the wolf standard, even if the retreat was acknowledged as tactical. Titinius's regiment had also been routed, but before the consular general had been killed, he'd ensured his army retained its pennant. At least Aemilius had been spared Postumius's ignominy. The coward had opened his veins, his shame bleeding from him together with his life.

Aemilius also had mixed feelings about his son's achievement compared to his own failure. The tribune and his knights were the only men to retain their spears and swords. The small band of cavalry was now lauded as the Horse Shield heroes.

Marcus held reservations about being praised as such. Camillus had assigned him to his personal staff on hearing he'd cheated death. Yet how could he claim a feat of bravery when he owed his survival to mercy?

Sharing the relief and joy of discovering both he and Drusus had survived had not lasted long. His promotion threatened a deeper rift between them. The Claudian had been promoted to a head decurion for his daring ride. But such a reward was insignificant compared to being a dictator's personal aide. And Mastarna's accusation of cowardice continued to weigh on Marcus. Soon he was avoiding Drusus whenever he could, lacking courage to confront him.

Medullinus crossed his arms. "So what are your plans, Brother? How exactly do you propose Rome defend itself?"

"How do we defend ourselves? By attacking! Scipio will march north to call Mastarna's bluff. And I'll clean up the mess left by you and your fellow consular generals in the matter of the Votive Games. I'll also assuage the gods of Latium by irrigating its floodplains." He pointed to the haruspex. "Just as Lord Artile prescribed months ago."

All turned to the priest. Throughout the discussions, the haruspex had given the appearance of being disinterested, examining the corner buttresses that supported the high ceiling as the men talked. Now he focused his attention on them. "General Camillus is correct. The preconditions for victory over Veii must be met as quickly as possible."

"Such plans are all very well, Brother, but how are you to achieve them with reduced manpower?" said Medullinus. "Two of our regiments suffered heavy losses. And the third has been decimated at your decree."

Camillus's eyes narrowed. "I make no apology about reminding soldiers that both the desire for conquest, and the threat of punishment, must motivate a man. And lack of men will not be an issue. I'll call for volunteers to swell the ranks of the legions. And

I'll use some retired veterans from the home guard who are still fit for battle."

Genucius frowned, adjusting his eye patch. "The executions have unnerved many. And now you plan to call more farmers to leave their crops? For worn bones to bear the weight of armor again? If so, something will need to be done about the booty denied them. Talk of peace is upon the lips of my fellow people's tribunes, too."

Camillus gripped the armrests of his chair. "Why is there always resistance from the commons! There won't be land to farm if we don't address this crisis! And the best chance to share the spoils is to seize the vast territory of Veii. Besides, I have a reform in mind that might please you and Icilius Calvus. I'll swell the ranks of the cavalry with eminent plebeians who can provide their own horses."

All the patricians bristled. The gods had visited calamity on Rome when plebeian generals were chosen. Now aristocrats were expected to ride into battle with men who'd not been born to hold bit and bridle. Marcus felt disconcerted as well. Wealthy plebeians might be able to ride a horse to hunt, but it was a different matter to control a stallion in battle.

He also expected Genucius to show surprise at Camillus's suggestion, but instead the plebeian nodded as though familiar with the prospect. "I'd be honored to be a knight. And such a proposal will go a long way to placating the people."

Camillus turned to the patricians, not waiting to hear their complaints. "Spurius, organize engineers to see to the irrigation. I will visit Satricum to offer Rome's apologies for its neglect of their gods and declare a date for duly consecrated games. And I'll promise to honor Mater Matuta by restoring her temple in Rome. The Latin Pact will be renewed. Thereafter we'll have allied troops to assist the Boar Legion at Anxur and Labicum."

He addressed Scipio next. "As Master of the Horse, you must once again surround Nepete, Falerii, and Capena. Let's take the fight to the Twelve and see if they indeed have a desire to breach Rome's wall. Postumius's deserters will go with you."

"And what are Aemilius and I to do?" said Medullinus. "Have you forgotten we're still consular generals?"

"And lucky to remain so. You'll assist Scipio. And Aemilius will act as prefect of Rome. His survivors can swell the ranks of the home guard for the time being. I will take Titinius's men with me south."

Aemilius glared. "I'm to be denied an active command, then?"

"You're badly wounded. Given your age, there's no shame in leading the home guard. And Calvus and his cronies may continue to stir up unrest. I'll need a calm head here."

Aemilius pursed his lips but said nothing again. Marcus doubted his father appreciated the reminder of his advancing years.

"And Veii?" asked Spurius. "Who's to command there?"

"No one. I want to lure Mastarna into a false sense of security. Once Rome has expiated its transgressions, and all our warfronts are under control, I'll once again turn my sights on his city. And when I do, I'll be the one to conquer it."

"Again I question how this is to be done," drawled Medullinus.

Camillus stood. "Freed from all other conflicts, our two legions and our allies will attack the northwest bridge. I'll lead a force of six thousand men to swarm over the wall of Veii at its weakest point."

"You only have six months, Brother," said Medullinus, brushing his thinning hair across his pate. "Where's the money to fund these strategies? How are already weary soldiers expected to continue fighting?"

"We need to push through exhaustion. Respite will come with victory. As will riches. In the meantime, the Senate must allow me to exhaust the treasury's coffers." He jabbed his finger at Medullinus. "And not you, nor anyone else, can stand in my way."

Marcus sensed the shock of those present. The consular general stood. "Careful, Brother. Rome does not tolerate despots."

"We all need to calm down," said Spurius. "Camillus is right. It's time to cast aside past grievances and jealousies for the good of Rome. He's been given half a year. Let's not question his authority."

Scipio added, "Listen to Spurius. Camillus needs men who will stand beside him, not undermine him."

Medullinus looked as though he'd been forced to drink a nasty-tasting tonic. "Very well. I will put enmity aside for the sake of the Republic."

Aemilius winced as he reached for his crutches, leaning on one to help him stand. "Your goals are bold, Camillus. And audacity may be our only chance. I'll support you for six months. But if Veii is not taken by then, I'll be proposing the Senate consider peace talks."

The dictator frowned, then nodded. "Accepted. But I don't plan to fail." He pointed to the doorway. "Go. You have your orders." He beckoned to Spurius. "You stay. We need to discuss our plans."

As the generals turned, Genucius rose from his stool. In the flurry of the others' exchange, he'd been forgotten. "And what are my orders?"

Camillus swiveled around. He seemed disconcerted he'd overlooked the politician. "You're now a knight. As Master of the Horse, Scipio will determine your role, given he's in charge of all Roman cavalries."

"So I'm not to be given a regiment? I thought . . . I thought . . ."

"Oh, and what exactly did you think?"

Genucius's brow furrowed. Then his voice hardened. "I thought you'd show good faith to the commons by appointing me as a general." He glanced across to Scipio. "It seems you would prefer a patrician with a weak spear arm to a man who helped you take the northwest bridge in the Battle of Blood and Hail."

Scipio scowled at the insult. Marcus thought it imprudent for the new knight to denigrate the general who would lead him.

Camillus didn't rise to the bait. "I'm giving you and all wealthy men of your class the chance to prove yourselves as knights. Isn't that fair?"

Genucius stood to attention and saluted, but his sullen expression rivaled that of Medullinus's. The plebeian had been accused of doing favors for Camillus before. Had the dictator not repaid him in kind?

As the soldiers departed, Camillus signaled to Spurius and Artile to draw up stools beside him, gesturing to Marcus to join them. And as the tribune took his seat, he couldn't help wondering whether the dictator enjoyed ruffling feathers, challenging those around him, keeping them on edge, and reminding each of them that he now ruled them.

FORTY-FIVE

Caecilia, Veii, Spring, 396 BC

The sound of cheering outside the palace startled Caecilia. Crouched beside her younger sons, she paused in the game of ships and heads. Larce was also distracted as he knelt on the terrace tiles, poised to flip the coin. "What are they shouting about, Ati?"

"I don't know. Stay here."

Arnth was unimpressed at being ordered to remain behind. Semni was quick to place her hands on his shoulders to restrain him from following his mother. "Come, little masters. Let's keep playing." Her expression was also curious, though, as was Perca's as she rocked Thia in her cradle.

Caecilia hurried toward the palace courtyard, Arruns following her. As she reached the atrium, she saw Tarchon emerge from the throne room, also puzzled.

A grinning Lusinies strode in from the portico. "It's Lord Mastarna!"

Caecilia did not wait to hear more.

An expectant crowd had gathered in the square, leaving a path clear to the double gates of Uni. Their cheers reached a crescendo as two riders maneuvered their way through the portal and then trotted toward the palace. There was no mistaking the king as he sat astride the great gray. Alongside him, Sethre Kurvenas rode his horse with confident grace.

Mastarna reined in his mount, swinging down to stand in front of his wife. He pulled off his padded helmet, letting it drop to the ground. Aching for him, Caecilia stepped close, taking in the smell of sweat and dust, metal and leather. He pulled her to him, pressing her so hard against the bronze of his corselet she thought her ribs might crack. At her gasp, he released her.

The crowd around them hooted and cheered. Ignoring them, Caecilia inspected him, checking for injury, but she saw no new scars. His tanned face was grimy, thick stubble shadowing his jaw. He looked so hearty. No gaunt lines or sickly pallor. He was the first healthy person she'd seen in a long, long time.

His dark eyes were soft with pity as he scanned her emaciated frame and hollow cheeks. He rested his fingers on her throat, tracing the delicate line of her collarbone before cradling her face between callused hands. "My sweet Bellatrix, there's nothing left of you."

She raised her hands to cup his face. "I hold everything between my palms."

Her kiss was hungry, telling him she was not just starved for food. Then, smiling, she drew back and ran her hand along the contours of the muscle cuirass. "You need to take this off."

He stroked her cheek, saying the familiar refrain, "Don't worry, I plan to." Then he leaned his forehead against hers. "And our children?"

"Alive."

"Praise the gods."

He turned and surveyed the people around them. "Veientanes, the routes to the north are open. Supply wagons will arrive soon. Eat well and drink deeply!"

They roared in reply.

Vel looped his arm around Caecilia's waist and escorted her up the steps, nodding acknowledgment to Arruns. The lictor bowed, a half smile on his lips.

Sethre dismounted and followed. Tarchon stood beaming on the portico, his eyes glued on the youth. However, when the royal couple reached the prince, he opened his arms wide to his father. Caecilia stepped aside as Tarchon hugged Vel. It was the first time she'd seen them embrace.

"I feared I'd never see you again, Father."

The king broke from him, clearly surprised at the heartfelt reception.

Caecilia smiled. "Is it any wonder your son should be pleased to see you?"

Mastarna's reserve disappeared. He thumped Tarchon on the back. "It's good to see you, too."

Lusinies added his welcome, clapping the king on the shoulder and gesturing toward the war council room. "Welcome back, my lord. Let's talk while we wait for refreshments."

As they entered the chamber, Tarchon placed his arm around Sethre's shoulders. Caecilia glanced at Vel to see his reaction, but he seemed unconcerned. In the thrill of reunion such a breach could be overlooked.

Sethre removed his helmet. His chin was covered in wiry stubble. And there were stitches puckering a wound along the side of his face. The green warrior had been blooded and would soon grow a full beard. He was allowed to remain as the group settled around the council table.

Caecilia sat next to Vel, who covered his hand with hers. "Where's Feluske?"

"Dead from the red scourge, my lord," said Lusinies. "Plague and starvation have stalked us. The desertion of the Roman troops only a week ago came as a welcome surprise. Your victory at Nepete saved us. The news of the League's approach instilled fear in them."

"But you're wrong," blurted Sethre. "The Twelve do not stand behind us."

Mastarna cast a stern look at his aide, unimpressed he'd spoken without consent. "I'm afraid what Sethre says is true. The Faliscans and Capenates approached the congress this time with some success. An agreement was reached that any city that wished to spare men to assist Veii and its allies was free to do so. We gained ancillary forces from three. However, the northern cities are now concerned with a more immediate threat than the Romans."

"What threat?" asked Tarchon.

"The Gauls are grouping at the River Padus. They are insinuating themselves ever southward just as the Romans are attempting to spread north."

Caecilia was stunned. There had been peaceful trade between the Rasenna and Gauls for years. What had caused them to become warlike? Did they, like the Romans, now covet the fertile pastures of the League? "So Postumius's force deserted for no other reason than rumor?"

Mastarna nodded. "So it seems. The tale of the rising of the Twelve proved to be as potent as an advancing army. But with the help of the other three Rasennan cities, Karcuna and I scored a decisive victory at Nepete. Thefarie did the same at Capena against Titinius, who was slain. The roads south were clogged with soldiers scurrying back to Rome." He squeezed Caecilia's hand. "Aemilius and Marcus were among them."

"So there will be no force to invade Rome?"

Mastarna frowned. "There's no need, Bellatrix. It will be some time before our foe recovers both its pride and strength."

A sense of foreboding spread through her. With news of the confederation's support, she'd believed her destiny was secure. Now, once again, the fickle goddess had set her wheel of fortune spinning in a different direction. "So no advantage can be gained from your victories after all?"

"Advantage? Of course there was benefit in our success. Our allies are now free from the Roman menace. And the northern trade routes are open. When I heard the Romans had deserted I rode ahead."

Her unease deepened. "So Rome will remain unconquered, then."

Mastarna stared at her. "There's opportunity for peace now, Bellatrix. Do you still want bloodshed when Veii is no longer surrounded? You're a fiercer warrior than I."

She withdrew her hand from under his. "I'm not ashamed to want the Rasenna to once again rule Rome. What if the enemy returns and the wolf once again bays outside our door? Three of the Twelve are with us. Why not command Thefarie and Karcuna to continue on with those allies?" She looked at Lusinies. "Why not muster all Veii's tribes to fight?"

She saw Vel's shock at her challenge. He scanned the thin frames of Tarchon and Lusinies before returning to meet her eyes. "And what type of men are we to lead, Bellatrix? Feluske is dead. We would lead a force of armed scarecrows. And without all in the Brotherhood, there's no chance of taking and holding Rome."

She reddened, ashamed she should press him. He was fit and healthy, but she could see the strain in his eyes. Who was she to urge a general to follow her strategy? What right did she have to strive for conquest just because she feared she'd taunted Fate?

"Then you believe the Romans are defeated, Father. That they will not return?" said Tarchon.

Mastarna dragged his attention from his wife. "I doubt it. We're in a position of power once again. And this war depletes Rome's resources and costs lives, too. The Romans suffered heavy losses in the north before they retreated. Let's see if they have any resolve to begin again once we've dismantled their fortifications. Let's see if the common soldier has the appetite to pay more war tax while shivering in winter and sweltering in summer far from home."

The sound of children's voices raised in excitement cut through the somberness of the conversation. Mastarna's frown vanished. He stood, gesturing Arruns to allow the princes to enter.

There was a scrape of chairs as the others also rose to bow and then depart the room.

Vel clasped Caecilia's hand. "Don't worry, Bellatrix, I believe Nortia has spared us."

Larce and Arnth rushed in, clambering over their father, who let them haul him to the floor: the great warrior conquered by a puny assault. Even Tas joined in, standing behind his father and wrapping his arms around his neck. And as Vel pulled Caecilia down to join the jumble of boys, she pushed apprehension aside to delight in the moment of sweet and heady reunion.

FORTY-SIX

Semni, Spring, Veii, 396 BC

The joy at the lifting of the siege had waned. Married life was not as Semni imagined. Constrained by their duties, she and her husband could not reside together. The barracks were no place for Nerie, and Arruns balked at sleeping next to the nursery. They snatched time together when Semni would visit his cell after the boy was asleep. It was a relief to feel no guilt when lying with him, but being denied the chance to wake beside him fostered frustration. She thought more and more of a life where the needs of others were not paramount. She did not want Arruns to be required to die for another man's family. And so, as the babe grew within her, so did her discontent.

In the few weeks since the king's return, she'd often steal into the loggia at night before visiting Arruns at the end of his shift. There she would confide her worries to the row of caryatids whose fair, solemn faces never expressed disapproval.

The night was mild, the stars blanketing the sky in a swirling milky mass. The moon was lucent and bright, illuminating the forum and its buildings. Standing at the gallery's balustrade, Semni wondered if she would see the same constellations if she traveled across the Great Sea to Canaan. Then she chided herself, knowing her dream of seeing distant shores was verging on delusion. She was better served looking forward to spending a short time in her husband's bed. But as she headed down the stairs, she was startled to find Arruns at the bottom. He clasped her hand. "What are you doing here? I've been looking for you."

Before she could answer, they heard voices in the courtyard: the soft feminine tones of Lady Caecilia, the deep bass of the king, and Prince Tarchon's, which was light in comparison to his father's. Twelve lictors followed the royal trio, stationing themselves at intervals at the outer doors and entrances leading from the open-roofed hall.

Arruns signaled Semni to be quiet by placing his finger to his lips, directing her to copy him as he pressed against the wall of the stairwell.

Lady Caecilia's voice was cheery. "It's such a beautiful night, Vel. Can't we sit beneath the stars for our council meeting? I'm tired of the fustiness of the war chamber. It only reminds me of grim times."

Aware they would be eavesdropping on official business, Semni glanced at Arruns, but he remained inscrutable.

She heard Prince Tarchon laugh, teasing the queen for such an indulgence. The king sounded good humored. "Very well, Bellatrix. If we're to talk of peace, then let it be under night skies."

A tremor of excitement buzzed through Semni. Impassive, Arruns gestured her to ascend the stairs. They crept into the loggia, crossing to the opposite side of the gallery to the one facing the forum. From there they could look down on the nobles in the courtyard. They crouched behind the balustrade. Her husband's stealth reminded her it was his job to merge into the shadows to watch and listen. She clutched his forearm, thrilled by the subterfuge. How much had he overheard in his time in Veii?

Two lictors arranged five bronze armchairs in a circle. Servant boys hastened to serve the king, queen, and prince wine.

General Karcuna was the first to arrive. He frowned at the arrangement, casting a doubtful look at the king when he heard he was pandering to his wife's whim.

Lord Mastarna raised his goblet to him. "I hear you're satisfied that Tarchon is eligible to be Sethre's mentor, Karcuna."

The tall general paused, inspecting the prince. The younger man met his eyes. Semni was impressed. In the past, the pleasure seeker would have fidgeted at such scrutiny.

"Considering Prince Tarchon has shown wisdom and resolve as regent, I'm prepared to consider a trial period," Lord Karcuna said. "But if he lapses into old ways . . ."

Lady Caecilia spoke before her stepson. "Those days are behind Tarchon. As is the enmity between our Houses. Campaigning with my husband has mended the rift, has it not?"

The princip bowed his head. "Indeed."

"Karcuna and I relished routing those Romans," said Mastarna. "It was good to see the Tulumnes and Mastarna clans fighting together instead of circling each other like hounds."

"Then Tarchon's mentorship of Sethre will cement our alliance," said the queen.

Lord Karcuna's cheek twitched. Semni found the tic disconcerting. "I'll be frank," he said. "Sethre is close to full manhood. The relationship might not last beyond a year. I doubt it's worth the trouble. I hope Tarchon won't hesitate to release my cousin from his bed when the time comes."

Semni blinked, surprised at the aristocrat's bluntness.

"I have given my word," said the prince. "I'll not seek to taint him. I'll honor any terms you set."

Lord Mastarna stood and extended his arm to the general. "I believe my son is sincere, Karcuna. I vouchsafe his conduct. We can agree to conditions later but let's seal the agreement now by hand." Lord Karcuna hesitated, then gripped the lucumo's arm. Then he turned and offered his own to Lord Tarchon.

As they resumed their seats, General Lusinies entered the courtyard. His battered countenance challenged Arruns's for menace. After the initial surprise at taking council in starlight, he smiled as he bowed his head to the queen. Sharing months of hardship had led to more than mutual respect.

Semni noticed Lady Caecilia was not cowed by the presence of the warriors. Elegant in her flowing purple mantle, she surveyed each man in turn, asserting her authority. Semni was amazed this woman was at ease talking of battles and treaties as much as dealing with nursery and hearth.

"The time has come to make peace with Rome," said the king.

"Let them come to us," said Lord Karcuna. "I don't see why we should be the first to treat."

The lucumo shook his head. "We're in a position of power. Why not take advantage of their chaos?"

General Lusinies grimaced. "But our spies say Camillus is raising a force to march north again. They say he's also planning to visit the war fronts in the south himself."

Lord Karcuna leaned forward. "We should not underestimate him. The rumor that all Etruria has joined us is now dispelled."

"We shall see," said Lord Mastarna. "Camillus only has six months as dictator. Why would he succeed in half a year when others have failed to do so for ten? However, I do think it's prudent that we send one of our armies north again."

"What treaty terms will we seek?" said General Lusinies.

"The same as those of the twenty years' peace before this war began," said the king. "Veii will gain access to the southern trade routes via Fidenae. Rome will be provided with our grain."

Lord Karcuna glanced at Lady Caecilia, then back to the king. "The old truce was predicated on us feeding Rome. But our crops are yet to be reaped. And there is no guarantee Camillus will not try to conquer the fields sown under his direction."

Lord Mastarna rubbed the scar from nose to mouth. "Camillus has made no move to return to Veii. And the longer he waits, the more daunting it will be to start again when he finds his siege lines stripped of stone and timber. Harvest time is only a few short months away. We should offer Rome what it had before."

Prince Tarchon stood. "Then let me act as Veii's ambassador."

His eagerness was met with awkward silence.

General Lusinies scratched his shiny bald head. "I speak plainly here. Prince Tarchon is hardly a decorated hero. Should we not send a warrior to deal with Camillus?"

"Tarchon has proven himself as a wise regent. And sending the king's son would show good faith," said Lady Caecilia, quick to defend him. "And the prince speaks fluent Latin. There's less chance of deception if an envoy doesn't need an interpreter."

"I agree," said Lord Mastarna. "We need diplomacy, not bluster. My son has never lacked intelligence, only good sense. In fact I think we should reinforce the message that it's time to put aside old hatreds." He turned to Lord Karcuna. "Sethre should be sent as well."

General Lusinies interrupted before the other princip could respond. "Do you want to antagonize Rome, my lord? Karcuna's father sparked the last Fidenate war."

"On the contrary," said the king. "It will show Camillus we're not afraid to send a relative of King Tulumnes to broker peace."

Prince Tarchon stared at his father, horrified. "I don't want to risk Sethre's life."

"By the gods, my lord," said General Lusinies to the lucumo. "Are you prepared to risk your son being taken hostage? Or killed?"

"Do you question my judgment?"

The general raised his hands. "I meant no offense."

Agitated, Prince Tarchon dragged his fingers through his hair. "Father, I'm willing to take the challenge, but Sethre . . ."

"Will you falter at the first hurdle when proving yourself as a mentor? Sethre Kurvenas is now your pupil. Let the youth learn about diplomacy from you as he has learned warfare from me. Besides, it may well be a guarantee of safety to send you both. It would be a brave act to execute two messengers with royal blood running in their veins. You must leave for Roman territory tomorrow."

The prince squared his shoulders. "Then I'll show Sethre what it means to step into a wolves' den and survive."

"Good." The lucumo turned to Lord Karcuna. "What say you? Are you prepared to send your ward to treat with Rome?"

The tic in the general's cheek flickered, but his voice was firm. "We'll show the Romans that Clan Tulumnes now breeds men of principle."

The monarch rose. The others stood to attention, but Lady Caecilia was slower to rise. "We must ensure our ambassadors are protected by our ablest soldiers."

"Of course they will be accompanied by guards," said her husband. "And I'll send Arruns as their personal protector. It would take more than one assassin to get past him should they attempt to kill Tarchon and Sethre in their sleep."

Semni gasped and cast a stricken look to her husband. Once again Arruns placed his finger to his lips. She forced herself to wait until the royal couple and councillors made their way from the courtyard. "I won't let you go. I can't let you go. You could be killed." She clung to him, her world collapsing.

He wrapped his arms around her. Cheek pressed to his chest, she heard his heartbeat matching the frantic thudding of her own. Yet after a time she realized he was excited, not despairing. She pulled away and stared at him. "You want this, don't you?"

He hesitated, but his zeal was apparent. The last time she'd glimpsed such anticipation was when he'd left for war with Lord Mastarna. But that was before he'd loved her. Before he'd helped her to birth Nerie. Before his child was seeded in her. "Don't you love me, Arruns?"

"Of course I love you, but I'm a warrior. You think I can become a trader in Canaan again? That man is dead, Semni. I'm like the serpent. I can't be tamed."

She covered her face with her hands, gulping back tears. His callused fingers tried to pry hers apart. "Don't weep. I'm not going to die. The Romans will not risk enraging King Mastarna by attacking his ambassadors."

"You can't say that for sure."

He smoothed her hair with an awkward motion. "Nothing is certain, Semni. I could have died of the plague in my sleep. Let's not spoil our time together. Come to bed. Stay the night. I'm sure Perca will look after Nerie."

She wiped her eyes and cheeks with the back of each hand, remembering that Lady Caecilia never cried in front of her husband when he went to war. She took a deep breath, determined to emulate her mistress. "Slowly, then. I want you all night if I'm to bid farewell in the morning."

He smiled, showing chipped teeth. "Then I'm to be denied sleep before my journey?"

She slipped her hand into his, tugging him to follow her. "Perhaps I'll let you have some. Enough to ensure you don't fall off your horse from fatigue. Not enough, though, to let you forget what you're missing while you're in Rome."

FORTY-SEVEN

Marcus, Outside Rome, Spring, 396 BC

The last time Marcus had seen Tarchon Mastarna, the Veientane had both attracted and disturbed him. On the brink of war, in the camp at Fidenae ten years ago, he'd seemed a soft creature, his dark, sloe-eyed beauty captivating. The sight of Caecilia embracing him was shocking. As her cousin, he'd never dared to be more familiar than hold her hand. In hindsight, he should have seen it as a sign that vice governed her, that she could never return to Roman decorum, that she had already been corrupted.

Today, there was no sign of the effete youth. Tarchon's stature was martial and proud. It was as though warfare had chiseled his features into even more handsome lines. Acting as regent of Veii in his father's absence had annealed his character. To walk into an enemy's home to barter for peace was not for the faint hearted.

The prince had not come alone. Marcus was surprised to see Sethre, the haughty young warrior who'd taunted him at Nepete. If the Veientane king wanted peace, then it was strange to send a representative from the Tulumnes clan brazenly wearing the winged lion crest. He also recognized Arruns, the lictor who'd thwarted him killing Mastarna at the Battle of Blood and Hail. The snake inked into the guard's face was as intimidating as his cold, hooded gaze.

Taken by surprise by the request to hold peace talks, Camillus had refused to grant Tarchon entry to the Temple of Apollo Medicus on the Campus, directing the delegation to meet at his country home instead.

The residence was modest, more a large farmhouse than a villa. The Furian family did not boast the heritage of the Aemilian family. Marcus had grown up on estates where grain was counted in wagon trains and vineyards stretched to the horizon. His father's crops, his father's land, his father's wine. One day to be his.

Glancing along the corridor leading to the kitchen, he wondered if Pinna was eavesdropping as usual. The fact Camillus brought her everywhere was yet another sign she was gaining too much influence.

There was another person hiding in the house. Artile Mastarna had been ordered to remain in the study while the negotiations were conducted. It worried Marcus that Camillus now consulted the Etruscan on both personal issues and matters of state.

After surrendering their weapons at the door, the emissaries entered the hall with its humble hearth shrine and simple well. The only adornments in the room were the dozens of silver spears and standards awarded to Furius Camillus, his military glory on display. Following the ambassadors were two servants carrying an enormous golden urn, a gift for Rome.

In the close confines of the atrium, the atmosphere was hostile. Tarchon frowned as he inspected the twelve lictors crowded along one stuccoed wooden wall. Arruns scrutinized his adversaries, positioning himself at the door to keep the exit clear. Marcus thought the action futile. None of the visitors would survive if Camillus chose to ignore the custom of treating a diplomat as inviolate.

Sethre eyed the lictors but remained composed, seemingly undaunted at being surrounded by his foe.

General Camillus remained seated on his curule chair as he observed the envoys enter. Both prince and dictator wore a cloak of purple—Veientane royalty meeting the supreme authority of Rome.

The general's tone was cordial. "Hail, Tarchon Mastarna."

The prince did not bow, reminding the Roman of his pedigree. "Hail, Furius Camillus. My father sends his greetings," he said in Latin.

Marcus had forgotten he spoke their language fluently even though his accent was thick and stilted. They would need to be wary. A man who needed no translator could overhear careless asides.

Tarchon turned to Marcus, his gaze roaming over the tribune's figure before returning to meet his eyes, staring at him for long moments. "We meet again, Marcus Aemilius."

Nonplussed by his appraisal, Marcus inwardly berated himself for maintaining eye contact for a fraction too long. He felt his face burn, determined to control the urge to imagine himself with the handsome Etruscan. He nodded. "Prince Tarchon."

The Veientane signaled the servants to place the huge vase in front of Camillus. "I bring a present as a sign of good faith."

The dictator glanced at the urn as though accustomed to such opulence. "Rome thanks your king for the gift," he said, then gestured toward Sethre. "And who is this?"

The prince turned and smiled at the youth, stroking his arm as he urged him to step forward. "This is my pupil, Sethre Kurvenas."

Marcus was startled, unsure whether he imagined the intimacy of the prince's touch or the adoration in his young companion's gaze. Were these two lovers? He remembered his conversation with Artile as they waited for the ferry. How the seer hated his brother for turning his beloved against him. He'd felt disgust that day for the priest's corruption of Tarchon. Was the prince following the example set by his uncle with an inappropriate relationship of his own?

Camillus's expression darkened as he studied the pair. "Vel Mastarna has sent the descendant of a king who murdered four Roman envoys? Is this some kind of mockery? I would've thought he would try to avoid reminding me of such bloody diplomacy."

Tarchon raised his hand in pacification. "My father is prepared to risk the lives of the sons of two royal houses. The grandnephew of King Tulumnes comes to treat in good faith, unlike his ancestor. Both Sethre's and my forebears were slain at the command of Mamercus Aemilius. We put such history aside for the sake of peace. Let's not tally the list of those who should be avenged on either side. If we do, then this war will be without end."

Camillus glared at the prince but motioned to the chair opposite him. "Take a seat."

A servant boy hurried forward to serve wine.

The ambassador sipped his drink. Marcus admired how the Veientane had diffused a fiery start to the conference.

Tarchon scanned the atrium, then turned back to face the two Romans. "You have humble quarters for a dictator."

"I'm no king. I've no need for luxury. "

"Still, I thought a visiting prince would be met in finer surroundings. I was surprised when word was sent that I would not address your Senate."

"As dictator, I chose to deal with this matter. Tell me, what are Veii's terms?"

"As before. Grain in return for access to trade routes. And, of course, withdrawal of your troops from Veientane territory."

The dictator tapped his gold ring. "What makes you think Rome wants your accord?"

Tarchon smiled. "Because the Wolf Legion lost its standard in the north. Because the Boar Legion struggles against enemies in the south and east. And because there is likely to be dissension between your classes as a result. How are you going to feed your people when all its farmers are bearing weapons?"

Camillus shrugged his shoulders. "A hungry belly does not worry Rome. And one defeat does not mean the loss of a war."

"I saw the flight from Veii myself. It seems Roman soldiers are adept at running backward." Tarchon's gaze moved to Marcus, once again assessing him for longer than the tribune found comfortable. "Except for Marcus Aemilius, of course. The Horse Shield hero. Your fame has spread."

The tribune didn't respond.

Camillus gestured to a servant to pour more wine. "Marcus is but one of many brave Romans who are prepared to fight. And those who deserted have borne the brunt of my ire. The decimation has provided a lesson to the legions."

Tarchon exchanged glances with Sethre before responding. "You reduced your army in punishment?"

"Sometimes harsh measures are necessary to remind a man of his duty. But I have no concerns about numbers. I've raised an extra levy, and the Latin Pact will provide us with allies. General Scipio has already mustered a force to ride north again."

"Do you forget that the League is now supporting us?"

"Ah, but I heard your Etruscan brethren have lost interest in Veii's cause."

"There are still enough to assist us."

"Perhaps, but not enough to stoke Rome's fears that it will be invaded."

The prince frowned. "So you're prepared to let this war continue? You Romans must grow weary of running on the spot! Ten years of combat and hundreds of your men killed for no gain."

Camillus stood. "I fear you have made a fruitless journey."

Tarchon stared up at him, surprise in his sloe eyes. "But it's the Senate that determines if Rome is to be at war or peace."

"A dictator has extraordinary powers. And I've been given a mission"—the general crossed his arms—"to conquer Veii."

Tarchon rose. "You'll never breach our walls. Your efforts will be wasted."

"Your city was on the brink of capitulation not long ago."

"Only after more than a year of deprivation. You have less than six months to succeed. We've supplies enough to see us through. And summer is upon us. Hot months without rain will take its toll on your people. You will soon beg for our wheat."

"There's little point in us continuing. I see now that Vel Mastarna was never sincere. He's insulted me by sending two emissaries who are molles—and one of them the relative of a murderous king!"

Tarchon clenched his jaw. "You've squandered our time. You should've advised us that I couldn't address the Senate."

Camillus pointed to the urn. "Take your gift. I'll collect it when I ride into your citadel. Why should I be satisfied with one vase when there is a palace of riches to fill our treasury?"

The prince glared at the dictator, then turned on his heel, barking at his servants to collect the tribute. Sethre hastened after him. Stony eyed, Arruns retrieved the envoys' helmets and swords from the lictors and handed them to his masters.

Astounded at how the negotiations had descended into vitriol, Marcus watched Tarchon strap on his helmet and help Sethre adjust his balteus and sword. Then the ambassadors stormed out into the encroaching night to commence the dangerous journey home.

After dismissing his lictors, Camillus dragged back the curtain to the study. "Lord Artile, come join us."

The priest hovered at the threshold, his shoulders slumped. The arrogance in his dark, liquid eyes had been replaced by dismay. Marcus was surprised at the extent of his despondency as the seer sank into the seat left vacant by the prince. Marcus drew up a chair beside him.

Camillus scowled at the haruspex. "What's the matter with you? Are you perturbed to see the man you corrupted has taken a beloved of his own?"

Artile looked up. "You know Tarchon and I were lovers?"

"I make it my business to glean all I can about the motives of a traitor. Marcus told me how you resent your brother and Caecilia for encouraging Tarchon to spurn you. I found it distasteful that you could betray a city because of a lover's quarrel, but I ignored your depravity because of your talents." He paused. "Or has your treachery always been predicated on some sordid love triangle? Did you know about the prince's passion for Sethre Kurvenas before you deserted Veii?"

The priest sighed. "I'd hoped it was an infatuation that would pass. I see today the boy has bewitched him."

Camillus snorted. "See, Marcus, I told you love makes a man weak. And a mollis even weaker."

His jibe jolted Artile from his mood. "It would pay you not to insult me. Especially since I can tell you how to destroy Veii without waiting to muster a force of six thousand men."

It took a moment for Marcus to register his words. So, too, the general. Then Camillus erupted. He stood and seized Artile by the scruff of his sheepskin cloak, dragging the priest to stand. "Are you saying you've only been half a traitor but now are willing to assume the entire role? Tell me what you know!"

Artile blanched, frozen under the dictator's grip. "I will, I will, just let me go."

Camillus released him and sat down. The seer rearranged his clothes, his hand shaking as he fumbled with the crescent fibula.

The dictator barked. "Stop fidgeting! How do I conquer Veii without storming its gates?"

"By tunneling under them."

Camillus grunted in frustration. "Is that all? I considered such a tactic years ago. The tufa blocks are three feet thick, and the ramparts are compacted with eleven feet of earth. What you say is worthless! I should send you back to your brother!"

Artile raised his black-tipped fingers in supplication. "No! What I say is possible. Remember the channel I showed you near the sanctuary?"

"A drain? Am I going to conquer Veii by using a sewer?"

Artile glanced between both dictator and tribune. "In a way, yes. That conduit is just one of many underground cuniculi around Veii. As I've mentioned before, there are huge galleries extending for miles beneath the surface that form a complex network of pipes, locks, and dams. More importantly, some caves provide direct access to the city drainage system on the plateau. How do you think Veientane spies managed to gain access to the city during the siege?"

Intrigued, Marcus edged forward on his seat. Camillus no longer glowered. "But my troops would need to wade waist deep through water to traverse such passages."

"If you wait until summer, the water courses dry up and the levels lessen. A little mud should not deter a Roman soldier." Confidence growing, Artile eased back in his chair and crossed his legs. "What's more, I know a way to access the citadel."

Camillus leaned forward, a hand on each knee. "How so?"

The haruspex smoothed his eyebrow, his caginess returning. "First I ask that you reward me for revealing the secret."

The general cocked his head to the side, voice caustic. "And what boon do you wish granted, priest?"

"To allow me to claim two slaves. My nephew, Vel Mastarna Junior—"

"Mastarna's firstborn? He's a child. What do you want with him?"

"Tas has the makings of a great seer. I wish to mentor him."

Marcus felt uneasy, conscious of how the priest had tainted Tarchon. He doubted the uncle would restrict himself to merely being the little boy's teacher. Camillus frowned but motioned the haruspex to continue.

"And I want Tarchon Mastarna, too."

The dictator's upper lip curled. "You'll need servants to hold him down if you want the prince to be your bedmate again."

"I want to make him suffer. To remind him every day that he has a master and he chose wrongly to show devotion to Mastarna and his bitch. And for loving *that boy.*"

"I'm not interested in your petty vengeance," growled Camillus. "And you're in no position to make demands. Tell me how I can breach the citadel."

The Etruscan hesitated. Marcus wondered if he was digesting his last scruple. Then Artile bent his head toward the general, his tone conspiratorial. "There's a shaft that leads up into the Great Temple from the base of the citadel. I escaped through it on the day of the Battle of Blood and Hail."

Camillus's eyes narrowed. "And how do we reach such a passage?"

"By digging a sap to connect to its opening. You'll need to occupy the quarry in the valley again. From there you can tunnel through to the overhang that hides the shaft entrance. The Veientanes won't think it unusual that Romans are once again wielding picks to cut stone to line trenches."

Camillus tapped his ring, absorbing the intelligence. "Our main camp overlooks the pit. It will be amusing to think we're undermining them beneath their noses."

Marcus's own excitement grew. "Once we've gained entry to the arx, our soldiers can open the main gates of the city."

The general thumped his knee. "While our other troops move through the cuniculi on the plateau!"

The priest was watching them, once again sure of himself. His smugness made Marcus want to strike him. This man had just condemned his own people to death, and he was smiling. Artile did not have the strength to wield a weapon but he was deadly.

Camillus stood and gripped the soothsayer's shoulder to force him to remain seated. "Why didn't you disclose this to me before?"

Artile winced at the pressure. "Forgive me, Furius Camillus. I didn't think it necessary to use the tunnels. I believed Rome would starve Veii into submission."

"Or maybe you were reluctant to see your former lover killed. Is that why you have held out on me all this time?"

The seer tried to rise, but the dictator continued to pin him to his chair.

"It's true. I did not wish Tarchon harmed. But now it's clear he's been beguiled. I want him to truly regret rejecting me."

Camillus squeezed Artile's shoulder even harder. He gasped in pain.

"You're not to keep anything from me again, do you understand?"

The Etruscan nodded. "You have my word."

The general released him, then patted him on the back. "You've done well. And if what you say is true, I'll reward you."

The haruspex massaged his shoulder. There was a mix of pain and anticipation in his dark eyes. "So you will give me both princes?"

The creases on Camillus's cheeks deepened with his smile. "All our dreams will be realized once Veii's citadel is mine."

Marcus stared at both men, feeling a twinge of conscience that subterfuge, not daring, would bring the Veientanes to their knees. "Do you feel no qualms, Artile?" the tribune asked.

The traitor stood, squaring his shoulders. He smoothed his eyebrow, composed, conceited, and cold. "My people believe that Fate is fixed. Our race is destined to dwindle away one day. And every man, woman, and child have their time. It's true for cities, too. And Veii's time is due."

A chill ran down the Aemilian's spine. He wondered if the general was wise to believe in this man. There was an evil about him.

Camillus stood between priest and tribune, slinging his arms around their shoulders. "It's time to celebrate, Marcus, not question Artile's soul. He's provided us with answers to both placate the gods and defeat our mortal enemy. And in summer, both of you will stand beside me at my triumph. In summer, Veii will fall."

FORTY-EIGHT

Caecilia, Veii, Spring, 396 BC

The hearth glowed in the darkness. Caecilia stared into the fire. It was the red heart of Mastarna's house. She wished the sacrifice she planned tonight to be performed in the dwelling she called home, rather than at the fireplace in the lofty palace. The flames jerked and flared, the shadows on the walls mimicking their pattern as she waited in the atrium for Vel to arrive.

Veii was healing. The painful memory of the plague and famine receding. There was fuel to keep homes warm from the nip of spring evenings. Bellies were full. Trade was returning to normal. The markets were noisy with haggling, the streets jammed with traffic.

There was once again a division between the quick and the dead, too. In the weeks after Vel's return, there'd been many funeral games to preside over. The despair suffered for over a year stoked the need to placate Aita. The Phersu was called upon often to reanimate the dead and appease the spirits.

Attending so many funerals made Caecilia even more grateful her children had been spared. She worried, though, that Larce was anxious when she was not near, careful to remain in her circumference. Always resilient, Arnth seemed unaffected by his encounter with death. He delighted in the return of Vel, clipping his heels whenever his father visited the family quarters. Tas was even more withdrawn. Now when Caecilia gazed into his tawny eyes, she recognized his thoughts: "I am mortal. When will I die?"

Thia did not recognize her father at first. She'd screamed when an armor-clad man loomed over her cradle, eager to kiss her. Composed when facing an enemy, the warrior was flustered by a baby. But the cadence of his voice quieted her. Since then, Vel's little princess would always burble and chirp when her Apa drew near.

There was now a buzz of excitement in the city. Vel had decreed the Spring Festival to be held. Once again, Veientanes could descend into the ravines and hills to revel in the new growth of the forest. The grapevines entwined on staked rows were blooming and would fruit in autumn. In winter, farmers would lay down the vintage. And in spring, Veientane wine would be consumed instead of liquor from distant cities. The cycle of the vine would continue. Once again the people would observe the death and resurrection of Fufluns throughout the seasons.

Loosening the strings of her purse, Caecilia drew out a tiny wooden figurine that her father had given her when she was born. Her guardian spirit. Her little juno. The talisman was a symbol of her Roman essence. When she'd first come to Veii, she'd prayed the spirit would protect her. Then she'd learned that Rasennan angels hovered unseen among humans, winged sentinels who served the gods and protected mortals. Such power made her little juno seem paltry. Even so, she always kept the idol beside her bed, reluctant to relinquish the safeguard. For a moment, she wondered what her father would think if he were alive. His one resolve was that Rome should conquer Veii. If he'd lived, she would never have been married to Vel. Should she be thankful, then, that he'd died so that she found love?

She clenched the juno in her fingers. There'd once been another amulet she'd used to protect her. Marcus's iron wristlet with the Aemilian horsehead crest. After the Battle of Blood and Hail she'd wrenched it off and buried it like the proof of an evil omen, her love for Marcus buried, too.

She took a deep breath. It was time to exorcise the Roman within her. The chains of belief that once bound her were now rusted. Tonight she would snap those brittle fetters forever. And tomorrow, she would submit to Fufluns.

She cast the little juno into the hottest part of the fire. For a moment she panicked, thinking she should fish it out with the rake, but then, as the blue-edged flames caught its smooth, polished surface, she found herself hypnotized. The chance to rescue it passed. If she retrieved it, the remnant would be misshapen.

She heard the murmur of voices at the outer door. Vel and Arruns. Her husband emerged into the dimness of the room, the firelight revealing his curiosity. "Why have you called me here? And what are you doing in the dark?"

She beckoned to him. "Come and see. I'm ridding myself of Rome." She pointed at the hearth.

He frowned as he peered into the fire. "What am I looking at?"

"My little juno. She's almost in ashes."

He could not hide his shock. "Why would you do that? She's the emblem of your spirit."

"So that I can be wholly Veientane. So that nothing will hold me in check at the Spring Festival."

He searched her face. "I know I asked this of you before I left. It was unfair. I don't expect you to surrender your beliefs."

"I do so gladly."

"What has changed your mind?"

"I nearly lost Larce and Arnth to the scourge. I also nearly died. I knew then I could not bear to be parted from any of you." She kissed him. "I want to be with you in Acheron."

He turned his attention to the burning talisman that was indistinguishable now from any lump of coal. He appeared pensive, shadow and light playing across the planes and curves of his craggy face. She slipped her hand into his. "I thought you'd be happy."

He laid his hand on her throat, stroking her birthmark with one finger. "Seeing you sitting before the hearth reminds me of when you were a bride. You're as thin as you were when I first wed you. You were so earnest, urging me to conduct the rites of fire and water. A Roman and a Rasennan. As opposite as those two elements. United under law but divided in mind and belief."

She closed her eyes, enjoying the sensation of his caress. "That girl is no more. There's nothing left of her within me."

Vel kissed her hand, then examined her fingernails. "These were bitten to the quick, your eyelids swollen from weeping, your fair skin mottled. You were terrified that night, as though you viewed me as some monster."

She smiled. "I prayed that I would not suffer at your hands." She placed his palm against her cheek. "Now I long for their touch, both when waking and in my dreams."

He clasped her hand and brought it to his lips, sucking each of her fingers in turn. The sensation of his warm mouth as it enclosed each tip was intense.

"Tomorrow we will seek epiphany as one, Bellatrix. Sharing the same beliefs in life and the same destiny after we die."

"So that we can love each other even after our hearts cease beating?"

"Forever." He kissed her throat. "Like Fufluns and Areatha."

"Wait," she said, breaking from him. She picked up one of the lamps, then tugged him to follow her through to the arcade with its trellised grapevine, past the moonlit garden and its bubbling fountain. Reaching their bedroom, she drew aside the heavy curtain, raising the lamp high so it illuminated one wall.

The painted leopard peered from its laurel grove, swallows flitting above its head. It had been their companion all their married life. Fuflun's beast. A guardian that would protect them on the journey to the Beyond.

The chamber was more shadow than light. She pulled Vel toward their bed with its plaid coverlet and placed the lamp on the side table. He smiled, grasping her waist and lifting her to sit on the edge of the thick mattress. She laced her hands around the back of his neck and brushed her lips against his. "Tonight, though, we are just Vel and Caecilia. Husband and wife. Our fidelity proven before the spirits of the House of Mastarna."

EVOCATIO

FORTY-NINE

Pinna, Outside Veii, Summer, 396 BC

Drusus trudged up the hill toward Pinna in the hot midday sun. He was covered with as much red dust as she'd ever been with grave soil. Trickles of perspiration carved lines through the grime on his face. His tunic and leather corselet were filthy, his boots dense with dirt. Behind him a detail of similarly stained men followed.

Every four hours a detachment of men would enter the bowels of the earth to mine the tunnel. The pace of the digging had been increased as soon as Furius Camillus had arrived at the main camp. His drive to complete the task energized the sappers despite the grueling schedule. Care was taken not to arouse suspicion. As far as the Veientanes could tell, the Romans were quarrying stone for the reinforcement of the siege lines.

As head decurion, Drusus did not wield a pick or cart away stone. However, as one of the supervising officers, he inspected progress at the end of every shift throughout the day. The rotation of men ensured fresh muscle power and no slacking. Nevertheless, four hours without break in the airless, dark confines took its toll.

Pinna ladled water from a jar into cups, handing them to the men as they passed. She gave one to Drusus who drained it in one swallow.

"I'll be glad when I don't have to creep into the belly of the earth. The tufa is soft enough to remove, but we need to shore up the structure as we go. We want to avoid a cave-in. It makes my skin crawl to be deep underground."

"How much farther is there to dig?"

He wiped sweat from his face, leaving a pale patch on his skin. "The engineers say we should reach the opening of the temple shaft the day after tomorrow as planned."

She smiled. "General Camillus will be pleased. He wants to attack on the summer solstice. He believes the dawn goddess will bless the assault if launched at daybreak."

He frowned. "Are you saying the general shares strategy with you?"

"You would be surprised what a woman can learn when tending to a man."

"You have become very sure of yourself, haven't you?"

"I don't plan to betray you, if that's what you fear."

Drusus scanned her face. "Yes, I believe you."

Pinna ladled more water into his cup. She was glad to be free of his malice.

The past few weeks had been thrilling. She'd been delighted to tread in the footsteps of her mother by visiting the sanctuary of Mater Matuta in Satricum. And her Wolf had promised to repair and reconsecrate the temple in Rome. Pinna was overjoyed her divinity would once again be housed in splendor.

All Camillus's plans were on track. Spurius had drained the floodplains around Lake Albanus. Rome's sins had been expiated. Latins were jubilant at reclaiming pastures of fertile, silted soil. And her Wolf had soothed their ire by declaring a suitable date for the Votive Games. The Latin Pact was once again being observed.

Allied forces had succeeded at both Anxur and Labicum. Garrisons were now established. The gods truly favored Rome.

Having settled matters in the south and east, Camillus had been impatient to assist Scipio and Medullinus. Pinna thought he would leave her behind in Rome; instead he insisted on taking her to Nepete. Under his leadership, the northern armies were trounced, slinking back to their hilltop fortresses. Yet with less than four months remaining in office, he decided to advance no further, satisfied the north now lay exposed. Scipio remained with a small force to maintain control. After Veii fell, Rome would take each city of the Twelve one by one.

Now Camillus was outside Veii, and he still wanted her with him. His newfound authority fed his lust as well as his ambition. She'd been surprised at his appetite, thinking he would be too absorbed with warfare to want her. Instead the prospect of triumphing fueled his desire. He ate heartily, slept little, talked into the night about strategy with his officers, and took her in snatches of time in between. Any other man would have been exhausted. With Camillus, there was untiring fervor and unrelenting hunger, for both victory and her.

Yet Pinna was concerned. She worried that gaining power was changing him. He listened less to others' opinions and made edicts without consultation. His self-confidence had tipped over into arrogance. No one dared counter him. No one could keep up with him either.

Drusus was pensive as he studied the quarry beyond the river before raising his head to survey the fortress on the cliff. His gaze rested on the palace with its terraced garden. "I'll finally see her."

Pinna studied his profile, not responding. She remembered how he'd clutched her in delirium after he was wounded, believing her to be Caecilia.

"Perhaps it would be kinder if I killed her. There is no way I can protect her once she's in Rome."

She rested her hand on his forearm. "She bears no love for you, Drusus. And you must do your duty."

He turned to her. "I'm scared."

"I don't believe that. You have faced battle countless times."

"I don't speak of death or injury. I fear the emptiness when there is no dream to dream."

"There was never any substance to that dream. Your love is unrequited."

His focus returned to the citadel. "At least my hate for Mastarna gives me purpose."

"Yes, the defixios have succeeded even if your love spell failed. You'll have your revenge."

Grimacing, he handed her the cup. "I'm to be deprived of the chance to kill him. General Camillus wants the king to be taken alive."

Pinna did not want to think too hard about her Wolf's decision. Strangulation awaited King Mastarna at the victor's triumph. She decided to change the subject. "You must be proud that Marcus has chosen you to be his second-in-command. It's a worthy promotion."

"Yes, but he's destined to wear the mural crown as the first to set foot in a besieged city."

She hefted the water jar onto her shoulder, the terra-cotta side hard against her head. She didn't want to be drawn into Drusus's jealousies either. "I must go. The general is waiting."

He resumed his observation of the palace, where the objects of his love and hate resided, both oblivious of the fate awaiting them.

• • •

Spurius's forehead was furrowed as he sat on the backless chair and selected a fig from the plate Pinna offered. "I bring news that Icilius Calvus and his associates are stirring discontent again.

They've caught the scent of the riches to be reaped from Veii. Now they say every citizen should profit, not just the troops."

Camillus drummed the fingers of one hand on his desk. "And what do Medullinus and Aemilius say to counter their argument?"

"That customary law should be observed. Everyone's tax burden will be relieved if the lion's share is paid to the treasury. Veii's vast wealth should replenish coffers that are almost depleted."

"That argument will be howled down," said Marcus, confident now to add to his superiors' discussions. "The people's tribunes will assert, as usual, that the commoners shouldn't have to rely on the Senate doling out money."

Pinna offered him a fig. He also ignored her. He'd done so for weeks. She thought his terseness unfair. After all, she'd kept her side of the bargain in healing Drusus.

Genucius cleared his throat. "Are you saying Calvus wants merchants and city idlers to end up with handfuls of gold?"

Spurius rolled his eyes. "Precisely."

"Then he goes too far! Only soldiers who risk their lives should be rewarded. They need to recoup their losses from being denied the chance to harvest their crops."

Pinna warmed to the plebeian's argument. She also believed only warriors were entitled to the spoils. She looked across to her Wolf who remained silent. She was disappointed he didn't immediately champion his men's right to retain their loot.

Spurius sighed. "Calvus is thinking ahead to the elections. He wants to garner the support of all. He claims everyone should be given the opportunity to march to Veii and claim their share. Failure to accede to this will only plant the seeds of rebellion."

Marcus was incredulous. "He wants to jam the road to Veii with scavengers?"

A note of anger crept into Genucius's voice. "Never mind that. I'm more concerned that patrician officers will seize booty and land while common soldiers must pay their portion to the State."

Pinna was surprised at the heat in his voice. She thought his rancor had lessened. After all, her Wolf had appointed him a general again. He'd been ordered to lead Postumius's regiment back to Veii to begin excavations. And he would direct his troops through the rock galleries under the city to share some of Camillus's glory.

Genucius had not finished his harangue. "And what's to be done about the Legion of the Boar? Why should they be denied their share because geography separates them from the spoils?"

"Enough!" Camillus thumped the table, startling everyone around him. "I haven't even breached Veii's wall, and there's already bickering over plunder!"

The officers fell silent.

"When am I to be free of Calvus's carping?" he continued. "I've enough to think about without such quarrels."

"Sir," ventured Marcus, "perhaps it's an issue best sorted out by the Senate."

"Are you saying I don't possess the ability to decide this matter?"

Marcus tensed. "Of course not, sir.

Camillus swiveled around to Artile. "What do you think?"

Pinna had forgotten the priest who sat in the corner, listening and observing as always. He was a constant malignant presence in their lives. The seer shrugged. "I doubt patrician or plebeian will be satisfied with either solution. Let your senators have the headache of determining what's fair."

The general tapped his gold ring three times. "Spurius, return to Rome and tell them I want this matter referred to the Curia." He transferred his attention to Genucius. "Are you content now?"

"I'd prefer you take a stand. I doubt the Senate will consider the matter properly. As usual, they'll decree that the plunder should be hoarded."

Again Pinna was surprised at his frankness. Camillus glowered at him. "We're on the eve of Rome's greatest conquest. Do you want to waste time arguing, or do you want to prepare your troops?"

Genucius's manner became conciliatory. "You're right. Let's concentrate on the attack rather than the chattering in Rome."

Spurius rose. "Then I'll leave as soon as possible. Although I had hoped to join your invasion."

Camillus smiled. "I'm sorry to deprive you. But now that Medullinus is back in Rome, he'll be inclined to listen to you more than any other man. So, too, Aemilius." He stood and gripped Spurius's arm. "When next we meet, Veii will have been destroyed, and the extent of our swag will be known."

He turned to Genucius. "Are you certain your preparations to infiltrate the cave galleries have gone unnoticed by Veientane spies?"

He nodded. "We've reconnoitered the tunnels under cover of night. Artile has assisted us with identifying the access points."

"Then prepare your men. Once they are inside the city they must fling open the gates to the rest of the regiment outside. Tell them we attack at daybreak on the summer solstice."

Marcus stood to attention. "And my orders, sir?"

"Brief your knights on the operation to climb up the shaft into the temple. Then relay instructions that the stockades are to be closed to traders. Also, the troops stationed along the siege lines must cease repair work and remain inside the forts. On no account must they engage the enemy. I want Mastarna to think our resolve is failing."

Marcus stood to attention and saluted. Genucius also, but the plebeian paused at the entrance to the tent, fixing his one eye on Pinna with his usual contempt before ducking his head to edge under the flap.

Camillus next spoke to the soothsayer. "I acknowledge you've greater expertise than I in taking the auspices, Lord Artile."

"I would be honored to use my haruspicy skills, Furius Camillus. I'll examine the liver of a bull instead of observing the sacred hens."

The dictator smiled. "Excellent."

After Artile had left, Camillus began writing his missive to the Senate. Pinna picked up a stick of sealing wax, warming it over the candle flame. "What do you really think should happen with the booty, my Wolf?"

He finished the letter, rolling it and pushing it into a cylinder. "I don't have time to cope with such disputes."

"It's not like you to have no opinion."

He took the stick from her and smeared the wax on the papyrus. "You're always so persistent. Very well, I hope the Curia heeds Genucius's case. Veii is too large a prize not to share."

"Then let it be so, my Wolf! Your men would be grateful. And, after all, you are dictator. Your decisions can't be countermanded by the Senate."

He laughed. "Would you approve of me then, little citizen? Do you think your father would, too?"

"He would've been honored to fight under your command."

"Then I'll think on it." He pressed his carnelian stamp into the wax, then stood and walked to the tent flap, handing the letter to his messenger outside.

Pinna focused on tidying his desk, glancing at the map upon which Artile had marked all the tunnels, the secrets to a city's annihilation.

Camillus stepped behind her, looping his arms around her waist, his chin resting on her shoulder as he also scanned the chart. "Do you truly think the dawn goddess will bless me?"

It was the first hint of doubt she'd heard from him in a long time. She was relieved arrogance had not seeped entirely through him. "Of course Mater Matuta will grant you victory, my Wolf. And you'll have the light of the longest day to achieve it."

"You make me strong," he murmured, kissing the nape of her neck, one hand cupping her breast, the other hitching up his leather kilt and tunic.

Pinna smiled and flipped up the back of her dress. She bent forward, knocking aside the paperweights as she stretched out and braced herself against the desk, ready to enjoy his power, exulting in her own.

FIFTY

Caecilia, Veii, Summer, 396 BC

Mastarna stood at the terrace wall, arms straight as he gripped the stone edge. He surveyed the horizon to the main Roman camp. Innocuous puffs of smoke drifted from the cooking fires. "I wonder what Camillus is up to. I have reports he's shut the stockades. All the Romans seem to be holed up in their forts or camps."

Caecilia rested her head on his shoulder and sighed. "It's suspicious. Why take Nepete yet only keep Scipio manning a skeleton force? Why lead an army of reinforcements to Veii if he plans no action?"

"I don't know. But Camillus is wasting time. Even with the influx of our farmers seeking refuge again, we've enough supplies with careful rationing. And we've ample water and fuel. Our citadel is unassailable. We can wait out the remaining months of his dictatorship, then once again negotiate for peace. A lasting truce is inevitable."

He continued to observe the encampment. Despite his assurances, Caecilia knew he was worried. His features were drawn from fatigue. There were more strands of silver at the sides of his dark, close-cropped curls. The failure of the peace talks rankled, but with ensuing months of freedom from the siege, it seemed Rome might be relenting. Caecilia had looked forward to summer with its azure skies and cicada song. But it was only a respite, not a release from conflict. On the kalends of June, the warning siren sounded. The Veientanes crowded along the length of the walls to stare at the Roman regiment returning. And at the head of the troops rode General Genucius. Morale deflated as swiftly as it had been buoyed. The gains made in the north had been lost. Vel was bitter that he had been taken by surprise.

Soon the entrances to the city were clogged with farmworkers and their families, hopes ruined that they might heft scythes for the autumn harvest. Travelers and traders on the thoroughfares ringing the plateau fled. Lock bolts were hammered into place on the double gates around the city. Vel immediately commanded Lusinies to strengthen the northwest bridge. The guards on the Uni, Tinia, and Minerva Gates were doubled. Archers were detailed to stand watch on the towers and spread themselves along the ramparts of the curtain walls. Raiding parties were sent on sorties. The race was on to reach the siege lines and cut off the Romans from beginning their repair work. However, the skirmishers made little headway. They faced the same obstacle of hilly terrain that had hampered the Romans from launching a frontal assault for a decade.

To Vel's frustration, Genucius managed to retake possession of the main camp and the quarry across the river. Caecilia thought it strange that the Roman general wasn't intent on tightening the cordon around Veii as had Camillus before him. He seemed unconcerned about letting trade trickle through the stockades. However, he did begin shoring up the trenches with stone despite Vel ordering forays to disrupt his engineers.

"Ati! Arnth is squashing me!"

The parents turned. The younger boys were playing leapfrog on the terrace, but Arnth had chosen to bring Larce crashing to the ground instead of vaulting over him. Sitting on a wicker chair at the loom, Cytheris raised one eyebrow at the familiar commotion but continued with her weaving. Perca hastened across to disentangle the brothers, but Arnth, stubborn as always, refused to budge.

Caecilia glanced across to Tas. He and Tarchon sat, heads close, discussing the Book of Fate. The boy hunched forward, listening to his half brother, oblivious to his younger siblings. His excitement at Vel letting him study the Holy Books had banished his discontent. All principes were required to read the Etruscan Discipline, even if only some were trained in its intricacies. Tarchon had been counseled, though, not to blow on the smoldering coals of Artile's promises and set Tas's obsession to be a seer aflame.

Mastarna drew the golden dice from the sinus of his tebenna. Caecilia was pleased that he'd resumed carrying them.

"Here, play with these," he said, extracting Arnth and handing the tesserae to Larce first. The older boy beamed at the unexpected preference, while the younger, used to being his father's favorite, stuck out his lower lip.

Just woken from slumber, Thia was chattering gibberish to Semni. Larce was the only one who was privy to his sister's secret language, translating what the baby said and amazed that everyone else was clueless.

Freeing Thia of her swaddling bands, Semni set the baby on the floor. The girl grasped the nursemaid's skirts, pulling herself to stand on wobbly legs. Then she tottered precariously across to Hathli, her new wet nurse. The stocky young widow steadied the child, turning her around and directing her back to Semni as a game.

Thick ankled and broad waisted, Hathli had sought refuge when her farmer husband was killed in a Roman raid. Then her sorrow doubled when her baby died in the plague. When the queen heard of her plight, pity filled her.

Mastarna smiled as he headed toward his daughter. He bent down and opened his arms. "Come, my princess."

The little girl smiled, revealing gummy gaps between a sparse scattering of small white teeth. "Apa," she chirped. She encircled her father's neck with chubby arms. There was no sign of the skinny, fretful baby of weeks before. Hathli's milk had nourished her back to health, although Thia was still smaller than most children nearly one year of age.

Vel planted a kiss on his daughter's cheek, then blew a raspberry, causing greater mirth and a torrent of garbling. He smiled at his wife. "What's she saying?" Caecilia shrugged. "I don't know, but she's giving you a lot of advice."

"Just like her mother," he said, grabbing his wife around the waist. "Ah, there's nothing quite like holding the two women in my life."

Caecilia smiled and reached up to smooth Thia's mop of tight curls. The little girl grasped her fingers, looking between father and mother to continue her conversation with them both.

Arruns approached. "Master, Lady Tanchvil is here to see you."

Vel frowned at the unexpected visit. "Tell the high priestess I'll see her in the council chamber." He handed Thia to Hathli, calling to Tarchon, "Join us, too."

Tas looked up, disappointed at his lesson being cut short. "May I go with you, Apa?"

"No. Keep reading. Tarchon won't be long."

Tarchon tousled the boy's hair. "Your father is right. And I'll be testing you when I return."

• • •

As always, Caecilia was struck by Tanchvil's grace as Arruns escorted the hatrencu into the council chamber. However, the augur was far from composed. She was wringing her hands, each long finger adorned with rings of gold.

Mastarna nodded and gestured for her to sit at the far end of the table. "Why do you seek an audience?"

"I've determined the meaning of the prodigy at Lake Albanus, my lord. The codex you brought me from the Sacred College at Velzna has been helpful."

"And what does the portent signify?"

"The rising of the waters was a warning to Rome that they'd neglected Mater Matuta and Nethuns."

"And what are the expiation rites for such transgressions?" said Tarchon.

"That's what concerns me. The waters of the lake must be drawn off so they no longer reach the sea. If this is achieved, then Veii will fall to Rome."

Tarchon turned to the king. "We heard the Latins have drained their floodplains. I thought it no more than irrigation. But now..."

Mastarna grimaced. "It seems they were diverting the water for holy purpose. No wonder the Latin tribes have joined forces with Rome again to hold the Aequians and Volscians in check."

Caecilia cast an alarmed look at her husband. "But how did Camillus know the answer to placating the gods? The Roman magistrates only have recourse to the three Sibylline Books. Those texts are limited on such matters."

"That's true," said Tanchvil. "But the oracle at Delphi might have been consulted."

Caecilia rubbed her temple, her head aching. Could it be true Veii might fall? "But why would our gods allow Veii's destruction, Lady Tanchvil? Why would they favor Rome?"

There was reproach in the hatrencu's voice. "You most of all must be aware that Queen Uni has been disregarded. The wine god is now revered more than her. Her festival on the kalends was forgotten. Instead the Mysteries of the Pacha Cult took precedence. It's dangerous to displease her."

Guilt surged through Caecilia, realizing she'd forgotten to worship Uni in the wake of the Feast of Fufluns.

Images of the initiation rites flashed through her mind. The Mysteries had not been as frightening as she'd feared. The games preceding it had recalled a time when Veii was carefree: a chariot race, a discus contest, jugglers and acrobats. And the procession into the woods to give offerings to Fufluns had been joyful. The masked actors following the high priest were dressed as maenads and satyrs. The nymphs danced and capered while the horse-tailed men stalked them, the leather phalluses tied around their waists jiggling. The pomp wended its way through ravine and woodland, leaving afternoon sun behind and greeting evening shadows. Holding their thyrsus staffs and torches aloft, the worshippers created a moving carpet of light up to the altar. The roasted aroma of the sacrificial goats was mouthwatering as the supplicants sated their hunger.

The wine had been unwatered. Strong and heady. Sweetened with honey. The first sip had tasted like fire. Caecilia refilled the drinking horn many times, seeking intoxication as quickly as possible. Giddy and laughing, her heartbeat was captured by the rhythm of the drums. Music enveloped her. Her senses thrummed with the moan of bullroarers, clash of cymbals, and trill of double pipes. Euphoric, she danced, eyes closed, snapping her head back and forth. Singing and gyrating, the revelers packed tight around her, their faces hidden by the guise of beast or satyr.

Kneeling before the enormous ivy-entwined mask of the wine god, she drank the holy milk that would purify her as she revered the sacred phallus. From the eyeholes of her mask, her vision was restricted, the terra-cotta pressing against her face. She could hear herself breathing. And when she stared into the blank eyes of the divinity's mask, she was liberated; she was no longer Caecilia.

Perspiration coated her from dancing too close to the bonfire, her sheer chiton clung to her flesh. Then he found her, wearing his bull's head mask, his half-naked body also slick with sweat. He'd carried her into the bracken. And there, lying on his goatskin, he taught her to see Fufluns. Her mind and soul merged with the divinity, her body an instrument to channel the god's spirit. When the elation ebbed, she grew greedy, needing the exquisite rush and heat and ecstasy again. Not satisfied with just one encounter. But the half bull was as possessive as he was potent. In the morning, she could not recall other than his lust as she woke, head aching, naked on his cloak, his arms around her.

Now the memory of the festival caused Caecilia to flush under Tanchvil's scrutiny. Yet should the followers of the Pacha Cult be ashamed of worshiping the dying god? Was Uni so jealous that she would seek to punish Veii because some sought epiphany? Surely there was room in the heavens for both immortals to be worshiped side by side? "I concede I've neglected Queen Uni, but it was with no malice. I still love and revere her."

"And as the chief priest of Veii," said Vel, "I seek to honor all deities and cults. However, I regret my failure to observe the mother goddess's rituals. I'll declare a holy day on the summer solstice to seek both her forgiveness and her blessing."

Tanchvil caressed the outstretched wings of the eagle on her torque. "I'm grateful, my lord. As the people will be when they hear. But the news of Lake Albanus is a dire warning. I fear you'll need to do more than beseech the divine Uni for her pardon. Veii must convince the gods that it's worthy of being saved."

"And how do you suggest I do that?"

"Observe the Fatales Rites. Call down lightning on Rome as I suggested before. Let me send my eagle, Antar, to the Veiled Ones to convince Tinia to hurl down his thunderbolt of destruction. Veii's fate may yet be deferred and disaster averted."

"I've already told you I don't believe in interfering with Fate. Nortia sets her course. She's fickle and changeable. We might as well beat our hands against air than attempt to persuade her. And the Veiled Ones seldom arm the king of the gods with lethal lightning."

Tanchvil rose. "I can only counsel you, my lord. But the Fatales Rites should not be dismissed so swiftly."

Caecilia thought how complicated Etruscan religion was with its layers of authority. Yet she didn't wish to discount the priestess's counsel. "Please, Vel. Consider what she's saying."

He clenched one hand into a fist on the table. "I recognize your concern, Lady Tanchvil, but, frankly, I can't see how Rome can conquer Veii. Appeasing the gods of Latium will not help Camillus break down our walls nor scale the heights of our citadel. And you seem to have forgotten Artile foretold Veii was only vulnerable if it failed to punish the traitor among us. Justice was served when King Kurvenas was killed."

"Hubris has been the downfall of many a lucumo, my lord. This city came close to surrendering not so very long ago. Catastrophe may yet be rained down upon us if we ignore divine warnings. You might be brave enough to flout the gods, but I don't see why your people should suffer because of your impiety."

Mastarna eased back in his chair, staring at the hatrencu, one hand still clenched. Caecilia reached across and placed her own over his. His fingers relaxed. She murmured, "Do this for our people, Vel."

Tarchon leaned forward. "Father, surely there's no harm in seeking a celestial guarantee."

The king's gaze traversed between queen, prince, and priestess. "Very well, let's show our enemy that our pantheon is greater than theirs. I will honor Queen Uni. I will placate her. And then, tomorrow, I will beseech the Veiled Ones to convince Tinia."

Caecilia squeezed his hand in gratitude. Her relief at his acqui-
escence was tempered with apprehension, though. So much was
at stake. Vel would need to be his most persuasive to achieve their
desire to destroy their greatest foe.

FIFTY-ONE

Pinna, Outside Veii, Summer, 396 BC

The ram, boar, and bull were garlanded with laurel, a sign divine Mars would bring peace through war. The truculent beasts were tamed by potions, their horns and tusks proving no danger. Having made the circuit of the camp's perimeter, Artile led the sacrificial beasts through the gate to the ritual space next to the general's headquarters.

To the west, the sun was sinking, a great half circle of orange-purple clouds cushioning its fall. Tomorrow the solstice would usher in the narrowing of days—and the demise of a people.

A warm breeze played on Pinna's skin, offering no relief from a day of heat and humidity. She watched the ceremony from in front of the command tent, brazen in her witness of blood sacrifice.

Holding his curved staff, Artile's kohl-rimmed eyes were trancelike, the pupils dilated. His teeth were flecked with shreds of the bay leaves he was chewing. His serenity was unnerving, his prophetic talent emanating from him, a prince among priests.

The bull was led forward, its horns gripped by two soldiers. Pinna thought it sad to see such an animal made drunken but knew that, should it bellow and try to break free, it would be an ill omen. Nearby, the boar grunted, but the ram was silent.

The priest was practiced in holy slaughter. Calling for Apollo to assist him, he sprinkled flour and wine over the beast's horns and head. His hammer blow struck the skull squarely. The bull crumpled onto its knees, stunned and helpless. The animal was then hefted onto the killing table by soldiers. Artile slit its throat with the sacrificial knife. Blood gushed into the runnels, draining into the sacred pit below. Then the haruspex carved the victim's belly open. The reek of the entrails assaulted Pinna's nostrils as they slithered in a sinuous tangle onto the altar. Hands and sleeves bloodied, the haruspex placed the liver in a patera dish and began his inspection.

Camillus and his officers and centurions clustered around Artile. He took his time, turning the dark, viscous organ over and over in his hands. Anticipation deepened. Then he raised his head and smiled at the general. "The veins are thickest in the quadrant where Queen Uni resides. It's a sign of greatest good fortune."

Camillus peered at the liver. "I thought an imperfection was a bad portent."

"The surface reflects the sixteen sectors of the heavens where each deity is located. It's not a simple case of blood clots and deformities."

"You say Uni favors Rome's cause?"

"Yes. The protectress of Veii must be angry with her people. I suggest you call to her. She may desert Veii if your case is persuasive. After all, Rome has righted its transgressions and is now purified."

Camillus was incredulous. "You suggest I perform an evocatio?" He scanned the citadel on the precipice beyond. The pink light of twilight bathed the Great Temple. Pinna thought it inconceivable that tomorrow she would stand next to it. Yet could her

Wolf convince the goddess to leave such splendor? To deny succor to the people who had long revered her above all others?

"Tomorrow there will be nothing to hold her," said Artile. "So woo her to transfer her power and influence from the weak to the strong. Why would she stay in Veii when it is Rome who will rule supreme? If she unites with her incarnation as Juno there, she will be all powerful."

Once again, the dictator surveyed the temple in the fading light of day. Shadows were creeping across the edifice, a grim foreboding of doom. "I'll offer to build her a fine house if she heeds the call. Rome will also worship her as a queen. Juno Regina. Holy and mighty."

Pinna scanned the assembled officers. Genucius appeared pensive as he considered the enormity of the act. Marcus seemed stunned. Farther back, she caught sight of Drusus among the decurions. He was smiling.

Artile pointed to the bull. "Don't forget to thank Apollo, Furius Camillus. The god of prophecy also must be acknowledged."

Camillus stood square on to the Great Temple. He raised his arms, his voice loud and bold. "Pythian Apollo, inspired by your holy breath, I go forward to the destruction of Veii, and I vow to you one-tenth part of the spoils. Queen Uni, I pray that you might leave the city where you now dwell. Forsake the Veientanes who have angered you. And in the wake of our victory, I ask that you follow me to Rome where I vow to build you a temple worthy of your greatness as Juno Regina."

There was no divine response. No rumble of thunder or flash of lightning. The earth did not tremble or the wind rise in force. The plea winged its way across the valley as the sun sank, plunging the city of Veii into darkness.

Camillus lowered his arms and closed his eyes, meditating for a moment, as though saying a personal prayer to also canvas divine favor. When he opened his eyes, they were fervid. "Commanders of the cavalry and infantry! Howsoever many of you are present to see this favorable omen, carry forth this message. The goddess of Veii has been called to abandon its walls. And I will ensure both Wolf and Boar Legions will share the spoils. Victory will be ours!"

Genucius's face split into a grin, but Marcus frowned at Camillus's announcement. Yet Pinna was pleased her Wolf had granted her wish to reward his warriors without waiting for the Senate's advice.

She gazed at the citadel. The moon was rising, and the star of Venus twinkled in the encroaching blue of the evening. On the arx, the lights of braziers and torches now sprinkled the darkness. Suddenly she was overcome with melancholy to think the people within were unaware their most famous haruspex had foretold their doom. Worse still, their protectoress had been wooed to perform the most terrible of betrayals. For Uni may even now be casting her eyes toward Rome, seduced by promises of a new home and greater reverence and power.

She shivered, thinking of how Marcus's soldiers would creep through the tunnel to undermine the impregnable fortress at dawn. Rapine and slaughter awaited. A destruction wrought by the man she loved.

FIFTY-TWO

Caecilia, Veii, Summer, 396 BC

Caecilia woke to the touch of Vel's hand resting on her bare hip. Roused from dreamless slumber, there was a fraction of confusion when traveling to the conscious world.

In the pitch black, the warmth of his fingers and the scent of sandalwood defined him as much as lamplight.

His breath tickled, his lips soft on the nape of her neck as he spooned against her. "It's time to wake, Bellatrix. We must be ready before dawn."

She welcomed the sound of his voice each morning. She would never tire of it; its timbre and cadence had seduced her even before she knew she loved him. She turned and laid her head on his shoulder, her hand resting on the soft, satiny grain of his scar. She did not want to rise. She wanted to forget about duty. All she wanted was to hold him in the hushed darkness, cocooned together.

Danger lay ahead of them today. They risked failing to convince the gods. Both of them needed to lustrate themselves before seeking Uni's forgiveness. Only then could they exhort the favor of the divine king and queen. Twenty white bulls would be sacrificed to the goddess in her citadel sanctuary in the morning. Twenty black ones to Tinia at his temple in the northern forum in the afternoon. There would be no rationing when it came to seeking heavenly approval. And at noon, her husband would beseech the Veiled Ones to convince Tinia to throw his thunderbolt. And if his plea was heard, Rome would fall.

Vel was also reluctant to rise. He stroked her arm from shoulder to wrist. "Hard to believe we've been married for eleven years."

She smiled, remembering how she'd trembled under the orange veil, peering through its coarse weave to see the husband Rome had chosen for her. An eighteen-year-old virgin wed to a man nearly twice her age. And then in Veii, they'd stood beneath a gossamer veil together. A symbol of union in life and death. One day their wedding shroud would cover them for eternity. "Eleven years married. It was a lifetime ago."

His fingers caressed her hair, then lingered on her throat. As always, he aroused her senses and desire.

"Perhaps I should never have given you the choice to return to me," he said, voice catching. "You would be safe in Rome if not for me."

A lump formed in her throat. "How can you say that? What kind of life would I have led there? Trapped in a loveless marriage to Drusus or exiled to a country villa by Aemilius? I don't regret returning to you. I thank Nortia for sending you to me in the first place and then for you rescuing me."

He cupped her chin. "What if Tinia doesn't answer my call? I have been impious. Arrogant."

"Stop it, Vel. There's no point in torturing yourself with misgivings. You're a just and wise ruler. You possess courage and daring. Tinia will heed you."

Rolling her onto her back, he lay on her, flesh against flesh, heat matching heat. Her Atlenta pendant was a hard shape against their chests. "I need you. You are stronger than I am."

She wrapped her legs around him. "Don't forget," she whispered, "that we are lions."

• • •

Their sleep was that of childhood. Lips rosy and slightly parted, the curve of cheek against the pillow, loose limbed. Caecilia raised the lamp so she could study them. Larce lay on his side, while Arnth was on his back, arms above his head as though in surrender. Caecilia smiled, thinking her youngest son was the least likely of her children to yield.

Night still held sway. Dawn an hour away. The golden thread spun through her mantle shimmered in the torchlight as she bent to kiss her sons. She would not see them again until the morrow. The rites of Uni would last all day and late into the night.

Bleary eyed and bare footed, Semni padded from the anteroom toward her. "Do you want me to dress them, mistress? I didn't think you wanted them at the ceremony."

"Go back to bed. I just wished to kiss them before I left."

Arnth did not stir at her touch, but Larce opened his eyes at her caress. "Sleep," she murmured, pressing her lips firmly on his cheek. "Sleep."

When she entered Tas's room, she noticed he was awake. He sat up straight when he saw her. "Ati, there were many wolves this time in the cave. They surrounded the bull. And Queen Uni stood with her lightning bolt raised."

Goose bumps pimpled her arms. Then she chided herself. Was it any wonder the boy dreamed of such animals? He was surrounded by the bull symbol of the House of Mastarna. And she often referred to Camillus and the generals of Rome as wolves. She placed the lamp on the side table and sat beside him, encircling him with her arms. "Ssh, it's just a nightmare. You will grow out of them soon."

He clung to her. "So you don't have bad dreams anymore, Ati?"

She nodded. "That's right, the night demon doesn't visit me anymore."

He shuffled down under the sheet.

"I'll see you tomorrow, my love," she said, kissing his head.

Hathli appeared in the doorway holding Thia, who was fussing. "I can't settle her, my lady. She has only slept for an hour or so. I've fed her but she won't go to sleep."

Caecilia grabbed her from the wet nurse, placing her palm against Thia's forehead. "Is she feverish?"

"Yes. She is running a temperature."

There was a spot of high color on one of Thia's cheeks. For a moment, Caecilia panicked, thinking the scourge had returned, but the redness was not a rash but concentrated in one place.

Rocking the child, Caecilia cooed, holding her against her shoulder. The little girl calmed at her touch.

"She's probably just teething, mistress," said Cytheris, joining them.

Caecilia pried opened her daughter's mouth. The lower gum was red and swollen. "But what if it's more?"

Cytheris shook her head. "You worry too much."

The mother was not prepared to fob off concern. "I nearly lost Larce and Arnth. I don't want to leave a sick child."

"Then take her with you, mistress. I'll hold her during the rituals. Now you must hurry to join the king. I'll bring Thia to the temple myself."

• • •

Moonset was tarrying. The thin sliver lingered as the sun broke free of the horizon to swathe the temple grounds with pale, clear light.

The royal party entered through the gates of the sanctuary. The rites dictated that only the king, queen, and prince should enter the temple to conduct the lustration. However, Tarchon had convinced his father to allow Sethre to accompany him, insisting that regal blood also flowed through his pupil's veins.

The royal family was clad in purple. Vel's crown was burnished and gleaming. He carried the eagle scepter in one hand.

Caecilia straightened her own coronet with its dozens of tiny beaten gold leaves. She knew it would give her a headache by the end of the day. Earrings shaped as bunched grapes dangled beside her cheeks, a symbol of her devotion to the wine god. And to show that she also honored Uni, a peacock brooch was fastened at her shoulder. Her thick brown hair was held by a netted snood. Cytheris had no time to curl it. Lovemaking and kissing children had eaten into the hours.

Cepens were busy preparing for the purification ceremony. Some scoured the stone killing table. Others stacked pitch-laced timber in the fire pits. Iron spits were erected, ready to roast the meat. Vats were being filled with wine.

As Caecilia passed through the precinct, she noticed the air was thick with a musky bovine scent. Not yet drugged, the white bulls snorted and shifted in the corral. Acolytes were threading bells onto ribbons, ready to decorate the beasts once the victims were tamed. The sacred geese waddled at liberty, honking in indignation when attendants chivied them out of the way.

Twelve black-clad lictors stationed themselves along the portico. Arruns had been left to organize his remaining men to ensure security throughout the parade to the northern forum. There General Lusinies would greet the king and queen at the end of the royal couple's journey to greet all their subjects on this special day.

Tanchvil greeted the party at the doorway to Uni's cell. A silver diadem crowned her loose, long gray hair. Her cloak was scarlet, painted with figures of Uni and Tinia. The dusting of kohl on her eyelashes gave a mystical quality to her gaze.

Cytheris ascended the steps with Thia. The princess was dressed in purple as befitting her station. The girl was asleep at last, worn out by her crying. Vel raised one eyebrow when he saw her. "Why is my little princess here?"

"She has a fever," said Caecilia. "I don't want to leave her out of my sight."

He frowned. "This is no place for a child."

"Uni is a mother goddess. I'm sure she would not be displeased we seek her protection for our daughter."

He gave a small smile and stroked Thia's hair.

Dawn's light had not yet fully infiltrated Uni's chamber. The cell was dim, the torches on the wall sconces still burning, although a slanted shaft of light streamed through the doorway, capturing dust motes. The room was cool but the air already hinted of another hot summer's day.

As Caecilia crossed the threshold, she saw the eagle on its perch. The bird lifted his wings, shuffling on the pole to adjust its grip. He was unhooded, his stare unblinking. She stepped back in alarm, noticing he was unrestrained.

"Don't fear, my lady," said Tanchvil. "Antar is obedient when untethered. I only sheath his eyes when there is a crowd." The priestess fed the bird a morsel from a pouch tied around her waist. Vel's entreaty would ride on the raptor's wings at noon.

The bronze-sheathed altar table was covered with the paraphernalia of worship: sacrificial knives and paterae of wine, milk, and flour. Two exquisite amber votives of Tinia and Uni were placed beside them. One page of a linen book lay unfolded. Tanchvil was ready to consult the Book of Fate.

High on its pedestal, the statue of Uni loomed above all, her head nearly touching the rafter. The deity was clad in a new goatskin cloak, and her pleated chiton was freshly painted. She, too, wore a crown of gold. In the gloom, Caecilia thought the maternal softness so evident in the divinity's expression had hardened. She was more warrioress than mother today, brandishing her lightning bolt like a spear. Caecilia felt apprehensive, remembering how dangerous Uni could be.

From the corner of her eye, she noticed Aricia through the open doorway to the workroom and beckoned to Cytheris. "Go and speak to your daughter before the ceremony begins."

"Thank you, mistress." The handmaid hastened to greet the girl. However, the visit was cut short when Tanchvil rapped out an order. Aricia squeezed her mother's hand and limped back into the workshop. Disappointed, Cytheris took her place at the side of the chamber, rocking the princess.

"Come. It's time to purify yourself," said Tanchvil, pouring water into a salver and directing the king to wash his hands. "Remember, the preparatory prayers must be accurate, my lord."

Caecilia knew there would be a grueling litany of perfected sentences. She hoped her husband would curb his impatience with reciting them. He needed to show as much reverence to Uni and Tinia as he did with Fufluns.

The shaft of sun had expanded to fill the entire sanctum. Caecilia was already perspiring with the humidity. Tarchon and Sethre took their places at the far side of the statue. She smiled to see how fine they looked together. Two noblemen, two warriors, two lovers.

Vel laid the eagle scepter on the altar and knelt on an embroidered cushion, extending his palm to her. "Come join me, Bellatrix. We will do this together."

"My lord, you must make the prayers of expiation by yourself first," cautioned Tanchvil.

"I wish my wife by my side. She'll prove once and for all she has renounced her birthplace and seeks its destruction. It will be powerful proof to Queen Uni that Aemilia Caeciliana is faithful to her, and to Veii."

The high priestess bowed her head. "Let it be."

Caecilia knelt beside him, craning her neck to look up at the goddess.

Tanchvil handed Vel a patera of milk. "Begin, my lord."

The king of Veii lifted the dish high in offering. His voice was deep, loud, and clear. "O Divine Uni. Queen of queens. Mother of Veii. Hear my prayers. I humbly offer the milk of life in expiation. Forgive me for my neglect. I beseech you to protect your people. And if you are so willing, I implore you to bless my quest to ask Tinia to call down lightning on Rome."

FIFTY-THREE

Marcus, Veii, Summer, 396 BC

Lark would soon exchange places with nightingale as Marcus and his cavalry assembled in the quarry under the cover of night. The dark hour before cockcrow was stifling.

All one hundred men knew their orders: Climb the shaft and break into the temple. Make their way to the top and bottom double Gates of Uni and overcome the sentries. Attack the palace and capture the royal family.

Marcus hoped no sentinel on the arx had acute enough eyesight to spy his brigade. They could not risk using torches. Only the light of the quarter moon illuminated the area.

His knights were not the only men waiting in the dark. To the west, north, and east, units of soldiers were assembled in tunnels ready to erupt through the drains into the heart of the city. To further hide the ruse, Camillus had ordered a simultaneous attack to be launched on the wall around the plateau. Marcus imagined bewildered citizens running to defend the gates, puzzled by the reckless assault when not a single Roman soldier had moved from his post for days. The barrage of noise and confusion as hoplites hurled grappling hooks, or thudded ladders against tufa stone, would divert attention from the imminent danger within.

As Marcus waited for the signal, he realized the blood debt claimed by Mastarna would now need to be repaid. Yet it was an impossible request. How could he seek clemency for Caecilia? And he tried not to think what might happen to their doomed sons and daughter. He hoped the general would only consider enslavement.

At least one child would be spared. Artile's wheedling voice had grated on the tribune's nerves as the Etruscan once again implored Camillus to give him Mastarna's firstborn. The uncle had shown no concern for the fate of the other children. He'd also called for the death of the high priestess of Uni. He wanted no rival surviving to convince the goddess to remain in Veii.

The men were growing restless, keyed up with anticipation. Marcus doubted any of them had slept more than a few short hours. The soldiers immediately behind him were the twenty Horse Shield heroes. Marcus had named Drusus as his second-in-command. Tatius showed no rancor at being passed over.

Still no signal. Once again Marcus contemplated the day ahead. Camillus's voice had been calm and heartless as he'd issued his other commands. No man was to be spared. Women and children were to be captured, or killed if they resisted. The palace, mansions, and public offices could be ransacked but not burned. All other buildings could be torched. Temples were to remain intact so the gods could be appeased before holy treasures were claimed. And most important of all, Juno's temple must go unscathed.

In the sweltering heat, Marcus grappled with his conscience in the face of such orders. He never thought the day would come when he'd be ordered to commit mass slaughter of unarmed people. There was little comfort knowing he'd bear no responsibility for his actions. He would be obeying orders.

Drusus whispered, "How does it feel to know you'll wear the mural crown tomorrow?"

Marcus frowned, keeping his voice low, aware he was breaching his own command to be silent. "It's not an honor I'll earn. I won't be scaling the wall of a besieged fortress."

"Whether over the wall or through a tunnel, you'll be the first to set foot into the stronghold."

Marcus's temper flared. "Now isn't the time for your envy."

The Claudian stiffened. "I'm just stating a fact."

"And I've preferred you over Tatius, even though he was more deserving. Now shut up."

Drusus fell silent. Marcus was sorry for his terseness. Yet for weeks he'd mulled over Mastarna's accusation. Little by little, he'd come to the conclusion Drusus may well have acted dishonorably. "Remember the general's orders," he murmured. "Forget your curse. Take Mastarna alive. Rome will exact retribution, not you."

Drusus fingers dug into Marcus's bicep. "I know my duty."

"Get your hand off me."

An owl hooted. The prearranged signal.

Marcus steadied himself. Drusus squeezed his arm again, no anger in his touch. "May Mars be with you, Brother."

"And with you, Brother. Now convey the order. It's time to go."

The entrance to the tunnel yawned before him. Marcus willed himself to step into the pitch black, the snaking line of men behind him. Crouching, he moved forward, reaching out to touch the walls on either side of the mine. He felt pick marks hewn into the surface. The smell of stone and dirt was strong. He thought the air would be suffocating, but the temperature was even. He heard grunts as some of the men hit their heads on the low roof. Sounds were amplified in the enclosed space: shuffling boots, swords knocking against rock. The stink of sweat, rich with apprehension and excitement, soon filled his nostrils.

The passage narrowed, the roof sloping downward. Marcus got down on his hands and knees. There was no turning back now.

He was hemmed in by men at his back and the darkness beyond. If one man froze in fear, or lashed out in panic, there would be chaos.

"We're nearly there," said Drusus. "The sap narrows before it opens to the drain."

There was a breeze. Marcus eased forward into the low-roofed overhang at the base of the cliff. He gulped in air, relieved to be free of the tunnel. Stooping, he scanned around him. He could hear the sound of the river beyond and see dim gray light at the entrance. The sun was rising. There was no time to waste. Drusus and Tatius joined him in the rock gallery, the others forced to wait their turn.

Drusus nudged him. "The opening to the temple shaft is here."

Fresh sweat broke out on Marcus's brow. He was standing beneath the very citadel itself. He peered up into a small rectangular aperture in the cave roof. Rough wooden rungs were hammered into the rock and disappeared into the gloom above. There was barely enough room to allow for the breadth of a man's shoulders. He swung his balteus over his neck so his sword dangled down his chest. He could not afford for the weapon to scrape against the side as he ascended. He hauled himself onto the bottom rung, forcing himself to reach his hand upward, then his foot, over and over into the blackness. He prayed he would not get stuck, encased in a vertical tufa tomb.

The climb seemed endless. His hands were dripping with perspiration, his tunic saturated. He was nervous that one of the rungs would break, sending him crashing into the men below. He could hear them panting with exertion, or muttering curses.

Suddenly his hand touched a smooth timber surface. The trap door. His heart thumped, blood pulsing in his temples. "I've reached the top. Wait for my command."

As he shifted his balteus back over his shoulder, Marcus heard muffled conversation above him: the unmistakable bass voice of Vel Mastarna as well as feminine tones. Caecilia.

He froze. He would be the one to capture her. He would be the one to subdue the king.

"What's happening?" murmured Drusus.

His words cut through Marcus's shock. He focused again. His plans needed to change. He doubted Mastarna would be armed, given he was in the temple. Still, it would take more than one man to overcome him.

He leaned over and whispered to Drusus and Tatius. "The king and queen are in the temple, so Mastarna's lictors will be close by. Tatius, you and your men attack the bodyguards and help me detain Mastarna. Drusus, you lead the other knights to the gates as planned. Be as stealthy as possible. Once we have secured the prisoners, Tatius and I will lead our turma to attack the palace. Spread the message. And remind everyone that those in purple must be spared."

"Let me take Mastarna," said Drusus.

"Don't question my orders."

The shaft buzzed with the murmuring of his commands as the message passed from the lips of one soldier to the next.

Balancing on the last rung, Marcus took a deep breath, then pressed his palms against the trap door and shoved it open.

For a moment he was blinded by light. The back of the statue loomed above him. He blinked, trying to rid his vision of the seared image of the goddess flashing before his eyes. He scrambled into the room and drew his sword, scanning for lictors, especially the tattooed Arruns. No bodyguards were visible. He could not see Mastarna, but he heard his voice coming from in front of the enormous statue.

A scream startled him. He twisted around to see a woman with a long, trailing plait holding a baby. Her eyes were wide in shock.

He was distracted again by the rasping cry of a bird. To his astonishment, an eagle rose above him, flapping its great gold-tipped wings. A tall, gray-haired woman called, trying to calm it.

She dropped the bronze patera she was holding when she saw the reason for the raptor's alarm. Marcus felt a swoosh of air as the eagle beat upward in the high chamber, then swooped through the open doors to freedom.

Drusus bumped into him. Marcus stood aside, letting the men disgorge from the shaft. One by one the Romans swarmed into the temple.

From the corner of his eye, he saw a blur of purple. Tarchon charged toward him, brandishing a wall torch. Marcus swerved, avoiding the flame. With a roar, the prince raised the brand again, sweeping it in an arc, then stabbed at the Roman, trying to set him alight. Marcus parried the makeshift weapon with his sword, knocking it from the Etruscan's hand.

Tarchon stared at him, expecting a death blow. Marcus slammed his fist into his stomach instead. As the prince doubled over, the tribune cracked him on the head with the hilt. Tarchon collapsed, his head thudding against the floor. He lay motionless.

Fists pummeled Marcus's back. He turned to find Sethre Kurvenas. He hesitated, reluctant to harm him. Before he could retaliate, though, a knight stepped behind the young noble and thrust his blade through his back. The youth slumped to the ground beside his lover, eyes vacant, blood pooling around him.

"You didn't need to kill him," he barked. "He was unarmed."

"I thought the order was to spare none other than those in purple."

Marcus grimaced, then gestured toward Tarchon. "Tie him up. He'll wake soon enough."

The baby was shrieking. Marcus glanced across to the woman with the child. She was cowering in a corner, dumb with fear. He frowned when he noticed the purple hue of the infant's clothes.

"Stop, please stop!"

It was Caecilia's voice.

Taking a deep breath, Marcus tightened the grip on his sword and headed around the statue, ready to capture the monarchs of Veii.

FIFTY-FOUR

Caecilia, Veii, Summer, 396 BC

Cytheris's scream was piercing.

Antar spread his wings, rising in raucous alarm.

Startled, Caecilia clutched Vel's arm, sending his patera clattering to the floor, milk splashing.

Terror overtook confusion. Thudding footsteps. A blur of armored men. It took a moment to realize they were speaking Latin. The eagle flapped overhead. Tarchon yelled. Panic clawed her chest when she heard Thia's cry, but shock paralyzed her.

Then, like some grotesque apparition, mouth wide with his roar, Claudius Drusus rounded the altar, sword held high.

Stunned, Vel took too long to react before beginning to rise. Hampered by his tebenna cloak, he changed his mind, launching himself at Drusus. The crown fell from his head, crashing to the floor and rolling away, as he tackled the Roman around the knees.

Drusus fell backward. Mastarna threw himself on top of him, punching his face. Blood spurted from the Roman's broken nose but he wasn't deterred. He grappled with the king, thrashing and bucking until he dislodged him. Then, scrambling to his feet, Drusus kicked Mastarna's right upper arm as Vel again tried to stand, his heavy cloak tangled around him. Before his rival could rise, the knight gripped the hilt of the sword in both hands and plunged the blade between Mastarna's neck and shoulder. Vel uttered a soft moan as the point tore through cartilage and muscle into his rib cage to pierce his heart. He toppled to the side, his body thudding on the tiles.

Dumbstruck, Caecilia watched Drusus retract his sword through her husband's flesh. Blood gushed out, spattering the floor, splattering her skirts. The murderer stood over his victim, his chest heaving.

A dry sob bruised her throat as she crawled over to Vel, trying to prop him up, but his weight was too heavy. "Don't leave me. Don't leave me." She shook him, trying to rouse him. Then, more frenzied, she gripped his blood-soaked tebenna, her hands reddening as she clenched the purple cloth.

Drusus grasped her shoulder and wrenched her away. His eyes roved over her, his breath ragged. She'd forgotten how tall and lean he was. Another wolf. She could tell there was something broken inside him. He shook her. "He's made you into a harlot!"

Suddenly another soldier stopped beside him, shoving him in the back. "You weren't supposed to kill the king."

Drusus twisted around. "Lead the men to the gates, Tatius. I've unfinished business here."

As the two knights argued, Caecilia tended to Vel. She cupped his face, kissing him. She said his name over and over, calling him back to her. From the corner of her eye, she saw the soldier called Tatius leave.

Drusus yanked her away and raised his weapon again. "Get off. It's time for retribution. Your husband will be a headless ghost."

Risking the downward arc of the sword, she threw herself onto Vel, covering his body with hers, hugging him tight. "No!"

Drusus jerked her shoulder but she clung on. He dug his fingers into her flesh. She felt her muscles tear, but she held fast, ignoring the pain, desperate to protect her husband. "Stop, please stop!"

She shrieked as he increased the pressure on her shoulder. She felt herself giving way. Then he let go as someone barreled into him, sending him sprawling.

"I told you not to kill him!"

She drew back. Marcus was standing over Drusus. The last time she'd seen him had been from the distance of the wall. Now, inches from him, she was struck by his size. A broad-shouldered killer. Once again, she clung to Vel, willing him to be alive. "He's a coward, Marcus. He's slain a king while in prayer. Now he seeks to mutilate him."

Drusus lumbered to his feet. "I swore I'd kill him, and I have."

Marcus growled. "It's bad enough you've disobeyed orders. Do you want to deliver Mastarna to Camillus in pieces?"

Drusus pointed at Caecilia with his sword. Blood dripped from his nose, mouth, and chin, the neck of his tunic saturated with it, his arms slick with sweat. "Look at her painted face and whorish clothes. He did that to her! I intend to make my curse come true." He took a step forward, blade poised to hack at Vel. Marcus blocked him.

"Leave him alone!"

"Get out of my way!"

Drusus pointed his weapon at Marcus. "You think you're better than me. But I won't be ordered around by you." He thrust at the tribune with his sword. Marcus grunted in surprise but parried the blow. His skill only enraged Drusus, who charged. Metal clanged and grated. Caecilia stared in bewilderment. She thought they were lifelong friends.

Through her shock, she heard Thia. The baby was hysterical. She looked beyond the edge of the statue to the back corner of the chamber. White faced, Cytheris tried to hold fast the wriggling child whose arms were outstretched to her mother.

Terrified to leave Vel, she called to Thia to stay with Cytheris. The maid nodded, stricken, as she cast glances between the queen and toward the workroom where her own daughter might lie dead. In a fresh rush of panic, Caecilia realized her sons were also in danger at the palace.

She returned her attention to the dueling soldiers. Marcus had gained the advantage, driving his friend back to one of the bronze doors with unrelenting blows. Then he stopped, panting. "By Great Mars, yield. I don't want to kill you."

The Claudian's eyes were manic. He yelled and lunged. Marcus feinted to the side. Then, as his attacker readjusted his aim, Marcus drove his sword into Drusus's armpit to his heart.

Drusus's weapon slipped from his fingers and crashed to the floor. He crumpled to his knees. Marcus dropped his sword and knelt, hugging him, holding him upright. The dead man's head flopped forward against his shoulder, his arms limp. Marcus lowered him to the floor. Then he knelt beside him, letting out a moan as agonized as a wounded animal's.

Caecilia rolled off Vel and sat cross-legged behind him, lifting his head onto her lap. She felt no pity for either her cousin or Drusus. She hissed at Marcus. "I thank the gods you stopped him."

"You mean 'killed him.'"

She nodded, defiant. "Yes. For killing him."

"You destroyed him long before I wielded the death blow."

She was astounded. "Why? There was nothing between us."

"For you, yes, but he loved you."

She was stung. How dare he blame her for the torment of a man who'd killed Vel. "I'm not responsible for his delusion. Nor for his cowardice!"

Marcus opened his mouth to speak but was distracted by the bucktoothed knight who'd accosted Drusus earlier. The soldier's surprise passed quickly enough at seeing his commander beside his dead friend. He placed his hand on the tribune's shoulder, his tone deferential. "I saw Claudius Drusus kill the king, sir. He disobeyed orders. Wait until General Camillus hears Mastarna is dead."

Marcus grimaced. "I shouldn't have killed Drusus. But he lost his senses. He attacked me."

"You did him a favor, sir. A cudgeling awaited him." He glared at Caecilia. "The general made it clear not to kill the king—or *her*."

Tatius's insult galvanized Marcus. He stood and scanned the group of soldiers. "Are the lictors dead?"

"Yes. There were only twelve of them, though. The others must be at the palace. All the priests are dead, too."

"And the two turmae Drusus was supposed to lead to the gates?"

"Every man acted as per your command. I sent them ahead. The infantry should be pouring through the Gates of Uni soon enough. Now we await your orders."

Caecilia was stunned. "But how? How have you breached our walls?"

"Through the drains. And once inside, our men will open the gates around the city to our comrades outside."

Her stomach lurched. There would be no place for citizens to retreat. The citadel fortress was no longer a refuge.

Marcus turned back to Tatius. She was chilled by her cousin's sanguine calm. Drusus was forgotten. His mind was on fresh butchery. "Leave five of the Horse Shield squadron with me to guard the sanctuary. I'll hold Caecilia here. The rest of your men attack the palace as planned. Make sure you secure the treasury. And find the princes. Now go!"

The clawing within Caecilia's chest was excruciating. "Please, Marcus! Don't let them kill my sons!"

He snapped at her. "You heard. There are orders to spare your family."

Her relief was fleeting. The boys would wake to sunlight and terror. And she was not there to protect them. Then her anxiety peaked again. "Are they only to be saved so Camillus can execute them at his triumph?"

Marcus flinched. "I don't know what the general has determined for your children. I only know the fate that awaits you."

She sucked in her breath, his bluntness reminding her how much he hated her. Shaken, she watched Tatius single out five soldiers to remain behind. Then the officer saluted Marcus and led the other knights from the temple.

"I'll be back," said Marcus to her. "I'm going to check the precincts." He signaled his men to go outside to the portico. He delayed following immediately, though, and instead kneeled again beside Drusus, belatedly placing his mouth on the dead man's in the hope of breathing in his soul. The kiss lasted longer than customary. The gesture puzzled Caecilia, as did Marcus's expression. There was a look of sorrowful love as well as regret.

Thia's howling had been reduced to whining. Cytheris held the baby against her shoulder, tears streaming down her face. Caecilia beckoned to her. The maid rose on shaking legs, stumbling over to the queen and sinking down beside her. She handed her the princess. "I'm going to see if Aricia is alive."

Caecilia clasped Thia, kissing her wet cheeks. Her daughter clung to her for a moment but then reached one hand down toward Vel. Not wanting the babe to be smeared with her father's blood, Caecilia shifted her higher. A fresh wave of disbelief and loss overwhelmed her. Thia wailed, "Apa, Apa." Realizing her own bloodied hands had already stained the child, Caecilia lowered the baby to the floor. Thia put her arm around Vel's neck, her cheek against his. When he did not respond, she chattered to him, tugging one of the bullas on his neck chain.

"Hush. Apa is sleeping." Caecilia guided Thia to lie down next to her. The baby placed her head on her mother's thigh, her hand stretched out to touch her father's hair. Tears welled, but Caecilia fought them back. She needed to draw on hatred until she also held her sons in her arms.

She scanned the chamber. The statue obscured her view of the back of the room. What had happened to Tarchon and Sethre? There was no sign of Tanchvil either. She suspected only the eagle had escaped unscathed.

Cytheris appeared, expression confused. "Aricia is not in the workroom."

Caecilia gripped Cytheris's hand. "The secret passageway. She must have used it. Thank the gods, she may yet be safe. But what of Tarchon and Sethre?"

The handmaid sat on the floor next to her. "The prince is unconscious. They've tied his hands and feet. Sethre is dead. And I saw Lady Tanchvil run out of the chamber when the eagle flew away."

Caecilia murmured a prayer that Tarchon was alive, although she wondered if he'd welcome waking to grief. Perhaps Sethre had been the luckier of the lovers to have died first. She gazed down at Vel, thinking the same of him. She felt as though a knife were slicing her insides. She closed his eyelids and kissed them. Then, in an echo of Marcus's gesture, she placed her mouth upon Vel's to catch his soul to release it. His lips were soft, no cooler than if she'd greeted him on a winter's day. She prayed she'd feel his spirit enter and spread through her like a balm. She felt nothing. He was already on his journey to the Beyond.

Her cry was raw and anguished. She closed her eyes, wishing she were dead. Cytheris shuffled close, placing an arm around her shoulders, saying nothing, knowing words were useless.

Thia stood and looped her arms around Caecilia's neck. Her trembling warmth reminded the mother that she must cease her keening.

The short, frantic blasts of a siren startled her. A pathetic warning signal. Caecilia's nerves jangled as she heard the Roman war cry and the bloodcurdling screams of women. The hoplites must have reached the forum. The cacophony of slaughter had begun.

FIFTY-FIVE

Semni, Veii, Summer, 396 BC

Semni jolted awake, her heart thumping. Had she heard a muffled scream?

She listened. Another deadened shout through the walls. More distinct. A different register. A man.

She scrambled out of bed. The light was muted in the window-less cell. Nerie was also awake. He made no sound, trembling, eyes wide, lids sticky with sleep. Semni stripped off her nightdress and pulled on her chiton before scooping him into her arms.

Ashen faced, Hathli appeared at the nursery's doorway. Arnth hovered at the threshold of his room. Larce stood behind him, eyes like saucers, clutching the younger boy's shoulder. Tas emerged from his chamber. His voice was high pitched. "What's happening, Semni? Who's making that noise?"

"I don't know." The nursemaid herded all the boys into the nursery where Perca sat upright on her bedroll, whistling. Semni looked around for Thia, panicked to see the cradle empty. "Where's the princess?"

"The queen and Cytheris took her to the temple." Hathli grasped Semni's hand and pulled her to the side. Her fingers gripped the maid's so hard she winced.

"We need to hide. I've heard those types of screams before."

"What do you mean?"

"When my village was raided by the Romans."

Semni's nerves thrummed. "But we're on the citadel. The Romans can't get us." She handed Nerie to her. "Dress the children. I'm going to find Arruns."

"We need to hide now," Hathli pleaded.

Semni shook her head. "Not until I find my husband." She turned to the boys. "Stay here with Hathli and Perca." She squeezed Arnth's forearm as she passed him. "Especially you, do you understand?"

He nodded, standing next to the country girl who clasped his hand.

The corridor was dim, the torches burning low in their sconces. The palace guards who had been stationed to protect the family quarters were missing.

As Semni crept along the warren of hallways nearer to the shrieking, a voice inside her told her to run, but she forced herself to go on. She needed to find Arruns. Quivering, she flattened herself against the jamb of a courtyard doorway and peered inside.

Soldiers with conical helmets were racing through the hall. The enemy she'd seen from afar was now in front of her. How had they breached the citadel? There had been no war horns to warn of their approach.

Blood splattered the tiled floor. Dead bodies lay scattered. Dressed in light linen corselets and armed only with spears, the palace guards offered little defense. And their yells were drawing more of their colleagues from their stations throughout the complex. Running straight into their enemy's hands. A lictor in front of the throne anteroom was trying to extract his ceremonial axe from the bundle of rods. Before he could do so, a Roman sliced his neck.

Two soldiers jostled a housemaid back and forth between them. She sobbed and begged. A third soldier, impatient with his comrades' sport, grabbed her by the wrist and pushed her face against the wall, ripping the back of her chiton. Semni looked away, only to see another of the servants dragged by her hair across the floor, her skirts leaving a drag mark in the thick slick of blood.

A warning siren was being sounded at last. Semni's chest hurt with the violent thudding of her heart. She searched for Arruns, scanning the bodies littering the floor. No tattooed corpse. Then she remembered. He'd been ordered to organize the procession. He would be in the stables at the back of the palace.

She turned, feet pounding along the hallways.

The boys and the maids huddled in the nursery. Nerie was whimpering, cheeks shiny with tears, nose running. Semni swung him onto her hip.

"You're right, Hathli," she gasped. "It's the Romans."

"Then there's no time to waste. We must hide."

"Shouldn't we try to escape the palace?" said Perca.

"They'll be in the forum. And we've four children with us. We need to hide until I can find Arruns. He'll know what to do."

Tas tugged at Semni's skirt. "We could use the secret passageway to the temple. Apa and Ati are there. He will protect us."

Semni was surprised at his coolness.

"What passageway?" asked Hathli.

"It's in one of the storage cellars."

There was a thud at the end of the corridor, shouts growing louder.

Larce squealed, "I don't want the Romans to get me. I want Ati!"

Semni grasped his hand. "We're going to play a game of hide-and-seek. Remember, we must be quiet." She kissed Nerie's forehead, desperate for him to stop his whining. "Ssh!" Her sharp tone silenced the child. He buried his head into her neck.

Hathli was strong enough to lift Arnth onto her hip. Tas clasped Perca's hand. "I'll show you the way."

The party of women and children ran along the colonnade alongside the terrace, winding through narrow corridors until they reached the steps leading down to the storage complex.

The air was cooler underground, shafts of light piercing the gloom at intervals through small light wells cut into the passage walls. With its huge half-sunken pithoi, the cellar was eerie. There was a ripe smell of hops and a dusty smell of grain. Most of the vessels were now filled to the brim. Semni closed the door behind them.

The Medusa's glare was hidden by two crossed planks of wood nailed into the terra-cotta cover. Semni gulped. She'd forgotten the portal had been blocked.

Hathli noticed her hesitation as she lowered Arnth to the floor. "Is that the entrance?"

Larce let go of Semni's hand and ran to the hatch. "It's locked!"

Tas was studying the gorgon, too. "It's my fault. If I hadn't used the tunnel, it would still be open."

Nerie was whimpering again. Semni jiggled him on her hip. She scanned the storeroom, searching for something to force off the slats. There was an iron bar on the side bench used to lever open the stoppers of the pithoi. She eased Nerie to the ground and tried to lift one. It was too heavy for her. Nerie dogged her steps, crying to be cuddled again.

Hathli, farm bred, hefted the bar and wedged the end under one of the boards. It would not shift. "We need a man."

Semni tried to calm herself. She couldn't believe they were only the width of two pieces of timber from safety. "I'm going to find Arruns."

"It's too dangerous," said Perca. "He could be anywhere."

"He might be in the stables."

Hathli placed her hand on Semni's arm. "You'll be swept along in the crush of those trying to flee outside. The Romans may already be in the side streets."

"But they'll find us in this cellar if they look hard enough!" said Perca.

Indecision paralyzed Semni at the thought of leaving Nerie. And yet they were trapped if she didn't find Arruns. She surveyed the stricken faces of the three boys. "Ssh, Perca, you're scaring the children. And Arruns will be trying to reach us, too. I know him." She kissed Nerie, prizing his fingers away to hand him to Hathli.

Semni headed to the corridor to the service lane. Servants were crowded in the warren. The enemy was starting to infiltrate the inner bowels of the palace. If she did not locate Arruns fast, she would be cut off from the children.

When she reached the exit, she stood to the side to let the crush of fugitives spew into the street. She smelled smoke. Curls of it spiraled into the air. The shrieking in the palace was nothing compared to the frenzied screams outside. She glanced down the road to the forum. She didn't think her heart could beat any harder or faster. It hurt to breathe. The square was teeming with Roman hoplites.

She turned the opposite way to the stables. She could hear the horses whinnying in alarm. Two grooms rushed past her.

A hand gripped her shoulder. She jumped in fright, then closed her eyes, expecting the slice of a blade or to be pushed to the ground and raped. Instead she heard Arruns's urgent voice as he pulled her around and hugged her. "Thank the gods!"

Before she could reply, he yanked her into the stable and closed the doors. "Where are Nerie and the princes?"

"They're hiding in the pithoi cellar. With Perca and Hathli."

He glanced in the direction of the temple. "The king and queen . . . the sanctuary must be overrun by now."

"It's your family who must come first. And the princes."

"Don't you think I've wanted to search for you? I couldn't make any headway through the service door with all those people blocking it."

A fresh wave of screaming distracted them. Semni peered through the crack between the stable doors. Romans were disgorging from the service exit, hacking at the Veientanes choking the street. A woman screamed over and over. Each shriek higher in pitch, jarring Semni's nerves. She cowered beside Arruns. "What are we going to do? How are we going to get back to Nerie?"

Arruns rose. "The delivery chute. We can reach it through the yard."

He flung open the stable doors, then ran back along the stalls, unlatching each gate and standing back to allow the panicked horses to escape. Then he held Semni close, protecting her from being trampled as he let the animals gallop into the lane to add to the mayhem. "They'll be a distraction as we cross the yard."

Her fear enabled her to keep pace with him as they raced to the chute in the palace wall. Semni peered into the service area below. She could hear Roman voices talking to each other, then moving off. "They're searching the storerooms!"

Arruns drew his dagger from his sheath. "We've surprise on our side. Follow me." He ducked his head as he crouched and ran down the ramp. Semni scurried down the incline, too.

"Stay close," he whispered. "Keep your back to the wall until you get a chance to run to the cellar."

They edged into the corridor. Semni gasped when she saw a Roman striding toward them. He halted in surprise. Arruns attacked before the soldier could raise his sword, thumping into him and knocking him to the ground. Then he drove his dagger into the man's gullet. Blood spouted from the sliced artery. Semni shuddered when she felt the warmth of the fluid hit her arm. The speed of the attack was as shocking as the expertise of her husband at killing. Arruns's face was spattered, but he remained impassive, flicking the blood away from his eyes. He gestured her to continue. She took a deep breath and forced herself onward, almost treading on his heels in her efforts to remain near him.

They crept closer to the Medusa chamber. With the prospect of a Roman looming at any time, the distance seemed miles. Suddenly, Semni heard laughter coming from one of the wine cellars. The door had been wrenched open, the lock broken. Three soldiers emerged. Arruns pulled her into one of the smaller storerooms. She held her breath as the enemy passed inches from them.

Arruns signaled her to follow him again. Holding her breath, she dashed past the wine cellar. There were no shouts. No footsteps running after her.

The pithoi chamber was only two more rooms away. Semni felt the urge to rush ahead, but as they neared it she noticed the door was open. Arruns halted and placed his hand across her mouth, warning her not to cry out. Her stomach twisted. For this time it was not Latin voices she heard but grunting, brutal and primal, and a girl sobbing "no, no, no."

FIFTY-SIX

Caecilia, Veii, Summer, 396 BC

"Get up, Caecilia."

Marcus had returned from his inspection of the sanctuary.

Thia clutched her mother and whimpered, hiding her face. Cytheris tightened her grip on her mistress's arm. Caecilia glared at him. "I won't leave Vel."

"Do as I say!"

His demand reminded her what it was to be a Roman woman. A spurt of anger shot through her. "What are you going to do, Marcus? Drag me away like Drusus did? It will be easy. I'm weak."

"Shut up. Do you think you can protect him forever? There are more than Drusus who want your husband to be a tormented ghost."

She swallowed, realizing her defense of Vel had been in vain. The dictator may have been deprived of the chance to execute a vanquished king, but he still had an opportunity to degrade his foe.

"Please, don't let Camillus desecrate his body! He must be cremated with due honor."

Marcus reached down and grasped her by her upper arms, forcing her to stand. Then he released her. She staggered a little, unsure whether he would reinforce his order with a slap.

"I'm not going to let him be decapitated."

She swayed, faint headed, unsure if she'd heard him correctly. "You won't?"

"I believe in paying a debt." He spat out the words.

He made no sense. "Debt?"

"You know what I'm talking about. The blood debt I owe Mastarna."

"I don't understand."

"Didn't he tell you? In return for sparing my life at Nepete, I'm obliged to grant you a favor. I doubt there's much I can do for you other than save Mastarna from mutilation."

She was astonished. The husband who'd chided her for keeping secrets had kept one from her. Gratitude surged through her that Vel would try to protect her. "But how can you prevent his body being defiled?"

"Burn him in one of the fire pits outside. It seems your people were preparing for a monumental sacrifice today."

She glanced up to Uni. Their attempts to appease the goddess had come too late. "Then let's do it quickly."

Marcus bent his knees to haul Mastarna onto his shoulders. He grunted with the effort of lifting the deadweight but managed to heft Vel from the floor. As he swung around to the door, the golden dice tumbled from a fold of the king's twisted cloak. Caecilia gasped and hurried to collect them.

Thia broke free of Cytheris and toddled to her mother, clutching at her chiton. "Hush," Caecilia murmured, "I'll be back soon. Here, play with Apa's dice."

As Thia settled beside Cytheris with her playthings, Caecilia noticed Marcus scrutinizing the child. "Hurry up," he said when he realized he'd been observed. "We need to do this now."

Caecilia walked to the doors, not caring that one edge of her mantle trailed through puddles of milk and blood. She skirted Drusus's corpse, seething, as she passed across the threshold.

The fearful din which had been muffled by the temple walls now assaulted her in a barrage: yells of triumph, shrieks of terror, the wailing of women, and the pitiful crying of children.

The grounds of the sanctuary were littered with acolytes who'd been cut down while tending to sacred tasks. A murderous sacrilege. The bulls reared in their corral, bellowing and butting each other in alarm. The sacred geese honked and flapped.

Three of Marcus's men stood guard behind the closed precinct gates, denying refuge to those fleeing from soldiers in the forum. The enemy numbers seemed to have swollen a hundredfold.

Her gaze traveled to the palace next door. Once again, she felt powerless. Her sons were inside, vulnerable. She could only pray Arruns might protect them—and that Camillus's soldiers would not forget their orders.

She dragged her eyes from the square, concentrating on following Marcus. For now, Vel was all that mattered. She swallowed, realizing she must pick her way through the dead lictors sprawled across the porch. Their rods and axes had not been enough to counter swords and surprise. She gasped when she saw Tanchvil among them. The priestess's throat was slit, her gray hair soaked in the blood pooling around her. "What type of men kill innocent women?" she shouted.

Marcus paused as he descended the steps. Head craned forward, he was sweating with the effort of lugging Vel. He barked at her to keep going, but Caecilia sensed his uneasiness at her question.

As she hurried after him, she glanced back at the two other Romans stationed on either side of the temple doorway. They were staring after their commander, expressions quizzical.

Marcus carried Mastarna's body over to one of the fire pits. Kicking the metal spit aside, he dumped the dead monarch on the pile of timber. Caecilia bit her lip, thinking how Vel should have been borne on a bier and lowered with reverence onto his pyre. She thought, too, that she should have bathed and anointed him, wrapping him in a shroud; instead her husband was swathed in bloodied purple and would be burned on a cooking fire.

She stepped down into the pit and crouched next to Vel. The stink of the pitch-covered logs burned her throat. She arranged the tebenna around him as best she could to hide his wound, trying to ignore how the cloth was stiff with blood. She clasped his hand and kissed his fingers before pressing his palm against her cheek. His battered features were relaxed. There was no sign he had suffered.

"There is no time for this," said Marcus, grabbing one of the torches that flared beside the pit.

She ignored him. She was not going to be rushed in saying her farewell. "I'll see you soon enough, my love," she murmured, kissing Vel's lips. "I look forward to your embrace."

Marcus stepped into the pit beside her and grabbed her forearm, holding the brand aloft in his other hand. "Enough." His voice was edgy as he glanced toward the Romans at the gates. It dawned on her he was disobeying orders.

"What are you going to tell Camillus?"

He pulled her to standing. "Do you want me to help you or not?"

She glanced across to the guards. "What about your men?"

"They're loyal to me. And your husband spared their lives at Nepete as well."

Caecilia was distracted by the sight of tendrils of smoke threading their way through the humid air of the sanctuary. She looked across to the precinct gates again. Flames were eating through a roof of a tavern in the forum. Her heartbeat spiked. It wouldn't take long for the fire to spread to the palace.

Now it was her turn to grip him. "Please, you must find my sons."

"How much more do you expect of me, Caecilia? I told you Camillus has said to spare them."

"Fires are being set. They may yet be in peril. Please, bring them to me."

He yanked his arm away. "I've repaid the debt. And the general gave orders not to burn the palace."

She cast another stricken look toward the inn. "By the gods! My children are your kin! Aemilian blood flows in them. Fire is fickle. Do you want the innocent to die? You saw Thia. She is but a babe. And Arnth is only nearing three, and Larce five. Tas is eight. They will be in our private quarters next to the terrace. They each wear golden bullas."

He hesitated. "Very well, I'll do what I can once I've finished here, but I give no guarantee." He stepped from the pit. "Now come on."

She gazed down at Vel. He appeared peaceful for a man robbed of life. She gulped, fighting to control her tears. "Fufluns, protect him. Guard him on his journey."

"Come, Caecilia." Marcus leaned down, offering her his hand. She stared at his extended fingers for a moment, then accepted his assistance. The act of kindness was brief. As though scalded, the cousins dropped each other's hands as soon as she'd clambered out of the pit.

"Better not watch." He put the torch to the timber.

For years she'd prepared herself to bid her last good-bye to her husband on his pyre. But when she saw the flames take hold, she lost courage. She would never be ready. She could not stand to see and smell Vel burn. She turned her back and walked away, unable to bear witness.

On the portico again, she rediscovered her nerve. She turned to face the precinct. The fire in the pit was raging. From a distance she could see the outline of Vel's body in the blaze. Suddenly, through her grief and shock, she felt satisfaction and pride. Her lover would be whole when he dined at the banquet with his ancestors. He would not be a ghost haunting the razed ruins of his city. He would be a king when Aita greeted him in Acheron. He was saved.

Fifty-Seven

Semni, Veii, Summer, 396 BC

Arruns removed his hand from Semni's mouth and moved into the cellar's doorway. She hesitated, scared to look inside but needing to check if Nerie was safe.

A Roman was straddling Perca, his back to the door, his hairy rump pale. He grunted with each thrust. The girl was struggling and begging.

Another soldier was raping Hathli, one hand around her throat. She was silent and unresisting. One of her arms appeared crooked and broken. The slap mark on her cheek was crimson.

Semni tore her attention away, scanning the room for the children, expecting them to be cowering in a corner, or worse, lying dead. She was confused to see no sign of them.

Arruns raised his dagger and threw it at the soldier who was holding Hathli down. It pierced the man's temple, driving into his brain. He slumped over his victim. Before Perca's assailant could react, the lictor sprinted across the room and stood behind the rapist, jerking and twisting his head until his neck cracked. He wrenched him to the side before the man could fall on the girl.

Semni ran and hugged her. Perca clung to her, unable to speak. Arruns dragged the Roman off Hathli. She lay motionless. Bile surged in Semni's gorge as she realized the wet nurse was dead, choke marks reddening her throat. The bastard had killed her as he violated her and then kept going.

In a spark of rage, Arruns kicked the dead man on the jaw. Then he focused on Perca, placing his hand on her shoulder. "Where are the children?"

The girl's chest heaved. "A pithos. Hathli made them hide in one while we waited for you."

Semni scanned the room of sunken containers. The day of the game of hide-and-seek returned.

Arruns glanced toward the corridor. "Close the door, then find the boys while I break open the hatch."

She eased the door shut and then raced to the pithos in which the boys had once hidden. Its lid was sealed. Her heart sank. Which one were they in? Then she noticed the ladder propped up next to a container in the back corner. She ran to the pot, rapping on its side, relieved to hear it was empty. "Tas, are you in there?"

A muffled voice replied.

She climbed the ladder and peered inside. Four sets of eyes stared up at her. Nerie stretched his arms and called to her from the depths. At his plaintive cries, the others erupted into a chorus of anxiety.

"Arruns," she hissed. "I need your help."

He was levering the first board with the iron bar. The wood splintered, the nails popping and flying outward. The plank thudded to the floor. Hearing her plea, he strode over, stepping onto the ladder, then leaning over to extend his hand down into the pot. One by one, each boy clung to the lictor's arm like a monkey, then dropped to the floor. Nerie was last. His father pulled him out, then tucked the toddler under his arm before backing down the rungs. The blond child reached for his mother, his grip so fierce around her neck she thought he would strangle her. Larce and Arnth clutched her skirts, eyes brimming with tears. Tas huddled close. He was dry eyed but fretful. Semni placed a hand on his shoulder. "Well done, Tas. That was brave of you."

He did not reply, his attention straying toward the front of the room where Perca and Hathli lay.

Semni pressed the younger brothers' faces against her legs, shielding them from the disturbing view. How much had the children heard? How terrified they must have been as they cowered in the dark pithos.

"I heard Hathli trying to stop them hurting Perca," said Tas.

She stroked his hair. "And now we all have to be as courageous as her, little master." She herded the boys over to Arruns, pointing at the Medusa's face that the lictor had now uncovered. Semni had forgotten the blankness of the gorgon's eyes and her gaping, cruel-lipped mouth.

Arruns hefted the bar again and prized off the second board. Then he raised the metal rod high, ready to smash through the terra-cotta, but Tas stepped forward, releasing the hidden clasp with one finger. The hinge creaked open. The dark void beyond was revealed. Semni shuddered, remembering the vanth.

"I'm scared to go in there," said Larce. "It's too dark."

Arruns pointed to the workbench. "Semni, get the lamp. I'll get a wall torch from the corridor."

All of them froze at the sound of footsteps thudding along the passageway. To their relief, no Romans crashed through the cellar door. Arruns darted into the hallway to retrieve a brand.

Lighting the lamp, he handed it and the torch to Tas once the boy had clambered through the hatch. His brothers followed. Arruns lifted Nerie across to them.

Semni looked around, realizing Perca had not moved. She hurried toward her.

The nursemaid sat dumb, staring at Hathli. Virginal blood stained the thirteen-year-old's lap. A fresh wave of pity surged through Semni. She leaned down and clasped the girl's elbow. "Come," she urged. "Hathli has gone to the Beyond. There's nothing more we can do for her. We need to hurry."

Perca rose, moaning in pain, and hobbled to the hatch. As Semni turned to follow her, she noticed a sack lying next to the pithos near the dead Romans. She picked it up and opened it, gasping as she recognized a jumble of the queen's amber beads, pearls, gold earrings, and bangles. Semni stared at the plunder, undecided what to do.

Impatient, Arruns joined her. "Take what you can. We'll need money to pay our way to safety."

"But they're Lady Caecilia's."

"Do you think she'll ever have need for them again?"

She flinched at his practicality, ruing that he spoke the truth. Pushing aside thoughts of her thievery, she shoved a handful of necklaces and bangles down the front of her chiton, tightening the sash around her waist to hold them secure.

Arruns ducked his head and stepped inside the secret room, offering his hand to help her through. The catch clicked. The torch and lamp flickered in the blackness. All of them were now in the lair of the vanth.

There were shouts as Romans broke into the storeroom. Their conversation sounded puzzled to find their comrades dead. One stopped outside the portal. Semni prayed he could not hear them breathing through the terra-cotta. She heard the word "Medusa" in a cautious tone, then retreating footsteps. The gorgon had warded off evil after all.

Semni felt the eyes of the vanth staring at her in the darkness. Tas raised the lamp. The demoness loomed, the pile of burned bricks beneath her. As Arruns raised the torch, Semni noticed a flicker of apprehension.

Tas swung around to face the opposite wall. "There's the passageway to the temple."

Semni was relieved to see only a few nails were loosely hammered into the second terra-cotta Medusa. The carpenters must have lost their nerve when it came to working in the cursed room. Arruns gave her the torch and began forcing the hatch door open with his dagger.

Suddenly she realized their fate was in an eight-year-old's hands. Tas's prior stealth and disobedience were now going to help them. But could the boy navigate the tunnel system to lead them to safety? And what purpose would be served in reaching the temple? The sanctum must be occupied by now. Lord Mastarna would not be in a position to help anyone.

Sharp, loud knocking on the other side of the cover startled her. Perca screamed. The children babbled in terror.

The rapping grew frantic. "It's me, Aricia! Let me in!"

The door was wrenched open. The acolyte was on her knees in the passageway, her lamp burning low in front of her.

The novitiate crawled into the vanth's room. "I was trying to come and warn you but the way was barred."

Tas threw himself at her, hugging her. "Where are Apa and Ati?"

Aricia drew away and clasped Tas's hand. "I don't know what happened to your parents, my pet. The Romans climbed into the temple through the shaft beneath Uni's statue. I was in the workroom. I escaped through the tunnel."

"Then they are dead."

"Is Ati dead?" Larce wailed.

"Enough," said Arruns, cutting off hysteria. "Aricia says she doesn't know. But your father is a great warrior. He would expect you all to be valiant." He turned to the girl. "Do you know any other way to escape the citadel?"

Aricia nodded. "Follow me to the Great Gallery. Keep one hand on the shoulder of the one in front of you. Be careful, the floor will slant downward as we move underground."

The human chain began its journey. Giving the torch to Arruns, Semni murmured a prayer, knowing her own courage was also being tested as she followed in Aricia's wake. She thought she would have to crawl; instead there was room enough for her to walk with her head bowed. She held Nerie's shoulder as he toddled in front of her.

The flames wavered, a draft catching them. Semni stepped into a large circular cavern and joined the boys in a semicircle around Aricia. She scanned the rock walls. There were entrances to other tunnels with different symbols above them. Tas pointed to two of them. "That one leads to the temple, and that one to our old house."

Aricia moved to the far side of the cavern and crouched. Her lantern revealed a rectangular opening in the floor. "This shaft leads to the bottom of the arx on the eastern side. From there we can access the river."

Semni shivered as she peered into the hole. There were wooden rungs inserted into niches in the sides. She could not see to the bottom. They would have to descend into pitch black by touch of fingers and toes. "How do you know that's where it leads?"

"Because Lord Artile told me."

Arruns edged next to her and gazed into the hole. Sweat streamed down his face. "How far down?"

"Perhaps a hundred feet."

"It's narrow."

Aricia studied his broad shoulders. "You'll fit."

He was hesitant. "How old is this shaft? Could any of the rungs be rotten? What happens if one breaks because I'm too heavy? "

Aricia rose, grimacing. "I don't know its age. And I don't know if it's safe. But what choice do we have? We'll have to risk it." She placed the lamp on the floor. "I'll need both my hands free to climb down and check."

She backed down into the hole. Soon, the black ringleted head vanished. They waited, all peering into the shaft, heads touching. And then they heard a faint voice from below. "The rungs are sturdy."

Sweat dripping from Arrun's chin, he hoisted Nerie onto his shoulders. Semni placed her hand on his forearm, aware he was anxious about descending into the maw. "I'll go before you if you want."

"No, I will. You go after Perca and the boys."

He stepped into the hole. Nerie gripped his forehead, whimpering as he disappeared from her sight.

Arnth pushed forward. "Me first."

Larce stood silent, not wanting to compete. Tas thrust out his chest. "I'll go first. I'm heir to the House of Mastarna. Apa would expect it."

Semni gestured to Perca as soon as all three princes had begun their descent. "Your turn."

She shook her head, weeping again. "I can't. I'm scared. I'm hurt."

Semni placed her hand on her shoulder. "Come, I'll be right behind you," she cajoled. "You don't want to be left here in the dark, do you? Why don't you whistle?"

Shaking, the girl edged into the shaft, emitting the tremulous, low-pitched noise.

Semni took one last look at the cavern. The torch had gone out; Aricia's was guttering, the lantern barely illuminating the stone floor. A sense of suffocation surged in her at the thought of being confined in blackness and stone. Then she reminded herself that Nerie was waiting for her. She slowed her breathing and edged her foot down onto the wooden rung, willing herself to reach for the next, and the next, and the next.

FIFTY-EIGHT

Marcus, Veii, Summer, 396 BC

Marcus strode from the portico into the temple precincts past its enormous podium and altar. He avoided checking the fire pit where Vel Mastarna's body burned. He needed no reminder of what he'd done. He found himself unable to control his trembling hands, rage and bitterness surging in him. He couldn't believe how Caecilia had caused his world to splinter.

The moment of Drusus's death was seared into his memory. If not for her, his friend wouldn't have been consumed with rage; if not for her, Drusus would never have disobeyed orders; if not for her, Drusus wouldn't have attacked him. And now he was dead. And he was his murderer.

Repaying the blood debt also fueled his anguish. The image of her begging for mercy for her husband wouldn't leave him. Blood staining her tight-clinging dress, face painted. Arrayed in purple. Decked with gold. A queenly whore.

A voice inside him told him to leave Mastarna to his fate. That he was risking his career for the sake of a cousin who'd caused him to slay his friend. And yet his integrity drove him to honor the pledge. Pity also for her anxiety for her children. Nevertheless, as Marcus bade his knights to open the sanctuary gates, he found himself angry that she'd pricked his conscience. He'd never thought of her sons as his cousins. Yet he didn't want the blood of innocent kin on his hands. And the threat of them being trapped by fire didn't concern him as much as soldiers who might forget their orders in their rampage.

As he strode into the forum, he was confronted by Romans dealing death to the defenseless. He was tempted to head to the Gates of Uni and run down the hill to fight the Veientane troops. He wanted to slay soldiers, not civilians. Instead he steeled himself to continue to the palace, knowing he needed to check on the progress of his knights.

Soldiers were swarming through the marketplace and broad avenues, dispersing onto side streets. The Veientanes fled before them, shrieking. The shouting of the Romans added to the din as they felled their victims. Corpses were strewn across the cobbles, blood streaming into the gutters. Despite being inured to the brutality of the battlefield, Marcus felt queasy that none of the dead men wore armor.

Women were dragged into the streets, their fingernails bloody as they scrabbled against the pectorals of their rapists. Soldiers were quarrelling over those who were fairest, impatient to take their turn. Richly appareled ladies were stripped of their jewelry, rings wrenched off their fingers, and gold chains torn from their throats. Children wailed as they watched their mothers being ravaged.

One hoplite pointed his spear at a baby boy crawling in the gutter. Marcus broke into a run, grabbing the butt before the man could stab downward. Then he shoved the man to the ground. The hoplite scrambled to his feet, belligerent, until he saw it was a tribune who'd pushed him.

"Concentrate on the men. There's no glory in skewering babies."

The man reddened and moved on. Marcus lifted the child and handed him to the mother, who clutched the boy to her breast and fled into an alleyway. Marcus tried not to think about their fate.

The sound of whinnying horses startled him. He turned to see the animals running loose, their panic adding to the fray.

A missile whizzed past his head. A woman had clambered onto a shop and was throwing tiles. As Marcus moved out of range, he scanned the roof ridges, noticing others doing the same. They were brave but doomed. Their aeries would soon be aflame.

Smarter, more experienced hoplites were concentrating on pillage. They emerged from the houses, bulging sacks thrown over their shoulders. A fight broke out as two of them squabbled over their haul. Marcus wondered how many Romans would be injured today by a comrade's blade.

The palace dwarfed all other buildings in the forum. Marcus had been stunned at the magnificence of the Great Temple, but it paled in comparison to the regal residence. He ascended the wide steps, trying not to gawk like a country yokel.

Once inside, he took stock. There were no hysterical shrieks or shouts echoing through the massive courtyard, only the sound of misery. The wounded sat groaning. Women sobbed as they cradled the dead. A girl huddled naked in a corner, rocking and blubbering, while a group of soldiers argued over a slave boy with a sweet face. The floor was littered with dead courtiers and servants. Palace guards and lictors also lay killed, their livery torn and bloodied, hapless protectors who'd never imagined fighting a foe in the luxury of the royal halls. Marcus scanned for children, relieved when he saw none.

He peered into a chamber flanked by two tall bronze doors, amazed to find an even larger room beyond. His eyes widened at the sight of a golden throne with a bull's head crest. Tatius emerged and saluted. "I've assigned one unit to secure the treasury, sir. All the palace guards are dead. We've killed eleven lictors, too."

"No need to guess. The tattooed henchman is missing?"

Tatius nodded. "No sign of him."

"And the princes?"

"Not found as yet, but some of my men are still searching. What are your orders?"

"Head down the hill. There are armies stationed in this city. Veii won't be conquered until they are vanquished."

Tatius grimaced. "There'll be complaints that they'll miss out on the best pickings. The infantry have flooded this place now."

Marcus glowered at him. "I'm sure the general won't let any patrician knight suffer who puts duty above his greed."

"I'll make it clear to them, sir." Then he screwed his mouth to the side. "You should see the treasury. It beggars belief."

Marcus studied the throne again. The ease of seizing a glut of riches would be euphoric for some. "The coffers better remain untouched. Double the guard there and here. And close these doors." He paused. "Tell one of your riders to capture a horse and ride into the city. Inform General Camillus the king is dead and the traitoress is in custody."

"Are you coming, sir?"

"No, I'm going to check the private quarters first. I want to report personally that all attempts were made to find the princes."

Marcus headed into an internal corridor to find the living area. His temper flared when he noticed the air was hazy from smoke. Camillus would be unhappy if he had to sift molten gold from a charred building.

Coughing, he held his forearm to his nose and hurried along the passageway until he reached the entrance to a large chamber with a terrace beyond. He was relieved to see the area was deserted, the floor devoid of corpses, especially tiny ones.

Laughter distracted him. A group of hoplites were tearing apart the royal bed chamber. His bellow startled them. "Go and find some water to douse the fire. The general wants the palace intact. And start securing prisoners."

For a moment, he thought avarice would make them forget discipline. They glared at him. Camillus had given them a right to the spoils. Who was this tribune to deny them?

"Others have already been here, sir. It's our turn now."

Marcus held himself rigid, his stare icy. The men saluted and then backed out of the chamber. He could hear them protesting to each other at being deprived of their swag.

Marcus ventured into the bedroom. Smoke had not yet penetrated inside. He surveyed the patterned ceiling of tiny flowers and walls with heavy horizontal lines of red, green, and blue. Chests of expensive wood were flung open, clothes strewn across the floor. Robes had been ripped from wall pegs. A lyre fashioned from amber lay with broken strings. Caskets of silver and bronze had been tossed aside, their lids scattered. All of them were intricately engraved, with clawed feet. He peered inside. Any jewelry had long been stolen. There were boxes of cosmetics, too, proof of the whorish appearance of Caecilia.

The bed was tall and wide with a plush mattress. The plaid cover had been ripped, the pillows scattered. The footstools pushed over. This is where his cousin had lain with her Veientane. Marcus felt the awkwardness of intruding on a place of intimacy as well as passion.

He crouched and searched under the bed, thinking it unlikely he would find a frightened prince. He spied an ornate silver mirror that must have slid across the floor. A man and woman embraced each other, gazes locked, lips almost touching. Their names were incised beside them in strange Etruscan script.

Marcus moved through to the terrace. There were no small persons huddling amid the garden or behind the fountain. He stood at the wall to look at the Roman camp opposite. How many times had Caecilia gazed at the people who had become her enemy?

He returned to the main chamber and headed into the corridor again. The cradle in the nursery was vacant except for a tiny doll. He glanced inside other rooms that had been abandoned, their occupants roused from sleep and fleeing. He felt a surge of relief there was no blood on the sheets. He smoothed his hand along the cloth. It was cold. Warm bodies had risen to leave some time ago.

Where had the princes gone? Havoc awaited them outside. Even with the Phoenician to protect them, he doubted they could be saved. At least if they were hiding in the palace, they could be identified as royal.

He closed his eyes and inhaled. He couldn't waste any more time combing through the residence. He owed nothing more to Vel Mastarna or his cousin.

Adjusting his balteus, and with hand on hilt, he turned back to the courtyard. Now his duty was solely to Rome. He broke into a run. A city waited below to be conquered. It was time to find some warriors to kill.

FIFTY-NINE

Semni, Veii, Summer, 396 BC

Rung after rung, Semni descended, easing down each time, worried the timber might break, not sure if she would make a misstep. The jewelry clicked and tinkled beneath her clothes. The climb was tortuous as Perca struggled and whimpered with pain. To Semni's relief, she saw a faint light below her, then felt her foot hit earth. In front of her was a low-roofed tunnel. Dropping to her knees, she crawled through it.

A huge arm encircled her waist as Arruns hugged her. Nerie wrapped his arms around her neck. The moment of reunion was brief as her husband broke from her and gave her their son to hold.

Semni gazed up at the sheer cliff towering above her, holly trailing across its surface. She felt giddy for a moment as she realized the height from which she had descended through the shaft. Black smoke billowed above, sullying the pale-blue sky. She was surprised to see the sun was far from its zenith. She assumed ages had passed but it was still early morning.

Beyond her lay a ravine covered by a scrub of new-growth oak and beech. A short distance away, they would find the river carving a path through a series of valleys. How were they going to traverse such terrain?

The group of fugitives clustered around Arruns, frightened to step away from the circle of his protection. Semni could not help feeling despondent. Surely four children, two women, and an injured girl were too many for one man to rescue?

Arruns was surveying the scenery, too. The anxiety she'd glimpsed in the cavern had gone. "Let's go. We need to reach the river," he said. "I plan to steal a boat. There are traders who carry supplies for the Romans along the river. They may take us north if we pay them."

Her eyes widened. "Or betray us. And the enemy patrol the north as well."

"There are Romans everywhere, Semni. We can only try."

"What about the forts?"

"There aren't as many on this side because of the depth of the ravines and the way the river runs so close to the wall. But I'll warrant most outposts will be unmanned. If the soldiers are allowed to claim booty, then every hoplite around here will be in the city stealing as much as he can. We need to hurry."

Semni scanned the gaggle of women and children. "The boys are already tired."

He glanced at his charges. "There's not much choice. We can't stay here."

"We'll stick out like sore thumbs. You, in particular."

"Don't give up before we've even started. Now, come on."

Perca moaned as she struggled to her feet, then staggered. Arruns hefted her into his arms.

Arnth seemed to have found an extra reserve of strength. He pushed past Tas to be the first after the lictor. Tas also showed resilience. He bade Larce to remember he was a prince, as the middle brother dragged his feet and whined. Larce straightened his shoulders, his competitive spirit rising to the surface.

Aricia fell in behind the boys as they pushed through the brush. Semni and Nerie trailed at the end of the queue. Soon she heard the sound of flowing water. Arruns stopped short, keeping cover in a thicket. There was a line of new willows trailing fronds in the river, green and peaceful. Semni licked her lips. She was thirsty, her throat parched.

Arruns scanned the ridge for Romans, then signaled them forward to the willows, lowering Perca to the ground once he'd reach the trees. The party scrambled under the bower, the thin fronds forming a roof of greenery above them.

"Give me one of the necklaces," he said.

Semni slid her hand down the neck of her dress and pulled out the queen's pearls. She noticed Tas's eyes widening as he recognized his mother's possession. Arruns stuffed the jewelry into the pouch at his waist.

"Stay here. I'll be back," he said. "Stay hidden in the willows. Be quiet."

She clutched his arm. "Don't leave us."

He peeled her fingers away and squeezed them. "I will return." Both knew it was a tenuous promise. And if he could not keep it, they would be doomed.

Arruns threaded his way through the scrub at the edge of the bank and disappeared. After everyone had slaked their thirst, Semni leaned her back against the willow's trunk. The clamor from the city drifted to them. She wondered if she would still hear it when she was far away, an indelible noise at the back of her mind.

"Rest," she said to the boys. "We've a long journey ahead when Arruns returns."

Tas remained anxious. "But what if we fall asleep? The Romans might get us."

"Hush. We'll watch over you," said Aricia.

Nerie settled onto his mother's lap. She stroked his fair hair until he fell asleep. Perca also curled up and closed her eyes. Tas remained alert, peeping through the leaves to keep watch for Arruns. The younger princes clustered beside him.

Semni covered Aricia's hand, keeping her voice low. "Do you actually know what happened in the temple?"

The girl's eyes brimmed with tears. "It happened so suddenly. One moment the chamber was hushed, with only the sound of Lord Mastarna invoking Uni. I couldn't see him or the queen because the statue was in the way. Then the rug hiding the secret shaft moved. The trap door rose in front of me and was flung open. There were so many of them. I was too shocked to cry out. They were stealthy, fanning out as each one broke free of the shaft. Mother was holding Thia and screaming."

"Did the Romans hurt them?"

Aricia covered her face with her hands. "I don't know! I was a coward. I ran and escaped through the passage leading from the workroom. I thought I might be able to warn you to get the princes out. But then I could not open the Medusa hatch." Tears trickled between her fingers.

She encircled Aricia's shoulder with her arm. "I doubt you could have helped anyone. You would've been captured if you'd shown yourself. You were brave to try and find us."

Aricia leaned against her shoulder. "Mother and I were going to spend time together at the feast. She said she was proud of me for training as a priestess."

Semni squeezed her. "Then you made peace. That's the most important thing to remember. We must pray the enemy shows mercy. And that they would not harm a baby."

Time crawled. Semni strained to hear any sound that might herald Arruns's return. Or worse, that Romans were approaching.

Tas suddenly turned to her. "I can see a boat."

All of them swiveled their heads around to Semni. Somehow she had become their leader. She placed her finger to her lips before scuttling forward to peer through the branches.

A barge was approaching. A Roman soldier was in its fore, another man at the tiller.

The boat drew closer, then slowed, turning its prow to the bank. Semni wondered if she should shout to the others to run. Then she noticed the soldier's profile—his hooked nose and the pattern of the snake upon his cheek. Arruns was wearing a Roman soldier's helmet and breast plate. There was fresh blood on his tunic and hands. Semni was beyond caring how many other killings her husband had needed to perform to secure the vessel.

He jumped out, guiding the craft's nose until it nudged against the bank. She crawled from her hiding place.

One by one, Arruns lifted the boys and women into the boat. Then he scooped some mud from the riverbank and smeared it across his face, covering the tattoo. He pushed off, wading in the shallows and nimbly jumping into the boat. Semni clung to the side of the prow as the craft rocked with his weight.

The trader watched them boarding, glancing around at the ridge above, and up and down stream.

"Can you trust him?" she whispered to Arruns.

"I've promised him more jewels if he takes us to the tributary beyond the north bridge. Then we can head overland to Lake Sabatinus and then on to Tarchna. I'm paying more than he can earn selling a shipment. We should have no trouble if I'm thought to be a Roman soldier as we pass the river stations. And there are only a few sentries on the lines." He gazed up to the citadel. "The rest are killing unarmed men and innocents."

For one last time, Semni gazed up at the arx. A black, hazy cloud hung over it. Ashes drifted in the air, settling on surfaces everywhere, even the skin of the water. The Romans were razing her city. A lump stuck in her throat. She would never see her home again.

Arruns lifted the heavy hides that covered the cargo hold. The space was empty. "All of you, lie down here. And make no noise.

Sound carries over water. Try to sleep. This trip will take hours. I'll give you fresh air when I think it's safe."

As the boys crawled inside, she thought how excited they would normally be at such an adventure. Instead they huddled together, trembling and sweaty in the stuffy confines of the crawl space.

Semni lay in the gloom under the hides, Nerie next to her. She could hear the sound of the vessel splashing through water, the creak of the sail. The fumes from the resin that caulked the boat's timbers were strong. She hoped they would not suffocate.

After a time, she became drowsy, struggling to keep awake. Her eyelids drooped, then shut. As sleep overwhelmed her, her last thought was whether she would wake to the land of the living or the world of the Beyond.

SIXTY

Pinna, Veii, Summer, 396 BC

All day Pinna waited in the camp, staring across to the high fortress, sick in the stomach, and sick at heart.

The shouts of alarm had been faint at first, drifting across the heavy humid air of the valley. By midday, the suffering cries swelled in volume. Now it was late afternoon, and the torment had not abated.

As always on a day of battle, the army wives congregated together, gaining comfort in each other's presence as they did their chores. Despite the ingenuity of the general's plan, they still worried their men might not return. Pinna did not join them; instead she walked to the bluff to observe the plateau. She doubted her lover would be injured. Mater Matuta would guard him.

Although nauseated, she remained riveted on the invasion unfolding before her. In the distance, she spied tiny figures throwing ropes over the curtain walls. Others leaped in desperation, risking broken bones instead of death by sword or spear. Their efforts were fruitless; soldiers awaited them.

From her high point, she saw the pall of smoke massing like a storm cloud as though Juno was raining down destruction. The dark sky made it hard to keep track of time. The hours stretched. The longest of days was an agony. The divine queen had truly been enticed from her home.

With no breeze, the smoke eventually floated to the camp, coating the tents with ash. And all the while Pinna pondered that her lover's ambition had now been made tangible. The residue settling on her hair was the cinders of a dying people, and a dying city.

She heard the rumble of wagons behind her, the crack of whips and muleteers shouting. A rider headed toward her, reining in his horse. His face was blackened by grime, his visage like some demon, runnels of scarlet streaking his face.

"General Camillus wants you to go to him."

"Then the Veientanes have surrendered?"

He laughed. "Surrendered? Veii has been conquered! Now the general has issued orders no unarmed men will be killed. Only those determined to bear weapons risk death."

"But why does he want me?"

"He didn't say. Only that you and Artile Mastarna should come to the palace." He pointed to the carts. "We have orders to start collecting the spoils to transport to Rome."

She hurried across to the convoy. Artile was already seated on the first wagon. He did not acknowledge her. His attention was solely on the concrete consequences of his treachery. His complexion was tinged green.

The driver urged the donkeys forward. Pinna gripped the seat beneath her as the cart bumped over the rutted road descending into the valley.

By the time she crossed the ford, she'd vomited twice. From the heights, the enemy had appeared small, but now she saw the corpses of those who'd tried to escape. She was shocked to see the river running red.

As she ascended the plateau to the city, she was assaulted by a discordant lament rising above an undercurrent of babbling misery. Eyes watering from smoke, she gazed up at the carved lions decorating the towers flanking the great oaken gates. The watchful guardians had failed their city today, rendered impotent by invaders from within. Artile did not bother to glance up at the stone beasts. There was a smear of sick on his mouth. His hands clenched in his lap.

The carts trundled into the main avenue of the city. Suddenly Pinna comprehended the enormity of her Wolf's achievement. Rome seemed like some country town compared to this metropolis. The sight would have thrilled her if she didn't have to witness the atrocities around her. She clutched the fascinum on her necklace. For the first time ever, she doubted her belief in Mater Matuta. It was hard to believe two mother goddesses could preside over such cruelty.

Fires had died down, buildings smoldering, their frames skeletal and scorched. Children were wandering, searching for mothers and fathers, their howling pitiful. Others tugged at bloodstained skirts, expecting an embrace that would forever be denied. Soldiers were scavenging, stealing from both the dead and the living. Others were rounding up prisoners. The female captives stood cowering, ropes around their necks. There were no elderly or frail in view.

Head aching, Pinna closed her eyes. The surfeit of butchery was too much to bear.

"Behold the palace of the great King Vel Mastarna."

She opened her eyes at Artile's deep voice. She glanced across to him and realized he was speaking to himself. Then she raised her eyes and gasped at the vast edifice before her.

The convoy halted, lining up in readiness for its cargo. Artile climbed down from the cart and headed to the portico without waiting for her. She scurried after him, noticing Camillus's groom holding the general's white stallion at the bottom of the broad set of steps.

"Pinna!" Marcus ran up the steps behind her. He was splattered with blood, his face filthy. "What are you doing here?"

"The general sent for me."

He scowled. "Come on, then. I've only just returned from the city."

Now she chased both men as they hastened through an impressive courtyard. Once again, she averted her eyes from the gore around her, following the men through tall bronze doors into a room whose walls were covered with murals.

A group of knights were milling around a closed set of studded double doors to a further room. She expected the soldiers to be buoyant after their victory; instead they were preoccupied, muttering to each other. The stink of them filled the air, their faces and clothes covered in soot, their arms stained red to the elbows. Artile did not even glance at them. He was agitated, wringing his hands. Pinna realized he must be anxious to see if Tarchon and the little prince had survived.

Marcus strode over to the cavalrymen, who saluted. "What's going on here?"

"We delivered some treasure to General Camillus. Now he and General Genucius have locked the doors," said a decurion, eying Pinna askance. "No one is to enter other than the concubine and priest."

Marcus hammered on the bronze. One massive door opened a fraction. Genucius acknowledged the tribune with a nod. "Ah, Marcus. Come inside, too."

The one-eyed commander shut the door once Pinna and the two men edged through the gap. Her mouth dropped open. She'd entered the heart of the realm. Before her was a huge throne on a dais with a smaller throne beside it. And in front of the podium, her Wolf sat on his curule chair, helmet on the floor beside him, cradling his head with his hands. Next to him was a pile of gold coins stacked higher than a man.

Tearing her eyes from the loot, Pinna ran to her lover's side and prized his hands from his face. Camillus raised his head. His expression was harrowed. His eyes were brimming with tears.

"What is it, my Wolf? Are you ill?"

He wiped the back of his hand across his eyes, then gripped her fingers. "Have you seen what I've done, Pinna? How the dead litter the avenues and squares? It's taken me all day to traverse every corner of the city. And all around me for miles were weapons, bodies, and lamentation."

Love for him welled. After witnessing his fervor yesterday, she expected him to be jubilant and callous. "You've won a great victory, my Wolf."

He searched her face. "Have I? I didn't win a battle. I trapped them like fish in a dam, then spiked them one by one."

"Remember you defeated the armies stationed here, my Wolf. You overcame warriors."

"Soldiers roused from slumber in the early morn before they had time to don armor. Scrambling to orientate themselves, waking to a nightmare. There were a few pockets of armed resistance. Most were easily quelled. Only the old campaigner, Lusinies, managed to mount a credible defense."

"As you planned. Remember the dawn goddess is on your side."

To her surprise he wrapped his arms around her, burying his forehead between her breasts. "Divine favor that overwhelms me. See the coins? They are but a glimpse of the riches held in the treasury."

She glanced over his head to Caius Genucius. He stood stroking his thick beard, eyes hard with hate. Marcus rubbed his puckered scar, then looked away. Artile waited behind a bronze-clad table laden with scrolls, impatient, brimful with questions.

She bent and whispered, "Rome will thank you for this conquest, my Wolf. You've delivered wealth that will help both rich and poor. Hunger will no longer stalk us. Would Juno have answered your call if she'd not wished the Veientanes to be defeated?"

She felt the tension in his body ease. He released her and rose, cupping her face between his palms. "As always, you know how to soothe me."

Artile was querulous. "Where's Tarchon? And Prince Tas?"

The general ignored him, focusing on Marcus. "What happened? Your messenger told me Vel Mastarna is dead."

Artile gasped. "My brother, dead? I thought he was to be captured!" He walked across to the tribune, seizing his forearm. "Is Tarchon dead, too?"

Marcus shucked him off.

Camillus roared. "Silence! I don't care about that mollis. Let Marcus Aemilius speak. Was Mastarna armed? Did he put up a fight?"

Marcus hesitated, clenching and unclenching his fists at his sides. Pinna wondered why he was so nervous.

"We found him at prayer when we broke into the temple. He wore no armor. In the confusion, he was fatally wounded."

"Who killed him?"

"Claudius Drusus."

Camillus's face suffused with color. "So the man who swore vengeance forgot his orders! Where is he now?"

There was pain in the tribune's voice. "Dead, sir. I killed him."

The general grunted in surprise. Pinna's pulse quickened.

"Drusus attacked me when I commanded him not to behead the king," continued Marcus. "So I defended myself. I wish he'd heeded me . . ." His lowered his head, his words trailing away.

Seeing his officer's distress, Camillus stepped across to him and placed his hand on his shoulder. "I feel for you, Marcus. He was your friend. But what you did was justified. Drusus placed personal feelings above Rome's."

Marcus raised his head. "I burned his body, sir."

"Drusus's?"

"No, Vel Mastarna's."

Camillus shoved the tribune's shoulder. "What!"

"I killed Drusus to stop him mutilating the king's body. I couldn't take the chance others would as well. Mastarna always treated our dead with respect."

"You've denied me the chance to look on him one last time! To display a conquered leader to our people!"

Marcus fell to one knee, head bowed. "I accept my punishment, sir. But there was no direct order concerning Mastarna's corpse. I burned him in a cooking pit. He deserved better."

"At least tell me you showed no mercy to your cousin."

"She's in the temple with Prince Tarchon."

Artile interrupted, his voice hopeful. "Then he's alive?

"He was breathing when I left him. I knocked him unconscious."

"Then let me go to him."

Camillus curled his lip. "Your brother lies dead, and your city in ruins—and all you worry about is a lover who spurned you?"

"I don't weep for my brother. Nor for his bitch. I'm the master of the House of Mastarna now."

"Have you seen the destruction about you? You're master of nothing."

The haruspex stared at him, the hollow look returning. "What about Vel Mastarna Junior?"

The dictator returned to his chair and picked up his helmet. "Your nephews have disappeared. I expect they'll turn up. There's no place to hide. Whether they will be alive remains to be seen."

"There are escape tunnels. Tas knows of them."

The general spoke sharply. "Tunnels? I thought you'd pointed out all of them."

"I told you about the main one to the temple. There's a warren of others on the arx that are too difficult to access." Artile's agitation increased. "Tas is only eight. He'll need help. The Phoenician lictor must have slipped the net with the boys." He pressed his palms together in supplication. "Please send out a search party. They couldn't have gone far."

The general buckled his helmet. "I'm not going to waste time on a manhunt. They could be anywhere by now. The invasion has lasted all day. The princes fled this morning."

"You're unwise, general. Boys are little foes who'll grow into warriors. And girls breed soldiers to wreak vengeance. Mastarna's children should not go free."

Camillus hesitated, then was dismissive. "I doubt they'll make it through the siege lines." He straightened his cloak. Self-doubt had vanished. "I've more important matters to deal with. It's time to speak to the captive queen." He offered Pinna his arm. "Come. You must accompany me to the temple as well."

Pleased her Wolf had not forgotten her, the concubine walked past the officers clustered around the now open doorway. Curiosity trickled through her disquiet. After a decade of wondering, she was about to meet Aemilia Caeciliana.

SIXTY-ONE

Caecilia, Veii, Summer, 396 BC

Caecilia's tears had dried but her eyes still watered. The chamber was hazy with fine smoke. She'd lost track of time. The light spilling from the portico into the chamber was an eerie orange. The humidity sapped energy from her.

Her wrists were raw from struggling against the rope that bound her hands. Her chest was constricted by the bonds strapping her to one leg of the altar table. A shot of pain pierced her shoulder every time she moved. After a while she recognized the futility of seeking escape. Thia's weight on her lap numbed her legs. Her throat was parched, and her head ached from the tightness of the coronet. She was surprised that she felt such discomfort when her heart had been torn from her.

Cytheris was also bound. She'd fallen asleep, her head slumped forward. The handmaid, who could always reassure her mistress, had been at a loss to provide consolation.

A lump formed in Caecilia's throat. She would lose Cytheris, too. She wondered if the servant would consider death preferable to slavery.

Dehydrated, Thia whined, trying everyone's nerves. The spot of color on her cheek was still visible, her touch feverish.

At least being tied to the far end of the altar meant Caecilia could see Tarchon. At first she thought he'd slipped away, but then she noticed the rise and fall of his chest. He was groggy when he opened his eyes, his words slurred. He was confused, then incredulous, calling out to check on her. His anguished cry when he saw Sethre was tragic. With wrists and ankles tied, he shuffled on his buttocks to his beloved's body, then lay on his side facing him, stroking the youth's cheek with his roped hands. After a time, he fell into a torpor.

She also dozed, exhausted by weeping and worry. Each time she woke, she was disbelieving. Her anxiety for her sons thrummed inside her.

The presence of Drusus's body in front of her was a goad. Her thoughts vacillated between hate for him and shock and sorrow over Vel. Each wave of grief was agony.

The Romans deputized to remain at the temple wandered in and out of the portico. She could see they were restless, bored with standing guard to prevent their fellow soldiers raiding the treasures in the sanctuary. One remained in the chamber ogling her, making her conscious of her clinging dress. She prayed he would obey Marcus's order not to rape the women, remembering her horror that her cousin needed to issue the command.

When the guard's eyes weren't roving over her breasts, he studied the rich trappings of the sanctum, in particular, Queen Uni's diadem, gold pectoral, and rings. She wondered if he would lever out the gems and hide them, hoping his superiors wouldn't notice. "Pity the gold is destined for the treasury," she murmured.

He glared at her. "Not this time; the general promised us a share."

She was surprised, then felt nauseous, thinking of the race to collect the loot. "Then you're missing your chance to steal your own."

"Shut up, bitch. You've already caused enough trouble."

Thia woke in fright and bawled.

"Shut her up," he said, nudging the baby with his toe.

Caecilia cried out, helpless to hold her daughter, sorry she'd taunted him. She crooned to the baby with a hoarse, wavering voice. To her relief, Thia quieted, standing on her mother's lap and clutching her neck, watching the guard.

She heard the scrape of boots as the guards stood to attention outside. Startled from sleep, Cytheris uttered a small cry as twenty-four Roman lictors marched into the chamber. Caecilia craned her neck to catch sight of her sons, heart thudding afresh when they did not appear.

Camillus was just as she remembered him. The lean wolf of Tas's dreams. She'd been waiting for him all day. In a strange way she longed to see him. To finally meet the man who'd stalked her so she could confront him.

Even after a day of overseeing slaughter, he stood immaculate in his armor, breastplate, and leather kilt. He had removed his helmet, his long hair oiled, beard clipped. As she watched him stride to the head of his entourage, she noticed his limp was barely detectable. He frowned as he passed Drusus's corpse, then his pace slowed when he saw Uni's statue, his eyes widening in awe. He bowed in reverence.

Marcus was at the dictator's side. Camillus must have forgiven him for burning Vel's body. He cast a furtive look toward the Claudian's body, the apple in his throat working, but his expression remained impassive.

A woman crept through the doorway and stood behind the general. Her pretty heart-shaped face was pale, the high arched eyebrows furrowed in a line as she took in the death around her.

Caecilia was surprised to see a female amid warriors. Who was she?

The woman also gazed upward in wonder at Uni. But as she turned her attention to Caecilia, the queen saw pity in her eyes, the first she'd seen from a Roman. Even when Marcus had helped her, he'd done so with resentment.

Camillus regarded the queen coolly as he picked up the eagle scepter from the altar table. He snapped his fingers to signal one of his lictors to set up his ivory chair. The dictator took his seat.

Caecilia forced herself to revert to Latin, her mother tongue, which she now considered an enemy's language. "I want to see my sons."

The dictator raised one eyebrow. "I don't think you're in the position to make demands, Aemilia Caeciliana."

She knew he wanted her to beg. She doubted it would make a difference. She glanced across to Marcus, hoping he would give her a hint that the boys were safe. He avoided her gaze, stony faced. She wondered why she should expect comfort from him. He'd kept his vow to Mastarna. He owed her nothing more. Her gaze traveled to the woman, who gave an almost imperceptible nod. Caecilia was unsure if she'd seen correctly. Yet the faint encouragement did not quell her anxiety.

Thia whimpered, tightening her grip.

"Let me hold my daughter. Do you think I'm capable of doing harm with my hands freed?"

Camillus hesitated. His companion murmured behind him. He appeared irritated at her interjection but gestured to the guard to untie the ropes. Again Caecilia was surprised. How did this female come to have such influence? Her shapely figure suggested the general probably enjoyed her, but she was clearly more than a bedmate.

Words of thanks stuck in her throat. She wrapped her arms around Thia's waist, kissing her. The baby settled on her lap, quiet but quivering. Caecilia returned her attention to Camillus, staring him down.

He laughed. "Do you think I'm frightened of a woman glaring at me?"

"I think only a coward slaughters unarmed people. You haven't won a battle here today. Trickery, not bravery, delivered Veii into your hands."

A hint of irritation flickered in his eyes. She'd seen it before at Fidenae years ago. She liked the fact she got under his skin.

He studied her from head to toe. She refused to feel ashamed. She was not prepared to be drawn back into Rome's rules and judgments. She was a Rasennan wife, not a Roman matron.

"Look at you with your sheer clothes and painted face. I didn't think a prostitute could become a monarch." Camillus turned to his men and smiled. They sniggered in appreciation.

Caecilia stuck out her chin. "I am no whore but a univira. Faithful to one man."

He sneered. "I doubt it. But any number of my men can soon relieve you of that distinction."

The woman behind him gasped. He turned and gave her a stern look.

Caecilia was determined not to show her fear. "I'm proud of who I am. Proud to be Veientane. I have no regrets I chose Veii."

"Husbands have a habit of dying, Caecilia. That's why you should have returned to your uncle's house. You should never have forsaken Rome."

"At least Vel Mastarna was spared the humiliation of being paraded at your triumph. And strangled at its conclusion."

Marcus tensed. Camillus also stiffened, looking across to the tribune, then back to her. "Regrettable, but at least I'll have the pleasure of seeing you executed."

She clenched her fists to hide her trembling. "Better a traitor to Rome than the martyr you wanted to make me."

"So you think yourself innocent? That you are some poor scapegoat?"

"No. I sought Rome's destruction." She swiveled her head to scan each person in the room. "Gladly."

"So you confess?"

"As if there will be any trial."

"You forfeited that privilege long ago. The Carcer dungeon awaits you, as does a view from the Tarpeian Rock."

As she tried to push thoughts of a brutal death aside, she noticed someone entering the sanctum from the corner of her eye.

She felt as though she'd been stabbed. Artile walked to Uni's statue and bowed with the conceited mien of the holiest of servants. She wondered how he didn't stagger with the burden of so many dead dragged behind him.

His eyes rested on her, gloating. Then his gaze traveled to the pool of Mastarna's blood in front of the altar without blinking. When he spied Tarchon, though, he panicked. He rushed to him, stepping in front of Sethre, and pressed two fingers against the prince's neck. He relaxed at finding a pulse then glared at Marcus. "You could've killed him."

Camillus barked, "Leave him. I have more concerns than worrying about your pet."

Tarchon opened his eyes at the priest's touch. Dazed, he took a few moments to recognize who hovered above him. When he realized, he struggled to sit, shock apparent. Then his face contorted with fury as he tried to break free from his bindings. "You bastard!"

Startled, Artile stood out of his reach.

Tarchon inched closer to Sethre, sliding his palms around one of the youth's lifeless hands, then defiant, he raised it to his lips.

The seer flinched, anger replacing his dismay.

Tarchon called to Camillus. "Rome must have been desperate to listen to this dog. He's not only betrayed his city but his own flesh and blood."

"Lord Artile is now a patriot of Rome. Your father should have taken care not to foster enmity with his brother."

"I don't know what lies he's told you, but he's a poisoner and pervert. There's good reason why my father despised him. As do I."

A look of distaste crossed Camillus's face. "I have little interest in such accusations." He beckoned to the haruspex. "Get over here."

Artile bristled at the command but obeyed. Caecilia was pleased to see the priest had become a lackey. However, the haruspex's haughtiness was restored when he studied her.

"Ah, Sister, I always told you that your fate led back to Rome. This is what becomes of flouting Nortia."

She gritted her teeth, hating he was right. "At least I'll be dragged to Rome instead of slinking there like a rat. I have not betrayed my people."

The priest scowled. "You're not Veientane. And Queen Uni chose to abandon her city because of you."

She frowned, twisting around to stare up at the goddess. "What do you mean?"

Camillus stood, pointing the scepter in one hand at the statue. "I called Uni to desert Veii. I promised her a temple in Rome as Juno Regina. She answered my prayer."

Caecilia heard Cytheris's sharp intake of breath and Tarchon's grunt of disbelief. She hugged Thia. What he said was fanciful, and yet it must be true. The mother goddess had been neglected and was unforgiving. The attempts to placate her had come too late.

Camillus walked around the altar table and knelt before the effigy. "O Mighty Jupiter and Juno Regina, I thank you for your favor. Know that this conquest was not unjust but of necessity to defend my people. Yet if you consider some retribution due for such devastation, I beseech you to spare Rome and let any penance fall upon my own head."

Wheeling around, he began to rise, but his foot caught in his cloak. Stumbling, he pitched forward, grabbing the edge of the altar to prevent falling. The scepter clattered to the floor.

"My Wolf!" The woman ran to his side, grasping his forearm.

He steadied himself and shrugged her away. "Leave me be, Pinna." It was clear he was unnerved, taking a moment to recover his composure. Then he straightened his shoulders and smoothed his cloak as he turned to the others with a smile. "My prayer is granted! A slight fall is my atonement for the greatest good fortune."

The anxious look on the woman's face remained. As did Artile's frown. Camillus ignored them. He picked up the scepter and walked around the table to stand in front of Caecilia again.

"The time has come for you to return to Rome." He signaled two lictors to come forward. "Give the child to Pinna. And bind the queen's hands again. Lead her and Prince Tarchon to the camp. Take the maidservant, too."

Caecilia screamed, straining against the ropes around her chest. "No, please, don't take my baby. Tell me if my sons are alive!"

At her mother's panic, Thia shrieked. Cytheris started to sob. Tarchon shouted abuse.

Pinna hurried across to Camillus. "Please, my Wolf, let her keep her daughter a little longer." She touched his arm, coaxing him. "Please."

His glare softened. "Very well. But don't feel too sorry for her. Her heartbreak is deserved."

Caecilia felt a wave of gratitude toward the woman who now approached her. She surrendered Thia to her while the lictor untied the ropes. Her limbs cramping, the queen wobbled as she rose to her feet. The dice fell from her lap. She bent and retrieved them. For a moment, black dots swam before her eyes as she straightened. She felt Pinna clasp her elbow to help her, bending close. "The princes have not been found either dead or alive."

Tears pricked her eyes. "Thank you," she whispered, claiming her daughter and cradling her. She prayed Arruns might yet save her sons.

Pinna stepped back and returned to stand beside Camillus. Caecilia sensed her unease. The woman who'd half tamed a wolf had a conscience.

"Place Aemilia Caeciliana in a covered wagon," called the dictator to his lictors. "I don't want her torn to pieces by a mob before I have the chance to display her in my triumph."

A guard shoved her to start walking. Cytheris and Tarchon fell in behind her, hands tied. All the prisoners shuffled, bodies stiff from their bonds.

As she reached the bronze doors, Caecilia stifled a sob, her throat raw. She didn't think she could bear to see the fire pit and the evidence Vel was truly gone. All that she now possessed were memories and loss—of her people, her friends, her family, and the man she loved.

TRIUMPH

SIXTY-TWO

Marcus, Rome, Summer, 396 BC

Marcus touched the scars on the inside of his wrist. He lacked the courage to dig deeper, to carve along the vein.

He relived the sword fight with Drusus constantly, shocked his friend would rather kill him than obey him. Thinking how easy it was to defeat a soldier who'd never truly recovered from his injuries. The sad memory of finally kissing the man he loved was soured by the fear he'd been too late to catch Drusus's soul. He felt the knight's dishonored ghost would surely haunt him forever. And he doubted the pain of losing him would ever ease. It did not help that he had too much time to think. Until preparations for Camillus's triumph were finalized, the troops remained camped on the Field of Mars. The Senate had not quibbled that Camillus deserved the recognition. He'd brought Rome's greatest foe to its knees.

The sound of horses nickering outside drew Marcus from his tent. Four white stallions were hitched to a bronze chariot in the parade ground. Camillus stood on the platform beside the driver, planting his feet apart to balance himself without gripping the edges. Genucius stood nearby, surprise obvious. Marcus felt uneasy. Only the king of the gods could drive such a quadriga.

He walked to the chariot, but before he reached it, he saw Medullinus striding toward them. Aemilius and Spurius trailed behind. None of them hid their outrage.

"Brother, are you mad? You can't ride into Rome as though you were Jupiter. Your hubris grows monumental."

Camillus remained on the platform above them. "I'm honoring Rome's divine ruler by choosing his sacred conveyance. I'm his mortal representative. I also pay homage to the sun god, Apollo. He and the dawn goddess granted victory to me."

"Victory to Rome," growled Medullinus.

The dictator shrugged. "In my triumphal march tomorrow, Rome and I are as one."

"You're merely a man, Furius Camillus," said Aemilius. "And one who may find his popularity disappearing fast."

The general's expression darkened. He stepped down from the vehicle, waving the charioteer on. "Don't tell me the people's tribunes are arguing about the cost of the triumph? There'll be four days of thanksgiving and feasting. It's unprecedented. And I'm paying half the cost from my own plunder. The Senate agreed the State will fund the rest."

"It's not the expense," said Spurius. "Calvus is spreading rumors against you. He says it's only through his advocacy that citizens were given a share of the spoils."

Camillus snorted. "Every Roman was given the chance to scavenge their share by decree of the Senate. They swarmed like flies on a putrid carcass the next morning after Veii had fallen. Isn't that right, Marcus?"

The tribune nodded, remembering his shock at the invasion of civilians clogging the Via Veientana at daybreak, eager to glean their pickings.

"Calvus claims you should have granted booty to all without equivocation," said Aemilius. "He's gaining kudos for representing the interests of all Romans."

Camillus exploded. "I was busy planning an attack!"

"Yet you permitted your soldiers to seize plunder without waiting for confirmation," muttered Medullinus.

Genucius interrupted. "The general made the right decision to support the veterans."

"Silence! I am dictator! I don't need to justify my actions."

Medullinus pointed to the chariot. "All this is going to your head, Brother. It's fortunate you must stand down after you announce the date of the new elections. A man who pretends to be a god can easily think he should be a king."

Camillus strode to his tent. "Let's discuss this inside." He then called to a nearby groom, "Fetch Artile."

Marcus murmured a greeting to his father as he ducked his head and entered the tent. Aemilius smiled. He enjoyed bragging that his son had won the mural crown. His glee that Caecilia had finally been detained made Marcus uncomfortable, though. His cousin's despair and courage had touched him after all. Hating her was no longer simple. She had been made real again.

Pinna was inside, embroidering palmettes in gold thread onto a purple toga. A purple tunic was folded next to her. At the men's arrival, she stood, responding to Camillus's command to serve his guests. All the politicians had grown used to her presence. Only Genucius stared at her with contempt. Marcus was astounded at how much influence she now wielded over the general. He couldn't forget the image of her comforting "her Wolf" as he wept. It was sickening. What had happened to the man who'd warned him of the perils of falling in love?

Marcus noticed with distaste that Pinna was wearing Caecilia's grape earrings, rings, and silver pendant. She'd not wasted her time decking herself with loot. They appeared garish on her. Having served them all, she resumed her seat, peering into the cradle next to her. Marcus stole a look at the baby. The little girl was sleeping. A pale doll with a mop of black curls and a row of tiny golden bees around her neck. Pinna resumed her work, but he could tell from the way she halfheartedly plied the needle that she was listening.

Camillus drained his cup and began pacing. "So what else are those people's tribunes saying?"

Aemilius heaved his rumpled toga onto his shoulder. "The commoners complain they had to buy captives at auction. They say they should have been allocated."

Camillus fumed. "Only soldiers were entitled to seize slaves. Besides, there were thousands of prisoners. Far too many for our troops to claim. There needed to be a sale. In the end those proceeds were the only ones paid into State coffers."

Artile had entered the tent. "I fear you're forgetting a far greater problem, Furius Camillus. You've failed to keep your promise to a god."

"But the new date for the Votive Games has been proclaimed," said Spurius. "The temple to Mater Matuta is to be reconsecrated."

"And Juno herself has been transported to Rome," added Camillus. "She awaits the erection of her own temple. And I ensured only surviving ordained acolytes of Uni touched her."

Artile smoothed his eyebrow. "What about your vow to Apollo? In your people's haste to claim their booty, no tithe was set aside for him."

Camillus ceased pacing, color draining from his face. Head bowed, he sank onto his curule chair. The three senators looked similarly aghast.

After all his posturing, Marcus was relieved to see a glimpse of humility in the dictator. "What are we going to do, sir? How do we give one tenth when there's not enough held in the treasury for division?"

Aemilius shook his head. "The loot should've been handed over to the State as is the proper process. This is what comes from breaking with custom."

Camillus raised his head. "After my triumph I'll resign from office. I've dealt with the crisis I was elected to resolve. I've delivered Veii to Rome. This is a matter for the Senate."

Medullinus scowled. "And so leave a mess for the next consular generals to correct."

Genucius snapped, "You can't have it both ways, Medullinus. Carping that your brother should step down and then whining when he does."

Spurius maintained his calm. "Brother, I'm afraid you can't ignore the issue of the tithe. You'll need to offer some advice to the Curia. You made the vow on behalf of Rome. You can't wash your hands of it."

Camillus frowned, then twisted around to look at Genucius. "I'm sorry, my friend. Every citizen will have to surrender one tenth of their plunder to the treasury. It's the only way I can see to solve this."

The plebeian flushed beet red. "You can't ask the soldiers to do that!"

"It must apply to all, otherwise there will be insurrection."

"He's right, Genucius," said Aemilius.

"I agree," said Spurius. "But the Senate needs to be consulted first."

Camillus turned to his older brother. "What say you?" Medullinus nodded, but Marcus saw his satisfied look at the dictator's predicament.

"Do you think Apollo will be satisfied with such tribute?" Camillus asked Artile.

"Yes, if all Rome contributes, your contract with the deity will be kept."

"Very well then, I'll announce it after my triumph."

"And so we come back to your spectacle," said Medullinus.

Spurius frowned. "He's merely being prudent. Let the people enjoy their holiday before receiving the bad news. Otherwise, there may be a riot."

Aemilius put his hand on Medullinus's arm. "Your brother deserves the accolade. He delivered the traitoress to us."

Camillus smiled. "How does it feel to see your niece in the Carcer, Aemilius?"

"Deeply satisfying. Especially when she's executed tomorrow."

The dictator glanced across to the baby. "And the princess? What do you want to do with her? Artile has no interest in keeping her as a slave. After all, she is your grandniece."

Aemilius's gaze hovered over the child's sleeping form. "I don't plan to raise a half-breed foe. And I want no reminder of the shame Caecilia brought on my House. The brat will be exposed on the Esquiline."

Marcus was stunned. His father had never expressed such an intention before.

"No!" Pinna rushed to Camillus. "You said the royal children would not be harmed!"

Aemilius glowered at her. "How dare you speak?" He transferred his scowl to Camillus. "Isn't it time you controlled your woman?"

Taking Pinna by the elbow, Camillus pushed her behind him. "Exposing the child seems extreme, Aemilius."

"I'm the patriarch of my family. She's my kin. And just a girl. It's no one's business but my own."

Pinna made to speak again, but Camillus snapped, "Be quiet. Go back to your sewing."

Marcus was not prepared to be silenced. "Father, please reconsider. The princess can be given to one of our servant girls to raise. Don't kill her. She can be sold as a slave when she's old enough if you don't want her under your roof."

Aemilius walked to the tent flap. "If I wanted your opinion, I'd ask for it."

Marcus bridled but said no more, thinking how cruel it was the little girl's fate should be left to his father and the priest. Again, he waited for Camillus to countermand Aemilius; instead the dictator nodded, announcing that Pinna would deliver the child to the senator's house after the triumph.

Medullinus and Spurius rose. Also callous, they offered no opinion as to Aemilius's edict. Artile followed, not even glancing at the doomed baby.

Stricken, Pinna rocked the cradle, murmuring to the child who'd woken.

Caius Genucius remained rooted to the spot. He was sweating profusely, drops glistening on the black mat of hair protruding from his tunic.

Marcus turned to go.

"Wait, Marcus Aemilius," said Genucius. "I want you to hear this."

Confused, the tribune glanced across to Camillus, who signaled him to stay.

Genucius crossed his arms and fixed his gaze on the general. "Are you really going to recommend the veterans pay a tenth part to the treasury?"

"I can't see a way around it. The army took the cream; the civilians, the dregs. To satisfy Apollo, the tithe has to be genuine."

The plebeian stepped closer. Marcus was surprised at his threatening stance.

"How long do you think you can manipulate me?"

Camillus tensed. "What do you mean?"

"Making me a knight but denying me a cavalry command at Nepete. I've always supported your patrician causes to the detriment of my class. But this is important to me. For the first time in

Rome's history, poor foot sloggers have seized their fair share. They should keep it. Let the city idlers surrender their lot."

"So you'd rather anger Apollo?"

"No, I'd rather the knights pay more. I saw the wagon loads of booty your handpicked horsemen were able to claim."

Camillus became heated. "Your hoardings from the conquest are far from meager."

"You should be made accountable for this negligence!"

"And you know a dictator is immune from prosecution!"

Genucius rubbed perspiration from his face. He pointed at Pinna. "Then know this. All this time you've been bedding a whore. Your faithful tribune and your piece of cunni have been plotting behind your back. And once I spread the news, you, the great vir triumphalis, will become the laughing stock of Rome."

SIXTY-THREE

Pinna, Rome, Summer, 396 BC

Pinna froze, heart hammering.

Confused, Camillus swung around to her. "What? What are you talking about?"

"Your concubine is a lupa. Her name is Lollia, daughter of Gnaeus Lollius. I've checked with the city magistrate. Her name is on the prostitutes' roll."

Pinna remained paralyzed, hating the hurt in her Wolf's eyes.

He grabbed her and shook her. "Speak to me! Is this true?"

"Yes. But I didn't lie about my father. I'm the daughter of a soldier."

He released her, shying away as though she were a leper. He rounded on Genucius, still incredulous. "You tell me now? Why not last year when you first chanced upon her in my tent at Falerii? Didn't you think to advise me I was plowing a field already seeded by a hundred other men?"

Genucius reddened. "She's vicious. She keeps tally of men's secrets."

Pinna rubbed her arms where Camillus had grabbed her. There were so many layers to her coercion. Her threats had always been to ensure a man's silence. Now such secrets were like chaff, choking her throat. What point was there in blurting them? Her Wolf was lost to her no matter what she said.

Anger overtook Camillus's disbelief. "And what is your secret, Genucius? I already knew you have a weakness for whores. What is it that she holds over you to forget your friendship and duty?" He cast a disgusted look at Pinna. "Or is it what you did with her that you wanted to hide?"

Genucius tensed. "I admit I've a few little perversions that harlots like her cater to. But I'm prepared to bear the brunt of ridicule if it means my fellow soldiers will see the man you truly are. One who would go back on his word and deprive them of hardwon spoils while strutting in a triumph. You'll be judged as a fool. Strung along by your junior officer's whore."

Camillus glared at Marcus. "You knew about this? You weren't also tricked when you took her as your army wife?"

Marcus stood speechless.

Genucius barked at Pinna. "Tell him, you slut. Tell the general how Marcus Aemilius shared you with Claudius Drusus. Tell him how all three of us took you in that lupanaria, one after another, on the same night."

"Drusus? What kind of sick joke is this?" Camillus grabbed Pinna again. "Is there any man in this camp you haven't fucked?"

She sank to the ground, catching hold of his hand. "I've been faithful to you, my Wolf."

He pulled his fingers from her grip. "Don't call me that, you filthy little liar. You were prepared to cuckold Marcus in the first place." He strode across to the tribune, thrusting his face close to his. "Genucius failed to warn me, but why didn't you? Did you remain silent in vengeance for me stealing her from you?"

Pinna interrupted before the knight could speak. "Drusus raped me in the lupanaria. Marcus Aemilius took pity on me and made me his concubine when I told him my father's story. He didn't want me to tell you how his friend assaulted me."

Genucius snorted. "Is that all? He protected you because Drusus raped you? Who would care?"

She bristled. "You claim to be such a champion of the people, Genucius. Yet you've been a patrician toady for years. Where were you when soldiers like my father were forced into bondage and my mother and I were reduced to prostitution?"

"Be quiet!" Camillus sank into his chair, holding his hand to his eyes as though under too bright a light. "Tell me the true reason you made her your army wife, Marcus. Did you really think I'd be concerned Drusus abused a lupa? I judge a man on how well he fights, not whether he frequents brothels." He glowered at Pinna. "Or how he treats the whores in them."

He might as well have wielded a cudgel against her. He had reduced her to nothing. And at last, she could winnow her emotions, blowing away the husk of her love for him. Her growing qualms since returning to Rome were justified. His charisma had hardened into arrogance and then been corrupted into hubris. "No, I won't be silent. Marcus acted only with good intentions. He shouldn't be punished for his kindness."

She walked across to the cradle where Thia lay listless on her side, sucking on the corner of her sheet, pining for her mother. She'd eaten nothing other than a little honeyed milk for days. Now Aemilius wanted to kill her. And the man she thought she loved was going to let it happen. All because of their bitter hatred for Caecilia—the sins of the mother visited upon the daughter. She lifted the girl, guiding her to lay her head on her shoulder as she rocked her. "Will you save the princess?"

Camillus frowned. "Did you really think I would let you raise the child of my greatest enemy, Pinna? Besides, it's Aemilius's decision."

She took a deep breath. She'd fought so hard to leave her past behind. But now she realized she should feel no shame. She might have been a night moth but she felt nobler than this general. She did not have the blood of a city, and now this baby, on her hands.

"All you need to know is why Drusus raped me in the first place. And that is because I saw him using black magic to damn Vel Mastarna and cast a love spell on Aemilia Caeciliana. I stole the defixios and threatened to nail them to the speakers' platform so all Rome would learn how weak he was. I know this because I was a tomb whore. I found Drusus planting the lead sheets in a sepulcher while I was trying to find a customer on a rainy night."

Camillus leaned back as though punched in the stomach. He stared at her, haggard. "You were a tomb whore? By the gods, I wanted to marry you! No wonder you were able to bewitch me with all your superstitions and charms."

She straightened her shoulders. "I'm a warrior's daughter, not an enchantress."

Genucius crossed to Camillus and placed his hand on his shoulder. "My friend, this is worse than I imagined. We've both been soiled by this harlot. Our reputations will suffer if it should become public. I spoke hastily. Let's talk about the matter of the tithe after the triumph."

Camillus nodded, more concerned with Marcus. He shouted, "Did you know she worked in a graveyard?"

The tribune stuttered. "No, sir. If I'd known she was a night moth . . . I would never have protected her."

His words were painful, but she could see him struggling with bewilderment. She'd not betrayed his love for Drusus. She may have been a she wolf, but she was not dangerous after all.

He dragged his eyes from her and addressed the dictator. "I admit I knew Drusus had damned Mastarna. He was besotted with my cousin. That's why he lost control when he saw Caecilia in the temple. He disobeyed orders, then attacked me when I tried to stop him from fulfilling every part of his curse."

Camillus unsheathed his dagger and stabbed it into the surface of the desk in front of him. "Are you also under Caecilia's spell? Did you pander to her by burning her husband's body? "

Marcus's voice wavered. "I owed Mastarna a blood debt. He spared my life and those of my men at Nepete."

Camillus yanked out the knife and pointed it at him. "And so she demanded you cremate him."

"No. That was my idea. I knew I could not help her or her children." He hesitated, nodding toward Thia. "And I was right."

The dictator rammed the dagger into the wood so it stood upright. "I can hardly deprive you of the mural crown without this becoming a scandal. So you'll show your true loyalty to me tomorrow. You'll be the one who throws Caecilia from the Tarpeian Rock. You'll be her executioner."

Pinna's jaw dropped. He truly had become a monster. Marcus glanced across to her, then back to Camillus. The pockmarks showed clearly on his ashen cheeks, his lips white. It must have taken all his strength to stand to attention and salute. "Yes, sir." Then he strode from the tent without a backward glance.

Camillus turned to her and straightened his arm, pointing at the tent opening. His eyes were hard, his voice low, once again the composed commander. "Take off the jewelry I gave you. You'll leave here with only the clothes you're wearing. And deliver that child to the House of Aemilius immediately. You're lucky I don't have you whipped. I want nothing more to do with you."

Pinna trembled, overwhelmed. She was destitute. Not even possessing enough to pay a lupa's registration fee to the city magistrate. She had come full circle. The life of a night moth loomed.

Turning her back to the two men, she laid Thia in the cradle. Then she slid the rings from her fingers and unfastened the earrings. Removing them was a relief. She felt purified. Camillus had insisted she wear them. Although she'd drawn the line at wearing the gold coronet while he'd bedded her.

She unclasped the delicate silver pendant that nestled beside her fascinum and Venus shell. The engraved huntress summoned an image of Aemilia Caeciliana to her mind. The kohl around the queen's honey-colored eyes was smeared from where she'd wiped away tears. Faded powder revealed a purple birthmark on her throat. Camillus had called her a whore, but Pinna saw only nobility as the captive stood defiant in her sheer blood-spattered dress. And the way Caecilia spoke to him had astonished her. Her words were full of contempt and rebellion even though she was wretched. The noblewoman's courage vanished, though, when she relinquished Thia. Pinna would forever be haunted by the mother's mournful weeping when she took the baby from her arms.

She tucked the necklace into Thia's clothes as she wrapped the little girl in the coverlet. As she lifted the child, the golden tesserae tumbled onto the sheet, the only playthings the little girl owned. Pinna palmed them, not prepared to let Thia go without. She knew somehow she would save this child. She'd assured Caecilia she would care for the princess. She was not going to fail her.

Turning, she found Camillus observing her. There was no sign he regretted losing her. A different man stood before her than the man she'd adored. She straightened her shoulders and thrust out her chin, emulating the Veientane queen. "No, Furius Camillus. It's I who want nothing to do with you. I thought I'd stolen your soul, but it's clear you have no soul to steal."

SIXTY-FOUR

Semni, Tarchna, Summer, 396 BC

Feet sunk into sand, Semni watched the rush and spread of water, intrigued by the surge and pull at her ankles. The susurration and rhythm of each wave hypnotized her.

She'd not expected the enormity of the sea. How it stretched to an empty horizon, its color, its sound. How it was living and breathing.

Nerie stood beside her, dancing on the spot, lifting each foot, and laughing as the water rushed in and out. Then he bumped down, scooped up a handful, and watched the wet sand drip onto his legs before the water once again covered them.

The tot was the only one who'd recovered from the events of the last week. His terror had subsided as soon as the refugees arrived in Tarchna, happy enough to be sleeping on a bed between his parents.

Semni wished having a roof over her head, and plenty of food, could heal her as easily. She'd washed off the blood and changed her clothes, but she dreaded nights when bad dreams would assail her, and mornings when she realized, day after day, they were real.

The voyage under the stifling hides took its toll. By the time the barge glided under the last bridge to reach the tributary north, all of them had been dull eyed and dehydrated. There had been moments of tension when they passed each river fort, but as Arruns had predicted, the Romans were too preoccupied with plundering Veii. Free at last to breathe in smokeless air, the fugitives had huddled in the stern of the boat to watch the dark forest silhouettes glide by. Semni had observed the pale twilight sky, trying not to look back at the dark cloud hovering over her home.

They must have made a strange sight. A tattooed Phoenician with a family that bore no resemblance to him. Semni worried they were too conspicuous. When challenged, Arruns said they were migrants heading for the rich lands of the coast. The queen's jewelry secured safe passage. And clean clothes and supplies. They bought a wagon in a village near Lake Sabatinus, joining the traffic heading west toward the Tolfa Hills.

Sighting Tarchna took her breath away. Acropolis and necropolis stood opposite each other. The living observing their ancestors. The dead protecting their descendants. And beyond, six miles below on the plain, stretched the blue-green Tyrhennian Sea and the bustling docks and emporiums of Port Gravisca.

When the king's uncle, Lord Atelinas, found them on his threshold, there was shock, then rejoicing. Vel Mastarna would be mourned, but at least his sons were reunited with kin. And the servants who'd saved the princes were offered refuge in the household. Yet to Semni, being granted asylum did not assuage grief. Her memories of her last day at Veii were constant, drifting through her mind like the shadows of clouds scudding over hillsides on summer breezes.

Taking Nerie by the hand, she helped him to toddle up the beach to where Arnth and Larce knelt digging. Perca sat cross-legged beside them, staring blankly. Semni wondered if the maid would ever recover from her ordeal. Arruns was the only man from whom she did not cringe.

On their flight, rumors were overheard as fellow travelers exchanged news as well as wineskins. Veii was no more. The king had died. The queen was due to be executed in Rome. Semni tried to keep the news from small ears. Nevertheless, the boys sensed that the worst had happened to their parents. Larce cried himself to sleep every night, calling for his mother. Arnth's tears were less frequent, but at every request, he was defiant and challenging.

Tas sat apart from his brothers on the beach, tracing spirals in the sand with one finger. He did not need to be told. His amber eyes would meet hers, sorrow glazing them even when not brimming with tears.

Semni also agonized over Thia. What had happened to the baby she'd nursed for one year? She could only pray the Romans would show her mercy, even if they had not spared her parents.

Aricia was collecting seashells on the shore, crouching to examine them. Her face was drawn, haunted by not knowing the fates of Cytheris and Lady Tanchvil. Even though word had reached Tarchna that Queen Uni was now Juno Regina in Rome, Aricia still wore the white-and-red robes of a cepen. Uni's high priest at Gravisca had welcomed her as his acolyte. She wondered how the girl could serve a deity who'd committed immortal treachery.

Semni settled Nerie next to Larce and Arnth, then walked across to sit next to Tas, giving him company but not expecting conversation.

Noticing the pair, Aricia ceased her inspection of the shells and limped over to join them. She slipped her arm around the prince's shoulders. "You must stop brooding, my pet."

"Apa and Ati are dead, aren't they?"

The two girls glanced at each other over his head.

Semni squeezed his hand. "We'll not lie to you, Tas. Word has come that your father was killed. The Romans are to execute your mother soon. Be brave. You're the eldest and must be an example to your brothers. It's up to all of us to honor their memory. And one day you will wreak vengeance."

Aricia kissed his hair. "Lord Atelinas has told us he'll hold funeral games for them soon. They won't be forgotten, my pet. Not while we revere them every year at the festival of our ancestors."

Tas clenched his fists, his voice choked. "If I was a soothsayer I would have known what my dream meant. The wolves in the cave were the Romans in the tunnel. I should've warned Apa."

"No one expected you to interpret the omen," said Semni. "And not even Lady Tanchvil understood what it meant. She thought it was a nightmare, not a vision."

Aricia bent her head close to his. "One day you'll be trained to be a haruspex and fulgurator, Tas. Then you'll have the power to interpret divine will. Your fame will spread to every city within the Twelve."

It was the first time in days Semni had seen his eyes light up. "I will become a great seer?"

Aricia nodded. "I'm sure the high priest will give you tuition."

Semni glared at her over the boy's head, then touched Tas's knee. "Go and play with the others. Enjoy this day in the sunshine and stop worrying about such matters."

He glanced across to the princes, reluctant to finish the conversation. Aricia had seen Semni's disapproval, though. She kissed the top of his head again. "Go, my pet. We will talk of this later."

When he was out of earshot, Semni rounded on her. "Now is not the time to put such ideas into his head!"

"He's talented. With training . . ."

"He's just a little boy who has lost his parents. By the gods! Let us finish mourning first!" Frustrated, she marched away.

A lone figure was standing at the water's edge at the far end of the beach, watching two ships passing in the sea lane beyond the shore. Their sails were full, prows carving the waves, their wash foaming behind them.

Arruns unfastened his belt, letting his long kilt drop, then strode into the water until he stood waist deep before diving beneath the flat green surface.

Thinking he might drown, Semni sprinted toward him, kicking up sand. Reaching his pile of clothes, she waited anxiously for him to resurface.

His head appeared, then he began swimming, gliding through the water with easy strokes.

Her breathing eased when she saw him heading back. Water streamed from his massive shoulders as he waded toward her, the snake revealed.

"I was worried you'd sink."

He frowned. "I'm a strong swimmer. I was in no danger." He picked up his kilt, wrapping it around him, and sat on the sand. Bending his knees, he rested his elbows on them, staring at the horizon, squinting against the glare.

Normally taciturn, he'd become morose since arriving in Tarchna. Surliness was his armor. No matter how much she sought his caresses, he was distant. She understood he was grieving but she wanted him to share his sorrow with her.

She sat beside him and leaned her head against his shoulder. The biremes sailed farther away, oars dipping. The beat of the drum as the overseer kept the rowers in rhythm grew fainter. She sensed longing in him. "Do you want to return to Sidon?"

He shook his head. "The princes need both of us." He glanced at her thickening waist. "And our son is yet to be born."

She was relieved. She couldn't bear it if he became a sailor and left Nerie and her for months on end. In the terror of the last week, the child growing within her had been a tiny glimmer of hope, a small piece of comfort. "At least he will not be born into war."

As if on cue, she felt the baby move, heralding his presence. She gasped, pressing her hand to her belly.

Arruns turned around, quizzical.

Another tiny nudge. "I've quickened."

He focused on her stomach. "Can I feel him?"

She smiled, untying her sash, and hiked up her chiton. His roughened palm was cool against her rounded flesh. She prayed their son would once again stretch his limbs.

The baby stirred. And Barekbaal the Canaanite, known as Arruns, the man who had saved the heirs of the House of Mastarna, the warrior with the serpent tattoo and the courage of a lion, raised his head and smiled.

SIXTY-FIVE

Caecilia, Rome, Summer, 396 BC

She woke to a yawning sense of darkness, of being blind even though her eyes were open.

Once again, she was aware of the heavy cuffs shackling her wrists. It was a redundant precaution. There was no way she could escape the dungeon in the Carcer. It was known as the Tullanium, a holding cell reserved for enemies of the State.

She gazed up to a rim of light which lit the edges of a hole carved into the stone ceiling. The torchlight from the jail above did not permeate farther than a few inches into the cell below. She used the aperture as a focal point to judge time. Gray gloom in the day; feeble illumination at night.

Mildew coated the rough-hewn rock walls and floor of the chamber. Water seeped through the stone. The Carcer was built next to the Great Drain. She was glad it had not rained. The smell of ordure combined with misery and desperation. The wails of inmates languishing in other levels of the prison sent chills through her.

After a week of imprisonment, she'd grown used to the odor. But her humiliation at having to foul a corner of the cell was constant.

She'd been surprised to find a wellspring in the center of the dungeon. Dehydrated after the long journey from Veii, she'd eagerly slaked her thirst. She was regularly fed as well. A meager mess of porridge lowered on a plank through the hole once a day. There were strict orders for the victim to be kept alive for the triumph.

"Never had a woman here before," one of the two jailors had commented when she'd been dragged into the central chamber of the Carcer. His hands had roamed over her breasts and bottom, grabbing her crotch. Her cheek was puffy and her lip split from where he'd hit her when she'd protested. She could not suppress a sob when he lowered her by the hands into the void, the pain in her shoulder excruciating.

Unable to fall asleep again, Caecilia sat up and leaned against the wall. Her shoulder was stiff and sore. Her bruises merged with the shadows. The rough woolen weave of the dress Pinna gave her was rank, the fabric damp, and her snood was ruined. She'd plaited her hair into one long, lank braid.

Physical discomfort meant little compared to the anguish that assailed her. Dreams reunited her with Vel and the children, but every time she opened her eyes, sorrow crushed her. With no chance of being reunited with Thia and her sons, she wanted to die. She longed to join Vel. Instead she faced a cruel death and a ghostly existence without him.

She mourned those alive, too, aching afresh when Tarchon had been separated from her. No farewell embrace was allowed. She wondered where they were detaining him.

At least she'd had the chance to kiss Cytheris before the maid was led to auction. With her last touch, the servant still offered comfort as they hugged each other. "You'll be in my thoughts forever, mistress. I'll always say a prayer for you and Lord Mastarna."

There was cycle to her emotions. Grief, torment, and guilt. Hatred, fear, and despair.

The memory of her last moments with Vel haunted her. As did her torment when surrendering Thia. Had her sons survived? Was all their suffering her fault? Was the punishment that awaited her justified?

Her loathing for Camillus and Aemilius gave her strength to endure. Even so, she was afraid. She faced being thrown from the heights. She didn't want to die in agony. Worse of all, she knew she'd become a specter denied reunion with her husband. She'd ensured Vel would reach Acheron. But who would prevent her body from being desecrated? Even the Atlenta myth offered no consolation. He was right. They would not live together as lions. Nor were they immortal like Fufluns and Areatha.

A flare of light drew her attention to the hole in the ceiling. A man barked at the jailor to rouse him. She was surprised to hear it was Marcus.

She heard the guard yawn. "I've got orders she's not to be moved."

"You dare question the command of a tribune? Bring her up now!"

The plank and rope hit the side of the hole, then dangled in front of her. She climbed onto the board, clinging to the cable as it jerked upward. She whimpered with pain as Marcus grabbed her under her arms and lifted her onto the floor of the upper prison.

Aghast, he scanned her injuries and deprivation. "Great Mars!"

"Ati, Ati!"

She turned, stunned to see Pinna balancing Thia on her hip. The baby stretched out her arms. Caecilia reached out to take her, but her wrists were restrained by the shackles. She grasped her daughter's hands, kissing them.

"Remove her fetters!" Marcus growled.

The keeper hesitated. "I got orders . . ."

"She's going nowhere. Let a mother embrace her child."

"I'll get into trouble."

Marcus drew a purse from the sinus of his toga and handed it to the guard. "This will make it worth your while. I'm paying for your silence, too."

The jailor drew the hammer from his belt and tapped the bolt to release the cuffs. He disappeared down into the lower level of the Carcer.

Freed of her irons, Caecilia clutched Thia, kissing her. The baby was not revolted by her mother's stink, burying her face into her neck, but Pinna stood back, gagging at the prison stench. Caecilia was confused. Why was Camillus's lover being so kind to her? And what had changed her cousin's contempt into compassion?

"Have you news of my sons?"

"They were never found," said Marcus.

Caecilia closed her eyes, breathing in Thia's sweet scent, relieved her boys might yet be alive.

Marcus placed his hand on her shoulder. "You've been beaten. Did they . . . ?"

"No. I told them I had the pox. Believing all Etruscan women are whores, they thought it the truth. But tell me, is Tarchon safe?"

"He's to be spared execution. Artile owns him now."

She felt nauseous. "Please tell him I love him. Tell him his father would be proud of him. And Lusinies?"

"To be strangled." Marcus's voice was clipped as he glanced around. "There's not much time. I'm not supposed to enter the city until I march in the triumph."

"And when will that be?"

"Have they not told you? It's tomorrow."

Her vision blurred for a moment. Her destiny was hurtling toward her. Thia lifted her head and touched her cheek, garbling to her mother. Caecilia focused again, kissing the babe's fingers. She turned to Pinna. "You'll look after my daughter as you promised?"

A troubled look crossed the woman's face.

Caecilia glanced between her two visitors. "What's the matter?"

Marcus dragged his fingers through his cowlick. She remembered the anxious gesture. "As patriarch, my father has decreed Thia is to die."

Her legs buckled. Marcus steadied her. "Don't worry, Caecilia. Pinna and I aren't going to let him harm her."

She was unable to stop quaking. She knew Aemilius loathed her but this was beyond bitterness. "But how?"

"I've told him I'll see to her death after the spectacle. In the meantime, Pinna will take Thia to safety."

"But he'll expect to see a body."

"There will be proof enough to satisfy Father," said Marcus. "Leave it to us."

Wary, Caecilia stared at Pinna. "How do I know I can trust you? You're Camillus's woman."

"No longer. I've left him."

Caecilia's respect for her rose. "Then you are wise."

Pinna glanced away, and Caecilia guessed there had been heartache in her decision. Then the woman recovered, reaching over to stroke Thia's curls. "I'll care for her as my own."

Caecilia swallowed. It was painful to accept that this woman would be Thia's new mother. She noticed the Atlenta pendant was tied around the baby's neck with a short leather thong. Nestled beside it was the bulla Vel had given the baby, the sacred bees. She recalled his brief caress of Thia's hair at the temple. He did not know it was to be his last. And he'd had no chance to bid his sons good-bye. "Do you still have the golden dice?"

Pinna nodded.

"Don't lose them. They were her father's. They brought us together." Tears pricked her eyes. "For her own protection, never reveal who we were. But please tell her that her parents loved her dearly. And that her father was a great warrior."

Pinna covered her hand. "I'll tell her that her mother was courageous, too."

"Her true name is Larthia," added Caecilia. "Let her grow up knowing she was her grandmother's namesake."

The sound of clinking in the stairwell heralded the return of the jailor.

"We must go now, Cilla," said Marcus. "Kiss your daughter."

She was startled by the lilting nickname, one used in a time of confidences and brotherly love. She placed her palm against his chest. "Thank you, Marcus. But why are you doing this? I thought you hated me. You've repaid the blood debt twice over already."

He stepped back at the intimate touch, his tone abrupt. "I'm not doing this for you. I do it because I don't believe in killing children. And you must thank Pinna for us coming here tonight."

Caecilia murmured her gratitude. The tiny woman wiped her eyes with the back of her hand.

The time had come to say farewell to Thia forever. Given this second chance, Caecilia decided not to show she was distraught. She wanted her daughter to believe this parting was only for a short time. Heart pounding, she took hold of the baby's hand, kissing it playfully before tickling her tummy. Thia responded with a gummy grin. "Go with Pinna. Be a good girl. I'll see you soon." She kissed the babe on the cheek and tried to hand her to Pinna.

Despite the playful tone, Thia protested. Heartbroken, Caecilia prized her away, coaxing her to let go. Finally Thia released her.

Pinna paused at the heavy wooden entrance doors. Caecilia flattened her palm and blew a kiss, sending the endearment spinning through space to Thia. She forced herself to keep smiling until she caught the last glimpse of her daughter waving good-bye with tiny dimpled fingers.

SIXTY-SIX

Marcus, Rome, Summer, 396 BC

Gulping in the crisp night air was a relief. The reek of the battlefield was nothing compared to the Carcer's. Marcus leaned back against the stone wall of the prison and closed his eyes. He doubted he'd ever be rid of the image of Caecilia in that grim place.

He felt Pinna's hand upon his arm. He opened his eyes. She looked pale and forlorn as she rocked the baby against her shoulder. That afternoon, reeling from her revelation, he'd been disconcerted when she'd appeared at his tent seeking help. He was astounded as to how many tiers of deceit she had practiced.

He steered her into an alleyway. "Remember what we agreed. Your past as a tomb whore has proven useful. Leave the corpse of a child from the Esquiline in my tent during the triumph. I'll show it to my father the next day. I'll tell him I smothered the princess."

"But he might see the substitute isn't Etruscan."

"He hasn't even bothered to look at Thia. I doubt he'll examine her corpse. A glimpse of dark hair, a patch of skin, closed lids. It's the deed he seeks, not the evidence."

"Thank you for rescuing her. And for providing me with yet another fresh start. I'll travel on to Satricum with the money you've given me."

"Let me know where you settle. Then I will send more."

"For a man who claims to despise Aemilia Caeciliana, you've done much to help her."

He tensed. "I told you. It's not for her sake but her child's."

"I don't believe you. You called her 'Cilla.' It wasn't a slip of the tongue but a remnant of affection." She paused. "Why didn't you tell her you will be her executioner?"

"Because I lack courage. But at least she'll die knowing I played no part in hurting her daughter." He placed his hand on Thia's head. The baby's hair was soft beneath his palm. He gave a faint smile and raised his eyes to Pinna's. "It seems we have another secret to share. No one must ever know this child survived."

"A secret without coercion. I like that."

"And we share the risk of discovery together. Go safely. Be careful."

She stood on her tiptoes and kissed his cheek. The contact shocked him. He couldn't remember the last time someone had touched him tenderly. He caught hold of her hand. "Why didn't you tell the general about my love for Drusus?"

"Because I promised you I wouldn't. And once the truth I was a lupa was revealed, my fate was determined anyway. Besides, I now see Camillus was never mine to possess. And, in the end, he was not the man I fell in love with. My desire was as hopeless as yours was for Drusus."

The pain of loss returned. "I slew him, Pinna."

She squeezed his fingers hard. "He was deranged. He was a coward. By the gods, he tried to kill you! His obsession was greater than his friendship. Forget him. You were tormented in life because of him. Don't bind yourself to him in death, too. Don't let him haunt you."

He stared at her, knowing he must heed her. He felt relief. A sense of freedom.

She drew her shawl over her head, covering Thia's as well. "Farewell, Marcus Aemilius Mamercus. I'll pray for you tomorrow. I'll pray for you always. I'll never forget you."

. . .

Marcus thought how beauty could be made haggard in the space of one long day of devastation. The wound that Tarchon suffered at the temple was healing, but there was a fresh bruise darkening the flesh around his eye. Welts marked his arms and legs. His wrists and ankles were fettered. Artile was taking no chances.

Marcus had watched the haruspex leave his tent shortly after sunrise. The auspices needed to be taken. And he was to preside over the ceremony on the Capitoline. The procession was due to start within the hour.

Tarchon sat on the ground surrounded by the loot Artile had claimed. Chalices, paterae, and candelabras. There were sacks of coins as well. The soothsayer was now a wealthy man.

The prince raised his hands, the chains clinking. "Have you come to gloat?"

Marcus frowned, glancing over his shoulder to the tent flap, wary of being interrupted. "I don't have much time. You'll be loaded into one of the wagons soon."

"To be displayed with the rest of the spoils." Tarchon lowered his hands into his lap. "I would have thought you'd be mustering with the other officers." He scanned the tribune's toga and tunic. "You're not wearing armor."

"No soldier will today. We enter the city as civilians." He pointed to the bruise on Tarchon's face. "I see Artile has been punishing you."

The prisoner touched the contusion. "He thinks he can beat me into loving him again. He'll end up killing me from frustration." He sighed. "I hope to spur him to do so. I've nothing left to live for."

Marcus knew he should not feel pity for a foe but failed. The memory of Tarchon caressing his dead beloved with bound hands was scored into his mind. It made him despair, knowing he'd never be allowed to love an equal. Or have the chance of being cherished in that way. "I regret my knight killed Sethre."

A flicker of surprise crossed Tarchon's face. "He's better off dead. I wouldn't wish him enslaved. He was the son of a king." He leaned his head back against the tent pole. "And I'd have been required to give him up soon enough. At least I can cherish the memories of the little time we had."

"What do you mean 'soon enough'?"

"We Etruscans have rules, too. As soon as Sethre reached manhood, I could no longer be his lover." He straightened and studied the Roman. "I pity you. I've seen your type before. Lonely and frustrated. Self-denial oozes from you. Fear, too . . . of giving in to temptation . . . of being caught."

Marcus felt his face burning. "You do well to keep silent."

"Do you think you can hide you're a mollis from me? Your secret hovers in your lingering glance and your shameful blush."

"I don't know what you're talking about."

Tarchon shook his head, once again leaning his head against the tent pole. "If you didn't come here to laud over me, what exactly do you want?"

"I bring word from Caecilia."

The prince sat up straight. "You've seen her? How is she?"

"She's grieving in the Tullanium. She said to tell you she loves you. That Mastarna would be proud of you."

"I wish I could tell her the same before she's murdered." He searched Marcus's face. "For a man who claims to hate her, you've been kind. Perhaps you've found love for her again?"

Uncomfortable, Marcus didn't reply. Once again he was being drawn back into memories of affection and family ties.

Tarchon persisted. "She loved you until the day you tried to kill Mastarna. It was only then she removed your iron wristlet. Before that, your amulet gave her comfort when she was homesick or frightened. And there was much for her to fear in Veii. She was under constant threat from the Tulumnes clan. And she suffered Artile's malice. He tried to pervert Prince Tas. And he fed her potions that made her barren."

Marcus's revulsion for the priest surged. And once again, cracks deepened in the veneer of his feelings toward Caecilia. But he needed to nurture hatred again. Otherwise, being her killer would destroy him. He squeezed the bridge of his nose to ward off tears. "I'm to be her executioner."

Tarchon sucked in his breath. "Why you?"

"Camillus has ordered me to prove my loyalty. Cremating Mastarna angered him. But believe me, killing her will be the hardest thing I have ever done."

"Then do the same for her as you did for my father. Don't let her be a ghost."

A trumpet started to signal final muster. Marcus knew he couldn't delay. What Tarchon was asking was nigh impossible. Denying Rome the body of the traitoress could lead to his own downfall. "I must go. What you ask is too difficult."

As he opened the tent flap, Marcus heard the chains clank behind him. Tarchon called, "Then if you won't grant her salvation, at least tell her you forgive her. Let the last human touch she feels be the hand of someone who loves her."

Sixty-Seven

Pinna, Rome, Summer, 396 BC

It was midday. The triumphal parade had not yet reached the Sacred Way. The sky was overcast yet the sun beat down when it broke through the clouds.

At least a thousand were crammed around Pinna in the Forum, straining their necks to catch sight of the dictator. Some had lined up since daybreak to gain the best position. The mood was buoyant. For once they had plenty of money.

Pinna arranged her palla again over her head and around her body. Thia lay hidden in a sling against her, slumbering after being given a draught.

Others had chosen to view the religious ceremony at dawn near the Circus Maximus. A dais had been erected where senators, magistrates, and knights sat on ivory chairs. An array of soldiers had then borne testimony as to the exploits of the vir triumphalis. She wondered if Marcus's words of praise stuck in his throat now he saw his hero as vain and vindictive. She knew he had qualms about being awarded the mural crown.

In the distance she could hear roars, the sound rolling toward them, as the pomp traveled from the Aventine. The three-beat rhythm of the drums grew louder.

She spied Prince Tarchon. Even though chained, he held himself with dignity, staring ahead, chin raised, shoulders back. He didn't flinch as the crowd jeered and pelted him with cabbages and onions.

General Lusinies was less composed. His head was bent, his shoulders defeated as refuse rained down on him. His journey would end when he reached the Carcer. The executioners awaited him in the Tullanium, ligatures at the ready.

The slaughter in Veii had deprived Rome of the sight of imprisoned Veientane warriors. The shortfall in military captives was compensated by hundreds of wagons bearing their armor and the rest of Camillus's treasure. The oohs of the crowd revealed their astonishment. They had scavenged the pickings. Here was the main.

Artile came next. He was beaming, enjoying the adulation of a crowd who no longer saw him as a dangerous false prophet. Pinna touched her fascinum, averting her head. Even though surrounded, she feared those hypnotic eyes would seek her out.

The two garlanded white cows were docile as Medullinus and Spurius led them. The Furian brothers were smiling at sharing in their brother's glory. Scipio, as Master of the Horse, rode on his stallion beside them. Senators and magistrates followed, as well as Camillus's two sons on horseback.

Twenty-four lictors bearing fasces appeared. Women threw handfuls of rose petals, the blossoms floating, their scent rich, creating a floral carpet for the approaching hero.

There were gasps as Camillus came into view. It was as though Jupiter rode in front of them. The four white stallions pranced as they pulled the golden quadriga onto the Sacred Way. Pinna thought of Apollo, the other god who was entitled to drive such a conveyance. The deity had aided the dictator to victory. Now Rome must fear divine retribution for forgetting him.

Camillus's face was painted with vermillion, his hair crowned with a laurel wreath. His feet were shod with red shoes with gold crescent buckles. The purple-embroidered robes were draped elegantly. Some other woman had finished her needlework.

The creases around his eyes and mouth were deep with the broadness of his smile. He wore a bulla to protect him from the envy of men and gods. A triumphing general was the only adult male who could wear one. Similar charms decorated the harnesses of his steeds and vehicle, double protection against evil and malice.

She partly covered her face with her shawl, not willing to risk him recognizing her, but she need not have worried. He avoided eye contact with the people, keeping his gaze focused above their heads as he waved.

The chariot passed by. Pinna realized it was the last time she would ever see him. And there was sadness underneath her sense of freedom. She wondered how long this faint yearning would last, or whether she could ever forgive him for changing. For no longer being her Wolf.

The legions of Rome followed, dressed in their tunics and togas, led by their officers. Genucius had trimmed his bushy beard and combed his unruly hair. He may have been a knight but true power was denied to him. Would he cause trouble for Camillus after all? She saw Marcus, his face grim beneath the gold mural crown with its turret decorations. Her heart ached for him, knowing the gruesome role he must play this day.

The common soldiers were smiling, joyous to enter the city and greet their families. Proud of their victory. Content with their loot. Pinna despised them for the murder they'd committed. Following tradition, they called out praise to Camillus as well as ribaldry at his expense. She knew joking would turn to anger when they discovered the general who'd championed them had also betrayed them.

The parade wended its way up the Clivus Capitolinus to assemble in the sanctuary precinct. In its wake, the gossip started. Their disapproval of Camillus's golden chariot and four white horses. How the dictator had rivaled the king of the gods. Did he now wish to be Rome's monarch?

The scene in the palace returned. How he'd stumbled while invoking the gods. He'd claimed he'd suffered a minor fall in place of a greater calamity for Rome. She doubted he'd averted disaster. The people would be furious over the tithe no matter how many horse races, games, and feasts Camillus provided. The city would once again be riven by internal divisions. Civil war might even ensue.

A roar distracted the crowd from their rumormongering. Pinna looked up. Lusinies's corpse had been thrown onto the steps leading from the Carcer to the Arx.

The roar turned to hateful howling and fist shaking. Calls of "traitor" and "bitch" and worse. A lump formed in Pinna's throat as she spied the frail figure of Amelia Caeciliana. Despite filth caulking her clothes, lank hair, and hollow eyes, the queen retained her dignity. Pinna both pitied and admired her. She wished Caecilia did not have to become a desolate spirit unable to merge with the Good Ones. She vowed to placate the specter by offering her violets and roses each year.

Thia stirred, fidgeting in the sling. It was time to go. The baby was too young to absorb this tragedy, but Pinna did not want to acquire the memory of Caecilia's final moments.

She began threading her way through the crowd. Clouds were darkening over the Senate House. Rain threatened to dampen the celebrations.

She didn't relish venturing onto the Esquiline. As a tomb whore, she'd become inured to traipsing past the rotting corpses of criminals and paupers. But she'd never grown used to the mewling of abandoned children. Or their ultimate silence. Their deaths always tore at her. More so because she was impotent to save them. She could not breastfeed them. And she and Mama never had food to spare. Pinna hoped Mater Matuta would bless her today for being able to rescue a child at last. It would take all her nerve, though, to search for a replacement matching Thia's size. She'd already steeped swaddling clothes in perfume in the hope it would disguise the smell of any decay. She prayed Aemilius's inspection would be as perfunctory as Marcus predicted.

Struggling to break free of the crowd, she finally retreated into a side street. She was perspiring beneath the weight of the tunic, stola, and palla. How strange that she wore the clothes of a respectable matron. From now on she would masquerade as the widow of a veteran who'd lost his life at Nepete. And she planned to enter Mater Matuta's temple in Satricum, believing the goddess would forgive a whore when protecting another mother's child. The deity always encouraged sisters to embrace their nephews and nieces as closely as their own children.

With Marcus's patronage she could live comfortably. She would slide into obscurity. Thia's identity as a Veientane princess had to remain hidden although the child's features might betray her race. At least the Latins did not hate the Etruscans.

There would be no more men. Nor did she want one. She knew she could not replace him, no matter how much she scoured away the vestiges of feeling for him.

Behind her, the shouts peaked into frenzied anticipation of the final push from the rock. She said a prayer for Caecilia, her heart saddened. She kissed Thia's head, settling her into the sling. The seed of love for this babe had already flowered. A new life lay ahead of them. Neither of them would be alone or unloved. The night moth's soul was free. She had a daughter.

Sixty-Eight

Caecilia, Rome, Summer, 396 BC

The light was blinding. Caecilia blinked; flashes of color disoriented her as she emerged on the threshold of the Carcer. The baying of the crowd rang in her ears, a city frenzied with rage. A venting of ten years of war, plague, and famine centered on her.

Shaking, she raised her shackled hands to cover her eyes as she was pushed onto the steps leading to the Arx. She stumbled, then righted herself, her eyes adjusting to the sunlight. She closed them again as she skirted Lusinies's body, murmuring a prayer for him, the horror of his strangled death throes in the Tullanium still vivid. The soldier assigned to accompany her gave her a nudge.

Her tread was heavy. She wondered how many others had made this climb. The stone steps must be impregnated with the sighs of the condemned. She clenched her teeth, determined not to reveal her despair.

There were more guards at the top of the stairs. They cordoned her off from the mob that flanked the road leading to the Capitoline sanctuary. Despite the escort, some people managed to lob rotten fruit. She winced at the blows, crooking her arm to protect her face. At least they were not stones.

A trickle of sweat slid between her breasts, a sheen coating her brow. As she approached the precinct, her gaze was drawn to the graceful lines of Jupiter's temple which nearly rivaled Queen Uni's. Now the traitor goddess was biding her time until her new home was built. Caecilia wondered if the Veientane divinity regretted taking a footstep across the Tiber. She would reside in a sanctuary lesser in grandeur than her temple in Veii. Camillus had dubbed her Juno Regina, but the deity was now merely Jupiter's consort. She would be relegated to the Aventine instead of residing in resplendence with him. Or would the divine Roman king feel threatened that the foreign goddess might usurp him?

Caecilia walked past the long line of wagons containing treasure to be consecrated to the great and mighty god. She swallowed hard, seeing the heaped panoplies of the Rasennan warriors who'd been felled by a stealthy attack.

And then she saw Tarchon. He stood up in the tray of a cart, raising his chained wrists to wave to her. She could see his mouth moving but couldn't hear him above the yells of abuse. His eye was blackened. Artile was already punishing him. She shouted that she loved him. Told him to remain strong. The words were engulfed by the tumult.

One guard shoved her, not prepared to let her dally. Her eyes widened as she spied the gold quadriga and four white stallions next to the temple steps. And there on the portico Camillus sat in his curule chair, flanked by a group of politicians.

Seeing his red-painted face and purple robes sent a shiver through her. Apart from the laurel wreath, it could have been a Rasennan king. Tears welled as she thought of how Vel hated the vermilion, and how little fingers could make a mess with the dye.

She scanned the men around him. Scipio. Genucius. Aemilius. The Furian brothers. Marcus also, wearing the mural crown. He glanced away when he saw her scrutiny. In broad daylight he wasn't as brave as he had been in the darkness of a jail.

Her gaze returned to Camillus and the man on his right-hand side. Not a soldier or senator but a soothsayer. Loathing rose in her to see Artile's smugness.

She took a deep breath, trying to calm her trembling, then drew her shoulders erect, imagining herself in her favorite chiton of yellow with fine leather boots and decked in jewels.

At the dictator's signal, a trumpet sounded. Camillus stood, lifting his arms to command quiet. Silence rippled across the crowd.

His eyes raked over her. "Did you see the fate of Lusinies, Aemilia Caeciliana? It's a shame I can't display your husband's body. The true enemy commander in chief."

"He's safe from your reach. He's been spared dishonor. And Lusinies died knowing he was subdued by an enemy who feared facing him in battle."

Camillus sat down and leaned his weight on one arm of his backless ivory chair. "No matter how many times you accuse me of cowardice, one thing is certain. The gods chose us. And I have the satisfaction of seeing Veii's queen executed, even if I was denied the chance to strangle its king."

She glanced over her shoulder at the quadriga, her cuffs clanking as she gestured toward Camillus's head. "Do you plan to replace the laurel wreath with a crown? After all, you emulate Mighty Jupiter himself."

He flinched. "I have no wish to be a monarch."

From the corner of her eye, she could see the patricians stiffen or murmur into another's ear.

"I thought a stint in the Tullanium would have taught you some humility, Caecilia."

Her stubbornness emerged. Anger also quelled some of her nerves. She turned to Aemilius, the man who'd washed his hands of her so he could grasp power. "You've grown long in the tooth,

Uncle. Do you still consider yourself a warrior? How does it feel to murder a kinswoman?"

"I disowned you long ago."

"Yet you've enjoyed my inheritance ever since. My father was a wealthy man."

Her scorn dented his composure. "And he'd be ashamed of you. Today you'll get what you deserve. You sullied both the Caecilian and Aemilian names. Your lust has brought catastrophe upon you and all whom you loved. You should have heeded the lessons learned as a child. Divine law preserves Rome. Even Veii's goddess has confirmed that. At least go to your death showing contrition for your treachery."

Caecilia scanned the self-righteous faces in front of her. Aemilius's taunt about her father stung but she had no remorse. She would not apologize. "It's the priest who is the traitor here. The blood of a multitude is on his hands. And you would be fools to trust him."

Artile smiled, then said in Etruscan, "On the contrary, the deaths of thousands are on your head. You defied Nortia. Rome was always your destiny. You angered Uni and so caused Veii's destruction. I will enjoy watching you die, Sister."

His gibe struck home but she pushed it away. "Chains will not make Tarchon love you, Artile. All you'll ever know is his hatred. And you can never have Tas. He is safe. Remember that when I haunt you."

Camillus held up his hand, impatient with the exchange in a foreign tongue. "Enough," he barked. "Aemilia Caeciliana, I sentence you to death for sedition." He turned to Marcus. "Take her to the cliff and throw her off."

A pain shot through her chest as she stared at the tribune. "You? You are to kill me?"

"I've been so commanded," he rasped. His soft brown eyes were those of the youth of the past.

"Marcus Aemilius shouldn't have shown mercy to your husband," said Camillus. "And so he'll now show his loyalty to me and Rome"—he gestured to Aemilius—"and to his father, family, and clan."

Suddenly Caecilia did feel regret. After all he'd done, her cousin did not deserve this. It should've been one of the practiced guards who did the deed.

Camillus motioned to Aemilius and Artile. "Let members of both Roman and Etruscan families witness her death."

The dictator walked down the steps into the precinct followed by the priest and senator. The rest of the nobles remained on the portico. In the sanctuary, people began chanting Caecilia's name.

Quaking, she realized her life was now measured by the number of steps she'd take to the edge. Marcus fell in beside her as they followed Camillus.

The air was thick with incense from huge cauldrons in the precinct. It would be a scent that clung to her as she died. As they exited through the gates of the sanctuary, they passed the flawless, white cows that were tethered to a post next to the altar.

The Forum stretched before her. The Comitium, Temple of Vesta, and Curia surrounded by the seven hills. Viewing them made her realize how small Rome was compared to the world she'd lived in for a decade. The memory of her first sight of Veii as she sat in the hooped cart on the Via Veientana flashed into her mind. The majestic city on the plateau rising above the wooded ravines.

Camillus crossed his arms. "Take her to the edge, Marcus. You'll be absolved of murder. You act for the State."

Aemilius placed his hand on his son's shoulder. "This is for the honor of our family. Justice is required."

Artile said nothing, too busy studying the sky. The clouds were darkening as though sympathetic to Caecilia's plight. They hovered blackest over the Senate House.

Marcus clasped her arm. "Come, Cilla."

Again, the soft diminutive. "Why didn't you tell me last night you were to be my killer?"

He glanced over his shoulder, checking he was out of earshot. "I didn't have the courage. But I'll make up for it now. I'm not going to let you become a ghost. You will join the Good Ones, Cilla. I'll ensure your body is bathed and shrouded. I'll cremate you. Say funeral rites. Your ashes will be kept in secret. And I'll give libation to you every year. No one will ever know."

Her knees buckled. He steadied her. "How? They'll throw my corpse on the Esquiline to rot. You'll be punished if caught."

He grimaced. "Bribery. Penniless cemetery workers can be paid off. I'm determined despite the consequences."

She clung to him, grateful. "Thank you. But why?"

"Why? Because I love you, Cilla. As does Tarchon. He bid me tell you that. It seems you have been surrounded by love for a long time now. I see now why you chose Veii."

Caecilia sighed in relief. She hadn't angered Nortia after all. She now understood the reason the goddess brought her back to Vel. For without defying Fortuna, she would never have found love. Never borne her children. And never been given the chance to live with them forever.

Camillus shouted. "Marcus Aemilius! Do it!"

Her heartbeat quickened. Marcus clasped her arm, his hand trembling. "I'm sorry I am the one to push you."

A flicker of light caught her attention as a single streak of lightning exploded on the Curia's roof. A thunderclap boomed. Tiles shattered and were sent flying.

Caecilia glanced back. Camillus was transfixed on the blackened furrow in the Senate House. Artile's face was ashen. Only one god in Rome had the power to throw a lightning bolt—Jupiter—Tinia. Had Antar delivered Vel's message?

Screaming erupted as people huddled together. Lightning meant one of two things: that a travesty had been righted or disaster would strike. Caecilia hoped it was a sign of both. There would be retribution for the devastation of Veii. And one day Rome might be conquered.

She was calm now. "Let me go, Marcus. I'll do this without you." She squeezed his fingers. "I love you also. I'm glad we are no longer enemies."

He was shaking. "Farewell, Cilla. I will not fail you." Then he released her and stepped back.

The precipice loomed only feet away. Her legs were unsteady, her pulse too fast. She thought of Tas and sweet Larce and Arnth, hoping they would be warriors, or old men, when she met them again in the Beyond. She also welcomed the thought of seeing Thia and how many grandchildren she had borne.

She closed her eyes, fearful if she looked down she would falter. Then she pushed off on one heel. She could not tarry. Vel would be waiting.

GLOSSARY

Acheron: In Greek mythology, the river of sorrow in the Underworld; in Etruscan religion, the Afterworld or the Beyond, a place to which the dead journeyed over land and sea.

Auspices: A religious ceremony where omens were interpreted by watching the flight of birds.

Bondsman: A debtor who forfeited his liberty to his creditor to satisfy his debts. He was enslaved until he paid back what he owed.

Bucchero: A type of glossy black pottery developed by the Etruscans.

Bulla: An amulet of gold or leather worn by both Etruscans and Romans to ward off evil spirits.

Cista: A small casket, usually cylindrical in shape, used for keeping cosmetics, perfumes, or jewelry.

Comitium: The open-air area in Rome where the plebeian and tribal assemblies met.

Consular General: A military tribune with consular powers or consular tribune. For many years in the early Roman Republic, military tribunes were elected instead of consuls because generals were needed on so many war fronts.

Cuirass/Corselet: Body armor consisting of a breastplate and back-plate made from metal, leather, or stiffened linen.

Decurion: One of three knights who led ten men in a *turma.* The head decurion commanded the turma with the other two decurions acting as his deputies.

Defixio: A lead sheet upon which the gods were invoked to either curse or enchant a person.

Fascinum: A phallic-shaped amulet worn around the neck.

Fillet: Bands of wool that a Roman matron would plait into her hair.

Fulgurator: An Etruscan priest skilled in interpreting the will of the gods through analysis of different types of lightning and thunder.

Haruspex: An Etruscan priest skilled in the art of haruspicy, i.e., dissecting a sacrificial animal's liver for the purpose of divination.

Hatrencu: A title generally associated with Etruscan women holding sacred office. The high status afforded to them suggests they held a traditionally more masculine role in society at large.

Hoplite: A citizen soldier in the heavy infantry who fought in a *phalanx* formation and was recognizable by his round "hop-lon" shield.

Juno, a: A divine essence that acted as a protecting spirit or the "guardian angel" of a woman. It could be represented in effigy or by cameo. Men called such a spirit their "genius."

Lar/Lares: A Roman guardian spirit that protected localities. A Lar was most commonly associated as being a household god that protected a Roman home.

Levis/Leves: Skirmishers in the army of the early Republic who were only armed with small, round shields and spears.

Lictor: In Rome, one of twelve civil servants who protected the kings, and later those magistrates holding imperium (supreme authority). They carried a bundle of rods called the fasces, the symbol of power and authority. The tradition of the lictor and fasces was believed to derive from the Etruscan kings.

Maenad: A female worshipper who appeared in the retinue of the god Dionysus (Greek), Bacchus (Roman), and Fufluns (Etruscan) alongside satyrs.

Military Tribune: A Tribune of the Soldiers was a young man who aspired to become a senator. He was chosen at the time of the annual magistracy elections and assigned to lead a part of a legion under superior commanders.

People's Tribune/s (Tribune of the Plebs): Ten officials elected to protect the rights of plebeians as they held the power to veto elections, decrees of the Senate, and actions of magistrates.

Phalanx: An infantry battle formation in which three rows of soldiers held overlapping shields and long spears. The phalanx formation was originally developed by the Greeks, copied by the Etruscans, and then adopted by the Romans.

Phersu: A masked man who performed blood sacrifices during Etruscan funeral games. He was the precursor to a Roman gladiator.

Princip/Principes: Etruscan aristocrats who held power to elect leaders and participate in government.

Pythia: A Greek prophetess known as the oracle of Delphi. She was inspired by the god Apollo and was reputed to make her utterances under the influence of hallucinogenic vapors emitted through a cleft in the earth.

Satyr: A male companion of the wine god Dionysus (Greek) or Fufluns (Etruscan) depicted with goat's ears and tail and sometimes a goat's phallus.

Sinus: The large fold of material in the front of a toga which could be used as a type of pocket.

Stola: A long, sleeveless, pleated dress worn over a tunic. It was fastened at the shoulders with fibulae and worn with two belts, one beneath the breasts, and the other around the waist.

Sibylline Books: A collection of holy books containing oracular utterances that were consulted by the Roman Senate in times of crisis. These were not prophecies but instead advice as to which expiation rites should be observed in order to avert calamity. The books were written in Greek and could only be interpreted by a select group of senators.

Tebenna: A rounded length of cloth worn by Etruscan men over a chiton. It was similar in appearance to a toga but shorter. The Roman toga was derived from this garment.

Thyrsus: A staff of giant fennel tipped with a pinecone and entwined with ivy, which was associated with the god Dionysus (Greek), Bacchus (Roman), and Fufluns (Etruscan).

Turma/Turmae: A cavalry squadron of thirty men that was split into groups of ten knights, each led by a *decurion*.

Zilath: Chief magistrate of an Etruscan city with similar authority to a Roman consul.

AUTHOR'S NOTE

The Etruscans have long absorbed me. I was inspired to write the Tales of Ancient Rome series when I chanced upon a photo of a sixth century BCE sarcophagus upon which a husband and wife were sculpted in a pose of affection. These lovers, known as "the Married Couple," intrigued me. What ancient culture exalted marital fidelity with such open sensuality? The answer led me to Etruria and the story of the siege of Veii. This conflict raged for ten years between two cities that lay only twelve miles apart across the Tiber. Amazingly, the customs and beliefs of these enemies were so different that it was as though an expanse of water divided a Renaissance society from one living in the Dark Ages. Given this disparity, I was inspired to create a couple from these opposing worlds whose love must not only transcend war but also withstand the pressures of conflicting moralities, allegiances, and beliefs.

For those new to the series, you might like to read my author's notes for *The Wedding Shroud* and *The Golden Dice*, in which I discuss topics such as the origins and religion of the Etruscans (including the Etruscan Discipline), bisexuality and pederasty, human sacrifice, and the status of women in Etruria and Rome (including information about prostitution and concubines). You can access these notes under the Learn More tab on my website, http://elisabethstorrs.com, together with pieces of research and photographs on my blog, *Triclinium*, at http://elisabethstorrs.com/category/blog/triclinium. An extended version of this note is also posted on my website.

The ancient sources I mainly consulted were accounts from Livy and Plutarch. Unfortunately, contemporaneous records of events in early Rome were destroyed centuries before these historians were born. As a result, they lacked the same access to primary sources that modern researchers do today. Furthermore, no extant body of Etruscan literature exists to enable us to judge the other side of the story. In effect, the conquerors of Etruria wrote about Etruscan history with all the prejudices of the victor over the vanquished.

The men of the Furii clan were patricians originating in Tusculum in Latium. The first to gain fame was Marcus Furius Camillus, who despite being wounded in the thigh, fought on against the Volsci at Mount Algidus. Lucius Furius Medullinus was also an esteemed general who historically had struggles with the Icilii clan.

Camillus, so called because he was a "camillus" altar boy, was named the second founder of Rome by Plutarch. Interestingly, he was five times chosen as dictator but never elected consul. Any intimate characteristics I've attributed to him are purely my own invention (as is his love affair with Pinna). Nevertheless, we know this general showed incredible political acumen, military innovation, bravery, and charisma. Plutarch praised him: "That even when the authority rightly belonged to him alone, it was exercised in common with others; while the glory that followed such exercise was his alone, even when he shared the command." This humility clearly followed his downfall after the hubris displayed in his triumph after the conquest of Veii. Indeed, the need to retrieve the tithe to Apollo from the populace caused vitriolic resentment. This escalated when the question arose as to whether the plebeians should remove themselves to Veii, leaving the patricians in Rome. Camillus strenuously opposed this, claiming that such a geographical division would lead to the demise of the Republic. As a result, he was temporarily exiled despite immunity from prosecution usually afforded to dictators for decisions made in office.

Camillus's tears upon seeing the enormity of his victory are reported, as is his plea to Jupiter that he should, if necessary, suffer retribution instead of Rome. However, his consequent small stumble was considered by Livy as "an omen of his [Camillus's] subsequent condemnation and capture of Rome [by the Gauls], a disaster which occurred a few years later."

The mystery of Lake Albanus forms an integral part of the legend, as does the betrayal by the anonymous Veientane soothsayer. The decrypted omen seems obscure, but the assistance Rome offered to its Latin allies to irrigate their land makes sense as a stepping-stone to conquest. The renewed support of the Latin League would have boosted manpower at a time when continuing warfare with the Volsci and Aequi was diverting Rome's resources from Veii. Given this, the rationale of gaining advantage by placating the Latin goddess, Mater Matuta, is also feasible. Accordingly, the idea that Pinna, a girl with origins in Latium, could convince her lover of the deity's power was irresistible.

The dictator's devotion to solar deities such as Mater Matuta is explored by Georges Dumézil in his book *Camillus*. He hypothesizes that Camillus worshiped the dawn goddess after seeing the success achieved at Mount Algidus by attacking at daybreak. Livy records the date of that victory in mid-June in the immediate period of preparation for the summer solstice, which was opened by the Matralia festival of Mater Matuta on June 11. Dumézil asserts that Camillus thereafter employed this tactic in all his campaigns.

The serendipity of research always delights me. After establishing Pinna's devotion to Mater Matuta, I delved into the background of the divinity and was drawn into a web of mythologies connecting mother deities and goddesses of light. This included Roman Juno and Etruscan Uni together with the dawn goddesses Thesan (Etruscan), Ino/Leukothea (Greek), Aurora (Roman), and the Phoenician Astarte. Immediately apparent was that all these goddesses helped women in childbirth and protected children while being associated with some aspect of the diurnal or seasonal patterns of the sun. And the strange rites of the Matralia, where matrons embrace their nephews and nieces instead of their own children, establishes Mater Matuta as a surrogate mother (as Pinna became at the end of the novel). However, for those who know Greek mythology, please note that, at the date at which the book is set, Mater Matuta wouldn't have been associated with her Greek counterpart Ino/Leukothea, who was the nurse of Dionysus, because the cult of Dionysus (Bacchus) was reputedly not introduced to Rome until 186 BCE.

The concept of an afterlife where the deceased's soul remained intact was not adopted by the Romans until much later in the Republic. Instead they believed in the Di Manes, the "Good Ones," who were a conglomerate of spirits existing underground who needed to be appeased to prevent them from rising up to torment the living. In contrast, the Etruscans had long believed in the concept of maintaining individuality after death in a world where the dead could look forward to rejoining their ancestors.

There is conjecture among modern historians as to the nature of Dionysiac worship in Etruria. Funerary art depicting symposium scenes of men and women enjoying a world of wine and music are interpreted as revealing how inebriation connects the participants to the "otherness" of a divine dimension. Hedonism is therefore linked to the concept of exorcising death in the celebration of a passage to the afterlife. These murals do not depict the more familiar portrayal of satyrs and maenads associated with Dionysus. However, the discovery of other representations of the attendants in the wine god's retinue in bronzes, vases, and sculpture provide evidence that this "Dionysism without Dionysus" transitioned into the more familiar orphic cult with its orgiastic initiation rites, which emphasized the inversion of social order. However, it's difficult to ascertain if the Etruscans indulged in the more savage Mysteries reputed to be conducted by the Greeks in addition to the civic aspects of a pomp, games, and sacrifice. It should be remembered, though, that the Greeks invented a gruesome mythology surrounding the wine god to discourage the obvious equality granted to women, slaves, and foreigners via the cult. Accordingly, the fact that the Etruscans afforded their women high status, independence, education, and freedoms well beyond the constraints of cloistered Greek women or second-class Roman matrons supports my supposition that the infidelity involved in Dionysiac worship could be acceptable when viewed as a sacred act. Indeed, as is consistently the case in the Etruscan pantheon, there is an emphasis of gods as married couples—hence Fufluns is often portrayed with his wife, Areatha (Ariadne), rather than with his wild retinue. Vel's gift to Caecilia was inspired by an engraved mirror showing the divine lovers with their lips a fraction from a kiss.

At the time my novels are set, the more life-affirming portrayal of the afterlife became a fearful one where demons threatened safe haven in the Beyond. This gradual change in the national psyche is presumed to be due to the encroachment of the Syracusans, and later the Romans, who succeeded in destroying a once invincible sea and land empire. The Calu Cult is my interpretation of this darker vision of gaining immortality through human sacrifice, which was undoubtedly practiced.

The tactic of using the cuniculi to infiltrate the plateaued city is given credence by the network of tunnels that riddle the territory around Veii, in particular the area of Formello, which span about thirty miles and are used to support drainage, divert flood waters, and distribute water during droughts. The more famous of these are the Burrows of Olmetti and Formellese and the Ponte Sodo. The Etruscans were incredible engineers who also created deep well shafts, although to my knowledge, there are none on the citadel now known as the Piazza D'Armi. However, archaeologists have discovered that, in a period earlier than the 396 BCE invasion, the Veientanes moved their religious center from the citadel to the highest point on the plateau, so it may well be that Camillus's forces managed to access the temple of Uni situated there through the cuniculi leading to the city proper.

Livy and Plutarch chronicle the story that the Veientane king was offering sacrifice at the time of the assault, but both are dubious as to its veracity, as Livy states, "This tale, which is too much like a romantic stage-play to be taken seriously, I feel is hardly worth attention either for affirmation or denial." Alas, as a novelist, the drama of the scene was too enticing.

Evocatio was a ceremony by which a Roman general lured the chief divinity of a foreign city to Rome through the promise of games and temples. The first and most famous example of this was by Camillus. Research also revealed that, although Rome adopted foreign cults, alien gods were not allowed within the holy boundary, or pomerium. The pomerium, however, did not always fall within the footprint of the city wall. This is the case with the Aventine Hill. Presumably Camillus built the temple for Juno Regina there rather than on the Capitoline because Uni was a foreign deity. Hence the traitorous Veientane deity was unable to truly place a footstep in Rome's sacred territory.

Very little remains of Veii, although more and more is being discovered by Iefke van Kampen and her team. I was honored to be shown around the beautiful site of the Portonnacio d'Apollo by her. The sanctuary is serene with its curative pool and cistern.

Various gods such as Minerva, Apollo, and Dionysus were worshipped there. The incredible terra-cotta statues I described that
once adorned the roof ridge can be seen at the Villa Giulia in
Rome, including the remarkable Apollo of Veii.

Finally, I must mention my favorite piece of Etruscan sculpture. It's an example of the symplegma, or "erotic embrace," which
is an apotropaic symbol invoking the forces of fertility against evil
and death. The relief depicts Larth Tetnies and Tanchvil Tarnai
lying naked on their bed beneath a transparent shroud, staring
into each other's eyes. I see Caecilia and Vel in this same way,
embracing each other even now, their love eternal. The thought
helps me hold back tears whenever I think of bidding farewell to
the two characters I've lived with for more than fifteen years.

Acknowledgments

Much love and appreciation to my husband, David, for supporting me in my writing and sharing my life for over thirty years, and to my wonderful sons, Andrew and Lucas, who have grown from boys into men over the duration of this series. Thanks also to their grandma, Jacqui. And I wish my mum and dad were still alive to read the series.

Enormous thanks to Jodi Warshaw at Lake Union, who has such faith in my books as well as patience with an author who can be reluctant to "murder her darlings." I also enjoyed the enthusiasm, critical eye, and wicked sense of humor of Tegan Tigani, who made the editing process fun. My appreciation also to my copy editor, Michelle Hope Anderson. And many thanks to all the wonderful Lake Union team who are always so generous, encouraging, and supportive—in particular the lovely Gabe Dumpit, as well as Tyler Stoops and Christy Caldwell. Danielle Fiorella also did a great job designing my cover. My proofreader, Elisabeth Rinaldi, should also be thanked.

Special thanks to the members of my writing group of many years—Cecilia Rice, Marilyn Harris, Katherine Delaney, and

Judith Crosbie—for their positivity. Also to my caring beta readers, Mary Lou Locke, Rebecca Lochlann, and Greg Johnston, for their valuable input.

My research was greatly assisted by esteemed Etruscologist Iefke van Kampen, who is always so generous with her time and hunted down sources on Dionysism in Etruria for me. I'm excited that I'm collaborating with her in merging fiction with fact in an exhibition curated by her at the Palazzo Chigi at Formello, in which my characters will voice the exquisite votive statues unearthed by her team at Veii in an audio-visual display. Thanks also to Larissa Bonfante, who responded to my obscure call across social media and helped me find her essay "Fufluns Pacha: The Etruscan Dionysus," which I could not access from Australia. And thanks to Filippo Gemmellaro, who so ably translated various essays from Italian. Love to Kate Duigan for updating the map and to Marcella Wilkinson for modeling the cover.

Last but not least, my love and gratitude to Natalie Scott and Joyce Kornblatt, to whom this book is dedicated. Both were mentors at the very beginning of my literary journey. Their words of wisdom remain with me always.

A complete bibliography is available on my website, http://elisabethstorrs.com, but sources of particular value for this book include the following: Eva Cantarella's *Bisexuality in the Ancient World* (New Haven: Yale University Press, 1992); *Etruscans: Eminent Women, Powerful Men*, edited by Patricia S. Lulof and Iefke van Kampen (Amsterdam: W Books, 2012); Larissa Bonfante's *Etruscan Dress* (Baltimore: Johns Hopkins University Press, 2003); *The Religion of the Etruscans*, edited by Nancy Thomson de Grummond and Erika Simon (Austin: University of Texas Press, 2006); Georges Dumézil's *Camillus* (Berkeley: University of California Press, 1980); Livy's *The Early History of Rome*, translated by Audrey de Sélincourt (London: Penguin

Books, 1971); and Plutarch's *The Lives of the Noble Grecians and Romans* (Chicago: Encyclopaedia Britannica, 1952).

ABOUT THE AUTHOR

Elisabeth Storrs has long held an interest in the history, myths, and legends of the ancient world. She studied classics at the University of Sydney, and she is a director of the NSW Writers' Centre and one of the founders of the Historical Novel Society Australasia. Over the years she has worked as a solicitor, a corporate lawyer, and a governance consultant. She lives with her husband and two sons in Sydney. Visit her at www.elisabethstorrs.com.